DUBLIN ZOO

JOHN MICHELL

PREFACE

Readers will note several factual anomalies in this book. These inaccuracies are deliberately included in the name, I hope, of a more compelling narrative.

An obvious example is the description of the Scunthorpe steel industry in the period immediately following the Great War of 1914–18, especially the supposed concentration on pig iron production. A subtler mistake is to be found in the curfew I attributed to Marseille during the period of the Second World War when southern France was under Vichy control. My research indicated something to the contrary, but my simple judgement was the plot worked better with a curfew included.

Honourable motivations likewise prompted other calculated misrepresentations. I sincerely hope these intended errors, along with any unplanned slip-up in the event, do not detract from the book's reading pleasure.

John Michell
www.johnmichell.strikingly.com

DISCLAIMER

This book is a work of fiction. Comments or actions attributed to public figures are either contrived or loosely based on historical events. In the latter case, summaries and accounts provided are not intended to be of academic quality, accuracy or balance.

Otherwise, any character's resemblance in the book to any individual living or dead is purely coincidental.

*Dublin Zoo opened its doors on September 1, 1831.
(The Zoo was) founded as a private society by anatomists
and physicists and supported by wealthy subscribers.*

www.dublinzoo.ie

CHAPTER ONE

'*A Dublin Zoo*,' Harold Bradshaw interjected loudly, a wry smile flickering across his face.

The judge stopped mid-sentence and momentarily returned the smile. 'It surely is,' he said softly. Audible gasps rippled through the Old Bailey court number one. His Lordship the Deputy Chief Justice Samuel Prendergast did not usually engage in banter with persons in the dock. And, moreover, his not unsympathetic tone indicated he understood the *Dublin Zoo* reference. As well he might – Samuel Prendergast was there twenty-one years ago when Harold's father, Albert, had adopted the expression.

Harold's jet black eyes were set in steel now that hardness had reclaimed him.

Like Harold, the judge's mask had also returned. 'Do you have anything else to say?'

Harold shook his head.

The judge's voice took on a decisive edge. 'You are hereby sentenced to twenty-five years' imprisonment with hard labour without eligibility for parole until you have served a total of eighteen years.' Justice Prendergast took a deep breath. 'Take him down,' he ordered.

Less than thirty minutes earlier the usher had called the court to order. 'The Central Criminal Court of England and Wales is now in session,' he bellowed. 'All stand.' Those assembled did as directed – lawyers and their clients, members of the press, and the swarm of interested observers crammed into the visitors' gallery. Friday 24 November 1937 was as grim and brooding as the thickset young man in the dock, dark of complexion and seemingly as wide as he was tall. Harold Bradshaw was two months short of his twenty-first birthday. The presiding judge strode purposively to his green leather chair, a coat of arms emblazoned on its high straight back. He was a tall, berobed in red and intimidating figure.

'Harold Raymond Bradshaw,' Justice Samuel Prendergast had begun immediately, 'you have been convicted on two counts of murder. It is now my duty to sentence you. In so doing, I have elected not to apply the death penalty as the law allows taking into account the vexed circumstances in which you shot dead Ignazio de Pascale and Lorenzo Martino. Before passing sentence, however, I should declare, in order to avoid any later suggestion of a conflict of interest, that as a young lawyer over two decades ago I once represented your late father, Albert.' The judge hesitated as if carefully formulating his words. 'I found your father to be a man of honour and integrity,' he said, his voice tinged with regret. 'Were he here today, he would be dismayed at this turn of events.' A pause followed as Justice Prendergast gathered himself. 'I now turn to the period of your incarcer ...'

At this point, Harold Bradshaw's interjection rang out.

Nearly eight years later, in July 1945 after the European war had ended, Labour's Clement Attlee displaced the iconic wartime leader Winston Churchill as UK prime minister. Those in British secret circles understood the election result would lead to the scrutiny of wartime activities ordered by Churchill independent of his war ministry and the Labour Party members within. Front of mind for a select few of Churchill's advisers was a secret plan implemented in September 1941 and the unwitting role played in it by Harold Bradshaw and some others. 'You wait,' one said to his nervous colleagues, 'there'll be an inquiry eventually.'

So warned, these same few advisers set about building alliances, seeking in advance to shore up their positions on the *matter*. In furtive huddles in non-descript government buildings and at other times whispered exchanges in gentlemen's clubs around the metropolitan borough of Westminster, the circle of indoctrination began to expand. Opinions were divided. Some agreed Churchill's 1941 initiative was bold, necessary and had been undone only by bad luck. And, they added, it did have two unexpectedly positive outcomes. But the doubters worried about principle and perceptions of decency. In particular, they worried about Harold Bradshaw, not only hoodwinked into participating in the operation but also coerced to boot. Hadn't Bradshaw and his parents suffered enough from Churchill's earlier misstep, the detractors agonized, in 1925 when Winston was Chancellor of the Exchequer?

It was 9 pm on Thursday 4 September 1941. Harold Bradshaw shifted uncomfortably. The steel seat inside the belly of the unlit and unmarked RAF special duty squadron Whitley bomber was cold and unforgiving. Rather than a one-hour flight from RAF Tempsford in Bedfordshire to Scotland for a practice parachute jump, this trip was three times as long and no training drill, all the way to Riom in central France provided the headwinds buffeting the Whitley did not cause it to fall out of the sky in the meantime.

The plane would fly a circuitous route, looping out over the Celtic Sea and across the Bay of Biscay to avoid the occupying Germans' observation posts on France's Atlantic coast before tracking along the Pyrenees Mountains separating Spain from southern France. At the range's midpoint, the pilot would turn left and fly due north to an area near Riom where the flat terrain and sparse population made it an ideal parachute drop site.

Harold rested his head against the webbing protecting the plane's fuselage from the back of passengers' skulls. He thought about the extraordinary circumstances that had brought him to the point where in three hours he would be parachuting into the dark and who knows what below. Just four years ago he had been sentenced to a long term of imprisonment for murder, only to be chosen out of the blue to do this job. What on earth would his parents think? The thought took Harold's mind to his father Albert's journey from rags to riches and back to rags again, and its sorry end for his mother and father alike.

Albert Edward Bradshaw, Harold's father, had been born into poverty in the Castle Garth slums of Newcastle upon Tyne in northeast England in 1894. Although poorly educated, he was a naturally intelligent young man. With the outbreak of World War I in 1914 and the government's decision to expand the all-volunteer Fourth Battalion of the Northumberland Fusiliers, Albert was quick to seize the opportunity. By then he was twenty and had already been six years down pit. The coal sickness that had claimed his father and reduced others to lifelong infirmity had instilled in him a burning determination to seek a different life. Albert's ailing mother and only sibling, sister Beatrice, tearfully waved goodbye as he left. By April 1915 Albert was in France and on the Western Front.

The Fusiliers Fourth Battalion was to incur horrific casualties. Albert's escape from the mines, he soon found, was a case of out of the frying pan and into the fire. Yet he had the good fortune to endure the horrors of the Western Front for only six months. The shrapnel that shattered his left thighbone in October 1915 might have caused permanent disability, but it did excuse him from combat duties early in the campaign. The trenches were no place for hobbling men dragging unresponsive legs behind them. Many Fourth Battalion others were not so lucky.

Albert's wound saw him evacuated to a field hospital in the French town of Provins. After surgery and two months' recuperation, he was posted to Paris in early 1916, reporting for duty as an orderly clerk at the head-quarters of the British Expeditionary Force, the BEF. Around this time, the French Government was finalizing plans with the anti-German Tsar Nicholas II of Russia for the deployment of a Russian force to the Western Front. Always big on pomp even in the depths of war, the French pressed their allies to be party to a ceremonial welcoming of the Russians. Marseille, 500 miles from Paris on the French Riviera in southeast France and far from the Western Front, was to be the Russian disembarkation point. To that end, the French Government established a reception office in Marseille to which it insisted, and then demanded, France's allies appoint liaison officers. The BEF High Command, ever-sensitive to any hint of Gallic hubris, acceded – but only half-heartedly. In an act of unspoken defiance it promoted the limping Private Albert Bradshaw to corporal, posted him to Marseille as its liaison officer and promptly forgot about him.

The Russian force was originally scheduled to arrive in France in the first week of March 1916. Accordingly, Albert was in place in Marseille by that time. He was billeted at a guesthouse on Rue Mazenod, the BEF High Command in its wisdom reasoning that an enlisted man like Albert would be ill at ease in Marseille's better hotels. Rue Mazenod ran through the city's rough and tumble port district. Initially, Albert rarely ventured from his accommodation except to make the daily walk to the reception office in the first arrondissement a mile away. French and Russian diplomats permanently staffed the office and an American diplomat, who had wrangled observer status, popped in infrequently to attend planning meetings. The other allied military personnel attaching to the office, Albert's supposed counterparts, were all officers. They and everyone else seemed especially status conscious. Before long limping Albert Bradshaw was being paid little attention or respect.

For two weeks Albert diligently reported for duty. At another time he might have accepted his marginalization as his lot in life. But now he was less compliant. Having witnessed the startling slaughter of the Western Front and on learning that, for reasons of Russian internal politics, the force's arrival was delayed, he elected simply to stay away. Better to be bored in his own company than in the strained surrounds of the reception office. The BEF High Command would pay for his lodging until the Russians arrived and he had no obligation to make reports back to Paris. Moreover, the weather on the French Riviera was turning for the better. So Albert decided to put up his feet and attend the office now and then, much like the observing American diplomat, checking to see when his commitments in Marseille would end and he could thankfully return to Paris.

The Whitley bomber dispatcher crab-walked down the plane's belly, stooped to a crouch in the confined space. His face six inches from Harold's, he mouthed the words *two plus*, indicating a little over two hours to go before reaching the Riom jump zone. Harold gave a thumbs up and the dispatcher retreated. It was cold and dark causing Harold to reflect on the loneliness and isolation experienced by his mother, Rita, when she came to England to live. How ironic, he thought, that fate should conspire to have his father marry a woman from Marseille, leading to him being plucked from prison to do the Marseille job.

Rita Tzanetis stood near the door to the kitchen of the Rue Mazenod guesthouse, studiously avoiding eye contact with anyone. Albert had not seen her before – with good reason. It was her first day of work. Unlike her wait staff colleagues, smartly dressed in white blouses and dark skirts and busily flittering about the dining tables, Rita's shapeless smock set her apart, marking her as the underling she was who picked up dirty dishes and returned them to the kitchen for washing.

'Good morning, sir,' Rita said as she gathered Albert's soiled crockery. Unable to speak English, she spoke in French although she was also fluent in Greek.

'*Humph,*' Albert grunted. Now three weeks into his stay in Marseille, he was beginning to struggle with the food. He pined like never before for a cup of good, strong English tea.

Rita interpreted Albert's grumpiness as annoyance with her. This alarmed her and made her worry about implications for her employment. Her parents were immigrants from Smyrna, then a Greek region of the Ottoman Empire. They had come to France fearing Turkish annexation of Smyrna and taken up residence in the dirt-poor seventh arrondissement, where Rita was born. The family remained there, eking out a living – Rita's parents and two brothers, four and two years her senior.

Rita in truth was not an attractive girl. At nineteen she was tall, gangly and awkward, which combined with her protruding nose and essentially featureless body affected her self-confidence. And now Albert's attitude had exacerbated the insecurity. 'I'm sorry, sir,' she said softly before scurrying off like a startled bird.

Albert did not understand Rita but sensed his abruptness had caused her timorous flight. This pricked his conscience. He regretted his rudeness and promised himself to make amends.

The next morning Albert came to breakfast armed with an English–French dictionary. The look of relief on Rita's face once she understood his apology instantly plunged Albert into love although, being unfamiliar with the emotion, he didn't realize it immediately. He laughed and Rita laughed back. All of a sudden the shortish, limping Englishman with the sinewy build, wavy fair hair and blue eyes was not such a bad fellow.

The stilted conversations using the dictionary were brief at first. But within a week Albert and Rita were talking daily. A bond formed. The couple proved remarkably competent in overcoming the language barrier and soon the bond became a friendship. As a juvenile in Newcastle Albert had once glimpsed Mrs Riley from next door naked from the waist up as she washed from a bowl in her sitting room; years later a girl had allowed him his one and only kiss. Yet despite his inexperience with women, Albert was at ease in Rita's company. Her reserve abated and their familiarity grew apace. Inside a fortnight they were strolling down to a disused finger wharf at the port after Rita's breakfast shift where they conversed in the shade of an old warehouse's cantilevered roof. In this way, Albert managed to convey why he was in Marseille and explain he would be leaving once the Russian force arrived.

Thereafter, Albert began to walk Rita home. At first he left her a short distance from her door. But when Rita suggested he meet her family, Albert agreed. This was not as successful as they had hoped. Albert was particularly unsettled by the hostility of Rita's eldest brother, twenty-three-year-old Axel. A large and powerful man of swarthy complexion, he seemed to resent Albert's intrusion into the family home and the attention he was paying to Rita. For her part, Rita was not about to allow Axel's attitude to affect her friendship with Albert. In a curious sort of way, his limp reassured her that his interest in her was genuine. And unlike her classmates at school, especially the more curvaceous of them, Rita had never had a boy so much as look at her. She was keen to explore the relationship, even if it had to remain chastely non-contact as the times demanded – a social more dramatically reinforced in Albert by his wariness of the threatening Axel.

Albert usually attended the reception office on a Friday. During one such visit on 21 April 1916 he learned the Russians would be arriving on the last day of the month. This gave him nine remaining days in Marseille. He informed Rita the following day, a Saturday. As was their habit, the two had wandered down to the disused finger wharf and sat with their backs against the wall of the abandoned warehouse. Suddenly, Rita was overcome by the thought of Albert leaving. She began to cry. Albert's protective instincts raced. He put his arm around her. It was the first time they had physically touched. Before either of them knew it they had kissed. Then, as if robots, they were inside the warehouse, entering through a door hinging crookedly half open.

Rita wore a black smock and underneath the rigorously fortifying underwear of the era. Soon the smock was around her waist. Albert didn't quite know where to concentrate. One moment his hand was on Rita's bloomer-like, lace-up knickers wrestling unsuccessfully with the uncooperative material; the next on top of her smock grasping for the tiny nodes passing as her breasts. Rita finally brought affairs to order. Shushing Albert to slow down, she partially unlaced her underwear until it was loose, her shy smile inviting him to draw it down. She waited patiently as Albert, hampered by his leg, wriggled into position. Eventually, both parties were naked from the waist down. It was over quickly. But in the following afterglow their drive soon rekindled and they coupled for a second time.

Neither Albert nor Rita knew anything about contraception, not even the rudimentary facts. By the time

Albert had returned to Paris, now reluctantly, Rita was pregnant, unbeknown to either of them. Overwhelmed by his sudden and unexpected fall into love, Albert did briefly contemplate desertion. But the offence carried the punishment of death by firing squad. The only viable course of action was to return to Paris and visit Marseille at every opportunity.

Seated in the belly of the shuddering Whitley bomber, Harold knew little about the background to his conception and much less of the actual act. What he did know, albeit again with a deficit of detail, was Albert and Rita had married in Marseille not long after their initial meeting. The marriage had been followed by an extended period of separation, one that involved Albert spending time in a British military prison in France. 'They locked me up for being absent without leave, AWOL,' Albert told Harold years later.

It was in Paris in mid-May 1916, a little under two months since first meeting Rita, that Albert was unpleasantly surprised. He was not expecting to see her nor any of her family until some months distant when next in Marseille. At dusk Albert exited the BEF headquarters on Rue de la Paix, close to the Ritz Hotel where the BEF High Command endured the rigours of war. The Thursday evening was cool, warranting a jacket. Suddenly, a savage blow to the back of his head felled him. This was followed by a series of kicks to his nether regions. Barely conscious but spared internal injuries by the coat he wore, Albert looked through the pain haze to recognize Rita's brothers. He also heard the message delivered by her big brother Axel.

'Rita is no longer pure,' Axel hissed in broken English, his face so close Albert could smell his garlic breath. 'She is with child. You must marry her. Our family's honour is at stake. The wedding will be on Saturday afternoon after next. If you do not come to Marseille, we will kill you.' Axel spat on the sidewalk close to where Albert's bloodied head lay. 'English pig,' he said, before he and his brother turned heel and walked into the night.

Albert staggered back to his enlisted men's barracks. He shuddered at the reaction of Rita's family to the pregnancy, picturing loud and fierce debates and even wilder gesticulation. He was not mistaken; the Tzanetis household had indeed been a hothouse of raging emotions. There had been talk of abortion or of sending Rita away for her confinement and the child being adopted out after birth. But both were deemed too expensive and complicated. Finally, it was decided Albert should marry Rita; most of the neighbours already knew a limping British Tommy had been courting her. She would have the child but Albert would then be expunged from her life by means of an explanation he had been killed in a tragic war-related incident.

The family's decision to force a marriage left Albert on the horns of an exquisite dilemma. His BEF superiors were not about to grant him leave; after all, he had just returned from an eight-week sojourn in Marseille, far from the war in the north. Yet Albert was in no doubt that Axel, Rita's imposing brother, would make good on his threat to kill him if he didn't comply with the family's demand.

Albert eventually reasoned that provided he could avoid a desertion charge, Axel was a greater threat than the British army. He hatched a plan to go absent without leave, it being dubbed in military law as *dereliction of duty* making it a substantially less grievous offence than desertion – one not involving the death penalty. The train timetable told Albert he could leave Paris early on Friday morning, with a scheduled arrival in Marseille mid-morning the following day. This would allow him time to marry Rita, leave Marseille on the Sunday morning and be back in Paris early Monday morning. As long as he was able to organize his work roster so as not to be on duty that weekend, he would be AWOL for barely more than one working day. Why, if he were really lucky his BEF masters might treat this short truancy as something requiring only a reprimand and the docking of a day's pay.

A little over a week later, on a hot Marseille Saturday afternoon in late May 1916, in a Greek Orthodox church not far from the guesthouse where they first met, a battered and bruised twenty-two-year-old Albert Bradshaw took Rita Tzanetis, aged nineteen, as his lawfully wedded wife. Decorum demanded Albert and his bride spend Saturday night at the family home. Albert spent it lying in the dark listening to Rita's father snore through the paper-thin dividing wall, not game even to think about consummating his marriage. Early the next morning, after drinking the sour tea and foul black bread grudgingly offered, Albert boarded a train for Paris. His feelings were mixed: he was pleased to be away from the brooding hostility of Rita's parents and the overt threat to his person posed by her brother Axel, but he was also disturbed at leaving the pregnant Rita to fend for herself.

Albert nonetheless was consoled by the fact that his plan had worked well to date. But he had counted his chickens far too early. Not long after leaving Marseille, his train pulled into a siding where it waited for over an hour. It was the first of many stops. As bad luck would have it, on that particular Sunday there was a raft of troop movements. Albert's civilian train was frequently obliged to give way to troop transports, sometimes for hours on end. It was nearly noon on Tuesday before he reached Paris. Exhausted and dishevelled, Albert raced to BEF headquarters where he tried to explain his unapproved absence. But a line had been crossed and he was speaking to deaf ears. Any hopes of a soft landing were gone.

CHAPTER TWO

Albert was court-martialled in June 1916, charged with desertion. It was then Samuel Prendergast entered his life as a freshly minted barrister. Harold smiled despite the Whitley bomber hitting an air pocket and dropping like a rock. His father would never hear a bad word about Samuel. And that would have remained the case, Harold was sure, even had Albert known that, twenty-one years on as a judge, Prendergast would bang up his only son for at least eighteen years. 'Without Samuel,' Albert liked to say, 'those bastards on the court martial panel would have had me shot in a trice.'

British army justice circa 1916 was unforgiving. But the army did randomly allocate Albert Lieutenant Samuel Prendergast as his advocate. Albert and Samuel were both twenty-two, although from different worlds. By any measure Samuel was a product of the British upper classes. His baronet father still held sovereign title to property in London, granted to the family in ancient times. Samuel had studied law at Balliol College, Oxford and passed his bar exam only weeks before enlisting in the army legal corps. Albert's was his first solo case and Samuel threw himself into his preparation. Each young man appreciated the other's frankness. Mutual trust and respect soon flowed.

The prosecution called eight well-schooled witnesses to lament the scourge of desertion and its injurious effect on morale and the war effort generally. The three tribunal members listened attentively, their collective mood rapidly darkening. 'So, Lieutenant Prendergast,' the tribunal president, a senior lawyer, asked when the prosecution finally rested, his heaving sigh on speaking embodying the tribunal's soaring ill will. 'Have you anything to say?'

Samuel grasped it would be futile to attempt to reason. Instead, he relegated good character argument to his closing address and opted for his fallback plan to attack via the legal veto, the president's power to reach a verdict independent of his two non-lawyer colleagues when legal reasons so required.

'Honourable members,' Samuel said, but looking directly at the president, 'the question before us is a simple matter of law.' He took a sip of water, affecting poise. 'It is not in contest that Corporal Bradshaw returned to the BEF High Command before it could initiate arrest orders. As such, I respectfully refer members to section forty, subsection three of the SOFA of 31 August 1914 governing His Majesty's armed forces in France.' SOFA was bureaucratese for *Status of Forces Agreement*. 'It states,' Samuel said, pausing for emphasis, 'that in the case of non-combat units, charges of *desertion by absconding* can arise pursuant only to the issue of an arrest warrant.'

The tribunal members hurriedly leafed through their papers. When positing Albert's guilt, the prosecution had relied solely on a separate legal document, *The Armed Forces Act 1904*. 'Yes, I note section forty, three of the SOFA,' the lawyer president said on reading it. 'But what of it? Where there is a conflict of law, the Act will always take precedence.'

Samuel was now at the crossroads. One poorly crafted sentence would see Albert shot. 'Learned president, I draw your attention to the recent case of *Peebles versus The Borough of Holborn*, where Moysten J held that where laws conflict, the later law is preferable to earlier iterations.' Samuel's was an audacious gamble. The precedent cited was tenuous, a lower court finding on a local government matter of no direct relevance to Albert's case.

The president appeared to be in two minds. 'Hand me up the transcript,' he said finally. 'I will weigh Justice Moysten's judgement when we adjourn to consider our verdict.'

The tribunal retired after closing arguments. Both its non-lawyer members immediately declared Albert guilty of desertion and deserving of the death sentence. The president was sorely tempted to agree with them. But he was an ambitious crown prosecutor in civilian life. And although sceptical of Samuel's legal gambit, he was also wary of career backlash – just enough to resist a desertion conviction and spare Albert the ultimate sanction. Exercising his legal veto, the president decreed Albert could be found guilty only of being AWOL. For this, the tribunal vented its spleen. Albert was sentenced to a year's hard labour at the British military prison in the French city of Tours, reduced in rank to private and fined fifty pounds to be garnisheed from wages re-commenced after his release from prison.

Albert was delivered from the tribunal hearing into the hands of the British military police waiting to take him to the Tours prison. Samuel was at once pleased and disappointed; Albert had been spared execution, but the sentence for an offence of two-and-a-half days AWOL was extreme. This bred in Samuel a belief he could have and should have done better. That is why, as Albert was led away, Samuel pressed a note into his hand. Samuel may well have given credence to the note one day reuniting him with Albert, but not for a second could he have imagined that twenty-one years later he would sit in judgement of Albert's not-yet-born son.

Albert had never expressed regret over the year he spent in the military prison, Harold reflected, musing out loud but barely able to hear himself above the roar of the Whitley's twin Armstrong Siddeley engines. Indeed, his father had often described his sentence as ultimately working to his advantage. 'Without being sent to Tours,' Albert used to say, 'I'd have probably never met Max Langdon or little Willie Gray, may he rest in peace.'

Most of the Tours prison population were shell-shocked British soldiers convicted of cowardice when their only crime was to have been overwhelmed by the carnage they had witnessed. The remaining inmates comprised an eclectic smattering of black marketeers, other ranks who had assaulted officers and drunkards who had managed to get themselves into trouble while on leave. The British military police in charge were largely ambivalent. The one exception was their distaste for prisoners who had beaten desertion charges – those perceived to have abandoned their comrades only to rub salt in the wound by escaping punishment for the betrayal. Victimization of this cohort was as widespread as it was vicious and invariably applied without regard to prisoners' individual circumstances.

It was for this reason that Albert quickly gravitated to two other members of the Northumberland Fusiliers, William Gray and Max Langdon. Both men were of a similar age to Albert and both natives of Newcastle – William, jockey-sized, with a naturally cheerful disposition and Max, taller, deeper of voice and more serious in outlook. William had a wound to his left upper thigh and Max one to his right shin. Technically, the wounds were not self-inflicted. William, you see, had shot Max and Max had reciprocated, both shootings occurring simultaneously on the count of three.

The pair's conduct in effect was an act of political protest. Both were veterans of the trench warfare characterizing the three bloody stalemated years from 1915 to 1917. With no one side able to gain the upper hand, the casualties were immense. Yet the respective High Commands continued to ignore the merciless sacrifice. Dismayed by this indifference, William and Max were driven to forge a pact.

In March 1916, they put the pact into effect. But once in the field hospital their injuries were soon revealed to be close quarters wounds. Charges of desertion followed. William and Max were lucky. It was a time relatively early on in the stalemate when *desertion by wounding* was defined by narrow reference to self-inflicted wounds, the foot being a particularly popular target. Aided by this and a sympathetic doctor, a major whose deliberately ambiguous report created confusion around how the wounds had been incurred, William and Max escaped the death penalty. The same could not be said for similarly creative others following in their stead, when the stalemate's persistence led to the adoption of a wider suite of capital offences.

For all its privations, prison was something of a finishing school for Albert. In particular, it honed his natural leadership qualities. Under Albert's direction, he, William and Max scrapped for survival, pooling their meagre rations and looking out for the ever-present threat of bashing. By the time the trio was released, within weeks of each other, William and Max knew they owed a huge debt of gratitude to Albert – their survival no less.

Harold was aware Albert had not returned to BEF headquarters in Paris after his release from prison in July 1917. Rather, he was posted as a hospital aide to a field sanatorium in Chantilly, close to the Western Front. *Ah, yes, the Chantilly sanatorium,* Harold thought from high above the Celtic Sea as the Whitley bomber relentlessly droned on. The experience had apparently been a nightmare and a blessing in disguise rolled into one. Not that Albert had ever talked about it much; his memories of the sanatorium were too harrowing for that. But when in the mood he would tell Harold about the diary and how he came to take possession of it. 'Never in my wildest dreams,' Albert would say, 'could I have guessed at its importance.'

The Chantilly sanatorium was a lunatic asylum in all bar name, where British soldiers suffering what modernity would call post traumatic stress disorder were triaged ahead of eventual repatriation to Britain. Albert's superiors knew of his prisoner background and treated him accordingly. He was subjected to each and every indignity they could conjure.

In March 1918 the Imperial German Army launched its Spring Offensive. It was its last chance to secure victory. Combatants fought under appalling conditions, even by the war's dubious standards. The number of patients arriving at the sanatorium increased exponentially, wretched souls coming in their droves. Most were shadows of the carefree young men they recently had been, many reduced to stumbling wrecks. *La Maison du Sanctuaire*, officialdom's cynical misnomer, became a darker place – a medieval throwback and chamber of endless horrors. It was here that Albert encountered Stanley Poppleton.

Stanley had not a mark on him. Not a scratch. Nor had he been gassed. Stanley was at the sanatorium because his mind had failed him in the cruellest possible way. His dark eyes flashed wildly as he muttered incoherently and saliva dribbled continuously down his chin. Stanley was just twenty-one.

Albert was working the night shift. One of his allotted tasks was to collect soiled bedpans from the wards, replace them with clean pots and empty and wash the contaminated items. Stanley shared a ward with twenty other men. It was around three in the morning in early May 1918 when Albert entered the ward to attend to bedpan duty.

'I don't like it here,' a cultured voice spoke.

Albert looked up, struggling to identify the speaker in the dim light. Stanley Poppleton was sitting up in bed exuding a serenity Albert found strangely unsettling. He found himself drawn to Stanley's bedside. 'And why's that?' Albert asked.

Stanley didn't speak. His only response was to smile. The smile was warm and hearty and Albert noticed Stanley was no longer dribbling. Had the light been better Albert would have also noticed his eyes were no longer darting. Albert was largely inured to the sanatorium's despair. Anyone who didn't adopt a self-defence mechanism would soon go mad. But the change in Stanley's demeanour somehow moved him. The cheerful calmness was both frightening and sad. To his surprise, Albert felt tears well in his eyes. 'Try to get back to sleep or you'll wake the others,' he said, a kindness in his voice he barely recognized.

'I want you to have this,' Stanley said. He produced from under his pillow a small, hard-covered notebook. 'It's my diary. I've kept it ever since I've been in France. I used to write in it when I was scared, often letters to my parents even though I never intended sending them. I just found it comforting.'

Stanley's composure now had Albert fully confounded. What had happened to the tormented madman who first arrived here?

'What do you want me to do with it?' Albert asked cautiously.

'Do what you think is best,' Stanley replied with the sagacity of a man three times his age. 'But don't give it to my family. Promise me that. My parents will be heartbroken enough and I don't want them to know I suffered or how scared I was.'

The way Stanley spoke about his parents, about their heartbroken reaction – as if he were dead – made Albert wary. He made a mental note to mention Stanley's behaviour to the ward psychiatrist when he came on duty later in the morning.

For now, however, Albert took the book from Stanley's outstretched hand. Its entries were in beautifully formed copperplate handwriting. Stanley had clearly been to a good school. Albert began to read, straining to see in the gloom. The first page was a letter dated 31 July 1916. *At Gommecourt*, it read. Gommecourt was a small farming village destined to go down in infamy as the scene of some of the bloodiest fighting of the Somme Offensive. It was the Western Front in its purest sense. *Less than a week since our arrival. Already three of my best friends have been killed, including Rupert Pomerory whom I have known since prep school. His neck was slashed open. I heard the blast and saw it happen. He took an age to bleed to death. I held his hand; all he did was to complain of being cold.* Albert fixed on the page, absorbed for some reason by the surname *Pomerory* when *Pomeroy* was the more commonly found.

Albert's preoccupation was such that he was slow to react when Stanley slashed the shaving razor across one wrist and then the other. Albert first stared, bewildered by the horror, and then lunged forward. But too late. The blood spurted like twin fountains. Seizing a blanket he tried to stem the bleeding. It was futile. As quickly as his deformed leg allowed, Albert ran from the ward, not realizing he was shouting *Dublin Zoo* as he went. He found the general duties doctor – passed out drunk.

Albert returned to the ward. There was no longer a need to hurry. Others came. Hugging Stanley's diary to his chest as if cold, Albert made his way to the sanatorium's front quadrangle. Leaning against the cool of a marble statue, he slid down its length to the ground still clutching the diary, tears stinging his eyes. It was then Albert pledged always to safeguard Stanley's diary. 'I do so in the name of my newborn child,' he whispered softly. The day before a letter had reached Albert informing him he had fathered a son and heir.

Harold knew he'd been born in Marseille and the reason for his given names. His mother had also been fond of telling him how he was such a big baby to bear. But both his parents were less forthcoming about Rita's family. Albert rarely touched alcohol. One Christmas during the good times, however, after a couple of port wines, he had whispered to Harold, then only about seven but bright enough to understand, 'You know I only learned of your birth sixteen months after it because your mother's family was very hostile towards me.' Then he had instantly clammed up and for the rest of his life never again raised the matter.

After her marriage to Albert, Rita remained in the family home for the next two months, seldom venturing out and always under the baleful, unforgiving eye of her mother. 'Harlot,' she hissed at Rita at every opportunity. When the baby bump became obvious the family closed ranks, telling the nosy parkers how Albert, bad leg notwithstanding, was now attached to the field headquarters of a unit at the Western Front.

The child was born on 28 January 1917 at a local clinic – a boy, a twelve-pound monster whose size and dark hue indicated dominance of the Tzanetis gene creating large, swarthy males. With that, the family told all-comers how only days earlier Albert became a prisoner of war when the Germans overran his field station. By majority vote, the disenfranchised Rita not participating, the family decided word of Albert's death would have to wait for now. It was one thing to say he had been captured around the time of his son's birth but too great a coincidence for him to die shortly after.

A condition of Albert's hard labour at the Tours prison was denial of the privilege to send and receive letters. It was not until he reached the Chantilly sanatorium after his release in July 1917 that he was able to write to Rita. Using simple English phrases, because both relied on language dictionaries to understand the other's written word, Albert explained the terms of his imprisonment and how as a proviso of his release he was forbidden to leave Chantilly. That done, his first question was to ask Rita about the outcome of her pregnancy.

Overcoming the vagaries of the French postal system, Albert's letter reached Rita's home in October 1917. But Rita's mother, the family authority on such matters, initially withheld it. Not until 28 January 1918 did she relent, giving the letter to Rita to mark Harold's first birthday. The upshot was no contact between Albert and Rita for nearly twenty months, from Albert's last writing in early June 1916 until the end of January 1918.

When Rita finally deciphered Albert's correspondence, she broached replying to it. Her mother resisted, arguing it was now time to tell the neighbours and others Albert had died while in German captivity. Rita countered that many women in Marseille had lost foreign husbands in combat, especially men from the colonies. A government office had recently been set up to assist families to repatriate remains to home countries for burial. That same office also presented bereaved wives with a plaque recording their husband's war service. Why, Rita cleverly pointed out, many houses in Marseille now bore the commemorative adornment. It would look odd if the family had no plaque to display; tongues would be sure to wag.

Rita carried the day. A letter reached Albert in early May 1918, the day before Stanley Poppleton's suicide, informing him he had fathered a baby boy. Rita had christened him Harold Raymond – Harold, she explained, to make him sound like a distinguished and sophisticated Frenchman, and Raymond in honour of Raymond Poincaré, the French president of the day. Both names would later translate seamlessly into English.

Albert wrote back telling Rita he would be unable to visit Marseille until the war ended and, as army rules stipulated, he returned to England to demobilize. Hampered by the slow and inefficient French mail system, the couple exchanged only one more letter before Albert demobbed in March 1919. Immediately thereafter he telegraphed Rita and set forth for Marseille. By now Harold's second birthday was six weeks past. Rita's family put on a brave show of welcoming the returning war hero. Even so, the shrewder of the relatives, friends and neighbours attending the celebrations chose not to ask too many questions.

But for all the politeness of their guests, Rita's family knew that so long as the child was in their midst, the gossips would inevitably discover the truth. Added to which the Tzanetis household had grown weary of the subterfuge. Accordingly, in June 1919 Albert, Rita and Harold set out for England, intending to settle in Newcastle. Rita was pleased to go. Her mother and brothers, Axel especially, had made her life intolerable. But at least they spoke to her. It was her father's wounded silence she most needed to escape.

CHAPTER THREE

arold knew that shortly after arriving in England his parents relocated to Scunthorpe in England's northeast midlands. Indeed, his earliest childhood memories were of growing up in abject poverty in the industrial city. Scunthorpe was an alien place for Rita. It was of profound regret to Harold that his dear mother had lost her mind there, and ultimately her life, never again returning to her native France. And what made this so bitter a pill to swallow, he thought not for the first time, was that Rita fell ill before the good times came.

Thanks to Albert's thriftiness and army severance pay, he and Rita were not entirely penniless when they reached Newcastle upon Tyne. But they were close to it; the burden of repaying the fifty pound fine incurred for being AWOL had seriously restricted Albert's ability to put money aside. What little they had would not last long. Albert's sister, Beatrice, now married with a husband and two children of her own, agreed against her better judgement for Albert, Rita and Harold to stay for a week until they found their own place. It was as Beatrice had feared. The house was too small, especially as Harold was such a big and mobile child. A trying arrangement soon became intolerable.

Albert set about finding work. But there were literally tens of thousands of ex-servicemen attempting to do the same thing; and Albert's injury made him an unattractive choice, even before prospective employers scrutinized his service record tainted by court martial and his custodial sentence. Keen to know how his old friends from the Tours prison had fared, Albert sought out William Gray and Max Langdon. He found them impoverished and reliant on charities, both telling Albert of experiences similar to his own, of employers loath to hire men with physical limitations and adverse service records.

In a matter of days Albert came to accept he would not find work in Newcastle. This and the tension with Beatrice's family convinced him to relocate his family to the industrial city of Scunthorpe, 140 miles to the south on the southern side of the River Humber. The area's industrial sector, reputedly, was booming. And Albert knew he had no time to waste; his paltry savings were all but exhausted. After paying respects at his mother's gravesite, the family boarded a train to Scunthorpe. Once there they took up residence in a single room, upstairs in a seedy boarding house in the city's gritty inner parts.

For the bulk of the Great War, Scunthorpe's steel industry was vertically integrated in the sense that it processed raw materials through to an end product of steel. This was highly inefficient from a commercial perspective. Despite plentiful iron ore deposits in and around the city, malleable steel could not be made without manganese, of which Scunthorpe had none. This led to the importation of large and expensive quantities of the additive, usually from faraway Cornwall. But the war effort, especially the need for shell casings, demanded the inefficiency.

With the war's end in November 1918, however, the manufacturing focus in Scunthorpe switched to the production of pig iron which, unlike steel, could be made using only the locally sourced iron ore. Not that pig iron alone had utility. Rather, it was a feedstock for making steel. But crucially pig iron could be moved in ingot form, which was infinitely more economical than transporting powdery manganese long distances. As such, steel mills in England with better access to manganese concentrated on making the steel end product, whereas Scunthorpe's mills focused on supplying the essential pig iron. Soon Scunthorpe's steel mills were belching smoke six days a week as the demand for pig iron ramped up, driven by post-war reconstruction in Britain and abroad.

Albert had assumed the need for manpower in Scunthorpe would soon yield him a labouring position. After all, the work was dirty, arduous and often unsafe. Those who could avoid it did. But the situation proved not to be markedly different from Newcastle. Albert's leg was again a problem. And his unfavourable service record deterred those few employers who did consider him. Albert even tried the Scunthorpe general hospital, offering it the benefit of his experience at the sanatorium. But to no avail.

How Albert came to meet a man called Leslie was never clear. It was likely at a soup kitchen where the down on their luck and unfortunate families regularly congregated. Leslie was a chancer, a man born to live on the fringes, always on the lookout for a quick and shady deal. Despite everything, Albert was not overly embittered by his war experiences and struggles with employment. But he was now faced with the prospect of his family's destitution. It was only natural he was prepared at least to consider expedient alternatives.

That's why when Leslie suggested he and Albert rob Scunthorpe's Frodingham railway station Albert did not dismiss the idea out of hand. 'It's an ideal target,' Leslie enthused. 'On Fridays its takings could be as high as fifty pounds.'

Albert proposed a reconnaissance of the railway station. It revealed an open ticket counter embedded in the near end of the station's brick administrative building. 'Piece of cake,' Leslie declared, seemingly failing to notice that cash taken was periodically transferred to a safe in the stationmaster's office via an internal door directly behind the counter.

'But Leslie,' Albert protested, 'if we threatened the ticket counter staff, they could run into the stationmaster's office and lock the door before we had time to vault the counter.'

'No problem,' Leslie said, determined not to be put off. 'I know where we can obtain a gun and force entry.'

The mention of a gun alarmed Albert and his interest in Leslie's plan paled. Even so, perhaps because he had nothing better to do, he did accompany Leslie to meet a man called Danny Potter. Danny's real name was Danik Potupa and he was originally from Belarus. A big, strong and ruthless man, he was also an astute judge of character. Danny used Leslie as a tout, someone who occasionally sold stolen goods for him. But he was under no illusions as to Leslie's many shortcomings. On hearing of Leslie's intention to rob the Frodingham railway station using a handgun to force entry into the stationmaster's office, Danny's eyes rolled in his head. Leslie was the last person on earth to whom Danny would sell a gun. With that, much to Albert's relief, the idea to rob the railway station quickly ran into the sands.

Shortly after, Leslie disappeared from sight. No one knew why or to where but it was safely assumed one of his get-rich-quick schemes had upset the wrong person. Nonetheless, Albert's encounter with Leslie was not entirely fruitless. Danny Potter, it transpires, had seen in Albert an intelligence and restlessness worth cultivating.

The dispatcher reappeared, tapping Harold lost in thought on his knee. He cupped his mouth next to Harold's ear. 'There's an hour-and-a-half to go,' he screamed. 'We'll be over the mountains soon. It'll get rough.' Harold looked up and nodded. He had checked and re-checked everything. There was nothing to do but sit and wait and hope, when the time came, it all went smoothly. His message imparted, the dispatcher left to buckle into his seat in the Whitley's front section. Harold gripped a steel strut as the plane pitched and rolled. *Steel,* he thought, *the making and unmaking of my father.* Before long Harold was again a boy, fascinated by his father's stories about building his business empire and the characters he encountered along the way – people like Danny Potter and Paddy Kearney.

Danny Potter was not philosophically opposed to legitimate business ventures; it was just that more money could be made illegally by avoiding certain overheads. That's why on receipt of a letter two months ago from his cousin Pavel, another Belarusian who had immigrated to Canada gripped by the gold lust, Danny had settled on a course of illegality. Pavel's letter told of the recent nationalization of the Canadian railway and plans by the now controlling authority to extend the network to Canada's far northwest, all the way to the frozen reaches of the Yukon Territory. Pavel had described in detail the huge amounts of high-quality steel necessary for building railway track, bridges and tunnels. And he claimed to know of several Canadian steel mills anxious to source good quality, reasonably priced pig iron. Danny's nose began to twitch and soon a plan had formed in his mind. He had now taken the first steps in its implementation.

Danny initially represented his venture to Albert as a legitimate undertaking. In this guise he took Albert to Scunthorpe's Prince George Hotel to meet a certain Paddy Kearney, an impish Irishman from Dublin of about thirty with a lived-in face, whom Danny introduced as his *transport contractor*. Paddy owned a lorry, a tilt bodied van. Had Albert enquired, he would have learned Paddy inherited the van from his English brother-in-law in Blackburn who contracted thoracic cancer. Paddy's inheritance was conditional on continuing his brother-in-law's cartage business in order to support the man's wife, Paddy's sister.

But all too often the van would lay idle when Paddy was on the drink. And when his sister gave up on him and returned to Ireland, Paddy decided a clean break was in order. He had driven the lorry clear to Scunthorpe over a year ago. The cartage business he established was barely viable, not helped by Paddy's propensity to drink himself into a stupor at every turn. This paucity of work meant that when Danny Potter came calling Paddy jumped at the opportunity.

By now it was mid-afternoon and Paddy was four pints downstream. 'Last *Tursday*,' he whispered to Albert after Danny went to the lavatory, his Irish lilt exaggerated by the drink, 'me and Danny broke into the Carmichael mill storage yard. In the wee hours it were. Dark as *fook*;

couldn't see a thing. We pinched 200 pig iron ingots, one imperial ton; took hours to load on the lorry. Poor old van nearly didn't make it but we got the load down to Danny's office in Tulip Road and hid it in the backyard.' Paddy took a deep sip of his Guinness. 'The next step,' he confided to Albert, 'is to drive the stuff to a bonded warehouse near the Port of Grimsby, when Danny says so.'

On his return, Danny continued discussing his venture as if it were a lawful enterprise. It was preferable, he explained, to transport the pig iron the twenty-six miles to the Port of Grimsby by road rather than barge it down the River Humber. 'Cheaper,' he said, slapping the Irishman's back. 'And also means more work for Paddy.' Paddy's wink told Albert that Danny's preference for road transport had more to do with avoiding a local barge operator asking questions about the pig iron's origin than it did other considerations.

The bonded warehouse where Paddy was to take the pig iron offered floor space on short-term rental. It was also where export items underwent customs clearance before being loaded onto ships. Danny's biggest headache was that the customs official inspecting his consignment had to do so in the presence of the shipper's agent, since without a form indicating payment of customs duty, the shipper was not permitted to accept the goods.

Duty on pig iron was levied at thirty per cent of the government-pegged wholesale price. An imperial ton of pig iron currently wholesaled for 100 pounds, the amount Danny intended his arranged forged bill of sale to reflect. Thus the customs duty payable was thirty pounds. Danny had settled on a plan for avoiding the impost. But he had been unable to identify the right accomplice to pull it off. He needed someone credible and reliable to play the role of a customs bureaucrat. Limping Albert Bradshaw, Danny had decided, was just the man.

Danny's judgement was sound. 'Fine,' was all Albert said as he and Danny left the Prince George Hotel, after Danny had offered him a fiver to assist in avoiding the *extortionate* customs duty.

On 30 July 1919, Paddy Kearney's lorry transferred Danny's Potter's stolen pig iron to the bonded warehouse at the Port of Grimsby. The next day, a Thursday, wearing a dustcoat bearing the insignia of HM Customs over a shirt and tie, Albert attended the warehouse where he met Danny and a man called John Bowe, the agent for Danny's shipper, Gale Logistics.

Danny first showed Bowe then Albert his forged bill of sale for 100 pounds, the official wholesale rate for a ton of pig iron. Bowe glanced at it briefly and nodded his approval. With that, Albert validated the document with his stamp, which he endorsed with his initials. Next Danny produced a bank cheque for thirty pounds – as good as cash in those days – to cover the assessed customs duty. Albert wrote out a receipt for payment using the customs slip given him by Danny the day before along with the stamp, customs attire, and the shirt and tie. He stamped and initialled both pages, giving the original to Bowe, the shipper's agent, and Danny the carbon copy. 'We'll load tomorrow,' Bowe said. 'The ship will sail on the night tide.' The men shook hands and went their separate ways.

Albert attended Danny's office on Tulip Road on Friday morning whereupon he received his five pound payment. Tulip Road was an unkempt side street in a rundown area of Scunthorpe close to the railway line running east from Frodingham station to Grimsby Town. Only those who had the misfortune to live in the area or a pressing need ever ventured there. Usually Danny wouldn't have bothered paying someone unimposing like Albert. But he had other plans in which Albert prominently featured. So when Albert handed back the items given him earlier, including the bank cheque with which Danny had purportedly paid his customs duty, Danny coughed up. Indeed, Danny was well pleased; in effect, he had just reduced his customs duty overhead from the nominal thirty pounds to five.

And the cost of Paddy Kearney's transport services? Well, Danny knew Paddy would try to gouge him. That's why he had chosen Paddy for the job, agreed to his excessive fee of twenty pounds, and why he was going to make an example of Paddy. This would ensure any contractor involved in Danny's future plans to ship other stolen pig iron consignments to Canada thought twice before following Paddy's lead.

It was for this reason Danny was found loitering outside the Prince George Hotel around closing time the day after his shipment of pig iron departed for Canada. It was a Saturday – a day which Paddy habitually spent in the pub. Just before closing time, Paddy was ejected onto the street. Danny watched him stagger down the road towards the laneway where his seedy lodgings were located, following at a safe distance until Paddy turned into the laneway. Away from the main road it was still and quiet. Danny came up behind Paddy and softly called his name. Paddy turned, drunkenly confused, before finally realizing it was Danny. He offered his hand, which Danny ignored. Instead, from a scabbard inside his trouser leg, Danny withdrew an iron bar wrapped in newspaper. After his coshing Paddy lay motionless on the ground, blood seeping from a gaping head wound. Barely conscious, he was powerless to prevent Danny from relieving him of the bulk of the twenty pounds paid for his trucking services, some eighteen pounds.

Later that night of 2 August 1919 Paddy was taken to hospital once a vagrant looking for a place to sleep stumbled across him and removed the small change in Paddy's pocket. Danny's intended message soon began to percolate.

Danny had now minimized his expenses to the extent possible, including of course by not paying for the pig iron in the first place. A methodical man, he documented each reduction in overheads in a ledger so that he might keep track of progress. By the time the pig iron left for Canada, Danny had outlaid a total of 110 pounds for unavoidable costs. True, he had been obliged by industry practice to send the shipment free on board destination – which translated into Danny shouldering liability for the load until it reached its destination port. Even so, his careful research had revealed he could offset the mandatory insurance fee by opting for second-class stowage. That the pig iron lashed to the ship's deck would be exposed to the elements during the voyage was of no matter; it did not rust.

Danny had earlier instructed Pavel to ask the buyer, the Fredericton steel mill in Canada's New Brunswick province, for a sale price of 290 pounds. This undercut the going retail rate of 300 pounds per ton for pig iron shipped from England to Canada's eastern seaboard. Danny's plan was to establish a relationship with the buyer whereupon his subsequent stolen shipments could be sold directly to the mill, bypassing Pavel and his ten pound spotter's fee. In this way, Danny would make up the profit shortfall associated with his cut-price rate.

The Fredericton people were not about to look a gift horse in the mouth and accepted Pavel's below market rate offer. This left Danny with a clear profit of 180 pounds, given he had outlaid 110 pounds to get the pig iron to Canada and the Fredericton mill had paid 290 pounds for it. He eagerly awaited the arrival of the mill's cheque for payment made out in pounds sterling as requested. Ever the canny one, or so he thought, Danny had impressed on Pavel that the cheque should be crossed as non-negotiable. In other words, the cheque would be made out such that only Danny, the nominated payee, could cash it.

The updraft from the Pyrenees Mountains was now causing the Whitley bomber to buck wildly. Hanging on for grim death, Harold remembered his father once telling him that, when the dust settled, there was a lot of debate around the Prince George and other of Scunthorpe's lesser hostelries as to whether Danny Potter should have hit Paddy harder, softer or not at all. 'On the principle that dead men tell no tales,' Albert had said, 'most decided option one was the only sensible choice.' Harold was nearly ten at the time of Albert's oblique passing reference to Nutter Collymore, the man who took revenge for Paddy Kearney's bashing. It was not until Harold was older, perhaps fourteen or fifteen and less likely to be disturbed by the violence, that his father told him the full Nutter story.

Cornelius Charles Collymore wasn't nicknamed *Nutter* for nothing. He was in fact barely three months off the boat from Ireland. Nutter's departure from the Emerald Isle had been a hasty affair. In May 1919 he'd shot dead a man called Fergus O'Donnell as Fergus was leaving his home in Kilkenny – in the middle of Wolfe Tone Street in broad daylight – as if he were a rabid dog. But Fergus came from a large if not so good Catholic family. Sooner rather than later his seven brothers, aided by an unhinged cousin or twenty, were on Nutter's trail. And once the family had done a whip around and raised a reward for information on Nutter's whereabouts, Nutter knew previously trusted souls would fall over themselves to give him up. It was leave or face the consequences, simple as that.

First stop for Nutter was Liverpool. But he knew he would not be safe there; Ireland was merely an overnight ferry ride away. So he took himself to England's northeast midlands, arriving in Scunthorpe in June 1919. He spent his first two weeks laying low venturing out only to buy drink for his hip flask, which he consumed in the confines of his cockroach-infested lodgings. But soon enough Nutter recovered his nerve.

Nutter's main skill was as an enforcer, someone good at knocking heads together. That is why the gambling supremos from Cork City had contracted him to convince Fergus O'Donnell to pay his delinquent gambling debts. But it was an unwise engagement, principally because Nutter was unstable; indeed, he was highly erratic. All too often a red haze he could never quite explain took over when practising his craft. The affliction first surfaced in Nutter's late teens and thereafter with sufficient frequency to earn him the *Nutter* sobriquet while still in his early twenties. And even now, at age forty, the disorder could be lethal when Nutter had a gun in his hand, as Fergus O'Donnell found out the hard way when Nutter blew his face away while supposed only to be scaring him.

For all that, Nutter had a good size rational streak to him. He realized that in a workingman's industrial city like Scunthorpe there would be demand for his services. People in such parts regularly sought relief from the hard slog of their lives. Some did it peaceably enough while others indulged in certain illegal pleasures guaranteed to result in enmities and the incurrence of debts of one form or another.

Scunthorpe also appealed to Nutter because it was a city in which the emigrating Irish did not settle in numbers. The absence of an Irish diaspora of which to speak offered a level of security virtually unmatched in all England; the last thing Nutter needed was a *boyo* getting a message back home to the O'Donnell clan. Paddy Kearney, accordingly, was one of a small contingent of Irishmen domiciled in the city. But those who did live in Scunthorpe gravitated to each other. And when Nutter learned a few Irish lads hailing from Dublin regularly took a pint at the Prince George Hotel, he decided that as a west coast man from distant County Kerry it was safe to break cover.

Nutter was a curious mix of psychopath and Irish sentimentalist. The trouble was you could never be sure which hat he was wearing on any given day. But when news of Paddy's bashing reached the Prince George in early August, the sentimentalist temporarily came to the fore. Along with Irish others, Nutter visited Paddy in hospital later in the week, bearing bottles of Irish whisky which the hospital authorities were only too pleased to confiscate. Paddy of course had clammed up when the police came calling but was more forthcoming in whispered conversation with his friends. Nutter knew it was only a matter of time before the police discovered Danny Potter was behind the bashing. Even so, the constabulary England-wide was renowned for not making much effort to investigate assaults involving the bog

Irish. Nutter immediately recognized the opportunity. He would atone for Paddy's injuries and in the process establish his credentials as a Scunthorpe hard man.

But a great learner of lessons Nutter was not. After killing Fergus O'Donnell, he would have done well to avoid firearms altogether. To be fair, though, that would have run counter to his natural instincts. No doubt he had dumped the handgun used to kill O'Donnell before making his escape to England. But he had kept two others, hidden in the lining of his suitcase. Now sitting in his murky rooms sipping neat whisky, Nutter removed his favourite tool of trade from its calico wrapping – a British Webley Mark Four revolver – and tenderly, as if bathing a baby, set about cleaning and oiling the weapon.

It was a Sunday night when Nutter performed his revolver maintenance. The next morning he set about locating Danny Potter. Nutter planned to kneecap Danny, that is shoot him in the knees, this most Irish of retributions designed to leave the victim incapacitated and in severe pain ever after. Only Nutter would know if he gave any thought to the risk of his red haze taking over. Whatever, Danny was shot dead the following Friday, 15 August 1919, in the middle of Scunthorpe, around noon in front of the Catholic church on Oswald Road.

The good folk of Scunthorpe were outraged. The *Scunthorpe Advertiser* led the charge. Politicians became involved. Under pressure to find the culprit, the Lincolnshire constabulary mobilized. A description was circulated. Soon an informant suggested an Irishman by the name of Collymore might have done the hit. From this point on Nutter was a marked man. The police took it personally. No lout of an Irishman was going to come into their bailiwick and start executing people, even if the target was a slime like Danny Potter.

A squad of heavily armed officers raided Nutter's rooms. There they found Nutter's remaining pistol still secreted in his portmanteau and the calico cloth in which he habitually wrapped his Webley pistol. Correctly presuming Nutter was still armed, the police broadcast a public warning that a dangerous fugitive was on the loose.

More quietly, an internal order circulated to the effect that unless Collymore surrendered meekly, officers were to shoot to kill. And that's how Nutter met his maker. When the police were alerted to a man answering Nutter's description making his way along the banks of the River Humber towards Grimsby, they descended in numbers. A challenge was issued to which Nutter, inundated by his red haze, responded with two shots from his pistol. A Constable Ordish, firing a Lee-Enfield rifle from a position safely out of range of Nutter, was credited with the kill.

CHAPTER FOUR

The Whitley bomber continued to pitch violently as it traversed the Pyrenees Mountains, heading for the midpoint where the pilot would turn left and fly up the centre of France towards Riom. By now Harold had grown accustomed to the plane's gyrations and no longer had sweaty palms. So acclimatized, he became engrossed in recalling his father's account of the events in the aftermath of Nutter Collymore's death. As ever when Collymore's name was mentioned, Harold marvelled at Albert's insight in identifying the business opportunity created by Danny Potter's murder. He was so proud his father had been sufficiently bold and resourceful as to grasp the moment ahead of any other.

Albert greeted Nutter Collymore's death with relief, having briefly feared Nutter might think him Danny Potter's accomplice and act accordingly. Even so, Danny's murder had denied Albert the chance of further work. Absent other prospects, Albert's mind turned to Scunthorpe's steel mills, working day and night to meet the existing demand for pig iron, and Danny Potter's enthusiasm for the new, huge and expanding, and essentially untapped Canadian pig iron market. Suddenly, Albert was energized by the thought of making a living by merging the two factors, by brokering the sale of Scunthorpe pig iron to Canada. But he had to act quickly, before the void was filled. And to attract local mills to the Canadian market, he had to make it economically worthwhile. It was Canada or bust.

Late on the night of Wednesday 20 August 1919, the same day he resolved to become a broker, Albert made a visit to Danny Potter's office on Tulip Road. The office was housed on the first floor of an old red brick building that had once been an iron foundry. The structure had been converted into six discrete units, three upstairs and three at street level. Two ground floor units sported heavily padlocked doors, suggesting their use as storerooms. The other ground floor unit and all on the first floor bar Danny's office appeared vacant. Albert entered the unfenced complex. He was nervous given the area's well earned reputation as a no-go place after dark but grateful that as a result the police almost never patrolled out here. An approaching freight train caused Albert to jump, reminding him again the office was adjacent to the Scunthorpe–Grimsby railway line.

With Danny's demise, Albert wasn't overly surprised to find the office had been ravaged. He lit the paraffin lamp he carried and surveyed the detritus. Anything of conceivable value had been removed; even the cheap bookshelves on the wall had been ripped out and taken away. Papers were strewn across the floor, flung aside from the purloined bookshelves. But it was the papers in which Albert was interested. For the next hour he sifted through the mess until he found one item he was seeking – correspondence between Danny and Mr John Bowe, shipping agent for Gale Logistics. The letter gave up that Bowe's office was located in Pier Street in Hull, some twenty-five miles away on the northern bank of the River Humber. It was nearly 4 am before Albert unearthed the other item he sought – an envelope containing a letter to Danny from his cousin in Canada, one Pavel Isachenko, on the back flap of which was Pavel's mailing address written in English. In the interim, Albert came across a ledger, its entries itemizing general costings and those specific to Danny's recent pig iron shipment. Instinctively, he stuffed it down his shirt before resuming the search for Pavel's contact details. It was a stroke of inspired intuition. The ledger soon became a vital source of pricing intelligence.

First thing next morning Albert wrote to Pavel, trusting he would find a translator if need be. He explained Danny's sudden death, from natural causes he said, and how he had taken over Danny's business. Albert was aware Pavel was unproven, having sold Danny's stolen pig iron in Canada at a reduced price. But knowing of no other candidate, he proposed Pavel become his Canadian commission agent at a rate consistent with Danny's ledger of ten pounds per ton sold. Albert's key stipulation, however, was that Pavel sell his pig iron at the undiscounted retail rate of 300 pounds per imperial ton. Albert despatched his letter by surface mail later that day.

The same night, by the glow of his paraffin lamp for his room had no electric light, Albert wrote to his ex-army friends William Gray and Max Langdon in Newcastle, care of the church-run doss house where he had last seen them. These were men on whom Albert could rely to provide inexpensive labour. He also knew William and Max would be skint. The next morning, therefore, he outlaid a precious five shillings from his fast diminishing five pound fee from Danny Potter to book dual passage on the 3 September rail service to Scunthorpe, thus giving his friends time enough to receive his letter and pick up their tickets at Newcastle Central railway station.

Albert planned that William and Max would sleep on the floor of the family's single room until permanent lodgings could be found, utilizing the outside privy and washroom shared with other residents. But Rita objected strenuously. At one end of Albert and Rita's room sat their dining setting, comprising four packing crates, and alongside it a small iron tub for bathing Harold. At the other end lay an improvised mattress of cardboard and newspaper. Next to the marital bed was the only decent item of furniture the couple owned, the cot in which Harold slept. And at the room's midpoint, a rickety brick fireplace acted as a kitchen where morning and night a fire was lit and food prepared atop a steel grate. 'No space in room, none,' Rita had proclaimed. '*Et le privé est-il adéquat?*' she added pointedly, foreshadowing the outrage of other tenants should William and Max try to use the building's overtaxed amenities.

Faced with Rita's insistence, Albert had no choice but to consider other options for William and Max. His attention turned to Paddy Kearney still in the hospital. Albert was planning to visit Paddy in any event but now made haste to the infirmary given he had an extra matter to discuss. By this stage Paddy's friends from the Prince George Hotel had tired of visiting. Irish sentimentality, in Scunthorpe at least, was of the ephemeral kind. The bored Paddy was only too pleased to give his visitor his undivided attention.

Albert began by outlining his business plan, having now closely studied Danny Potter's ledger. The ledger, Albert said, revealed a cost of 230 pounds all up to legally ship a ton of pig iron to Canada's eastern seaboard. At the going retail rate of 300 pounds, this returned suppliers a profit of seventy pounds per ton. The ledger also indicated an average per-ton profit across all other pig iron markets of eighty-two pounds. Albert told Paddy his aim was to ship pig iron to Canada at a total cost of 210 pounds per ton, inclusive of a twenty pound per ton brokerage fee. At the retail sale rate of 300 pounds, the resulting ninety pounds per ton profit would be the means for attracting Scunthorpe suppliers to the Canadian market. But achieving a 210 pound base, Albert warned, called for savage reductions in logistics overheads, including in local transport and labour. Cheap labour he had arranged through ex-army friends; he was now inviting Paddy to be his local transport counterpart.

Without waiting for Paddy's answer, Albert moved straight to his extra discussion item. He proposed William and Max sleep in Paddy's lorry until they found better digs. It would be a rough existence, Albert conceded, relying on a night bucket for basic needs and a once a week dip in the River Humber for their personal hygiene. Albert also suggested Paddy's lorry be moved to the street in front of his residence and parked there. Time was limited, Albert explained, and William and Max needed to be close by to plan and consult. There was no time to waste commuting. William and Max would sleep in the van's enclosed back, venturing into Albert's room only to drink tea and fry bully beef, at least while there was money to buy provisions. Soon, Albert knew, they would all be relying on soup kitchens to exist.

Paddy said nothing for a time, raising Albert's concern he was about to voice objections. To the contrary, Paddy could scarcely believe his luck. After nearly three weeks of internment, he had tired of the hospital and its overbearing matron. And by now his head wound had nearly healed, and he was sure the draining concussion headaches would stop soon. Furthermore, in just the past week the two landlords in his life had disowned him: the owner of the Prince George Hotel where Paddy's van had been garaged in return for his drinking every penny he earned in the pub, and the owner of the rooming house where Paddy had not paid rent for weeks. The former had demanded Paddy shift his lorry now he was not providing custom whereas the latter had welcomed the opportunity to evict him.

Finally, the Irishman spoke. 'Come and get me when William and Max arrive,' he said simply. 'It'll be time and more to be gone from here.' Despite his many flaws, Paddy was a man of principle. When he shook Albert's hand a deal was sealed as if he had signed a contract drafted by the finest lawyer in the land.

Skinny and drawn, William Gray and Max Langdon arrived in Scunthorpe as scheduled on Wednesday 3 September 1919. Albert took them directly to the hospital where Paddy signed out. Within two hours the four men were at the Prince George Hotel, with Albert firmly entrenched as the group's leader. The big red van with the huge front radiator and enclosed tray section dwarfing the open driver's cabin took some coaxing into life, but with Paddy's skilled handling it finally left the hotel.

Shortly after, Paddy, William and Max took up residence in the back of Paddy's van parked in the street outside the crumbling two-storey dwelling housing Albert, Rita and Harold's spartan accommodation. It was an unusual arrangement even by inner city Scunthorpe standards.

It was in the period immediately after moving Paddy's lorry that Albert first noticed the change in Rita. At different times, infrequently at first then more often, he began to catch her staring into space, vacant and unhearing. Rita was a prisoner of the couple's penury and her language barrier. Albert decided she was lacking in adult company, spending too much time alone with two-year-old Harold. He resolved to focus on his business with greater urgency, believing once the family was on its financial feet life would normalize and Rita with it. Albert was right to suspect Rita's isolation. But he underestimated its insidiously cumulative effect. Day by day, Rita was inching towards the brink of catatonia from where, anon, the proverbial straw would break the camel's back and tip her into a state of permanent trance.

Harold's briefers had repeatedly warned him how the war had pitted the French people against each other. For a clandestine agent, they had told him, France was a dangerous place where the smallest mistake would invite a collaborator to inform on him, spelling certain disaster. But seated in the Whitley bomber, the aircraft flying smoothly now the Pyrenees Mountains were behind it, Harold was at a happy phase of his father's story. He had purged his mind of the dangers soon to confront him in favour of pleasant memories. It especially pleased Harold to recall Albert's reflections on the Gale Logistics agreement, one of the key early steps on his way to building an empire.

Paddy's lorry rumbled into Hull around noon on Thursday 4 September 1919. It stopped briefly to allow Albert to alight and then moved on. Albert strolled up and down

Pier Street, never losing sight of the Gale Logistics office. When he saw John Bowe leave the building on his lunch break, wrapped sandwich in hand, Albert made a beeline for him.

'Mr Bowe,' Albert said, once he'd caught up to the shipping agent, 'did you know you were recently a party to a criminal offence? I need to talk to you about it.'

Bowe did not initially recognize Albert, whose ragged appearance belied he'd once acted as a customs inspector for Bowe's benefit. But the allegation was sufficient to stop Bowe in his tracks. 'Who are you?' he demanded heatedly.

Albert reminded Bowe of his part in Danny Potter's shipment. 'Without checking the validity of the bill of sale or verifying the credentials of the inspecting customs officer, you agreed to ship Danny's consignment of pig iron. That places you in contravention of the UK Customs Act. For that you are at risk of deregistration as a licensed shipping agent. You have two options. One is to allow the police to investigate and probably lose your job; the other is to listen to my proposal.'

Bowe's face turned ashen grey. The mere thought of losing his job terrified him; he had a wife and two young children to feed. 'What do you want?' he said, his voice wavering.

Albert let Bowe stew as they walked towards the Hull docks. Bowe's appetite had deserted him. He dumped his cheese and pickle sandwich in a refuse bin as they went. Only then did Albert tell him of Danny's theft of a ton of pig iron and his scheme to avoid paying customs tax on it. Albert outlined his own role in the matter and family reasons for doing so. By the time the two men reached the waterfront, he had detailed his plan to become a legitimate broker shipping pig iron to Canada. But to attract Scunthorpe suppliers to the Canadian market, Albert explained, he needed cheap shipping rates. In return for an exclusivity agreement, Albert proposed Gale Logistics give him a premium of twenty-five per cent on the usual cost of shipping to Canada's eastern seaboard.

'A ton of pig iron can be shipped to the Canadian east for eighty pounds plus eight pounds insurance if it goes free on board destination, second-class stowage,' Bowe said. Albert knew this was true because it matched the cost of shipping and insurance recorded in Danny Potter's ledger. 'You're asking for a discount of twenty pounds on shipping,' Bowe continued. He shook his head and grimaced. 'Twenty-five per cent is out of the question. Mr Gale would baulk without even considering it.'

Albert tactically gave ground. 'I've enough problems of my own without taking on yours,' he said. 'You deliver me a twenty per cent premium or I'm going to the police, simple as that.'

Bowe looked at him slyly. 'I'd almost certainly escape prison if you went to the police but for impersonating a customs officer you'd be sure to go inside. Your family would be left destitute.'

The truth of this did not fluster Albert. 'Mr Bowe,' he said evenly, 'my position is as dire as you say; you can tell that just by looking at me. But that is my strength, actually. You are wrong if you think I have more to lose than you. The simple truth is no one will give me a job because of my leg injury and the fact that I spent a year in a military prison. Unless I can start a viable business, my family and I are all dead in the not-so-long run. Alternatively, you and your family can expect a good life so long as you keep your job. Accordingly, Mr Bowe, it is you who has everything to lose and me who has nothing at stake.'

Standing there on the northern bank of the River Humber, black clouds dotting the sky, Bowe felt the weight of the world on his shoulders. He knew Albert was serious, leaving him no way out. 'I'll give you a fifteen per cent discount on the eighty pound shipping rate provided that, in addition to the initial one-ton shipment, you ship a minimum of thirty tons of pig iron over the course of a calendar year commencing on 1 October 1919 and ending 30 September 1920. But the first shipment of 200 ingots must be on the high seas by the first of October, otherwise Mr Gale will assess you as an unreliable client unable to meet deadlines and veto the deal. That's the best I can do.'

The 1 October deadline seriously troubled Albert. Letters to and from Canada took over a month in transit, meaning his letter to Danny Potter's cousin Pavel, proposing Pavel become his commission agent, would arrive in late September. Therefore, even were Pavel willing and able to find a Canadian buyer his response would not be received until well after 1 October. Yet Albert assessed Bowe had been pushed to his limit. 'The offer's not ideal,' Albert said, feigning indecision. 'But I'll accept it.' He had, in fact, no other realistic option.

Bowe didn't answer. Instead, he took Albert's outstretched hand. Albert wasn't deterred by the agent's clammy grip; it told him Bowe wouldn't dare break his word. Albert walked away feeling no particular elation. True, he had made a significant step forward. But now with the first shipment due in a mere twenty-seven days he had to find a local supplier willing to enter the Canadian market on the unproven promise of an above average rate of return. More to the point, in the same timeframe he had to find a guaranteed Canadian buyer, one prepared to pay the going retail rate of 300 pounds a ton for pig iron shipped from England free on board destination, second-class stowage.

CHAPTER FIVE

Harold continued to revel in the memories of Albert's run up to the good times as the Whitley bomber maintained its northerly heading towards Riom. He especially thought of the name Albert had bestowed on his business and how it spoke of his father valuing his family above all else. Not that it had all been plain sailing. Albert had often told the story of the hard-won lucky break that followed soon after the Gale Logistics deal. 'It was destiny,' he used to say. 'But it didn't come easily.'

In 1919 Scunthorpe's steel industry had not yet undergone consolidation. As a result, six small, privately owned steel mills existed alongside the three big operations later to eat those smaller players managing to survive. Mulling things over on the way back from Hull in Paddy's lumbering lorry on 4 September, Albert decided the majors would deal in volumes too big for him. He would target the smaller private mills. But, Albert reasoned, he would need a supplier with access to Canadian buyers. Only then could he meet the pressing 1 October deadline imposed by Gale Logistics' John Bowe. And if he could not find a supplier able to deliver him a Canadian buyer? Well, it would be a *Dublin Zoo* and his business dream would be over before it began.

Albert rose early the Friday morning after visiting Hull intent on approaching the Carmichael mill, the very same mill from which Danny Potter had once stolen 200 pig iron ingots. It was a private mill some two hours of walking from his home. Albert wore a collar and spit-buffed his boots for the occasion.

Albert entered the Carmichael mill to find its front counter unstaffed. He stepped into the area beyond the counter to see a man seated at an office desk reading a newspaper. Albert tapped lightly on the door. 'Excuse me,' he said politely.

The man was in his late forties, broad chested and with a bristling moustache. He looked up and saw Albert. 'Is that damn new girl late again?' he growled exasperatedly to the air.

Albert jumped in while he could. 'I'm looking for the mill owner,' he said. 'I have a plan to broker the sale of pig iron such as to return at least an additional eight pounds per ton profit.'

'We have an absentee owner,' the man said. 'I'm Nettlefold, the mill manager.' Nettlefold looked at Albert, weighing him, but otherwise saying or doing nothing.

Albert dared to hope. Nettlefold might not be the mill's ultimate decision-maker but he would have the owner's ear. 'I'll only take a minute of your time,' Albert said.

'Sit down,' Nettlefold said cautiously. Albert limped forward, sat and began to outline his business plan, deliberately not mentioning his destination market. To his endless encouragement, he detected Nettlefold's interest pique.

The conversation deepened. 'Noticed your limp,' Nettlefold said after a time. 'The war?'

'Battle of Loos, October 1915,' Albert replied. 'Shrapnel.'

'Ah ha,' Nettlefold said engagingly. 'Which regiment?'

Albert's heart sunk. Nettlefold's question had taken the conversation in a dangerous direction. 'Northumberland Fusiliers,' Albert said, hoping soon to change the subject.

'Really?' Nettlefold said with gusto. 'I was in Paris with headquarters planning for the Seventeenth.' The Seventeenth Battalion was a Fusiliers service unit that built and repaired Western Front railway track. For those in the field the work was exceedingly dangerous, much less so for those in headquarters planning. 'We gave those Huns a nice old licking, didn't we?'

Nettlefold's enthusiasm for the war crushed Albert's hopes in an instant; he knew for certain his service record would be a problem. Albert's instincts were on point. When Nettlefold asked for Albert's service papers and saw he'd spent time in a military prison, the goodwill evaporated. 'Can't help you,' were Nettlefold's frosty final words.

Albert left the Carmichael mill frustrated to have been rebuffed because of his service record. By the time he reached his street he had decided to focus on finding a private mill owner too old for military service, one less influenced by tainted war records. Moreover, Albert reasoned, in truth more in hope than conviction, over time older owners would have amassed Canadian buyers among their industry contacts.

At home, Albert found William and Max bored and listless after a day spent in the back of Paddy's truck. Paddy was not there but returned shortly after to advise he had secured a job selling newspapers, starting immediately. An Irish pal of his was going home and had alerted Paddy to the vacancy. For Albert, this was welcome news in an otherwise bad day. The few pennies Paddy would earn would buy badly needed porridge, tea and bully beef at a time when his family and the others all might well starve.

After gruel for dinner, Albert, Paddy, William and Max sat in the back of Paddy's lorry. Albert outlined his plan to target private mill owners too old for military service. He proposed William and Max visit the two villages adjoining Scunthorpe that each hosted a private mill. 'Pretend to seek work off your war service,' he said. 'Ask about if the local mill owner served in the war.' William and Max were eager to be gainfully employed. 'But shave and polish your boots,' Albert cautioned, 'or people will think you vagrants.' He paused and smiled. 'After all, you are representing ARH Brokerage Services.' Paddy's lorry rocked with laughter. All in it understood the ARH acronym. It meant Albert, Rita and Harold – the picture worth a thousand words Albert had painted when earlier naming his business.

On Saturday morning 6 September the four men went their separate ways – in Albert's case to two other private mills to offer higher rates of return in exchange for access, aiming to trawl for an owner too old for military service. A prim young man staffing the first mill's front office counter was immediately disdainful. Unspeaking, he pointed to a counter sign reading *No unsolicited callers* before turning his back in rude dismissal. Albert's was a repeat experience at the second mill, if more genteel. A kindly woman at reception told him to wait. She left the area to return minutes later carrying a cup of tea. 'Here, dear,' she said, 'drink this. You look half starved to death. Then best be on your way.'

Albert made the long trek home, pondering lessons learned. If he was ever to get before owners unencumbered by war service, he decided, he had to bypass any praetorian guard, gatekeepers and mill managers alike. With Paddy, done with his first day of newspaper selling, Albert waited for William and Max to return from the village of Ealand some nine miles away. Long before their homecoming, a weary Paddy retired to the lorry.

'Anything to report?' Albert asked softly once William and Max had finished their supper of heated rainwater porridge. At the far end of the room Harold slept in his cot and Rita lay in waking silence on the makeshift bed she shared with Albert.

As ever with William and Max, William did the talking. 'Not much,' he said soberly. 'Although we did find out the Ealand steel mill owner is too old to have served in the war.'

'How so?' Albert said, subdued by William's lack of animation.

'Well,' William said, 'a Salvation Army fellow at the *Cock and Crow* told us a chap by the name of Basil Pomerory owns the Ealand mill. Not Pomeroy, the Salvo said, but *Pomerory*. Apparently he's over seventy. After his grandson was killed at the Somme, the dead soldier's father, Pomerory's son, got on the bottle. Basil came out of retirement to save the mill.' William shook his head. 'But even though Pomerory didn't serve, it doesn't help us. The effect of the war on his family is certain to have him look down his nose at our service records.'

Suddenly, William and Max saw intensity in Albert's eyes. 'This Basil,' Albert said, his senses jangling at the mention of the Pomerory name, 'what did you say his name was?'

'Pomerory, not Pomeroy, according to the Salvo. What's the significance of that?'

'When I was at the Chantilly sanatorium in France during the war a young man called Stanley Poppleton gave me his diary just before he committed suicide. In it he wrote of being with a lad called Pomerory when Pomerory died at the Somme.'

William and Max watched as Albert moved to the far end of the room, treading lightly to avoid disturbing Rita. But even though her eyes were open, staring vacantly at the ceiling, she appeared not to notice his movement.

Albert returned with an item folded in newspaper. 'This,' Albert said, holding up Stanley's diary, 'might well be the key to establishing ARH Brokerage Services. We need to tell Pomerory that in all likelihood we have information on his grandson, after which I would hope to pay him a visit. If I've learned anything over the past two days, it's the importance of making our pitch directly to an owner. Get some rest, gentlemen. Tomorrow we will reconnoitre the Ealand steel mill.'

With that, Albert stooped to pick up a piece of yellowed paper that had fallen from the diary. Upon reading the short message on it, he nodded in recognition.

CHAPTER SIX

For a reason he did not understand, Harold suddenly thought of the Whitley bomber being painted entirely in black matt. 'Makes us harder to spot, especially when there's cloud about,' the flight lieutenant pilot had told him at RAF Tempsford prior to departure. The thought of racing through the night sky in an unlit, all-black aluminium and canvas tube caused Harold's happy mood to vanish. As if by association, he thought about Albert stumbling across Basil Pomerory. Certainly, it was a high point in his father's life. But equally, Albert never recovered from the fact it ultimately came at the cost of Willie Gray's life.

On the morning of Sunday 7 September 1919, after bread and dripping and a cup of tea, Albert, William and Max left for the Ealand steel mill. Paddy was missing even though Sunday was not a newspaper-selling day; he had woken with yet another debilitating concussion headache. It took the three men several hours to reach the mill on an industrial estate adjacent to the Ealand village. A mile or so away, and a world apart from the mill's griminess, was the pristine Clearwater Lake. They passed by it while en route, stopping briefly to admire its beauty.

Looking through the surrounding wire fence, Albert and the others saw a complex of red brick buildings all with rusted, corrugated iron roofs, some with tall brick smokestacks spewing dark smoke into the air. The mill was accessible only off Bonnyhale Road, a byway snaking to its one vehicular entrance, a heavy sliding steel gate painted green. A wicket gate in the main gate's bottom right hand corner offered pedestrian access.

Albert stood facing the green steel gate. 'Basil Pomerory will surely be chauffeured to work,' he mused, 'and tomorrow is Monday, a working day.' He awkwardly pirouetted. 'Paddy will also be working if he's well enough. But you two should be here at 7 am. Willie will stand at the big gate and block Pomerory's car when he arrives, long enough for Max to shout a message to him in his gunnery sergeant's voice.' William and Max's eyes sparkled. It told Albert of their enthusiasm for the task.

Albert expected William and Max to return by noon on Monday after delivering the message to Basil Pomerory. But by mid-afternoon anticipation turned to foreboding and by nightfall Albert and Paddy were pacing the street, fearfully concerned as to William and Max's whereabouts.

And when two policemen did finally bring Max back, he was in a state of shock.

'We'll be back tomorrow morning', the sergeant in charge told Albert and Paddy, 'to take a full statement from Mr Langdon.'

It was a good hour before Max was able to speak. 'I was standing up Bonnyhale Road,' he said eventually, 'and saw a posh maroon Hillman saloon car coming towards the mill. When it passed, I could see this old cove sitting in the back. I guessed it was Basil Pomerory and signalled Willie to head for the mill's front gate. I started towards the entrance as quickly as I could with my gammy leg. When I looked up William was in position and had blocked the Hillman's entry. The chauffeur turned and spoke to the man in the back. I didn't hear what the old man said but he was holding up the back of his hand tilted at the wrist and waving his fingers forward, telling the driver to keep going. Next thing I know Willie's under the car. By the time I reached him the car was inside the compound and the front gate had been closed. I yelled to the security guard stationed outside, "All we wanted to do was tell Pomerory we possibly have some information about his grandson." But he just ignored me. A couple of others came out through the wicket gate, checked on Willie and then went back inside. Like me, they could tell he was dead. I sat there holding Willie, for how long I'm not sure. Next thing I know there's a copper asking me what's happened.'

Albert's mind flashed back to his court martial in France and his adoption of the *Dublin Zoo* expression.

Never since, until now, had he felt the chill touch of fate's black hand. 'Get Max to bed, Paddy,' Albert instructed the Irishman. 'He needs to rest.'

True to their word, the same two policemen reappeared the next morning, Tuesday 9 September 1919. Max was finally sleeping after a night of sweating nightmares. They let him be. Instead, the sergeant drew Albert to one side, leaving his young constable companion staring doubtfully at Paddy's dilapidated lorry. By now Paddy had departed for work.

'Basil Pomerory is a highly respected figure in Scunthorpe,' the sergeant said. His rehearsed flatness did not escape Albert. 'Whatever happened out at Ealand, there is no evidence he or his driver were at fault. But being the upstanding citizen he is, Mr Pomerory did indicate if your friend Mr Langdon was prepared to accept a small gratuity to cover any expenses associated with Mr Gray's death then both parties could consider the matter closed.' The sergeant was impassive as he stared at Albert. But the shame in his eyes was unmistakable.

'How much is Pomerory offering?' Albert asked.

The sergeant became defensive. 'I'll not stand for you speaking to me as if I'm Mr Pomerory's errand boy,' he responded angrily. 'You should speak to his representative. His name is Tompkinson. You'll find his office in Bell Lane.'

Albert watched the police depart before returning to his room. Rita was cooing softly to Harold in French. Albert smiled as the boy answered. Although unable to understand him, Albert appreciated he was already forming sentences. And indeed Harold was, but unbeknown to Albert with near fluency in the distinct Marseille vernacular.

Fatherly pride swelled in Albert. He placed his arm affectionately around his son's shoulders, looking closely at him. For the first time he detected in the boy a resemblance to Rita's fearsome brother Axel. Just over four months from his third birthday, Harold was not tall, reflecting Albert's genetic influence on his physical make-up. But he was noticeably solid for his age. Like all Tzanetis males, Albert decided, Harold would be powerful, strong and dark of complexion.

But Albert was driven and had no time to dwell on Harold's emerging likeness to Axel. The war had long caused him to stop asking why young men should die needlessly. Yet the image of William, his cheery pint-size friend, lying under Basil Pomerory's car had cut Albert deeply. 'I need to go out, *chère*,' he told Rita. 'Feed Max hot porridge when he wakes, *s'il vous plaît*.'

Rita appeared to grasp Albert's gist. Her smile, however, as he kissed her cheek caused him to stop and stare. It was vacant, as if he were a stranger greeting her politely, and her remoteness struck at Albert's already wounded heart.

Harold looked at his French-made watch. It was cheap and scratched, perhaps once his grandfather's, and ideally suited to the junior travelling salesman he was to become on the ground in France. Without illumination inside the Whitley bomber the time was hard to make out. Squinting, Harold estimated there were about forty-five minutes until jump time when he would drop into the cold and dark. With that time fast approaching, he was nervous and trying to keep sinister thoughts from intruding. Harold pictured Albert's sad face at any mention of William Gray's death. William's loss had hit Albert hard and remained with him for the rest of his life. Even so, Harold found it comforting in his current circumstances to recall his father's wise words. 'Willie's death also proved that it's darkest just before the dawn,' Albert had said.

Albert headed down busy Jackson Road. He had no idea how to get to Bell Lane but planned to ask Paddy who knew Scunthorpe like the back of his hand. After twenty minutes, Albert spotted him, a scrawny figure badly in need of a bath, decent food and new clothes. Paddy had newspapers folded over his right arm and held a single paper aloft in his left as an advertising token. Albert was shocked by Paddy's appearance. Did they all look *that* bad? It was a salutary reminder to ignore the voice of doubt and other distractions, not the least of which was Rita's mental decline, and press on with his brokerage plan. He owed it to Paddy, Max, the memory of William and, above all, to his family. Otherwise, they were all doomed to die like the sewer rats they'd become.

'A lot of homeless people use Bell Lane,' Paddy told Albert, offering directions. 'There's not much around but derelict buildings. I'm confused why this Tompkinson would have his office there.'

Albert set off. Just before noon he entered Bell Lane. It was as Paddy had described. A decrepit man lay flat on his back in the middle of the laneway snoring loudly, an empty rum bottle by his side. Halfway down, Albert spotted two discoloured plaques mounted on the wall near a doorway. One announced the ground floor presence of a fishmonger, now obviously long gone, and the other directed enquirers to the first-floor office of *Mr Reginald Tompkinson, Private Investigator*.

Albert opened the creaky door and stepped into a small, damp foyer. On hearing movement above, he mounted an unstable stairway. Tompkinson was standing in his office doorway, waiting for him. He was a large man with receding ginger hair and a florid face. A huge stomach protruded from his straining shirt, framed either side by the braces holding up his trousers.

'Heard you on the stairs,' he said in a cold and uninviting voice.

Albert motioned to his leg. 'The war,' he replied. 'I'm not too bad on the flat but climbing stairs can be difficult.'

Tompkinson ignored the explanation. 'What do you want?'

'I understand you represent Mr Basil Pomerory?' Albert said.

Tompkinson considered this but didn't answer.

Albert went on. 'I believe Pomerory is offering compensation for the death of William Gray, who was killed by Pomerory's car.'

'So you're Langdon?' Tompkinson asked after another pause.

Tompkinson's confirmation he was working for Pomerory set Albert's mind racing. *What on earth was Pomerory doing employing this roughneck? He could afford the best people going.* 'Yeah, I'm Max Langdon,' Albert answered.

Tompkinson rubbed his stomach. 'Mr Pomerory,' he said, 'has authorized me to pay you two pounds, ten shillings on condition you sign a legal release absolving him and his employees from liability for Gray's death.'

Two-and-a-half quid, Albert thought contemptuously. *What bollocks. How much had Pomerory really authorized him to pay?*

Tompkinson opened the top drawer of his desk and took out a typed single page. 'Sign and date this,' he said bluntly, placing a fountain pen next to the document blank bar for its minimal text. 'No need to read it. It's all legal mumbo jumbo.'

Albert was conscious of Tompkinson's bulk standing intimidatingly close to him. He could smell the man's body odour. 'I think the nib on the pen is broken,' Albert said.

Tompkinson snatched the writing implement. 'There's nought wrong with the bloody thing,' he growled menacingly. 'What are you up to, chum?' he asked, suspicion fuelling his aggression.

Albert acted scared but in fact had coolly opted for caution. Tompkinson was too big and vicious to tackle head on. 'Nothing,' he replied. 'It looked damaged to me, that's all.' Albert would never know that his calmness in the face of physical threat was a trait which had been passed on to his son. For now, however, Tompkinson glared and thrust the pen at him. Albert scrawled the name Max Langdon at the bottom of the page and dated it Tuesday 9 September 1919. But the distraction had been sufficient for Albert to scan the paper. The words *five pounds* had featured twice.

The glowering Tompkinson retrieved a cash box from a wooden filing cabinet and opened it with a small key attached by a chain to his waistband. He extracted two filthy one pound notes and some coins and placed them on the desk near Albert. Albert stuffed the notes in his pocket and began to count the coins, sliding them into the palm of his left hand using the first two fingers of his right. 'Here,' he said, holding up one of the silver coins, 'this supposed two bob piece is actually a 1915 Danish krone. Look, it's got Danish writing on it.'

Tompkinson exhaled exasperatedly. 'You are mistaken,' he said slowly and threateningly. 'Best you get out of here, you pathetic little cripple, before I throw you down the stairs.'

Albert hopped away as quickly as he could, a sense of relief washing over him once in the street. But he was also wary Tompkinson might have arranged for someone to relieve him of his booty, much as Danny Potter had done to poor old Paddy, and did not stop for breath until he reached the relative safety of Jackson Road. And when he did, anger began to grip him: anger that Pomerory had valued Willie Gray's life at a measly five pounds; anger that Tompkinson had stolen more than half of this inadequate payout; and anger that he was no closer to locating the pig iron supplier with access to a Canadian buyer he needed to find within the next twenty-two days.

Still, as Albert soon recognized, much was to be gleaned from the visit to Tompkinson. Clearly, Pomerory was banking on Max signing the so-called legal release and thinking he had forever forfeited the option of going to the authorities. This could only mean Pomerory feared being held legally responsible for Willie Gray's death. And Pomerory's use of a thug like Tompkinson to coerce signing of the release, Albert decided, confirmed this conclusion. The private detective had been hired because Pomerory could credibly deny an association with him once he took possession of the signed document and passed Tompkinson a crisp new fiver. Moreover, Albert realized, the signed release was effectively a receipt, Tompkinson's avowal to Pomerory he had paid out five pounds. This last thought Albert stored away for the rainy day when he might square up with Tompkinson.

Albert also knew the release he had signed as Max Langdon was not worth the paper it was written on. That Pomerory's legal vulnerability was alive and well compelled Albert to head for the Scunthorpe Post Office. He was now grateful instinct had prompted him when leaving home to bring along the time-aged piece of paper that had fallen from Stanley Poppleton's diary when showing it to William and Max three days earlier.

Albert calculated that of the two pounds eight shillings received from Tompkinson, the Danish krone aside, all bar five shillings would be set aside for back rent, food and petrol for Paddy's van. Even so, he elected to spend the gargantuan sum of two and six to send first class the economically brief telegram he carefully drafted at the post office. The extravagant expenditure supposedly guaranteed next day delivery.

Albert's telegram was directed to a London address. In June 1916, in France, when the military police had led Albert away after his court martial, the note pressed into his hand by his advocate Samuel Prendergast had read: *Contact me at my parents' home in London, 14 Blaydon Close Kensington, if you ever need my help. Keep your head down while in prison. Good luck. Samuel.* After serving his term in the military prison, and later on taking possession of Stanley's Poppleton's diary at the sanatorium, Albert had placed the note inside the diary for safekeeping. Until the preceding Saturday night, he had forgotten it was there.

The dispatcher reappeared. He crouched close to Harold and held up an index finger, placing the palm of his other hand on top of it, indicating half an hour to go. In the name of security, the Whitley's crew was forbidden from engaging with the *Joes* they transported to France. But the dispatcher was a seasoned operator who knew the value agents placed on a smile and a wink at a time when their fear and self-doubt were peaking. Harold was no exception. The dispatcher's kindness caused him to reflect on the generosity of spirit extended to his father by Samuel and Millicent Prendergast. 'Without Samuel and Millie,' Albert had often told Harold during the good times, 'we'd still be living in rooms in Scunthorpe and slowly starving to death.'

Samuel Prendergast kissed his wife Millicent. Wednesday 10 September 1919 had been a difficult day. *Gumbletons* was the most prestigious barristers' chambers in London, perhaps in all of England. But six months ago the Chief Justice had thrown out an appeal lodged by Mr Gumbleton on behalf of a husband-poisoning female client. Ever since, Gumbleton had become antagonistic towards Samuel. And with the female client soon to face the hangman's noose, things were sure to get worse.

It all stemmed from the fact that Samuel had been Gumbleton's junior at the trial. He had studied the brief of evidence and become convinced of the client's guilt. But when Samuel had tried tactfully to suggest to Gumbleton that he advise the client to plead guilty and focus on mitigation at the subsequent sentencing hearing, on avoiding the death penalty, Gumbleton had ignored him and sought outright acquittal. And he now resented that Samuel had been right. 'The situation is fast becoming untenable,' Samuel told Millicent.

Millie Prendergast was a society woman these days, something she tolerated more than enjoyed. She had once been a civil servant, unusual for a woman of that era, and moreover one of considerable ability. But that had stopped eighteen months ago when she and Samuel married and civil service rules obliged her to give up work. She smiled at Samuel. 'If things are that bad, darling, I do think you need look for other opportunities.' But Millie also knew Samuel's father had organized his position at the firm and Samuel was conflicted by the thought of leaving.

Samuel didn't answer, as if pushing the matter aside for now. Instead, he took the mail neatly stacked on the sideboard and settled in an armchair, leafing through the envelopes. The telegram marked *First Class Delivery* caught his eye. 'Well, well, well,' he said on reading it.

Millie looked up. 'Oh, yes, your parents' butler walked it around earlier.' Samuel and Millie's home was just around the corner from Samuel's boyhood home. Unmarried at the time, Samuel had written the family home address in the note he had handed to Albert at the conclusion of Albert's court martial.

'What is it?' Millie asked, detecting that Samuel's interest in the telegram had overcome his despondency.

'Someone I defended during the war, actually. Albert Edward Bradshaw. I only got half the result I should have and frankly felt guilty about it. The best I could do was to give him my contact details and offer to help in the future if I could. My conscience.' Samuel smiled self-deprecatingly. 'I'm surprised he's in touch. I'd long assumed we'd gone our separate ways.'

'What does he want?'

'I'm not sure exactly,' Samuel said, 'beyond that he has a legal matter on which he is seeking urgent advice.'

Samuel handed Millie the telegram, green post office shield at its head and black-typed message below. She read it out loud: 'Got a *Dublin Zoo*. Stop. Need urgent legal help. Stop. Can you come Saturday 13 September? Stop. Reply c/- Scunthorpe PO. Stop. Meet you at Scunthorpe station. Sgnd: Bradshaw A. E. 12532.'

'What the bloody hell is a *Dublin Zoo*?' Millie asked, a mixture of puzzlement and good humour on her face.

Samuel laughed. 'One of the bailiffs at Albert's court martial once worked at the zoo in Dublin. Apparently, a baboon got loose one day and caused awful chaos before they finally shot it. Quite the drama it seems. The bailiff thereafter began describing any problematic situation as a *Dublin Zoo*, using the term as an adjectival noun. During the hearing, when things were looking grim for Albert, the bailiff would whisper commiseration. "You've a *Dublin Zoo* on your hands, laddie," he'd say. Albert began to joke about it and eventually adopted the expression. A form of gallows humour, I suppose, given for a time it really did look like the tribunal would hand down the death penalty.'

'Can you be sure the telegram's genuine?' Millie said.

Samuel loved Millie's discerning mind. 'I feel so,' he said. 'The numerals in it are Albert's service number. He used to lament it amounted to bad luck because the numbers add up to thirteen.'

Millie could see Samuel's memories had transported him back to the court martial and his defence of Albert

Bradshaw. He was in a world of his own. 'Was he a good man?' she asked gently.

'He was,' Samuel replied reflectively. 'A very good man dealt a very bad hand of cards.'

'Right then,' Millie said. 'Looks like we have a weekend to negotiate in the wilds of North Lincolnshire. I'll get the social secretary to book us to Scunthorpe – up Saturday, back Sunday, and a hotel for Saturday night. It will be fun. Once I have the details, you can send this Bradshaw chap a telegram advising him of them.'

'As you wish, darling,' Samuel replied, smiling broadly.

CHAPTER SEVEN

By the time Samuel and Millie's train arrived in Scunthorpe it was already late afternoon Saturday 13 September 1919. With winter fast approaching the sun had gone, rendering the railway station cold and gloomy and thick with sulphureous steam engine fumes. Samuel surveyed the station forecourt, searching for Albert's face as he remembered it. A station porter stood nearby with a trolley on which sat two large suitcases.

The touch of a hand on his arm made Samuel jump. He turned to see a pair of sunken eyes set deep in an emaciated face topped by a tassel of hair matted down by the cloth cap the man held now he was indoors. Samuel's first instinct was to think the fellow was a beggar until he spoke. 'It's been a while,' Albert Bradshaw said, a smile coming to his gaunt face on witnessing Samuel's all too obvious shock at his appearance.

'Good God, is that you, Albert?' Samuel said, his usually nimble mind unable to revert to the *Good to see you* phrase he had planned to deploy in salutation.

'It's what's left of me,' Albert agreed.

Samuel introduced Albert to Millie. She greeted him warmly, giving no hint of perturbation at Albert's woebegone state.

By now Samuel's mental dexterity had returned. He quickly summed up Albert would feel uncomfortably out of place if he suggested dinner in the dining room at the Grand Hotel, Scunthorpe's premier lodging facility.

'Darling,' he said, addressing Millie, 'would you mind ducking outside with the porter and finding our driver? He's supposed to be waiting near the entrance. Tell him to put our luggage in the car and wait for us.' Samuel discreetly placed a half crown coin in Millie's gloved hand – two shillings and sixpence with which to tip the porter. 'Albert and I will repair to the station's tearoom. You should join us there.'

'Albert,' Samuel said once the pair had found a table, 'I can see things have been difficult for you. Before you tell me why you want to see me, I want you to have something to eat; I insist.'

Albert had nearly finished the first of two Cornish pasties and was on his second cup of sweet milky tea when Millie returned. She stabbed at the stale savoury Samuel had bought for her before pushing it aside in favour of her tea.

In accepting two pasties, Albert's eyes had been bigger than his belly. Having barely eaten a square meal since demobilizing from the army his stomach had shrunk. He slipped the uneaten second pasty into the pocket of his grimy coat and wiped his lips with his serviette. 'It's time I explained myself,' he said. 'Before I detain you good folk longer than I should.'

An hour and two more pots of tea passed before Albert had finished. His story began with his release from the military prison in France and subsequent experiences at the Chantilly sanatorium. It ended with his recent visit to the private investigator Reginald Tompkinson, the decision to send Samuel a telegram and his objective to exploit, with Samuel's assistance, Basil Pomerory's legal vulnerability over Willie Gray's death. Albert explained that, at a minimum, he hoped Pomerory's liability would lead to justice for William. But he would be less than honest, Albert admitted, if he didn't also hope it might be the means for establishing his business. All the while Samuel and Millie listened in earnest concentration, Samuel occasionally pencilling notes in his pocket book.

By now the tearoom was beginning to close its doors. The trio walked out into the cold night, Samuel and Millie ignoring Albert's deft pluck of Millie's uneaten savoury from its plate as they departed. 'I'll need to sleep on this, Albert,' Samuel said, 'to think it through properly. Even so, time is short and an action plan needs to be in place before Millie and I leave here on the 9 am train tomorrow. Come to the Grand Hotel at 6:30 am. We'll discuss the way forward over an early breakfast in our suite.'

Samuel and Millie ate a light supper at the Grand. They were on their cognacs and coffee when Millie drew a deep breath. 'I can read you like a book, Samuel Prendergast,' she said, smiling fondly at her husband. 'It's time for you to do what you must. You will resign from Gumbletons first thing Monday morning and for the immediate future devote your energies to bringing to account those responsible for William Gray's death and to establishing Albert's brokerage firm. Try not to worry about your father's reaction. It may take some time, but one day he will accept you had to follow your calling.'

Samuel's heart swelled. He took Millie's hand. 'I love you so much, Millie,' he said, his words simple yet conveying an intense depth of feeling. The two returned to their suite, whereupon they made passionate love deep into the night.

The hotel doorman looked on in unspoken disapproval as Samuel ushered Albert into the hotel foyer and up the stairs to his suite. Dawn was beginning to break. Millie was busily preparing plates from trays on the sideboard. Albert could not believe the amount of food on offer. He took the serve of scrambled eggs and smoked salmon Millie offered and sat at the dining table she had set.

'I have decided,' Samuel said without ceremony, 'not to involve the police for the time being, although make no mistake justice for William Gray will be done. Rather, in the first instance, I plan to speak to Pomerory's lawyer here in Scunthorpe. I will point out that, if subpoenaed, several witnesses including Pomerory's chauffeur, workers at the mill, the police sergeant he has in his pocket, and even the private detective fellow, Tompkinson, could implicate him in the matter of William Gray's death. I will also make clear I am prepared to approach the Lincolnshire Chief Constable to advocate for a charge of murder. But were Pomerory to make a genuine show of contrition, I would also be prepared to assist his legal representatives seek lesser charges.'

'What type of act of contrition?' Millie asked.

Samuel had on his lawyer's face. He addressed Millie as if in court and she the presiding judge. 'William Gray died because he shared Albert's dream of escaping a life of grinding poverty. He was fully committed to establishing Albert's brokerage firm. Furthermore, he had no known family or other likely benefactors. For that reason, if Pomerory undertakes to sell pig iron to Canada using Albert's brokerage service, both the ton that must be shipped on 1 October and the additional thirty tons Gale Logistics requires over the first year of Albert's operation, I would accept that as a suitable act of contrition.'

Samuel turned to Albert. 'Do you think that is fair, Albert?'

'I do,' Albert replied, but hesitatingly. 'What about the buyer aspect, though? I'd always hoped to find a Canadian buyer through the supplier's contacts.'

'Firstly,' Samuel replied, his eyes focused on Albert, 'we all agree this Belarusian character Pavel Isachenko, whom you wrote to in August, will be unable to help with the initial shipment due at the end of this month. Secondly, even if Basil Pomerory is willing to be your supplier, we don't know if he will have access to a Canadian buyer. With time so tight we need buyer certainty. An idea occurred to me overnight for obtaining this, for the initial consignment at least. Millie and I must return to London for a week but will return next Saturday. While there I will explore the idea.'

Samuel searched Albert's face and saw the assent he was seeking. 'Looking ahead,' Samuel continued, 'it's possible you and I will need to go to Canada to find customers for subsequent consignments. As you correctly point out, there's no guarantee Pavel will receive your letter or want to be your agent. Nor do we know if he will be capable of selling into the retail market. The Fredericton mill, naturally, jumped at the offer of Danny Potter's stolen pig iron at below market rate.'

Samuel paused for effect, looking at Albert with piercing intensity. Millie watched on with expression-less admiration; here was her precious husband, the tall, brilliant and handsome barrister in full flight. 'Just as there is a need for haste, there are also inevitable set-up costs. I don't want any misplaced pride on your part restricting our progress, is that clear? I am your lawyer and you are my client. Once on your feet, I'll be expecting you to repay every penny I advance you.'

Albert was taken aback by Samuel's directness. The polite, upper crust Englishman could be the autocratic professional when he wanted. Not that Albert minded submitting to Samuel's authority. After all, he had once placed his life in Samuel's hands. And now Samuel's mention of a possible Canadian buyer for the first consignment had filled Albert with optimism, replacing the gnawing doubt he was determinedly ignoring about finding a buyer through a local supplier.

Samuel took a chequebook from the inside pocket of his blazer, wrote a cheque for twenty pounds and handed it to Albert. From the corner of his eye, Samuel noted Millie's barely perceptible stiffening. The young couple had less than eighty pounds in their working bank account, and now Samuel had given away more than a quarter of it. 'First thing tomorrow morning,' Samuel told Albert, 'I want you to open a bank account. You'll need this to make and receive payments for the pig iron you broker. And buy yourself a suit, shirt and tie, and decent boots so that you're presentable at business meetings. You'll also need an office, preferably one allowing Paddy and Max to live in or above it and with space to securely park the lorry. No one will take you seriously while your workers are living like bohemians in the street. Have a look about and commit to paying a month's rental if you find something suitable. I'll look after the lease when I return.'

Millie chimed in. 'You should also buy your family and colleagues some decent food and proper clothes, Albert.'

Before Albert could answer, Samuel added, 'Yes, do that too.'

Albert's head swivelled as he switched his gaze from Samuel to Millie and back to Samuel. Finally, arms extended, he turned the palms of his hands upwards. 'Do you mind if I have another cup of tea before I get to it?' he asked, chuckling softly.

On the train back to London, Millie gently chided Samuel for his impetuosity. 'Do you think you'll ever see your twenty quid again?' she asked. 'I can't imagine your father will be too pleased when he hears you've already sunk money into Albert's venture.'

'You know Mill,' Samuel said, looking into Millie's eyes, 'at breakfast this morning I felt fully grown up for the first time in my life, finally able to take a decision independent of father, God bless him.' He kissed Millie's forehead. 'Even if father rejects my proposal, our house was bought through a special distribution paid to me by the family trust, placing the title in my name. With your blessing, I'm prepared to take out a mortgage if necessary.'

Millie snuggled against Samuel, her head on his shoulder, gazing reflectively at the passing countryside. 'I would hate to see it come to that,' she said. 'If you did mortgage the house I fear a rift between you and your father that would never heal. I do think you should resign from Gumbletons forthwith and want to be by your side to help with Albert. But there will be hardships. The monthly trust allocation we receive covers the cost of paying staff and running our household. But without your salary, our only disposable income will be my weekly allowance.' Samuel noted Millie's use of technical jargon, speaking like the trained economist she was. 'That will keep us off the breadline but not by much. And I would be reluctant to ask my own dear papa for an allowance increase simply because of the decision we've made.' Millie brightened and kissed Samuel deeply. 'You really should have told me you were so harebrained before asking me to marry you.'

It was the Tuesday night, two days after Samuel and Millie's breakfast meeting with Albert. Samuel had telephoned his parents on Monday evening to suggest dinner, saying he had something important to tell them. His mother had been delighted. 'We simply do not see you and Millicent enough these days,' she said, secretly hoping for news of a pregnancy. 'Come tomorrow night; we'll have an early supper, just the four of us.'

Sir Kingsley Prendergast was in uproar. The baronet merchant banker was in his late fifties. A large and imposing man with a walrus moustache, he was the Chairman of *Collins Eastley*, the UK's largest merchant bank. Rumour had it that Sir Kingsley was worth more than five million pounds. But he had made his money by not giving it away and was deeply intolerant of any perceived foolishness in matters of business.

'Please be quiet, Sarah,' he said sternly to Lady Prendergast, Samuel's mother, when she tried to tell him not to shout. 'First, Samuel comes in here and announces he has resigned from Gumbletons. Now he tells me he wants a thousand pound line of credit with my bank. All because of a fool scheme dreamt up by some fellow up north with no business experience or documented plan, into which Samuel has already ploughed money and committed to plough more. And then, when I object, he says he's prepared to commit the cardinal sin of using personal assets to finance the venture if I won't help. I flatly forbid it. I will disinherit him if he so much as places a lien of a halfpenny on the house bought by the trust. And furthermore, I will have the trust deed amended so he no longer receives a monthly allocation. If that's not enough, the ultimate absurdity is he wants me to approach George Perley with a view to finding a Canadian industrialist who will commit to buying a ton of pig iron sight unseen to be shipped at the end of this month. The whole thing is complete madness and I want no part of it.' Sir George Perley was the Canadian High Commissioner in London. He had once been Vice-president of the Canada Atlantic Railway Company when it was privately owned.

Samuel responded to his father's tirade with respectful firmness, but his disappointment was evident in the face of Sir Kingsley's intransigence. Pudding and dessert wine were served. Lady Prendergast and Millie conversed brightly while Samuel and Sir Kingsley ate in silence. In keeping with custom, as soon as the table had been cleared the men were supposed to take brandy and cigars in the study and the women coffee in the drawing room. But both men sat motionless. Lady Prendergast stood, addressing the maid who hovered awkwardly. 'Mary, Madam Millicent and I will have coffee in the drawing room now, please.' She gestured towards Sir Kingsley and Samuel with a dismissive sweep of her hand. 'And these two can please themselves.' With that, the women departed leaving Samuel and his father immersed in the study of their hands clasped in front of them.

Like most mothers, Sarah Prendergast was protective of her son and only child. At first she had had reservations whether Millicent Chambers was the right woman for him, primarily because Millie was from a mercantile family. In Sarah's eyes, this made her a member of the *petty bourgeoisie*, someone belonging to the social stratum below the Prendergasts. Kingsley, after all, was a banker to the commercialists and not as such a man who actually engaged in the tawdry business of wheeling and dealing.

Moreover, Millie worked. Lady Prendergast might have forgiven her this had she been the champion of a charitable cause – as might befit a respectable upper class woman – but not a salaried civil servant, for goodness sake. Apparently, Millie was working on a project to establish a national Ministry of Health to regulate and standardize the care provided by the current collection of often ramshackle independent hospitals dotted across the country. The young ones had met in October 1917 when Samuel's legal work for the army brought the two into contact. It was obvious they loved each other. Indeed, it was Millie's unaffected affection for her son that caused Sarah to begin to thaw.

After making discreet enquiries to ensure that Millie's was a well-to-do family, with interests in sugar plantations in Trinidad as it transpired, Sarah's reservations abated. She and Kingsley gave their blessing and the couple married in March 1918. Since then, the two women had become close; only the subject of when children might come along was off-limits at Millie's polite but firm insistence.

'What the goodness has got into Samuel?' Sarah asked once she and Millie were alone.

'Mama Prendergast,' Millie replied, 'Samuel is an extraordinary man, one who is destined for greatness – of that I am certain. He doesn't resent the wealth and privilege of his upbringing, but equally he is moved by the social inequality he encounters. But nor is Samuel idealistic, naive or a welfare advocate. Rather, he wants to give people opportunity and purpose and see them succeed by virtue of their own efforts. He and I are so alike; it's what drew us together when I first met him. He has grown unhappy working at Gumbletons and, candidly, I encouraged him to leave. This venture involving this poor chap, Bradshaw, gives meaning to his life. But it would break his heart and mine if pursuing it meant his father disowned him.'

Lady Prendergast considered this at length; she had watched Samuel closely when he explained Albert's venture to his father and sensed his passion. And Sarah was not in the best of health, even if she had told no one about this, not even Sir Kingsley. Above all, she wanted her boy to be happy. 'Kingsley can be very pig-headed when he wants to be. But his bark is worse than his bite. Leave him to me.' She paused. 'I will ensure Samuel receives the line of credit he needs and that Kingsley finds a buyer for the iron whatever it is. And don't worry about Kingsley's threat to cut off your monthly trust allocation. That will not happen. But, Millie, I will be your ally only for a year. If after that Samuel is still whistling in the wind, I expect him to return to regular employment in the law. And in that regard, I want your solemn promise you will compel him to do so.'

Tears formed in Millie's eyes. She rose and kissed the older woman on the cheek. 'Thank you, mama, thank you from the bottom of my heart. This means so much to Samuel and me.'

'And one further thing,' Sarah said.

'Anything,' Millie answered with uncharacteristic rashness.

'You and Samuel are to have a child within the next three years. I am now fifty-two years old and my physician is telling me my blood pressure is far too high. I want a grandchild while I'm alive and well and able to dote over it. Do we have a deal?' Like her husband, Lady Prendergast knew how to drive a hard bargain when she needed one.

Samuel awoke the Wednesday morning after dining with his parents feeling worn out and frustrated. He had hardly slept and marvelled that Millie seemed to have slept like an angel. He readied himself to go to the office; there was still a lot to do in finalizing his affairs at Gumbletons and he wanted it all done by Thursday. Millie was taking tea in the conservatory when he came down. She looked beautiful and refreshed.

'I can't understand why you're so cheerful,' Samuel grumbled. 'Albert needs capital to get his business started. At the very least he'll have fuel costs associated with getting the initial pig iron consignment to the port so that it can be on the water by 1 October, not to mention the upfront costs he'll eventually recover from the supplier like customs duty, shipping and insurance, and floor space rental at the bonded warehouse. And from the moment he's in operation, he'll also have office rental, wages and all nature of ongoing overheads. The fact is that without a line of credit, I'm not sure where his start up money will come from short of mortgaging this house against father's express wishes. And on top at that, at this point I have no idea if Basil Pomerory will agree to supply the pig iron or whether we will find a buyer. It's all proving a bit much.'

'Darling,' Millie replied gently, 'I do agree with your father on the business principle, that we should not be financing Albert from our private funds, specifically by mortgaging our house. But these things have a way of working out. You press on and do what you need to do.'

Samuel shook his head. Millie was such a grounded person. How could she be so sanguine in the circumstances? Then it dawned on him. 'You and mother have cooked up something, haven't you?' he said, his spirits suddenly soaring.

'Sam,' Millie said, using her preferred form of address when wanting to be serious with her husband. 'Your mother is going to speak to your father, that's all I know. But if I'm any judge, you will get your line of credit and papa Prendergast will also find a buyer for the consignment scheduled to ship on 1 October. As you know, however, there is still the matter of finding a supplier willing to tackle the Canadian market with Albert as his broker. I would encourage you to focus on that aspect.'

Samuel was now too excited to eat. He kissed Millie lovingly and left, urging his driver to make haste as they commuted towards the City.

It was Friday afternoon, 19 September 1919, when Samuel's mother called in. Samuel had made good use of his last days at Gumbletons, finalizing handover notes on the various briefs he had been handling and following up with the Lawyers Guild of London whom he had contacted first thing the preceding Monday. His approach to the Guild had been to request it to enquire urgently of its Lincolnshire counterpart as to the name of the lawyer known to represent a local industrialist, Mr Basil Pomerory. Samuel did not disabuse the Guild of the notion that his approach concerned a matter currently before chambers. It was a close-run thing, but to Samuel's relief it worked out. By Thursday afternoon he had the name of Mr Randolph Castle of Castle and Partners in Exeter Road, Scunthorpe.

Lady Prendergast made small talk for a time, doing so with amusement in her eyes and directing a wink at Millie. Finally, when Samuel could no longer sit still, she reached for her handbag and placed a chequebook and a small envelope on the coffee table in front of her. The chequebook's white cover bore the name *Collins Eastley* in prominent black lettering. Opening the envelope, Samuel found a single-page note headed *Office of the High Commissioner for Canada*. It was addressed to Sir Kingsley, whose initials adorning the salutation indicated he had read it. Samuel quickly scanned the handwritten text: *Bryers Calmain VP Redstone Rolling Mills, Ontario will accept consignment fob destination, second-class stowage ex Port of Grimsby 1 October 1919. Agreed rate of sterling 300 per imperial ton. Not very enthusiastic, mind. You owe me a drink when next I'm at the Connaught. George.* Below were the consignee's shipping address and a request for the consignor's bank account details.

CHAPTER EIGHT

By far, Harold's most treasured memory was his father's pride in the birth of ARH Brokerage Services – a monumental achievement against all odds. Hunched forward in happy reminiscence, he was suddenly conscious of the parachute harness he had strapped on at the dispatcher's direction at the time of the thirty-minute signal. As he adjusted the heavy pack to prevent it pinching at his shoulders, Harold pictured Albert the night he returned home after his watershed meeting with Basil Pomerory. He especially remembered the silver Danish krone coin in his father's extended hand. It was a memory seared deep within Harold as an infant, a vivid recall of the first time he heard Albert use the *Dublin Zoo* expression.

First thing on the Monday morning following the Prendergasts' visit, Albert attended the Royal Humberside Bank with his cheque for twenty pounds where he opened an account with a five pound deposit, taking the remaining fifteen in cash. Albert emerged from the bank to where Rita, an inquisitive Harold and Max awaited. They walked to the grandly named Princeton Emporium and spent the rest of the morning buying new clothes and footwear, discarding their old for new there in the store.

By the time of his last purchase, a new outfit for Paddy, absent working, Albert's fifteen pounds was less than six. The party then repaired to the Scunthorpe bakery where they ate fresh sandwiches washed down by cups of tea. It had been a long time since they had consumed decent food. Yet while Albert and Max laughed at two-year-old Harold's evident delight in the treat, the same could not be said for Rita who seemed lost in a world of her own.

After lunch Albert hailed a taxicab to take Rita and Harold home, along with the package containing Paddy's new clothes. He watched the taxi putter off, fretting silently. To be sure Rita faced language difficulties. But her behaviour was becoming increasingly odd and the vacant look in her eyes more permanent. Only when the car had disappeared from sight did Albert address Max. 'We need to take a walk,' he said, 'down to Tulip Road to Danny Potter's old office.'

Albert headed determinedly in the direction of the Frodingham–Grimsby railway line, Max struggling to keep up. The two hobbled on, walking parallel to the railway for thirty minutes until they turned left into Tulip Road. There they came upon a two-storey, soot-covered, brick building. 'This is where Danny had his office,'

Albert said, pointing to a door on the first floor. Since his late night visit nearly four weeks earlier, the office's door and windows had been barricaded. Walking to the back of the building, Albert was pleased to note a large yard, albeit overrun by weeds, which if fenced could securely accommodate Paddy's lorry. This was the same yard where, in the long grass under hessian sacks, Danny Potter had briefly stored his stolen pig iron.

Albert and Max returned to the building's front facing Tulip Road. A narrow pathway led to a set of rusted stairs. They climbed to the first floor landing and began peering through cracks in the strips of plywood covering the windows of Danny's office. A voice startled them both. 'Can I help you gentlemen?'

A man of about fifty stood at street level. A sedan car was parked close by, having arrived unnoticed as Albert and Max scaled the stairs.

'And you are?' Albert asked.

'I'm Kennedy, owner of this fine establishment.'

Kennedy's irony was not lost on Albert. The block's investment return had clearly not met expectations. 'We'll come down,' Albert yelled out.

Kennedy was neither hostile nor friendly, more like cautious. 'We're looking for office space,' Albert said, gesturing at Max. 'Mr Langdon and I deal in the brokerage of industrial metals. We heard about this place and came to inspect it.'

'There's currently four units available,' Kennedy said. 'But I doubt they'll remain vacant for long,' his averted gaze admitting to little likelihood of imminently leasing any unit. 'How did you hear about my block?' he asked, changing the subject.

Max was usually the quiet type. Uncharacteristically, he joined the conversation unbidden. 'A chap called Danny Potter once rented here,' he said knowledgeably, even though Nutter Collymore had shot Danny before he and William arrived in Scunthorpe.

'Are you associates of Potter?' Kennedy broke in aggressively. 'The bastard owed six months' back rent at the time of his death.'

It was now Albert's turn to change the subject. 'Do any of the units have water connected?' he asked.

Kennedy was torn between pursuing his case for rental arrears and the possibility of attracting a new tenant. He chose to be forward-looking. 'No water to the units, but there's an ablution block with a privy at the rear. It needs a bit of work but under the right circumstances could be made serviceable.'

Albert felt tingling. It was his intuition telling him the block was the perfect fit, not just now but also later, for his grand plans. 'Who leases the padlocked ground floor units?' he asked.

Kennedy shifted uneasily. 'They're not rented as such,' he said. 'I use them for storage when I need it. There's nothing that couldn't be moved if you liked the look of one or both of them.'

Albert ignored the offer. 'How much to rent Danny Potter's old office for three months with an option to extend?'

Kennedy did his figures. But before quoting he said, 'And you'll pay Potter's back rent?'

'Come on, Max,' Albert said. 'We're wasting our time here.' He began to walk away.

'Wait,' Kennedy called. 'Forty-five pounds for three months.'

'Twenty, and with a functioning ablution block.'

'Thirty,' Kennedy countered, 'taking into account the cost of renovating the washroom and privy.' His offer was met with a silent stare from Albert, who was proving to be a natural negotiator. 'Twenty-five's the absolute best I can do,' Kennedy said, blinking first.

'Done,' Albert said, extending his hand. 'I'll make a five pound deposit now in return for the keys to the office. When the restoration of the ablution block is complete, I'll pay you the balance in four instalments of five pounds each.'

Samuel and Millie were amazed at the change in Albert when they arrived back in Scunthorpe on the night of Saturday 20 September. A week of eating good food and a change of clothes had done wonders. Samuel briefed Albert on developments in London, the line of credit and the Canadian buyer he'd secured for the first pig iron shipment.

In turn, Albert told Samuel about the office accommodation agreement and its financial terms. It was decided that on Sunday morning the five of them – Albert, Max, Paddy, and Samuel and Millie – should inspect the office. Since paying the deposit, Albert and Max had removed the hoarding, cleared out rubbish, cleaned windows and fitted a new lock to the door. All work had been financed from Albert's bank account, the balance of which now stood at three pounds from its previous five. Max in particular was proving to be a dab handyman.

'So me and Maxy boy are to live in this office, then?' Paddy whispered to Albert on the return journey to the Grand Hotel after the group's Sunday morning visit to Tulip Road. Together with Max, they were squeezed in the back of Samuel and Millie's chauffeured limousine.

'Yes,' Albert replied. 'I hope in time we can rent the unit next door and use it as your living quarters. We're on borrowed time where you and Max living rough in my street are concerned. I've seen how people walking by glare at the lorry. Someone will soon take matters into their own hands.' Albert didn't tell Paddy of his vision to one day buy the entire block, knock it down and build his own sparkling office complex.

'And I'm also to give up the newspaper selling?'

Albert could hear the apprehensiveness in Paddy's voice. He recognized Paddy had become accustomed to the work and found security in it. 'It's your lorry, Paddy, and you're the only one who can drive it,' Albert said. 'Without you and the lorry we are nothing. Even if you lent it to us, Max and I can't drive it because of our leg injuries.' As he spoke, Albert recalled his shock at Paddy's appearance when recently sighting him on Jackson Road. It wasn't just building his business that concerned Albert.

The Irishman was already enfeebled by the ongoing effects of the concussion headaches he was experiencing as the result of Danny Potter's bashing. He would be dead in three months if he went his own way. 'Come with us, Paddy,' Albert pleaded. 'Let's see what you, me and Max can achieve together.'

Back at the Grand Hotel, the group took lunch in Samuel and Millie's suite. 'It might be the day of rest,' Samuel said, once those assembled had finished eating, 'but we have work to do. It's imperative we have our lines straight for the visit to Castle and Partners tomorrow morning.'

Lost in nostalgia, Harold was now absorbed in piecing together the last steps in his father's glorious rise. Suddenly, he became panicky. What if he didn't finish Albert's story before launching into the night sky? If a contingent of German troops was waiting for him and not the *Maquis*, the French Resistance, his life would be over, give or take a few hours of torture, and he never would complete it. Harold willed himself to steady; there was ample time to finish provided he got on with it. With that, he forced his mind to the diary his father had obtained from Stanley Poppleton at the sanatorium in France. It was at this point in Albert's story, Harold reflected, that the diary really came to the fore.

Samuel and Albert were on Exeter Road by 8:30 am on Monday morning 22 September 1919. Samuel carried a leather briefcase and Albert a small rectangular parcel folded in newspaper. They soon located the Castle and Partners office. The tactics settled on over Sunday lunch were for Albert to accompany Samuel. Albert was the owner and managing director of ARH Brokerage Services and the approach to Randolph Castle, the law firm's managing partner, concerned an ARH employee. Castle had no need to know that ARH was as yet unincorporated.

ARH's incorporation was in fact a low priority for Samuel right now. The effect of incorporation was to protect a company director's private assets in the event of company failure, leaving only the company's assets available to creditors. But currently neither Albert nor any of the others likely to become ARH directors owned personal assets of value, certainly none in need of legal protection.

'I'm afraid Mr Castle is in a meeting,' the Castle and Partners receptionist said.

'We will wait,' Samuel replied. 'But please tell him we wish to discuss a matter of vital importance to one of his major clients.'

It was an hour and twenty minutes before Samuel and Albert were ushered into a meeting room. Randolph Castle was a tall man well over six feet in height. He wore an expensive, dark blue, woollen suit. A large red pocket-handkerchief matched his necktie and a fob watch secreted in his waistcoat pocket attached at his girth. Samuel guessed he was in his late forties, a formidable opponent with extensive legal experience.

'Prendergast is my name,' Samuel said. 'Samuel Prendergast. Formerly of Gumbletons in London. I am now legal adviser to ARH Brokerage Services of which Mr Bradshaw here is the managing director.' Castle shook hands, a guarded look on his face. He knew Gumbletons employed only the best and brightest legal minds.

'I'm here because of an incident involving a client of yours, Basil Pomerory,' Samuel said. 'One in which Mr William Gray, an ARH employee, was killed by Mr Pomerory's motor vehicle.'

Castle interrupted Samuel by holding up the palm of his hand close to Samuel's face. It was an act of aggression and a stamping of authority rolled into one. 'That matter has been settled,' he said dismissively. 'An associate of Mr Gray's who witnessed the accident has signed a waiver absolving Mr Pomerory and his employees of responsibility for the incident. Now if you will excuse me, I have a busy day.'

Bluffing, Samuel thought, *too much belligerence. He knows Pomerory has something to hide and was probably the architect of the scheme to buy off Max Langdon.* 'Don't be too hasty, Mr Castle,' he said softly. 'The waiver allegedly signed by Gray's associate, Langdon, was not signed by Langdon at all. Who did sign it is unimportant. But the simple fact is there is no valid waiver. Moreover, the real Langdon is prepared to testify that Pomerory instructed his driver to run down Gray. And don't think it will come down to one man's word against another's. We will subpoena the driver, who will regard the threat of a perjury charge as a very different proposition to giving a false statement to a compliant police sergeant in Pomerory's pay. Similarly, we are only too willing to subpoena the mill workers manning the gate on the day Gray was killed. Then there's the role of the private investigator, Tompkinson, which you arranged.'

Castle stopped in his tracks. He was as tough as Samuel had assessed – and smart with it. He also knew Samuel spelled trouble, not just for Pomerory; his role in the Tompkinson matter, if revealed, would surely invite Law Guild scrutiny. Castle smiled coldly. 'Your move, Mr Prendergast. What do you want?'

'The first thing I want is to speak to Pomerory, here in this office at 2 pm. We will be back then. Good morning.'

Out on Exeter Road, Albert congratulated Samuel. 'Brilliant, Sam,' he said. Samuel noted for the first time Albert's familiar form of address. 'To be honest, I wasn't confident we'd get today's meeting with Pomerory as we planned for yesterday.'

Samuel smiled distractedly. He was already preparing for the meeting. 'Let's go and have lunch,' he said. 'I want to jot down some more points for this afternoon.' Albert drank only tea while Samuel ate and worked. Now that a meeting with Pomerory had been arranged he was too nervous to eat.

Pomerory was taller than Albert had imagined. And despite his nearly seventy-three years, he was upright and confident and carried a patrician air. He and Castle sat on one side of the table in Castle's conference room and Samuel and Albert on the other. There were no formalities beyond Castle waving a hand at Samuel, inviting him to commence.

'Mr Pomerory,' Samuel said, 'we are here because we believe you are a party to the death of William Gray.'

Castle jumped in. 'Mr Pomerory has not made and will not be making any admission of liability in respect of William Gray's death,' he said.

'His presence at this meeting is admission enough, Mr Castle,' Samuel said, his eyes never leaving Pomerory. 'Our response to this confession is a demand that Mr Pomerory make an act of contrition. To spell that out, if Mr Pomerory is sufficiently contrite Max Langdon will give evidence to the effect Mr Pomerory was careless in causing Mr Gray's death and that he did not act with reckless intent. With his good name and, we assume, the absence of any relevant prior conviction, Mr Pomerory could expect to walk free with a fine or, in the worst case, a suspended sentence for involuntary manslaughter. Otherwise, we will throw Mr Pomerory to the wolves. In the event, Mr Castle, your role in the Tompkinson episode will also come under scrutiny, along with that of the corrupt police sergeant who led the investigation into Mr Gray's death. Conspiracy to pervert the course of justice is the best Mr Pomerory could hope for, with a charge of murder more likely than not. And you, Mr

Castle, would certainly be disbarred and possibly incarcerated alongside Mr Pomerory.'

'This is just blackmail,' Castle seethed, his mouth distorted in outrage.

Castle prepared to go on. But the sound of Pomerory's voice stopped him. 'You play a good game, Prendergast,' Pomerory said. 'But you don't frighten me. Let me tell you why.'

Pomerory stood and poured himself a glass of water from the jug on the sideboard before resuming his seat. 'Just on six years ago, in 1913, my wife died. I was naturally devastated but the effect on our two adult children was even worse. The youngest, my daughter, was unhappily married and unable to have children. She ended up running off with an American artist, a female American artist.' Pomerory smiled at Castle's shocked expression. 'She lives in New York City in some type of debauched commune. Effectively, she is lost to me. My son, on the other hand, was happily married with a son of his own. The boy, by name of Rupert, was doing well and my son was running the family steel mill, the Ealand mill. At the outbreak of the war my grandson Rupert enlisted, wanting to do his patriotic duty. After he was killed at the Western Front in 1916, his father, my son Richard, could not cope. You see his mother's death had weakened his spirit. The death of his son coming on top of it was enough to destroy him. He began to drink heavily. Soon his marriage was in trouble and the mill struggling to meet its government contracts. I was retired by this stage but still fit. I stepped in. There was not much I could do about Richard or his marriage, but I could get the mill back on its feet. Richard now lives alone in a private nursing facility in London.'

Pomerory smiled at Samuel and Albert. 'You will appreciate, therefore, I don't have much to live for. Yes, the mill keeps me occupied but soon I will have to retire for good. Then there's nothing. I agree with you, Mr Prendergast, I could face serious charges if I do not bow to your demands, leading to the high likelihood of imprisonment. But before it came to that I would take a walk out by Clearwater Lake with my hunting rifle, never to return.' He paused, not for effect Albert realized, but because of the effort involved in revealing the most private of truths. 'I'm sure this exposition of my personal circumstances will lead you to understand I really do mean what I say.'

Albert cast a sideways glance at Samuel. For once he seemed unsure of himself. Like Albert, Samuel instinctively believed Pomerory and understood he could not be coerced into an act of so-called contrition.

'In view of what I've just told you, you're probably wondering why I bothered to come to this meeting,' Pomerory said, saving Samuel and Albert from their uncertainty.

'Well, yes,' Samuel conceded, 'in the circumstances I am.'

'One of the fellows on the mill security detail reported that after the accident the Langdon chap had said to him something about having information on my grandson. I did not give much credence to the report. My belief was the incident with Gray and Langdon was some sort of scam. The war's damaged a lot of people and made them desperate.'

Aye, brother, aye, Albert thought.

'But when Mr Castle told me about the demand for a meeting, and in particular your involvement, Mr Prendergast, this suggested the claim about information on Rupert might actually be genuine. So here I am. Ready to buy whatever you're hawking in return for your forgetting about the William Gray matter.'

At the tactics meeting in Samuel and Millie's suite at the Grand Hotel the day before, after Sunday lunch, Albert had raised Stanley Poppleton's diary and its reference to Rupert Pomerory. He had argued the diary might be a point of leverage with Pomerory. But whereas Millie, Max and Paddy had been attracted to the idea, Samuel had seemed less keen. As ever, his mind had been firmly focused on matters legal.

Now in the Castle and Partners conference room, Albert spoke for the first time, surprised by the confidence in his voice. 'Mr Pomerory, we are not here to blackmail you or sell you a memory of your grandson.' Albert took Stanley Poppleton's diary from its newspaper wrapping and placed it on the table. 'I am one of those people made desperate by the war. So is Max Langdon as was William Gray. I have a war injury and other history such that no one will employ me, as does Langdon and so did Gray.

We are trying to start a business to support ourselves, as brokers selling pig iron to Canada. I need urgently to find a supplier willing to enter the Canadian market using my services. The point of the Langdon and Gray exercise was to attract your attention so that I might give you this diary in return for access to you and make my case to become your broker.'

Albert slid the diary across the table in Pomerory's direction. The older man looked curiously at it. He opened the first page and studied it. 'The owner of this diary was at Gommecourt with Rupert when he died?' he asked looking up at Albert.

'Yes. You'll see the diary belonged to a friend of his called Stanley Poppleton. Stanley gave it to me shortly before he died. I haven't tried to find Stanley's family to give it to them because he made me promise not to. He said the effect of the diary on his parents would be too much for them.'

Pomerory nodded in understanding. The room fell silent while Pomerory read and re-read the entry. 'This diary means a lot to me, Mr ... er,' Pomerory said, looking up.

'Bradshaw.'

'Mr Bradshaw. I would like to hear exactly how you came to be in possession of it.'

Ever the pragmatist, Samuel saw the opening. 'Mr Pomerory, you and Albert will have ample time to talk about the diary, I assure you. But first, will you agree to Albert brokering the sale of a ton of your pig iron to Canada for 300 pounds at a total cost to you of 210 pounds?' Samuel did not mention Albert's brokerage fee would now be thirty pounds absent payment of a ten pound agent's commission to Pavel. 'There's a tight shipping deadline involved,' Samuel said, 'and we need an answer while in this meeting.'

Samuel referred to his notebook's calendar. 'Today's Monday 22 September. If Albert's lorry picked up an imperial ton of pig iron first thing next Monday morning, a week from now, it could undergo customs inspection that afternoon at the Port of Grimsby and be loaded on Tuesday 30 September. This would have it on the high seas by 1 October.' Samuel re-studied his calendar. 'Yes, yes, that would work.'

Samuel looked up to find Pomerory now weeping and engrossed in the diary. 'Mr Pomerory?' he said, gently pressing.

Pomerory looked up. 'What?' he asked, his thoughts elsewhere.

'The pig iron. Could Albert pick up 200 ingots next Monday?'

'Oh, the pig iron. What was it? You want me to sell an imperial ton to a Canadian buyer, was it?' Samuel nodded. 'Fine,' Pomerory said, turning to Castle. 'Prepare a heads of agreement engaging Bradshaw as my broker would you please, Randolph?'

That night, after a celebration pint at the Grand Hotel, Albert returned to his accommodation. How much more welcoming the street would seem, its grey bleakness notwithstanding, once the eyesore that was Paddy's lorry was removed. In his room Albert found Rita in her now accustomed trance, lying on the bed, eyes open but seeing and hearing nothing. Harold was standing upright in his cot.

Albert admired Harold's growth and less avidly noted how he seemed more to resemble Rita's brother Axel with each passing day. On the spur of the moment, Albert took the Danish krone from his pocket, the one Pomerory's agent Reginald Tompkinson had foisted on him. He held it in front of Harold. The boy reached out his left hand and took the coin, the action confirming Albert's suspicion Harold was left-handed – a southpaw.

'This is your good luck charm, Harold,' Albert said, 'a reminder of what your old man managed to achieve.' He gently took the krone from Harold's hand and placed it beside his cot. 'Every time life throws you a *Dublin Zoo*, look at this coin and think of me. It will give you strength and protect you.'

The brightening of the boy's face and, for an instant, a gleam in his eyes suggested understanding. But Albert quickly dismissed the notion. Harold was not yet three and far too young to understand anything of the sort.

Albert readied for bed. On lowering himself to a sleeping position, he looked up and was surprised, startled even, to see Harold, whom minutes earlier Albert had laid on his back, again standing upright in his cot. '*Dublin Zoo*,' the boy said distinctly, before sliding down and reassuming a sleeping position.

CHAPTER NINE

Harold's backside was sore. For nearly three hours he'd been jammed into a rock hard steel seat. Although there were only minutes left until he jumped, he decided to take advantage of the Whitley bomber's smooth passage to flex his back while he could. Clasping a supporting strut, lest the plane make an unpredictable lurch, Harold smiled. After the meeting in Randolph Castle's law office, Albert's business quickly took root. 'It's as if nothing can stop me,' Albert would say during the good times, always shaking his head as if he found it hard to believe. Harold especially remembered the newspaper clippings of the official opening of the new ARH Brokerage Services complex on Tulip Road, those Albert would show him when journeying back to the salad days.

Albert and Basil Pomerory forged a productive commercial partnership in the weeks following their initial meeting, even if personally the two remained somewhat at arm's length. Early into the affiliation, Albert told Pomerory how the private investigator Reginald Tompkinson had fleeced them both. Pomerory nodded grimly. 'Leave it with me,' was all he said. The landlord who called by shortly after looking for office rent was told by a local street dweller that a battered and bruised Tompkinson was last seen hastening towards Frodingham railway station, one arm in a cast and a suitcase in his good hand.

Thereafter, armed with Pomerory's promissory letter guaranteeing supply, Albert and Samuel travelled to Canada in early November 1919, venturing first to London where Samuel lodged paperwork to incorporate ARH Brokerage Services and thence to Southampton where they boarded a passenger liner. Five days later in Hamilton, Ontario they met with the Redstone Rolling Mills management, the buyers of Albert's initial one-ton shipment. Pleased with the purity of the first pig iron batch, the Redstone executives were happy to sign a contract with ARH Brokerage Services for the supply of 100 tons of pig iron over the next year, which accounted for all of the Ealand mill's productive capacity, earning Albert 3000 pounds in brokerage fees in the process.

In December 1919 Basil Pomerory appeared in the Scunthorpe Assizes charged with careless conduct causing death by motor vehicle. His appearance followed a series of meetings between Samuel and Randolph Castle, Pomerory's lawyer. The police prosecutor went softly owing, he said, to Pomerory's coming forward, evident remorse and good character. A fine of 200 pounds was levied, and in lieu of a custodial sentence Pomerory was placed on a six-month good behaviour bond.

Yet for all the success and growing strength of their business partnership, the reserve between Albert and the older man never completely abated. From Albert's perspective Willie Gray had paid too high a price for complete forgiveness. This visibly manifested in late 1924 when Pomerory unexpectedly died from a heart attack. Like others close to the mill owner, Albert was shocked by the sudden development and, in truth, not a little saddened. Even so, Albert's principles dictated he should not attend Pomerory's funeral.

Max Langdon formally became a director of ARH Brokerage Services. In 1921, at Albert's behest, he oversaw the demolition of the old building on Tulip Road and in collaboration with a London architectural firm the design and construction of a new ARH head office on the site. But Paddy did not make the transition. By the time his brain tumour was diagnosed in mid-1920, it was too late. Paddy's lorry, now long retired and mounted on a platform, took pride of place in front of ARH's new Tulip Road complex. And in the office foyer, prominent memorial plaques recorded the momentous contributions of William M. Gray and Padraig P. Kearney to ARH's establishment.

Two years on, in 1923, Max married a girl from the Isle of Wight whom he had met while on holiday there. Her family owned a dairy farm and her father was ailing. Max resigned from ARH, selling his holding to Albert, and bought a share of the farm business. Shortly after, he and his wife inherited the rest. Max ran the Isle of Wight property until his death in 1970 at age seventy-seven.

And Albert and his family? Well, Albert especially grew with the business. By the time Harold commenced school as a five-year-old in February 1922, the family had taken up residence in a large home on the shores of Clearwater Lake. After which, Rita now permanently catatonic spent her days staring out at the lake and rarely venturing from the house. Unfortunately, as it transpired, Albert had purchased the house through ARH rather than funding it personally. At the time there seemed only blue sky ahead and compelling tax advantages existed in the company owning the asset for ten years, after which the house would be sold to Albert at market price and become his private property.

By the start of 1925 and soon to turn thirty-one, Albert had a staff of ten and was selling huge volumes of pig iron to Canada. ARH was now conservatively worth 250,000 pounds. And it was about to be worth a lot more. In his capacity as ARH's sole director, Albert was in due diligence to buy the Ealand steel mill from the estate of the late Basil Pomerory.

Samuel and Millie returned to London for Christmas 1919. Their contact with Albert thereafter wilted; neither they nor

Albert had a minute to spare in their busy lives. Inevitably, the parties grew apart, the Prendergasts last sighting Albert when he ventured south to attend the christening of the couple's first child around the time Samuel took silk in 1922. Samuel and Millie never again visited Scunthorpe, although they dearly would have liked to have made one final visit in June 1936. But living in the United States at the time while Samuel was on judicial exchange, they were to learn of Albert's tragic death only on their return to London at the end of the year. Both were devastated. The respect and affection Samuel and Millie held for Albert, however, transcended his death. It was indissoluble.

The footnote to the birth of ARH Brokerage Services was a brief conversation Albert had in 1923 with an executive from the Fredericton Steel Mill in Canada's New Brunswick province. The Canadian mentioned in passing that the mill had once bought a ton of pig iron from a Scunthorpe supplier at below the market rate. An Eastern European fellow, Belarusian he thought, name of Pavel, had arranged the sale. The mill had hoped to make further purchases. But Pavel had skipped town leaving no forwarding address.

'Was Pavel given a cheque for sterling for the one sale,' an intrigued Albert asked, 'made out to a man called Danny Potter?'

'No,' the executive replied. 'He asked for the whole payment in cash, in Canadian dollars.'

The man couldn't understand why Albert found this so funny.

It seemed to Harold an age since the dispatcher had given the half hour signal. He would be back at any moment, when there were precisely ten minutes to go. At that time he would open the drop hatch in the bottom of the plane's fuselage, the so-called Whitley hole, a circular exit point just three feet in diameter. Once the hatch was open and his parachute's static line attached to the aircraft frame, Harold would sit on the floor next to the hole. The jump light, presently extinguished, would be red initially before switching to green. The instant it changed Harold would plunge feet first through the hatch. Harold shrugged. The good times had lasted six wonderful years before slowly withering over the next four and finally evaporating. He was older when the fall came and there were fewer gaps in his memory. *It wasn't a difficult time,* Harold thought. *No, it was much more than that. It was a complete and utter catastrophe.*

March 1925. The manager of the Scunthorpe branch of the Royal Humberside Bank was well pleased. The area manager had just called to congratulate him on the deal. The loan taken by ARH Brokerage Services for a massive 500,000 pounds was easily the largest his office had ever negotiated. Shortly after, the *Scunthorpe Advertiser* carried a front-page story reporting the sale of the Ealand steel mill to ARH Brokerage Services. At dinner that night Albert proudly told Harold – now eight and a dead ringer for Rita's brother Axel – how his father had become an industrialist. Albert and Harold had grown used to conversing among themselves over meals prepared and served by the house staff; the ever-silent Rita seldom gave any indication of hearing them.

In the preceding years, Albert had taken Rita to a series of doctors, none of whom could find physical fault with her. A psychiatrist in London, a rat-faced man with rimless glasses and a long goatee beard, told Albert Rita was like a prisoner too long in solitary confinement. He doubted her diseased mind would repair but assured Albert she was in no pain or discomfort. Albert left it there. Nothing more could be done.

As for Harold, he was proving to be a very bright boy. 'He consistently tops all subjects,' Harold's primary school headmaster told Albert. 'And his language skills are extraordinary; his French is far better than his teachers or tutors, who tell me he speaks in the Marseille vernacular.' Albert was gratified but deeply regretted Rita was too unwell to be aware of Harold's development. 'I would recommend you consider him undertaking secondary schooling at Eton as a precursor to attending Oxford or Cambridge University,' the headmaster continued. 'I should think a career in the diplomatic corps beckons.' Unusually large for his age, if not overly tall, Harold was also excelling at rugby, his calm physicality daunting students even three years his senior.

The Speaker of the House of Commons gave the call to the Right Honourable Member for Epping. A plumpish man in middle age rose to his feet. His name was Winston Churchill. He was Chancellor of the Exchequer in the conservative Stanley Baldwin government. It was 28 April 1925. The speech Churchill delivered detailed Britain's return to the gold standard and how the value of British sterling henceforth would be pegged to the price of gold.

In the weeks, months and years that followed, debate raged back and forth. But there was no denying Churchill's decision had more to do with whimsy than it did economics – dreams of returning Britain to the glory days before the Great War when sterling was all powerful, feared and loathed on global financial markets. Simply put, Churchill's decision made the British pound expensive relative to other currencies. Suddenly, British exporters were faced with stiff competition in overseas markets as goods produced in England and exported abroad became costlier than those produced by foreign rivals.

Exporters able to reorient their sales to the UK domestic market were less savaged. But enterprises involved solely in export were severely hit – none more so than ARH Brokerage Services. Albert's company was now also heavily indebted by its purchase of the Ealand steel mill. American competitors made hay as virtually overnight Canadian buyers experienced a near doubling in the price of pig iron imported from England. Albert's exclusive focus on the Canadian market began to hurt him badly. As contract after contract lapsed, ARH's earnings plummeted, and owing to the cost of English pig iron, Albert had no alternative market to which he could turn.

Even so, Albert had been careful to diversify his investments, devoting substantial capital to purchasing commercial property, and bonds and other interest-bearing instruments. For four years he battled to keep his empire afloat. But the Wall Street crash in October 1929, spawned some say by Churchill's 1925 decision on sterling, and the resulting Great Depression rendered all his efforts in vain. Not only did ARH's Canadian markets disappear completely behind protectionist tariff walls, but soon most of the commercial property Albert owned in Scunthorpe and elsewhere in England fell vacant. In time, the properties became little more than worthless doss houses for the rapidly growing armies of homeless vagrants.

In 1931 the Royal Bank of Humberside called in the 500,000 pound loan used to purchase the Ealand steel mill. Albert suddenly found himself pursued by marauding creditors. The mill, the ARH Tulip Road complex and the family mansion at Clearwater Lake, which was still a company asset, were security for the loan. They were seized and anything in them that could be sold was sold. And when the Royal Bank of Humberside itself went under in 1933, the three assets were irretrievably lost. Albert's financial emasculation was completed when the issuers of the debentures into which he had ploughed substantial cash first froze interest payments and then collapsed one by one, taking every penny of his capital with them.

By the end of 1933 all the family had to its name was a small collection of valuables Albert had packed into suitcases and a three-room cottage in rural Eastoft on Scunthorpe's outskirts. Albert had purchased the property in Harold's name just before all his assets disappeared into the financial abyss.

Indeed, financial ruin did for Albert what the Great War, time in prison and years of hardship could not. A sickness of mind began to grip him as his empire crumbled before his eyes. Albert's driving ambition to rebuild his business slowly became an unhealthy obsession. At first, his descent into insanity was disguised because those around him knew it would be impossible for limping Albert, now nearly forty, to obtain salaried work in a labour market beset by thirty-two per cent unemployment. Only later, when well past the tipping point, did his cruel decline fully reveal itself.

Harold recalled the days leading to his eighteenth birthday in January 1935 and their distressing uncertainty. He had long become accustomed to his mother's unresponsiveness, but the deterioration in his father, the dominant presence in his life, was a new and disturbing development. Albert's penchant for rising early, donning a suit and tie and making the twelve-mile round trip walk to Scunthorpe was something Harold had initially admired. But now standing in the belly of the Whitley bomber, waiting for the dispatcher's return, he remembered starting to fret over his father's increasingly irrational behaviour. At the time, Harold recalled, he didn't know this was just the beginning. Much worse was to follow.

Throughout 1934 Albert kept the household financially afloat by selling, one by one, the valuables he'd retained. But now most of the assets were gone and the day of reckoning was fast approaching. If some money didn't come in soon, the whole family would be in jeopardy. Harold had completed his secondary schooling not at Eton as hoped but at the local grammar school. Even so, his outstanding grades guaranteed him a place at any university in the land. And Harold knew just how much Albert wanted him to attend university, a sentiment his father expressed more forcefully the more he atrophied. But Harold also knew he had no choice but to forego university and take a job. There was no alternative.

Harold chose the evening of his eighteenth birthday, 28 January 1935, to break the news. 'I've just secured a position as a delivery boy for Trimble's butchers in Scunthorpe,' he told Albert. 'Now I have this job, father, I think I should defer my university studies until things are better.'

By now Albert's distorted mind was locked and inflexible. He was impervious to logic and would not be let down lightly. 'I am an industrialist of great standing,' he raged. 'No son of mine is going to work as a delivery boy. You will go to Oxford this year as planned. I'll not hear another word about the matter.'

'But father, we can't afford it,' Harold protested. 'We have no money and nothing of value except for the samovar.' Harold was referring to an exquisite, silver and enamel, nineteenth century Russian mini samovar, the brilliant workmanship of its elaborately patterned surface enhancing its beauty – and value. Albert had bought it for fifteen pounds on a trip to London over a decade ago; *a steal* he had boasted to Harold. And indeed, it was the family's last possession of any monetary worth.

Albert made no response to the mention of the antique. Instead, he limped close to Harold, his shoulders threateningly hunched. Albert had never previously had cause to raise a hand to Harold. That was why Harold was caught unawares when Albert's clenched right fist swung through the air. It caught Harold flush on the nose, leaving the younger man staring incredulously at his father. Albert's eyes were glazed over as he stood back a pace, hopping about as if he were a boxer who had landed a telling blow, only for his deformed leg to force him to perform a grotesque parody of the real thing.

Suddenly, a shriek rang out. It was the high-pitched, blood-curdling scream of a mythical werewolf on the North Yorkshire moors. Harold turned to find his mother literally pulling clumps of hair from her head. Albert appeared not to have heard the shriek and continued to jig awkwardly, winding down like a child's spinning top as he ran out of energy. Harold was horrified. He could barely comprehend what was happening: his father now mad as a March hare hopping unevenly from one foot to the other, while simultaneously his beloved but troubled mother disintegrated in front of him.

Harold removed himself from the house. Outside, the night was pitch-black and the air cold and crisp. He walked a good 200 yards from the cottage and stood looking up at the star-encrusted sky. It was then Harold made his pledge. Come what may, he would protect and care for his parents so long as he had strength in his body. He knew what they had endured to raise and nurture him; he owed them his fidelity and so much more.

In spite of everything, Harold smiled on returning to the cottage. Albert and Rita were both seated in the two shoddy armchairs furnishing the cottage's small sitting and dining area. The light of a flat-wick lamp played on their faces and an unnatural calm permeated the room. 'Hello, son,' Albert said, looking up and smiling at Harold. 'How was school today?' Albert, Harold realized, had no memory of the events fifteen minutes earlier.

A routine of sorts quickly developed. Each day, Albert made the trek to Scunthorpe, jaws grinding incessantly and his distorted gait and bedraggled appearance now more prominent. It was the walk of a madman. Albert appeared not to notice Harold had taken up his job as a butcher's delivery boy, working six days a week beginning at 6 am and ending late afternoon. For her part, Rita retreated into her cocoon of silence. On Sundays, Harold occasionally read to her from her selection of French language novels. But he could not tell if she heard him or not. Otherwise,

Harold earned just enough to put food on the table sufficient for the family to survive.

The dispatcher reappeared, holding both hands before Harold, fingers and thumbs outstretched, giving notice it was ten minutes until jump time. With harness attached, he slid open the door covering the Whitley hole. The jump light flashed on. Its red light bathed the dispatcher as he attached Harold's parachute static line and directed him to sit on the floor next to the narrow hatch. Freezing cold air rushed to meet Harold, chilling his face. Soon he'd be out there, in the cold and dark. It was a grim thought prompting grim memories.

The 1930s was a dismal time the world over as the Great Depression maintained its ruinous grip. By 1936 Britain's industrial heartland was still on its knees and into its seventh year of calamity. Returning home one night in the early summer of that year, Harold noticed the door to the family cottage was ajar. A premonition of something terrible washed over him.

Throwing his butcher's delivery bike on the ground, he rushed inside. Rita lay on the floor, blood still seeping into a pool around her, the result of a horrific wound to her forehead. Her pale stillness told Harold the worst. He looked around him. The doors on the dilapidated chiffonier in which the family's few possessions were stored had been ripped from their hinges. Harold could see the samovar was missing. He stared back at Rita prone on the floor. A shocking clarity came to him. His mother had been killed for the valuable antique.

Harold covered Rita's lifeless body. Tears flowing down his face, he cycled towards Scunthorpe, looking for Albert who would now be on his return journey. 'Father,' Harold said on finding him, 'come with me. We must go to Scunthorpe.' Albert was hot and tired and wanted to go home. But by now Harold was a powerful man, even though just nineteen. With the protesting Albert kicking and squirming, Harold effortlessly hoisted him on the bicycle's crossbar and feverishly rode off.

'Yes, young man, what can I do for you?' asked the officer at the Scunthorpe police station front counter. For a moment he thought Harold had made a citizen's arrest, judging by the way he held an older man in a rumpled suit by his back collar.

'Our cottage at Eastoft has been robbed,' Harold panted.

The policeman sighed. Robberies these days were ten to the dozen. He took a form from under the counter. 'Fill this in, sir,' he said, handing Harold a pencil.

'No wait, wait,' Harold said urgently, struggling to keep his composure. 'The robbers killed my mother,' he said. 'This is my father. He's ill. I didn't want him to go home and find my mother. She's out there lying on the floor covered in blood.'

'You're saying there's been a murder as well?'

'Yes.'

The policeman stepped back, his eyes widened and shocked. 'It's 7 pm,' he said. 'All the detectives are out at the moment. Sit down over there until I can contact someone.'

It took over three hours before Harold and a cantankerous Albert, squeezed in the back of a police van along with Harold's bicycle, returned to the family cottage. The two detectives who had taken Harold's statement sat in the vehicle's front seat. Both reeked of beer and, on reaching the cottage, stumbled about when inspecting the crime scene. A hearse arrived to remove Rita's body, with profound effect on Albert. For all her silence, Rita had been part of his worldly fabric. At three in the morning, Harold heard his father's wailing, finding him crouched in the sitting room rocking back and forth. Albert's keening reminded Harold of the distress he'd seen in wounded animals.

Harold had barely slept by the time daylight came. He was tired and troubled but had no option other than to go to work. If he didn't, ten others were waiting to take his place. Harold made Albert as comfortable as possible, placing bread, jam and a pot of tea on the small dining table. Albert, however, refused to eat. On leaving the cottage, Harold lightly kissed his father's cheek.

When Harold returned from work that afternoon, his first thought was to wish he'd hugged his father that morning when he had the chance. Albert Bradshaw's face was blue from the perfectly knotted bed sheet around his neck suspending him from the ceiling. Albert had seen a few nooses in his time at the sanatorium in France. Rigor mortis had already set in when Harold cut him down, indicating his father's suicide occurred shortly after Harold had left for work.

CHAPTER TEN

For a time after the joint funeral of his parents, Harold maintained hope the police would find those responsible for their deaths, indirectly in the case of his father. But by the height of summer, in August 1936, two months on from the robbery, no progress had been made. Harold knew then the culprits would never face justice. With that, the lamentable failure of his pledge to protect his parents weighed more heavily on his shoulders. Sitting in the darkened confines of the family cottage late one August night, Harold concluded he had an unmistakable obligation. Discharging this responsibility centred on his taking up the offer made by Max Langdon when Max journeyed from his dairy farm on the Isle of Wight to attend Albert and Rita's funerals.

Sitting on the floor of the Whitley bomber adjacent to the open drop hatch, Harold pondered the powerful motivation of revenge. It was ultimately why the *Maquis*

took the risks they did and why on that night in August 1936, when he accepted the police would never solve his mother's murder, he had been so steadfast in deciding to atone for his parents' death. The noise of the jet stream frigidly whistling by was deafening, but it had no effect on Harold. He laughed and the dispatcher smiled back, thinking Harold was bidding him good-bye. In fact Harold was remembering that five years ago, at age nineteen, he had had no idea how to carry out his revenge plan and how he had bumbled around looking for an opening. It had finally come, he recalled, but in the most unexpected way. And coy about it to this day, he also thought of how he had lost his virginity in the process.

Back in August 1936 Harold's job as a butcher's delivery boy brought him into regular contact with many of the people working in Scunthorpe's pubs and cafés. Short of ideas on how to implement his revenge plan, Harold decided to ask certain of these individuals to keep an ear cocked for rumours conceivably bearing on his mother's death. One such person was Bessie Murphy, a kitchen maid at the Lion and Castle public house.

Bessie was not Irish but rather a former land girl from the north of England. She was eighteen, short and plump with curly red hair, and fancied Harold terribly. It would be fair to say Harold's squatness was not every female's cup of tea. But to certain tastes – especially women attracted to strong thighs toned to perfection by endless hours of pedalling a butcher's delivery bike – he was a dream come true. In Bessie's eyes, the contrast of Harold's dark complexion with Scunthorpe's more commonplace sun-starved males only added to his appeal. But although Harold was friendly enough, he'd never taken any romantic interest in Bessie, prompting her to hatch a plan.

'Harold,' she said softly, placing the sausages and forequarter chops he'd delivered in the ice chest, 'I have something important to tell you, about your mother. Not here, but later. Meet me in the laneway behind the pub tonight, half after ten, after closing time.'

Harold wasn't sure what to make of the surreptitious arrangements. But the mention of his mother was sufficient to win his agreement, it never once occurring to him that Bessie might have romance in mind. 'I'll be there,' he said.

The night air was thick with coal fire pollution when Harold stepped cautiously into the laneway behind the Lion and Castle. A sound coming from behind a section of uneven paling made him jump. 'Harold,' Bessie whispered sharply, 'come here and squeeze through the gap in the fence, quick.'

Once inside the grounds of the darkened hotel, now an hour closed, Bessie held a forefinger to her lips. She led Harold across the yard to a window left ajar. With something resembling athletic dexterity, she hoisted herself inside, motioning for Harold to follow. It was dark and Harold could see nothing. But the strong smell of carbolic soap told him they were in the hotel laundry. Bessie closed the window. The immediate intimacy of being in close confines with a young woman caused Harold's hormones to race. As such, when Bessie placed a hand on either side of his face and drew his lips to hers, he kissed her hungrily.

Before he knew it, Harold's hands were wandering all over her body. Bessie took two steps back and lowered herself to the floor. Kneeling on the bath towels she had earlier crafted into a rough bed, she dragged the unresisting Harold to her. Harold was sweating from the laundry room's humidity. It was actually a relief to remove his jacket and shirt, even if instincts other than cooling himself had now taken over. Before long Bessie had joined him in the state of undress. As Harold's eyes adjusted to the gloom, the sight of Bessie's pendulous breasts aroused him further. And when she reclined completely naked on the improvised bed, legs apart, he thought his head was going to burst. A force he had never known overtook him.

In the northeast midlands in 1936 it was a puritanical time and virtually unheard of for women to take the sexual initiative. That was why, once his lust was sated and his head had cleared, Harold returned to his morning conversation with Bessie, still not grasping why she had lured him to the hotel and assuming she did have something important to impart.

'What was it you wanted to tell me, Bess?' he asked.

And to be fair to Bessie, she did have one snippet of information, even though it was designed only to hook Harold and then keep him in the snare. 'A couple of rozzers were in the pub a few nights ago. Nice and sloshed they were. I heard one say a prostitute called Gabriela had told him she overheard two fellas bragging they'd done the murder out at Eastoft. The other copper just laughed. Said something like far too much hard work in trying to get a conviction on the word of a working girl.'

For Harold, learning that two men had murdered his mother was at least some progress. Even so, it was a modest advance. 'That's all?' he asked.

'Yeah, I'd only come in from the kitchen and happened to be walking by. I couldn't very well stand next to them and start earwigging, could I?'

'No, I suppose not. Where would I find this Gabriela?'

'Don't know. The copper didn't mention her last name and anyway it's probably not her real name.' A pause as Bessie sought to put her strategy into effect. 'But I know lots of people around the town. If you promise to step out with me, I'll be sure to ask about.'

Harold didn't answer. His mind was tumbling and turning and frankly, despite the sex they'd just had, he was also shocked that Bessie should be so forward as to ask him to court her.

'That would also include you coming here a couple of times each week,' Bessie added, pointing to the laundry floor.

Harold voiced his agreement, too readily for his own liking. To be sure, his acquiescence did stem from a sincere hope Bessie might cast light on the identity of the men who killed his mother. But deep in Harold's heart an uncomfortable truth lurked – the sensuous delight of his first sexual experience had also been a factor in his eager concurrence. 'But you should know,' Harold said, anxious to block out disconcerting thoughts about dishonourable motives, 'I've no money to be taking you to the cinema, cafés or anything of the sort.'

'Don't worry,' Bessie said with a frankness that reignited Harold's consternation. 'I let the publican lay on top of me once a week for five bob a go. That will pay for our outings.' Bessie sensed Harold's rising incredulity. 'He's a widower,' she hastened to add, as if that explained everything.

Unlike the sexual dimension of their relationship, Harold found stepping out with Bessie unfulfilling. She was cheerful enough but of limited horizons; little of what Bessie said interested him. The one time Harold called her *chère* she suspiciously scolded him. 'Why are you talking to me like some Frog toff, then?' she demanded to know. But Harold knew he had to stay the course; his single solo effort to find the prostitute Gabriela had ended in an embarrassing street scene when he declined the services of the woman he had approached.

Harold and Bessie settled into a routine of several outings a week and a twice-weekly liaison in the hotel laundry. Bessie knew the sex was the glue keeping their relationship together. After a month, however, she detected Harold's growing exasperation at her continued deflection of his questions about Gabriela. She calculated the point was fast approaching where her sexual attraction would no longer keep him engaged. Only then did Bessie decide to come clean on Gabriela, hoping to breathe new life into her association with Harold.

It was late the following Saturday afternoon. As pre-arranged, Harold met Bessie at a local chip shop. Their bounty wrapped in newspaper, they sat on a bench in one of Scunthorpe's few public parks. Harold's delivery bike rested against a nearby tree – a silent sentinel watching over them. He enquired about progress on Gabriela, his question now somewhat pro forma. 'Actually, last night I ran into a couple of working girls I know,' Bessie lied, 'and asked about this Gabriela.' Sensing Harold's interest rise, she nestled her head against his shoulder. It was late September 1936 and the night air was chill.

'Any luck?' Harold asked, his voice lightly pitching up.

'Not really,' Bessie replied. 'Working girls use all sorts of names. The two I spoke with last night both agreed Gabriela was probably a name chosen at random. The next week she would be out working under another name.'

Bessie felt Harold's breath expel in disappointment. 'One thing, though,' she said, drawing on information she had been withholding for weeks, 'the girls told me the coppers tend to frequent the Plantation Room. It's down on Palmerstone Street. You know, *palm plantation*.' When Harold didn't respond, Bessie continued. 'Anyway, it's a tough area and the rozzers think they're unlikely to run into any upstanding citizens.' She giggled. 'None at least who are likely to admit to being seen in the Plantation Room.'

'So there's a good chance the copper you overheard in the pub a month ago met this Gabriela at the Plantation Room?'

'That's what the girls seemed to be suggesting.'

For the uninitiated like Harold, the Plantation Room was about as daunting as it got. Palmerstone Street was poorly lit, in fact hardly lit at all. The club sat in the midst of several derelict buildings, a stark reminder of the Great Depression's economic destruction. In the dim light a neon sign with several letters blacked out tepidly illuminated its tattered facade. The place reeked of hopelessness. At ground level a portable sign in the shape of a large chevron bore the dual edicts *No weapons, No minors*, and below this economical text an arrow directed customers to the venue's entrance.

It was just after 9 pm on the Wednesday after Bessie had alerted Harold to the possible lead. He entered as unobtrusively as he could, finding himself in a dingy, smoke-filled open area adjacent to a long bar running half the length of one side of the room. The club was barely one third full. All the customers were men. They sat on rough-hewn steel chairs painted white at tables of identical construction. Seating at the bar was apparently forbidden. Directly opposite the bar, a corridor leading away from the main room could be seen. Its entrance was guarded by a large man dressed in black, a nightstick inserted in the belt of his trousers. He struck a deliberately threatening pose. Scantily dressed young women dispensed drinks and cigarettes on silver trays, while others sat at tables with patrons.

Harold took a seat at a table, grateful for the subdued lighting. To his surprise he found the tables and chairs were bolted to the floor, quickly realizing this was to prevent their use as weapons in a brawl. Sweat was coursing from his armpits and his mouth was dry. He watched as every now and again a girl accompanied by a customer disappeared into the corridor guarded by the man with the nightstick.

'What's your preference, darling?' a hard-edged female voice asked, causing Harold to start. He looked up to see a woman of about thirty, an unaffectionate creature with stained teeth.

Harold cleared his throat. His plan, to engage one of the girls in conversation, now seemed woefully inadequate. 'Well ...,' he said, trying to devise a new strategy on the run.

The woman was impatient. She spoke with a bored air, not bothering to look at Harold as she did. 'A quid for the works which includes a drink for you and the girl first. Ten bob for a hand job and the drink. Special rates for rough stuff and French, and certain girls only. Whatever you want, the sessions are for half an hour maximum.'

With that, the woman looked directly at Harold. The sight of his clean-cut appearance surprised her. Most of the club's customers were crude, unkempt and ill mannered. Her street-smarts told her he was not undercover vice squad. In any event, the club owners had enough of Scunthorpe's coppers in their pockets to ensure advance warning of a raid. She concluded he was a young man on a mission.

'First time is it, sweetheart? I'll find you someone really nice to pop your cherry.'

Before Harold could answer, the woman made a beckoning motion with her hand, yelling, 'Ester, Ester, come here.'

Ester was younger than the woman but no less hard of face. 'This gentleman requires a special service,' the older woman said. 'Take it slowly with him; we don't want him shooting his bolt in the first ten seconds.' Both women tittered before the first woman departed leaving Harold alone with Ester.

'Where you from, petal?' Ester asked, using her usual opening gambit.

'Eastoft,' Harold replied, wishing he could lie more easily. Before Ester could answer he continued. 'I was looking for a girl called Gabriela, actually. One of me *marras*,' he said, using the north of England slang term for *friend* in an effort to appear relaxed, 'told me Gabriela was good value if you get my drift.'

Harold's man of the world act didn't impress Ester. 'I can be Gabriela if you like,' she said, a trace of irritation in her voice. 'Why don't you give me a quid, then we can have a nice drink before we get on with it.'

The sweat emanating from Harold's armpits trickled down his rib cage. He simply didn't have a pound to give Ester. And now with his plan dashed to engage a girl in conversation for nothing, he still hadn't come up with an alternative strategy. Honesty was the only option. 'My name is Harold Bradshaw,' he said, 'and I'm looking for this Gabriela because she may know the identities of the men who killed my mother during a robbery at our house three months ago. You might have read about it in the papers. I'd gladly buy you a drink if I could but all I've got to my name is a couple of pennies.'

Like the woman before her, Ester quickly recognized there was something different about Harold. His open freshness caused her to warm to him. And, indeed, she had read about the murder of Harold's mother. The truth be known, Ester was a lesbian who lived in constant fear of being uncloaked. Her work at the Plantation Room was cover for an affair she'd started with a trouser-wearing librarian. But after nearly six months in service, she was close to the end of her tether. The sometimes violent and always demeaning behaviour of the clientele had led her to hate those who patronized the club. The thought of Harold's mother suffering violence at the hands of similarly loathsome men sparked her sympathy.

'Wait here one second,' Ester said. With that, she strode to the man guarding the entrance to the corridor leading to the bedrooms. After a short conversation, she returned. 'Gabriela was a name briefly used by one of the girls, Freda someone,' Ester said. 'She's with a client at the moment.' Ester looked around her again. The security guard was now watching. She raised her arm and clicked her fingers. Another girl bearing a silver tray appeared. 'Okay, he's finally coughed up a quid,' Ester said to the girl with a pretended air of exasperation. 'Bring us two whiskies, neat.'

It was the first time Harold drank alcohol. But clearly not Ester's – she knocked back her shot in a single gulp.

Harold hated the taste the instant the fluid hit his tongue. 'Here, you can have mine too if you like,' he said, sliding the glass in Ester's direction. She tipped most of its contents into her empty glass and slid Harold's glass back to him, so that they each had a glass containing whisky in front of them. Harold never did finish his drink. The nip he consumed was the one and only time in his short life that he ever drank alcohol.

The security guard directed Freda to the table where Harold and Ester sat in supposedly preliminary conversation. A big thug of a man from Leeds, he could sense something was going on and intended to find out what it was.

Freda was even younger than Ester, leaving her still fresh of face. Harold studied her. *I can see why the rozzers prefer you,* he thought. Ester spoke first, introducing Harold to Freda.

Freda greeted Harold pleasantly enough. But when Ester explained why Harold was at the club, Freda froze. 'That big tosser over there,' she hissed in alarm, nominating the gawking security guard with her eyes rather than the movement of her head, 'is a fucking mate of theirs. He'll tell 'em if he thinks I'm blabbing. The bastards will kill me.' Freda shook her head in frustration. 'I took a big risk in telling that useless fucking copper what I knew. The bastard swore he'd tell no one.' Freda began to tremble in a combination of anger and fear. She looked at Harold. 'Now you tell me he's yapping in the pub about it, while his lazy sods of mates say the lead I gave them is too flimsy to follow up. Glory be, what fucking tosspots.'

Harold was taken aback by Freda's colourful language. In his innocence he had never imagined a woman would swear like a sailor. Freda could see that her language had shocked Harold. Despite her agitation, his naivety amused her; it was as if he were a little boy. A chord had been touched. 'Meet me next Sunday afternoon inside the Oswald Road Catholic church at 5 pm,' she said against her better instincts. But in that same instant her sense of self-preservation took over. 'I'm now going to stand up and slap your face. The story I'm going to tell the snooper over there, after he has chucked you out, is you asked for Phoebe, my name this week, and have just said you want to Greek me.' Freda turned to Ester. 'You'll back me, right Ester?'

'Certainly will.'

Harold's mind was racing. He knew about French sex, it being a popular subject among male students during his senior school years. Indeed, unlike most of his classmates, he was sure, he had actually gone on to experience oral sex, courtesy of Bessie. The verb *to Greek*, however, meant nothing to him, other than an intuitive understanding it was a sexual act more risqué than its Gallic counterpart. But Freda soon rudely interrupted his thinking. Jumping to her feet, she slapped him hard across the face. 'You fucking pervert,' she screamed. 'Get away from me you sick bastard. I don't do that for anyone, especially for deviants like you.'

The next thing Harold knew the security guard's nightstick had delivered him a powerful blow across his shoulders, the pain taking his breath away. This was followed by a forceful frogmarch across the room, a door being kicked open and, finally, Harold looking up from the gutter where he had just been deposited. 'If I ever see you again, mate,' a thick West Yorkshire accent warned, 'I'll break every bone in your fucking body.'

Sporting a large bruise extending from one shoulder blade to the other, Harold entered the Catholic church on Oswald Road just before 5 pm on Sunday 27 September 1936. He was immediately ill at ease. The grandeur of the stained glass windows, the polished stone floor replete with long red carpet and the elaborately decorated altar, behind which towered a huge cross, contrasted with the church's grim exterior in a way that unsettled Harold. Everywhere he looked, the religious icons captured in bust adorning the nave's walls and high vaulted ceiling seemed to be glaring at him, challenging him for the interloper he was.

Religion had not played a role in Harold's upbringing. But he could clearly remember as a child his mother professing to a belief in the afterlife, before she became ill and thereafter said nothing about anything. As for his father, Harold had once asked him during the good times if he believed God had contributed to his success. Albert's response was to snort contemptuously. 'There's no God, son. Can't be. Not after what I've seen.'

Harold sat in a pew about midpoint in the nave. There were barely a dozen other worshippers present. He felt rather than heard Freda in the aisle as she genuflected before sliding onto the bench beside him. 'I come here every Sunday to ask for God's forgiveness,' she said softly, 'for the work I do.'

Harold didn't answer. He had no idea what he was expected to say.

'Two brothers called Tattersall, a couple of Yonners I believe, did over your mother,' Freda said without further delay. 'I heard them bragging about it to the security guard fellow you seen the other night.'

Harold understood Yonners were people from Oldham, located about ten miles from Manchester. Oldham had once been the epicentre of UK textile manufacturing but ultimately ended up with an unhealthy reliance on a single industry. Once textiles could be imported more cheaply, the industry went into decline and then the Great Depression destroyed it. Large numbers of marginalized young men left Oldham, taking to the northeast midlands looking for work. Most lacked even a basic education, this barrier to employment causing many to turn to crime.

'Where do they live?' Harold asked. 'These Tattersalls.'

'No idea,' Freda replied, 'and don't want to know. Them fellas are animals; I'm taking a huge risk telling you what I know.' Memories of a violent childhood and a drunken, raging father overtook Freda. 'If it were your pa that got done over, I wouldn't have said nought.' A pause. 'Men,' she spat.

'You have my word no one will know what you've told me,' Harold said, the flint-hard steel of reassurance in his voice surprising him.

Freda instinctively understood Harold's sincerity. She gently touched his face. 'May God walk with you, Harold,' she said.

Harold began to leave.

'They'll be on the dole for sure,' Freda called out softly. 'You might find them that way.'

Monday morning at work Harold casually asked his employer, Mr Trimble, the price he thought his family's cottage would fetch at sale. Mr Trimble took an interest in real estate and could often be heard lamenting to customers about depressed housing prices. 'No electric light, no running water, karzi way out the back,' he said, stroking his chin in earnest consideration. 'I doubt you'd get a penny over 200 quid for it currently.'

That night Harold wrote to Max Langdon, Albert's old army friend and business partner whom Albert had first met in the Tours military prison in France. When attending the funerals of Harold's parents, Max told Harold should he ever wish to sell the cottage he would buy it at market price, knowing Albert had earlier bought the property in Harold's name.

Informed by Mr Trimble's estimate, Harold offered the cottage for sale for 150 pounds, telling Max he was eyeing a shift to Edinburgh where he had a job opportunity.

Harold indicated that, subject to an agreed sale, he would travel to the Isle of Wight to exchange the title deed for the 150 pounds, suggesting Max have the money to hand because his visit south might come at short notice. He did so knowing Max would not think the arrangement too strange given the prevailing distrust of banks.

But it was not Harold's all too real reservations about banks that prompted his proposed settlement arrangements. Rather, it was his need to control the timing of the sale. He could not leave Scunthorpe until he found the Tattersall brothers and had done what he needed to do. But once the necessary was done, he would need to leave in a hurry.

Harold's letter, therefore, asked Max to answer by telegram, saying an early response to his offer was essential to progressing his anticipated shift to Scotland. Max's in principle agreement to the sale was in fact the central element of Harold's revenge plan. It not only facilitated his immediate departure whenever the time came, but it also underpinned his plans for the period thereafter. And if Harold never found the Tattersalls? Well, his plan would have failed and the sale would have to lapse.

Harold posted his letter the next day while on his morning delivery rounds.

CHAPTER ELEVEN

The day after posting his letter to Max Langdon, on completion of his Wednesday morning rounds, Harold pedalled down to the government office dispensing unemployment benefits, otherwise known as the dole. Harold knew the payment had been introduced in response to the lingering Depression. Even so, the line of ragged people, all men, stretching endlessly into the distance amazed him. He rode his bicycle past the waiting recipients, much like a mounted cavalry officer reviewing his troops. People from Oldham, Oldhamers, as Harold knew, habitually dropped the *g* from certain spoken words, so that *shilling*, for example, became *shillin*.

He came across a likely-looking candidate. 'Do you know the Tattersall brothers?' Harold asked. 'I have to give them five shillings for some work they did for my boss.' He was hoping the man would repeat *shillings* as *shillins*, thereby self-identifying as an Oldhamer.

But his target was too quick on his feet. 'Yeah,' the man said, 'I know where they live. Give me the money and I'll make sure they get it.'

Harold moved on without answering, determined to refine his approach. But for now he had to return to the butcher's shop to help prepare the afternoon deliveries. Mr Trimble would be starting to wonder where he was.

The next day, the Thursday, Harold again went to the unemployment office. Just as he was beginning to despair of another fruitless effort, he sighted a small, worn man in tatty clothes standing in the line accompanied, unusually, by a woman, smaller still and prematurely aged. Something about the couple's downtrodden state resonated with Harold. 'Do you know the Tattersall brothers from Oldham?' the now dismounted Harold asked the man.

'Those dogs,' the man replied sullenly, looking straight ahead.

Harold took three pennies from his pocket. 'It's not much but it's something,' he said, offering the coins to the man. 'All I want to know is where they doss.'

The man ignored Harold, continuing to look straight ahead.

'They're *sleepin* rough at the vagrants' camp near the Iron's football pitch,' came an exasperated woman's voice. It was the man's companion. 'Now give me the money,' she demanded. The Iron was the nickname given to the Scunthorpe and Lindsey United Football Club.

Harold had to get back to work. He tipped the pennies into the woman's hand and rode off. Her no-nonsense manner reeked of the truth, leaving Harold certain he could locate the Tattersalls. Now only Max Langdon's response to the sale offer was outstanding. Over the ensuing days Harold sweated, occasionally drawing strength from his father's description of Max as a man of unswerving integrity.

Finally, the much-anticipated telegram arrived, on Tuesday 6 October 1936, exactly a week after Harold had posted his letter. For all Harold's worry, Max kept to his word: *Proposed sale arrangements agreed* was his terse message. Later that day, Harold took a large butcher's knife from Mr Trimble's shop. At night by lamplight, he whetted it to razor sharpness on one of the shop's stone sharpeners. Harold returned the borrowed sharpener on Wednesday morning but not the knife. He was primed and ready. Early next Saturday would be Harold's date with destiny – it was the weekend and the Tattersalls would be sure to be sleeping off a Friday night on the tiles.

There must be less than a minute to go, Harold thought, looking up from his sitting position on the floor of the Whitley bomber to check if the jump light was still red, even though the surrounding red hue told him it was. His thoughts turned to that Saturday morning five years ago when he revenged his parents. He recalled it in minute detail, remembering his surprise at how his plan had worked flawlessly. It took Harold less than the thirty seconds he had left in the aircraft to relive the whole experience, so clear was it in his memory.

Harold arrived at the vagrants' camp about 6 am on Saturday 10 October 1936. He carried in his pocket a train ticket for passage on that day's 10:40 am service to London, bought the night before. Hidden a mile away in a dense clump of trees was his delivery bicycle. Harold carried the borrowed butcher's knife in a gunny sack, old hessian sacking fashioned into an over-shoulder carry bag. His intention was to inflict a wound on each of the Tattersall brothers, terrible injuries leading to a lifetime of chronic disability such that both would regret having ever been near his mother. He would then drop the knife and his delivery bike at Mr Trimble's shop before proceeding directly to Frodingham station. Crimes involving camp dwellers were commonplace and rarely provoked investigative urgency. He'd be in London well before the police reacted.

Harold planned to spend the Saturday night in London, lying low. Having previously visited there with his father, he knew where he would sleep – on the bank of the River Thames among the shifting community of homeless people he had seen squatting under Blackfriars Bridge. First thing Sunday morning he would take a train to Southampton then a ferry to the Isle of Wight. All things being equal, Max Langdon would have the 150 pounds ready for collection. Harold would retrace his steps to London. Aided by the funds he anticipated having, he would meld into the vast city and start a new life.

Harold had hardly slept the night before. After buying his train ticket that Friday evening, he went to Bessie at the Lion and Castle Hotel. They spoke on the street outside, blowing steaming breath now it was mid-autumn. 'I've found out that the men who killed my mother have gone to Manchester,' Harold said, laying down a smokescreen in the expectation, misguided as it transpired, the police would eventually interview Bessie. 'I'm heading there first thing tomorrow morning,' he said. 'I shouldn't be away more than a few days.'

But he'd shuffled while speaking. Bessie was not one to miss cues. She knew Harold was announcing the end of their relationship. 'You lying bastard,' she swore softly. 'But it was good while it lasted.' A worldly-wise smile came to her face. 'Old Jacobson has asked me to marry him.' Jacobson was the hotel publican, Bessie's employer and the widower with whom she transacted weekly, earning her five shillings. 'He's thirty years older than me,' she said, shrugging. 'But when he dies I'll get the pub. So sod off Harold Bradshaw and don't come back.' With that, Bessie turned heel and disappeared into the hotel.

Harold's plan to disable the Tattersalls had its origin in stories told to him by his father about soldiers acutely disabled in the war. 'A fate worse than death,' Albert used to say. 'They'd have been better off dying.' Harold had grasped at a young age that Albert's memory of such suffering was why he seldom complained about his own injury.

With the seed of his plan long unwittingly sown, Harold's studies of basic anatomy at school and later the examination of animal carcasses at Trimble's butchery provided the finishing touches. Put simply, Harold planned to slash the rotator cuff tendons in the shoulders of each Tattersall brother. Wounds sufficiently deep would sever the tendons and, in 1936, there was no known surgical technique to repair them. The tendons in question controlled movement of the arms such that severely damaged tendons resulted in major impairment, even loss of arm function. Properly administered, the wounds would ensure the Tattersall brothers had only limited arm use for the rest of their lives; scratching their noses would be a challenge, let alone bludgeoning sick and defenceless women.

At first Harold was nervous, sweating despite the fact he wore shirtsleeves in the chill morning air. The gunny sack containing the knife was slung over his left shoulder. But on entering the camp, Harold's tenseness gave way to calm, a sensation he had first experienced at school when taking to the rugby field. A group of men stood around an open campfire.

'Tattersall boys?' Harold asked, deliberately brusque and unfriendly.

'Who wants to know?' one of the men replied with matching aggression.

Harold of course was a southpaw. He strode to the man and with lightning speed pounded his dominant left fist forcefully against the man's mouth. The blow propelled the man backwards, his feet leaving the ground. He laid moaning, blood seeping from his bottom lip. Suddenly, all around the fire were staring fearfully at Harold. Harold stood legs apart, his square jaw jutting belligerently. The fact he wore no coat in the cold and had shirtsleeves rolled to the elbow accentuated his squat, muscular frame and only added to his menace.

'Well?' Harold said, addressing another man.

'D-d-down there,' the man stammered, intimidated. 'The tent with the red flap.'

Harold walked away slowly, drawing the butcher's knife from his gunny sack as he did. The men around the campfire could see this. They watched silently, stilled by Harold's cold calculation and the threat implied in his unhurried stride.

Inside the tent, Harold saw two forms wrapped in dirty blankets. A disgusting night bucket sat between the shapes, reeking nauseatingly. Harold kicked at one of the forms. A dazed man with a filthy matted beard and hair to match looked up. 'What the fuck?' he cursed. As Harold had anticipated, the man was sleeping off a drunken Friday night.

'Tattersall?' Harold asked.

'Aye, Rory Tattersall. Who be you?'

Harold ignored the question. 'What did you do with the antique vase you stole in the robbery at Eastoft?' He was sure the Tattersalls wouldn't know what a samovar was.

It took a moment for Rory to understand. When he did his anger further flared. 'We sold the *fuckin* thing, you daft cock,' he said, trying to get to his feet. He was still fully clothed. 'Freddie,' Rory called to his brother, repeating the call with shrill alarm when he saw the knife Harold carried. But Freddie was dead to the world.

Harold kicked Rory Tattersall hard, knocking him back down onto the bedding. 'Who killed the woman?' he asked quietly.

'Freddie,' Rory replied in an instant. 'I told him not to do it but he wouldn't listen.'

Harold knew Rory was lying but didn't care. He now had all the confirmation he needed. Rory screamed in fear as Harold seized his Adam's apple and then in pain as the butcher's knife sliced through clothing and flesh. The noise caused Freddie to stir and Harold could hear voices outside the tent. He placed his foot on Rory's chest and with a butcher's skill sliced through his unwounded shoulder.

By this stage Freddie was awake and sitting upright, staring in disbelief at what he was witnessing. Harold rounded on him, transferring the knife to his right hand and punching Freddie hard with his favoured left. The hungover Freddie was slow to react, his nose exploding with a crunching sound. With that, his boot on Freddie's chest, Harold quickly repeated the slicing procedure, through one shoulder and then the other.

On leaving the tent Harold walked through the middle of the gaggle of men who had gathered. His jaw was set hard and his dark steely eyes stared straight ahead. The bloodied knife he held at his side. The men parted like biblical reeds, allowing Harold to pass. No one challenged him. Harold continued to walk slowly, feeling eyes burning into the back of his neck. Only when at the camp perimeter did he begin to run.

Harold quickly washed the knife in the first puddle he encountered en route to his bicycle and returned it to the gunny sack. On reaching the bike he donned the jacket tied to its handlebars, checked the title deed for the cottage was still in its inside pocket and, once satisfied, headed for Trimble's butchery, legs pumping powerfully.

Mr Trimble's shop had a small backyard protected by a wire fence. But Harold did not have the key to the yard. So, as planned, he lifted the bike over the fence and threw the gunny sack containing the knife over on top of it. That done, he ran in the direction of Frodingham station, stopping to gather his breath after sprinting half a mile. Then he smoothed his hair, wiped his sweaty brow and donned the cloth cap he took from his coat pocket. So prepared, he walked the remaining distance to the station as if he had not a care in the world.

Harold's was an anxious wait at Frodingham station. He sat on a wooden slatted bench painted dark green facing the railway track, his cap pulled low over his eyes. He tried to sleep. But each time he heard the ominous sound of approaching boots, worry it was the police shook him awake. Even when his train to London finally departed Harold remained on edge. But by the time it stopped to pick up passengers at Doncaster, thirty miles from Scunthorpe, he was sufficiently relaxed to buy a cup of tea and a bun from his five shillings and sixpence saved laboriously a penny at a time. Another coin also nestled in Harold's pocket. Its monetary value was zero but in its own way it was priceless. It was the silver Danish krone given to him by his father back in 1919. And now that he had attended to the Tattersalls and made good his escape, Harold came truly to believe it actually was the good luck charm Albert had promised it would be.

As the train rattled south to London, Harold began reflecting on the morning's events. A strange feeling overcame him. Not quite pleasure, but certainly not self-disgust. Satisfaction, perhaps. In particular, he thought of the fear he had instilled in the Tattersalls and the men first encountered at the campfire and his calm when doing so. Violence delivered with composure, Harold decided, was markedly more effective than when meted out intemperately. Then he slept. His dreams were dominated by the sound of his knife slicing through flesh. Suddenly, Harold awoke with a jolt, not in nightmare but because of the dawning realization of his uncommon capacity to calculatedly inflict harm. He knew from schoolboy rugby that many others had the physical prowess to cause harm, but none he knew could rise to violence unless angry, thereby limiting their self-control and capacity for calculation. By the time Harold reached London, he knew he was somehow different. He had been gifted an advantage over other men – a seemingly unparalleled ability to resort to violence when calm and exert it with a precision guaranteeing its effective application.

The Scunthorpe police had indeed been slow to investigate the assaults on the Tattersalls. And when they did, the brothers were not about to admit to anything implicating them in Rita Bradshaw's murder. Everything they owned had been stolen by the time two officers arrived at the camp in the late afternoon. Both brothers were suffering serious blood loss, obliging the police to apply tourniquets until the wounds could be sutured. The first aid might have been life saving but for the Tattersalls it was a mixed blessing. Theirs was a dark, merciless world of dog eat dog, where the only rule was the rule of violence. Unable to lift their arms above shoulder height, they could not defend themselves when their many enemies came calling.

Nor did the police ever pursue the lead given them by Freda, the Plantation Room prostitute, that in time would have revealed the brothers as Rita's murderers and linked Harold to the assaults. As a result, neither Bessie Murphy, Harold's first lover from the Lion and Castle Hotel, nor his employer, Mr Trimble, was ever questioned. And although Scunthorpe gossip and simple deduction – and in Mr Trimble's case the pushbike and butcher's knife thrown over the back fence coupled with Harold's disappearance – eventually told both all they needed to know, neither party came forward. The Great War and Depression had jaundiced Bessie and Mr Trimble's outlooks, and many others with them. In the absence of a state able to protect its citizens each in their own way believed in an eye for an eye.

Mr Trimble's knowledge died with him five years later. Although shortly before his death he did tell two others why the *Dublin Zoo* expression was so dear to Harold's heart. And prior to speaking to Trimble, these same two others also discussed Harold with Bessie Murphy, by then known as Bessie Jacobson – the name she'd used ever since her marriage to the Lion and Castle landlord in late 1936.

CHAPTER TWELVE

Inside the Whitley bomber, the jump light turned green, causing the dispatcher to mouth the word *Go*. From his sitting position Harold slid vertically, feet first, through the open Whitley hole and into the unknown, arms stiffly by his side as if standing to parade ground attention. It was close to midnight on Thursday 4 September 1941.

Relieved to have avoided the commonplace hazard of cracking his skull on the way out, once outside the aircraft Harold tried to remember his training, leaning back and adopting a star position. 'One thousand, two thousand, three thousand,' he screamed into the night sky.

After a seeming eternity, Harold felt the upward pull of his parachute signalling the canopy was deployed, allowing him to dispense with the star posture. Then there was silence, dark and cold. Harold looked around, hoping to sight the parachute supporting the suitcase containing the samples of cloth, pins and thread and his personal effects, all vital to his travelling salesman cover, which the dispatcher would have thrown out of the Whitley behind him. But unable to see in the dark, he gave up and scanned the ground below looking for the Resistance torchlight that would guide him to earth.

Harold spotted an orange speck below and then another, and his anxiety eased. Without the lights, he risked cannoning into the ground with no parachute roll on impact, at the possible cost of fractures to both ankles. Harold manipulated the parachute toggles so as to manoeuvre towards the midpoint of the torches flashing on and off at three-second intervals. *Five seconds more,* he told himself once the torchlight steadied, warning him he was close to landing. He angled his feet to the right, bending them at the ankles in preparation for his preferred left side roll.

The weakly illuminated ground rushed to meet Harold. He hit it harder than expected, but his roll still managed to absorb most of the impact. Harold was quickly to his feet, gathering in the parachute before the wind caught it and dragged him away. Then he heard people running towards him. Much to Harold's relief, their breathless conversations were in French.

Those preparing Harold for his insertion had issued him apparel and footwear that was cheap, French-made and befitting the cadet travelling salesman for a Paris-based haberdashery company he was to become on the ground. Harold also heeded the instruction not to take anything of a personal nature with him – with one small exception. Secure in the breast pocket of the cheap suit he wore beneath his covering overalls was the Danish krone coin, the good luck charm given to him by his father on the night of the birth of ARH Brokerage Services. He had touched the coin a split second before spearing into the night sky.

'A little more warning would have been nice,' a man said, while roughly yanking Harold's parachute and overalls off him. Harold had no idea what he was talking about but didn't ask.

Another figure appeared. 'I have his case,' he told the first man. 'Let's get out of here.'

Harold and the two men ran swiftly to a copse of trees. While one buried the parachutes and Harold's overalls, the other flashed his torch. From out of the dark an unlit van of some description appeared. Harold was literally thrown in the back and the vehicle bumped forward traversing a section of rough terrain. Then there was the crunching sound of driving on a gravel road for around an hour until a barn-like structure was reached into which the van entered. For ten seconds, the three *Maquis* crammed in the front seat sat quietly. Then came a knock on the window followed by the rear door opening and a man carrying a hurricane lamp with its wick lit low commanding Harold forward with a wave of his hand.

'You fucking idiots,' the man from behind the lamp hissed at Harold. 'We could all get killed trying to organize a reception and onward travel at short notice simply because your people don't know one week from the next.'

Harold was flummoxed by the man's anger and unsure what had provoked it. 'Sorry,' he said, not knowing for what he was apologizing.

The man spat, shaking his head. He pointed to a ladder leading to a loft on which a covering layer of thick hay could be seen in the dim light. 'Up there, quickly,' he ordered.

Suitcase in hand, Harold scaled the ladder followed by the man with the lamp. 'There's water there,' the man said, pointing into the gloom. 'If you have to piss, then piss in the straw; if you have to shit come down stairs and do it, but only if you have to. No lights and no noise. Try to sleep. Someone will be back at dawn to take you to Riom city. Downstairs near the front is a washtub. Shave, wash your face and brush your teeth before dawn so you're ready to leave immediately. Our instructions, however fucked up they were, are to get you on the train to Lyon looking like a commuter who's had a decent night's sleep.'

'Okay, and thanks again,' Harold said, now realizing there'd been some sort of administrative mix-up. He hoped it wasn't an omen. It was of course. Unbeknown to Harold the error had been deliberately made by certain persons in England intimately involved with his insertion into France.

'At least your language is good,' the man said, marginally mollified by Harold's fluent French spoken with a Marseille accent. With that, the lamp was extinguished and the men left on foot stealing into the dark, locking a padlock on the barn door as they went.

Now alone, Harold felt a spasm of fear ripple through him. Here he was perched in a loft somewhere in rural France, unarmed and virtually powerless to resist if the Germans came for him. He calmed himself with the breathing exercises they had taught him. And although the fear abated, loneliness soon replaced it. Harold lay on the straw fully clothed too wound up from the adrenalin rush of his parachute jump to sleep. 'Be sure to cleanse your mind of negative thoughts when you first get there,' his instructors had told him. 'Think of something that gives you comfort, happy memories.' Harold's thoughts turned to Katrina, sifting through the complicated sequence of events leading to his initial encounter with her. He began by thinking of the idyllic greenness of Max Langdon's farm on the Isle of Wight.

It was two in the morning on 5 September 1941.

Five years earlier, Harold's perceived need to sleep rough on his first night in London had been unwarranted given the tardiness of the Scunthorpe police investigation into the assaults on the Tattersalls. But he was understandably cautious. Dusk was falling when he reached Blackfriars Bridge, only to find those having already claimed this slice of the Thames riverbank resentful of his arrival. In his determination to lay low, Harold had failed to consider this possibility.

To be sure, his size and menacing stare deterred any would-be aggressor. Even so, Harold worried about what might happen while he slept. He moved further down river, only to find other suitable sleeping spots also occupied. Eventually, he managed to catch a precious few hours' rest squeezed between the Victoria Embankment and the brick exterior of Temple tube station, his jacket buttoned to the neck in the cold. Tired and a little paranoid, he washed his face in the Thames as Sunday dawned. Then he headed south across the river to Waterloo station where he ate breakfast before purchasing a ticket to Southampton Central. Three hours later, Harold was on the Isle of Wight.

The farmhouse was a good 500 yards from the point where the bus dropped Harold. He was grateful for the driver's cheery cooperation, without which he would never have located Max Langdon's property.

Harold could hear dogs barking and a woman's voice commanding them to be quiet when he rang the homestead's front door bell.

'Yes?' the female voice interrogated him from behind a locked screen door.

'I'm looking for Mr Max Langdon.'

'Why's that?' came a response laden with suspicion.

'My name is Harold Bradshaw. I wrote to Max recently about the purchase of my family's cottage in Scunthorpe.' Harold was feeling very self-conscious, wishing he had been able to shave and change into a clean shirt.

'Wait there,' the voice ordered disapprovingly.

Harold surveyed the lush green pasture extending from all points around the farmhouse as far as the eye could see. Herds of farm animals could be seen in the distance, seemingly contented cows to Harold's inexpert eye. The serene panorama contrasted jarringly with his own complicated situation and for an instant Harold envied Max, overpoweringly so.

The sound of a rear door closing gently caught his ear, followed shortly after by its closure again, this time less carefully. Fragments of a hasty conversation between a man and a woman reached him. Then without warning, the front screen door opened, making him jump. A tall, middle-aged man in overalls limped from the house. He extended a hand. 'How are you, Harold?' the man asked in a gunnery sergeant's voice.

'I'm good, Mr Langdon, thank you,' Harold replied. Albert had taught him always to be respectful to his elders. 'Sorry for arriving like this, unannounced like.'

Max surveyed the young man in front of him. *Every picture tells a story*, he thought. 'Whatever you've been up to, I hope you haven't brought the coppers with you,' he said levelly. 'Between us, Sybil's not very happy I agreed to pay you 150 quid for the cottage. If the rozzers were to arrive hot on your trail, I'd be sleeping in the milking shed for a month.'

Harold's instincts told him he needed to complete the sale and leave, before Max changed his mind. He produced the title deed for the cottage from his pocket. 'I've filled it out,' he said, holding the paper aloft. 'All you need to do is sign here.' Harold awkwardly stabbed a finger at a section of the document.

Max could now see the grazes on the knuckles of Harold's left hand. They confirmed his suspicions that something troubling was afoot. He ignored the paper Harold held out. 'Harold,' Max said finally, 'I offered to buy the cottage only because I felt I owed it to Albert to help you if I could. But in making the offer, I envisaged any sale would be a straight-up process, which clearly this isn't. I really don't know what you're up to with this cock and bull story of moving to Edinburgh and now turning up like this. But obviously none of it is above board.'

Max stared hard at Harold, questioning him. 'I swear the sale is fully legitimate, Mr Langdon,' Harold said, 'and nothing of what's happened can blow back on you.' Harold took a deep breath. 'But the truth is I've got a *Dublin Zoo* right now.'

Max made no answer, principally because the lump rising in his throat had swathed him in powerful memories. *A chip off the old block*, he thought. Cautiously more than grudgingly, Max accepted the deed and placed it in his rear pocket. 'We went through a lot together, me and your Dad,' he said, reaching underneath his overalls into his shirt pocket from where he extracted a wad of notes.

Harold reached out to take the money. Max clasped Harold's hand with a vice-like grip and looked him deep in the eyes for a good ten seconds. Only then did he release his hold and let Harold take the money. 'Good luck, Harold,' Max said. 'I have a feeling you'll be needing all you can get of it.'

Harold shook Max's hand and walked away. As he went, he considered Max's warning about his future need for an abundance of good luck. Harold felt for his Danish krone, the lucky charm given to him by his father. 'My father will protect me and give me strength so long as I've got this,' Harold said out loud, surprising himself with the strength of his conviction.

It took Harold nearly two hours to make his way back to the Isle of Wight ferry terminal in Cowes. Southampton was barely half an hour away but Sunday services ran only infrequently. Harold felt increasingly exposed. It was obvious the effects of the Great Depression had lingered less in southern England than in the industrial midlands, the number of down and outs along the Thames notwith-standing. People generally were not only better dressed and healthier-looking but also seemed more optimistic. His broken-down appearance was like a sign on his forehead he was not from these parts.

Wishing it were time for the ferry to depart, Harold was startled to see two uniformed policemen walking towards him. His first instinct was to run but he knew he had no option other than to stay put. Leaning forward on the bench he occupied, clenched fists under his chin and elbows on his knees, Harold stared resolutely at the Solent strait separating the Isle of Wight from mainland England.

To Harold's dismay he saw out of the corner of his eye one of the policemen studying him as they approached. He willed himself to sit still, his relief palpable when the officers passed without stopping. Without further incident, Harold reached Southampton and was grateful when his onward train docked in London. Although the experience with the police in Cowes gave him confidence his description had not been circulated, he was still anxious to avail himself of the capital's anonymity.

Harold had originally planned to use some of his 150 pounds to book into a halfway decent London hotel for a few days until he found somewhere permanent to live. But he had not factored in the relative affluence of southern England, causing him to worry his scruffy state might arouse attention even at a hotel of moderate standard. As it was, while sipping tea and eating a pie in the Waterloo station canteen, Harold was all too aware of the wide berth given him by other diners. He left the station contemplating another night of sleeping rough.

Deciding to head away from the Thames in light of the previous night's experience and his now considerable hoard of cash, Harold headed south as twilight closed in, onto Kennington Road. He walked head down, avoiding eye contact. Turning a bend in the road, the lights from a floodlit building caused him to lift his head. Harold soon found himself looking at the Imperial War Museum. He did not know the museum had formerly been a hospital or that it had formally opened only three months earlier. Nor did he know that the building's conversion was incomplete at the time of its official opening. Now the race was on to finish the project, obliging the behind-schedule contractor to work around the clock.

Harold happened upon a doleful-looking man with a red flag and a hurricane lamp controlling the movement of lorries into and out of the site. He quickly summed up the man was no stranger to adversity. 'Any ideas where I might sleep?' Harold asked the workman. 'Too cold and crowded down at the river.'

The man was Welsh. 'There's a place close to here called the Brixton Lodge. I stayed there when I first came over. Not too flash, mind, but clean enough and out of the weather.'

Harold decided to chance his luck. 'Is the landlord likely to ask any questions?' he said.

The man laughed. 'Doubt it. Provided you can pay in advance, you'll have no problems.'

'Where is this place?'

'Keep walking down Kennington Road and then take Brixton Road for another two miles.'

'Thanks Taff,' Harold said, 'much appreciated.'

CHAPTER THIRTEEN

The screech of a barn owl startled Harold. He laid stock still for a good two minutes, listening for the sound of human movement. There was none. The nervous reaction reminded Harold where he was and of the dangers he faced. Still at this point, all he had to do was catch the train to Lyon later in the morning where he'd spend two days building cover, even if for security reasons the Resistance had been told he was only briefly transiting the city. No doubt there would be document checks along the way and while in Lyon. But provided his papers were in order, he'd be doing nothing to draw attention to himself. The real work would begin when he reached Marseille. Then who knew what would happen? Calm again, Harold's thoughts went back to the day when he and Billy Fiddler walked down to Inverness Terrace in Bayswater, London. And when they did images of Katrina rushed to him, one after another in rapid succession.

The Brixton Lodge was readying to close its doors for the night when Harold arrived. A stern middle-aged woman with wise eyes looked up as he entered. 'Three nights you say?' she confirmed after Harold enquired as to availability. 'Six pounds all up includes use of the washroom and a towel. No drinking, no fighting and no refund if we have to ask you to leave.' The woman watched as Harold turned his back and extracted ten pounds from his wad of notes. She took the note, holding it to the light. 'If the police come calling,' she said, looking over her shoulder as she disappeared into a back office, 'our policy is to cooperate with them.' She returned holding four one pound notes. 'Top floor dormitory, row one, bed sixteen. Washroom on this floor. And if I were you, I wouldn't be losing sight of that money of yours. Sleep with it is my advice.'

The dormitory took up the building's entire top floor. Beds were arrayed in three neat rows – one, two and three, with sixteen beds in each row. About two-thirds of the beds were occupied. Some occupants stared warily at Harold as he walked to the end of row one. The hostel, he decided, was a step up from sleeping rough, but not by much.

Harold spent most of the night lying awake, listening to the falling rain, his cash in the bed by his side. When he did sleep, it was only for a few hours. Many men were up with the dawn and noisily preparing to head off to wherever they were going – some to jobs, Harold assumed.

The rain was still falling lightly as Harold headed down Brixton Road; he was glad to have slept indoors and now thought better of the hostel. It being Monday morning, shops were beginning to open. Harold purchased items for shaving, a new set of clothes and a sailor's canvas duffle bag. He returned to the hostel washroom where he washed, shaved and changed into his new clothes. The duffle bag over his shoulder now containing his money, shaving tackle and dirty clothes, Harold left the hostel in search of food.

Over breakfast at a grubby teahouse, Harold considered his next steps. His priority was to find somewhere permanent to live. He also had to find a job before his cash ran out although this was easier said than done given he could not be open about his background. And thirdly, apropos of his background, he needed to ascertain where he currently stood with the law. The last matter he sought to address by purchasing a newspaper. Back in the hostel, the rain now pelting down outside, he lay on his bed scouring the paper for mention of the London police seeking a fugitive from Scunthorpe in connection with a serious assault. None was forthcoming. Had Harold read the article headed *Court News*, over which he skipped, he would have found reference to the elevation of Justice Samuel Prendergast to Deputy Chief Justice of the Central Criminal Court of England and Wales, effective 1 January 1937.

The absence of newspaper reports and his survival the previous day of the Cowes policeman's passing inspection combined to raise Harold's hopes the police were not searching for him. But he was not yet prepared to accept this. As such, he decided to seek a labouring position at the Imperial War Museum, assuming if one were available it would entail only cursory background checks.

Harold left the hostel the moment the rain stopped. But on reaching the museum he found to his annoyance the building contractor's site office was shut. And no sooner had he begun to retrace his steps to the hostel than the heavens re-opened. Drenched by the torrential rain, Harold sat in a nearby bus station shivering, miserable and soaked to the skin. A man wearing an expensive mackintosh and carrying an umbrella hurried into the shelter.

'Terrible weather, what?' he said in greeting.

Harold smiled briefly in response, his teeth chattering.

The man looked at Harold, wondering why he was out in the elements without a raincoat. 'Here, have this,' he said, offering Harold his umbrella. 'I've another at the office.'

Harold was caught off-guard by this unexpected act of generosity and felt obliged to offer an explanation for his waterlogged state. 'New to London,' he said, gesturing with his left thumb in the direction of the museum, 'and was hoping to get a job on the site.'

'Difficult, I understand,' the man replied, shrewdly assessing Harold. 'Public monument with all sorts of valuable artefacts lying about the place. You'd need a police check first.' A bus arrived. 'Cheerio,' he said over his shoulder as he boarded.

The rain eased a little allowing Harold to return to the hostel under his newly acquired umbrella. He went straight to the washroom to towel off. There were few people about prompting a snap decision to take a hot bath, hoping to ward off catching cold. The hot water was luxuriating, but Harold was dejected all the same. If labouring jobs at the Imperial War Museum site involved police checks, would this apply elsewhere? After twenty minutes, he dried off and donned the dirty clothes he'd worn previously. Back upstairs, Harold hung his wet clothing over a lukewarm metal heater affixed to the wall.

The voice of an older man caused Harold to open his eyes. The bath had relaxed him, causing him to doze as he lay on his bed. 'Do you mind if I have a look at your newspaper?' the man asked timidly. He spoke with a Cumbrian accent.

Harold inspected the person standing before him. He was small and physically withered, about sixty Harold judged, with skin of a peculiar yellow colour. 'Yes, that's fine,' Harold said. 'Where are you from?' he added, the man's inoffensiveness inviting conversation.

'Carlisle,' he replied.

'What brings you to London?'

The man smiled sadly. 'I'm dying from cirrhosis of the liver. Got a son down here I haven't seen in years – Robert, or Bob as we liked to call him. Thought I'd come down and try to find him. Someone told me about this place. Got here three nights ago.' A moment's hesitation and then the man extended his right hand. 'Billy,' he said. Brixton Lodge protocol dictated that surnames were not readily bandied around.

Harold also hesitated. 'Harold,' he said, taking Billy's bony hand once he'd summed up it was safe to reveal his Christian name.

The conversation proceeded. Harold finessed his story, explaining how the recent death of his parents from natural causes and a dearth of work in Manchester – skirting mention of Scunthorpe – had prompted him to come to London. He also told Billy of his visit that morning to the Imperial War Museum to seek work, only to be disappointed.

'Last I heard of my son,' Billy said after a time, 'was that he had a job in Bayswater, in a shop on the Queensway selling shoes.' Billy paused while he tried to summon the right words. 'I'd like to go and look for him. How would you feel about coming along?'

It suddenly dawned on Harold that Billy was scared. Ill and unfamiliar with London, the thought of venturing out alone daunted him. Harold was torn. He felt sympathy for Billy, but at the same time he needed to concentrate on finding a job and a place to live. Harold shrugged internally. He had the financial means to extend his stay at the hostel if necessary; an afternoon out with Billy would not be too great an imposition. 'If the rain stops we can go this afternoon, if you like,' Harold said. 'My clothes should be dry by then.'

Harold and Billy walked out of the Queens Road underground station, taking the Queensway exit. It was cold and gloomy, but the rain had gone. Harold carried his duffle bag over his right shoulder, his umbrella in his left hand. The pair strolled down the Queensway looking for shops selling shoes. But mostly they encountered blocks of brown brick flats with steeply sloping slate roofs, a selection of dubious cafés and other shops, and some public buildings such as the post office. On reaching the domed Abbott's department store near the end of the Queensway without sighting a single shoe shop, Harold suggested they make enquiries. A helpful if superior woman told them she did recall a footwear store on the Queensway at one point. But new owners had taken over Abbott's back in 1927 and greatly expanded its line of merchandise. 'The Selfridges, you know,' she sniffed. As a result, many smaller stores had gone out of business.

Harold and Billy stood in silence on the Queensway contemplating what next. 'He's queer, my lad,' Billy said finally.

'What's that?' Harold said only half listening. An illuminated sign a block away had caught his eye and distracted him. *The Sunset on Inverness* it blared.

'Bob, my son.' Billy started to cry softly. 'I'll never see him again. I know that now.'

Harold was unsure how to respond. He patted Billy's shoulder. 'Let's take a look at this place down here,' Harold said pointing to the sign, hoping to take Billy's mind off things.

The building housing the bright sign fronted onto Inverness Terrace, a narrow street running parallel with the Queensway. This explained the *Inverness* part of *The*

Sunset on Inverness. And the meaning of *The Sunset* soon became apparent when Harold and Billy reached the establishment's closed front entrance. *The Sunset. A prestigious club experience to be enjoyed after dark* announced a sign of white lettering on a blue background, neatly framed and expertly mounted on the club's exterior wall next to its large timber and iron front door.

With nothing else attracting their interest, the pair was about to move off when with a creak the heavy front door began to open. It opened about halfway before the head of a woman peered around it. 'Are you here in relation to the security position?' she asked Harold. He could not have known it then but the woman's name was Katrina.

Katrina was not a girl by any means, more likely late thirties. But she had captured that confident attractiveness women can have at this stage of life. Harold's lips formed to say *No.* Before the word could issue, however, a voice from behind him said, 'Yes, he is. I'm Billy Fiddler, Harold's agent.' Billy hadn't forgotten Harold's evident frustration when earlier recounting he had been unable to obtain work at the Imperial War Museum.

Katrina looked puzzled. 'I thought we were getting a Fergus?'

'Fergus couldn't make it,' Billy said, sharp as a whip.

Katrina shrugged. 'Come in, then,' she said.

Harold and Billy entered a busily over-furnished foyer. Katrina ushered them through the closed door of an office running off it. Seated behind a large mahogany desk was a man in his mid-fifties. His dark, wavy hair was streaked with grey. The attire he wore suggested moderate business success, whereas his florid face more emphatically betrayed a likeness for drink. To the right of the desk, at its front, sat a younger man of powerful build. He was clean cut, handsome and forty at most. A second chair was placed at the desk's front left.

'This is Mr Lenaghan, Mr Frank Lenaghan, owner of The Sunset on Inverness,' Katrina said, gesturing at the man behind the desk. 'And this is Mr Miller, our chief of security.'

Without introducing herself or explaining her role, she made to withdraw. 'You didn't say there'd be two of them,' Lenaghan the owner boomed, speaking to Katrina as if neither Harold nor Billy was in the room. 'Get us another chair, for God's sake.'

With that, Miller the security chief bounded to his feet and gallantly assisted Katrina. If Lenaghan noticed the warmth in her smile of gratitude he gave no obvious indication.

'So you're Fergus O'Toole?' Lenaghan said to Harold once Katrina had gone and those left were settled.

'No, Fergus couldn't make it,' Harold said following Billy's lead.

Lenaghan vigorously shook his head. 'For fuck's sake,' he muttered. He took a deep breath. 'What's your name, then?'

'Harold.'

'Harold fucking what?'

'Harold Bradshaw,' Harold replied, wondering if he'd just committed a grievous error and gratified when the disclosure of his full name provoked no particular reaction.

'Address?'

The use of his proper name made Harold reluctant to give out the Brixton Lodge address and reveal his current whereabouts. 'I'm new to London,' he said evasively, 'and still have to find a place to live.'

'Harold's been staying with me in Carlisle the last few weeks,' Billy piped up, coming to Harold's rescue.

'Who fucking asked you?' Lenaghan spat at him before turning back to Harold. 'Give me the Carlisle address, for Christ's sake.'

'19 Trimble Street,' Harold replied. Nineteen was his age and Mr Trimble, of course, his former employer.

'And where have you worked?'

Harold had the hang of it by now. 'I've done a bit of work in pubs up north …'

'Give me the name of one.'

'The Lion and Castle in Durham, my home town,' Harold replied, fervently hoping Lenaghan wouldn't bother to investigate since he had never been to Durham. And the Lion and Castle was indeed the pub in Scunthorpe where Bessie Murphy worked and she and Harold had delightfully fornicated for a month or so.

'That's right,' Billy interjected. 'Did a great job too. I know the manager. I'll get him to call you if you like.'

Harold was at once appalled and delighted by Billy's gall. Not so Lenaghan. 'If you so much as open your mouth again, Miller here will bounce you into the street. Do you understand?'

Billy looked suitably contrite but was pleased all the same. His interruption had diverted Lenaghan's attention from Harold's claim to have lived and worked in Durham.

'How about club work?' Lenaghan asked once he regained his composure.

'My last job was at the Plantation Room in Scunthorpe, from January to September this year,' Harold lied. He was prepared to risk mentioning Scunthorpe and the club knowing he had escaped interrogation on his supposed Durham background only by Billy's good grace.

Lenaghan, however, didn't question Harold. Instead, he looked at Miller. 'Know it?'

'Yeah,' Miller said, 'or know of it, rather. Down market place, blood house knock shop apparently. Run by a couple of low-life Yorkies, Sharpe and someone else.'

'References?' Lenaghan enquired of Harold.

'Didn't end too well, actually,' Harold replied, drawing on his Plantation Room experience. 'I gave it to a customer who told one of the girls he wanted to Greek her. I belted him and threw him in the street. Sharpe sacked me as a result. Said I was bad for business.'

'I see,' Lenaghan said thoughtfully. 'You should know that if I give you this job, there's a need to allow the customers a certain amount of leeway. The trick is to spot the troublemakers in advance and not admit them in the first place.'

Miller spoke uninvited, addressing Harold. 'Are you a drinking man?' he asked.

'Don't drink or smoke,' Harold replied with a frank honesty evident to all in the room.

Miller continued, 'What about the ladies?'

A *Mr Trimbleism* came to Harold's rescue. 'My rule,' he said, 'is never get your butter where you get your bread.'

Miller looked at Lenaghan and shrugged. 'Okay by me.'

'Wait outside,' Lenaghan ordered Harold and Billy.

They sat in the foyer, saying nothing. Eventually, Katrina reappeared. 'You can start tomorrow,' she told Harold. 'Be here at 4 pm prepared for a twelve-hour shift. We'll give you a uniform to wear. Six quid a week, with accommodation upstairs, late breakfast included, for two guineas a week if you want it.' Harold nodded. 'Your own room but you share a washroom with the two other junior security staff.' Harold nodded again. 'Miller has his own quarters at one end of the corridor and Frank and I have a suite at the other.' Katrina sensed Harold and Billy's curiosity. 'I'm Katrina, Mr Lenaghan's ... ah ... ah ... companion.'

Harold and Billy left the club and headed for the tube station. They had walked no more than fifty yards when a prematurely balding man as squat and powerful as a Great War tank scurried by. The man held a piece of paper in his hand and carried the harried look of someone late for an appointment. 'If I'm not mistaken,' Billy sniggered, 'that's Fergus O'Toole.'

Harold laughed heartily before turning serious. 'I really needed that job, Billy; this morning made clear I would struggle to find work. I'm eternally grateful to you. I wouldn't have got through back there without your help.' Within a year Harold would have cause to reconsider this vote of thanks, but in the moment he was totally sincere.

'From an early age it was clear my son was different,' Billy said, now also serious. 'Maybe that's why I drank; I don't know. But I'd lost Robert before he was fully grown and must now accept that's how it's meant to be.' Billy smiled sadly and placed his arm around Harold's shoulders. 'It gave me so much pleasure to help you, Harold,' he said. 'For a moment I felt like a proper father and not the terrible parent I've been.' Billy released his hold of Harold. 'I'll go back to Carlisle tomorrow. I'm ready to die now and thankful I've had this last chance to do right for someone I'd be proud to call my son.'

The pair returned to Brixton in silence, each lost in his own thoughts. Billy declined Harold's offer to eat together, saying he wasn't hungry. In the early hours of the next morning, Harold awoke and for a time watched Billy sleeping peacefully. But when daylight came, Harold's eyes opened with a start. Billy's bed was empty.

CHAPTER FOURTEEN

Harold arrived at The Sunset on Inverness smack on time the next day. He carried with him all his worldly possessions. Miller, the club's head of security, answered his knock on the door. Neither Lenaghan nor Katrina was around. Harold was squired upstairs to a storeroom where items of black clothing were packed neatly on shelves. Below the shelves, on the floor, was a row of heavy boots. Harold chose his uniform: three shirts each with the words *The Sunset* emblazoned on the shirt pocket; two pairs of trousers; and a pair of boots. He was then shown his sleeping quarters and given a tour of the facilities he was to use. 'Put your gear in your room and change into a uniform,' Miller told him. 'When you've finished, come down to my office.'

Katrina was hovering when Harold walked down the stairs. 'Welcome to The Sunset,' she said cheerfully. Aided by her figure-hugging, red crepe dress Harold noticed for the first time her trim waist and not inconsiderable chest.

'I'm looking for Mr Miller's office,' Harold said.

'Dan ... ah Mr Miller's office,' Katrina said, quickly correcting herself and pointing to the back of the building, 'is down there.'

Miller and two others, both dressed in the club's black uniform, were waiting when Harold entered the office. 'Godwin and Swift,' Miller said, gesturing in the direction of the two young men sitting in defensive hunches in front of the desk behind which Miller sat. Neither made an effort to greet Harold.

'Bradshaw,' Harold offered to the vacuum.

'Right,' Miller said. 'Now Bradshaw's here, I'll revert to the oversight role. This means I'll be recommencing spot checks; so be on your game, otherwise you'll end up out on your arse like that slacker Ronaldson. For your information, Bradshaw, your normal starting time is 6 pm; punters start arriving around half six. We do not permit new arrivals after 2 am and the club closes at four. The normal system is for one of you three to man the front door while the other two patrol the club lounge area, the floor as we call it.'

Miller turned to a rough floor plan pasted on the wall behind him. A line demarcated areas *A* and *B*. 'But for now, Gody and Swifty will rotate between the front door and area *A*. You, Bradshaw, will stick to area *B*. Rules are simple. Any misbehaver is to be turfed, but gently mind. Ditto for any that get pissed or, in the case of unaccompanied clients, annoy the hostesses or refuse to buy them drinks. If in doubt, check with me. This is a classy venue and we'll tolerate no riff-raff, present company excepted.' Miller's attempt at humour appeared lost on

Godwin and Swift obliging Harold, keen to conform, to stifle a snigger.

The briefing done, Miller suggested they might like to have a cup of tea before things got busy. Godwin and Swift left the office ahead of Harold, ignoring him. Harold surveyed them as they walked up the stairs in front of him. He estimated they were both at least six years his senior. Godwin was tall with thinning brown hair. He sported the undefined but unquestionably powerful build of a lumberjack. Swift, in contrast, was typically Anglo-Saxon with fair hair and pale skin, his aesthetically angular build contrasting pleasingly with Godwin's blunt force. Harold followed them into a dining room consisting of wooden tables and chairs. Godwin then Swift poured tea from a large enamel teapot on the sideboard. Harold did likewise. But when he made to sit with them, Godwin growled like an angry bear, a low rumbling coming from deep inside him.

'You stay away from us, you *Pit Yakker* cunt,' he hissed, misrepresenting Harold's origins with his derogatory use of the popular London term to describe natives of Durham. Details of Harold's interview yesterday had clearly filtered through. 'Ronnie Ronaldson was a mate of ours,' Godwin snarled, 'and we don't appreciate scabs like you taking his place.' Godwin glanced at Swift, who quickly adopted a fierce expression and directed it at Harold. It was immediately obvious to Harold that Swift was totally intimidated by his thuggish colleague.

Harold moved to a separate table. While drinking his tea, his mind harked back to his recent train trip to

London when he had fled from Scunthorpe. He could scarcely believe it was only three days ago. But it was not the short passage of time that was uppermost in Harold's thoughts. It was his awakening on the train to his gift – his calm capacity to employ violence, calculatedly and commandingly. Harold glanced at the hulking Godwin before pushing the matter from his mind. Right now he had a job to concentrate on.

Come half past six, the club started to fill as Miller had foreshadowed. Harold patrolled the floor's area *B* trying to look nonchalantly familiar. As instructed, he did not speak to any of the young women employed to host unaccompanied male customers in return for their purchase of exorbitantly priced drinks. After the first hour Godwin replaced Swift in area *A*, for Swift to reappear an hour later. Around 9:30 pm a light orchestra took to the stage with a suave older man in a tuxedo performing vocals. Harold had never seen the likes of it and was soon mesmerized. Next thing he knew Miller was by his side, speaking in sharp reprimand and telling him to keep moving.

Thereafter, Harold avoided looking at the band and roamed continuously. He marvelled at the difference between The Sunset's clientele and the Plantation Room. Here, most were older men of well-to-do appearance, some accompanied by wives or companions and some not. Nor was there a comparable level of tension in the air.

Close to midnight a dropped glass drew Harold to a table of four men and two hostesses seated just on his side of the imaginary boundary separating areas *A* and *B*. The same noise attracted Swift who had only recently returned from another stint of front door duty. Harold waved forward one of the bar staff to sweep up the broken glass. As he did, Swift spoke quickly and fearfully. 'Watch out for Godwin. He's a vicious nutter.' With that, Swift scurried away.

Just like Tuesday night, Wednesday and Thursday nights were largely uneventful. Friday and Saturday nights, however, were altogether different propositions. The crowds were bigger and rowdier, the orchestra played longer and couples danced enthusiastically.

On the Saturday night an unaccompanied client, a large bluff man expensively dressed, became unhappy when the girl hosting him declined to dance. 'I own half of Woking, you ugly cow,' he screamed. Miller watching from the bar nodded to Harold.

Harold approached. 'What do you want, then, sonny?' the man sneered.

'Sorry, sir,' Harold said, 'but I'll have to ask you to leave.'

'*Sorry, sir, but I'll have to ask you to leave,*' the man mimicked in mincing parody. Then harder and with threat. 'Why don't you fuck off and come back when you've worked out your cock is not just for pissing out of.'

Harold feinted with his right fist before driving his preferred left into a point just under the man's rib cage. The punch travelled no more than six inches. The man doubled over, the breath exploding out of him like a geyser. Harold steered him, gasping, to the club's cloak station in the foyer. In the man's waistcoat he found a small ticket and gave it to the girl in charge. A hat and overcoat were produced. Placing the former on the man's head Harold walked him from the building, handing him the overcoat once outside. On re-entry Godwin blocked Harold's path, their shoulders meeting solidly as Harold passed. Glancing back, Harold saw only pure hate in Godwin's unblinking stare. This confirmed for Harold what he already knew: that Godwin was a problem requiring eventual resolution.

Harold was once more in position on the floor. Miller sauntered by without stopping. 'Good job with *Mr I own half of Woking*,' he said. 'Nice touch, just the right amount of hammer.'

Three months elapsed. By late January 1937 floor walking was no longer tiring Harold's legs or hurting his feet, and he had grown accustomed to the routine of working until 4 am on all days, bar Sunday – his day off when the club was closed – and sleeping until noon. Apart from Godwin's glowering hostility, things were going well. The relatively few unruly customers with whom he dealt were generally fat and flabby and the worse for drink, powerless against Harold's physical strength and lightning quick hands. Moreover, Harold's calm ability to calibrate the degree of force he applied to individual situations had not gone unnoticed by management. Even the owner, Frank Lenaghan, who rarely appeared in the club at night – and then usually in the company of an important client – had complimented him on his work.

For his part, Miller privately told Harold of his plans soon to entrust him with front door duties, on a rotating basis with Godwin and Swift. 'The front of shop,' as Miller put it, 'gives the customers an important initial impression. I'm now satisfied you're ready to step up.'

Inside the barn near Riom in France, Harold's thoughts were competing with each other. He was torn between continuing his reminiscence and the need to sleep. Finally, the latter won out. He had to be alert. The smallest slip-up when in Riom or later on the train to Lyon stood to be calamitous. Harold closed his eyes. But they refused to yield to his will, stubbornly so. Before long in Harold's mind it was again the last Saturday night in January 1937, the thirtieth, two days after his twentieth birthday. Unannounced, Lenaghan and Katrina had just come down to the club from their suite upstairs.

Lenaghan and Katrina did not make their way to the reserved table directly in front of the stage as Harold thought they might. Rather, they disappeared into the foyer. Minutes later, they returned in the company of another couple, a man and woman both stylishly dressed. Clearly, Lenaghan and Katrina had been waiting at the entrance to greet their guests. The quartet made their way through Harold's area to the reserved table. Harold watched them, intrigued by the usually brusque Lenaghan's effort to engage the visitors, the man especially. The guests were both in their early fifties, Harold estimated. The air of authority the man exuded was unmistakable and his olive complexion suggested he was not English born.

No sooner had Lenaghan and the others taken their seats and ordered wine than the stage lights flickered to life and the orchestra and vocalist entered stage right. Halfway through the performance Harold had a matter with which to deal. It was nothing serious – just a man who had over-celebrated, fallen asleep at his table and begun to snore loudly. Harold gently shook the inebriate, all the while smiling with professional courtesy at his embarrassed wife. He walked the roused man through the club and into the foyer. Swift was on front door duty. Harold winked at him as he assisted the customer into the street. Standing in the chill night air, gently supporting the man while waiting for his trailing wife to collect coats, Harold was surprised to see three large black limousines parked directly in front of the club. 'What's the story with the limos?' he enquired amiably of Swift once the clients were on their way.

'It's the couple with the boss,' Swift answered with matching warmth. 'According to Miller, it's some mafia nabob from Little Italy over in Camden and his missus. Miller told me to be nice and polite to them. Apparently, this geezer has just taken over as top dog and he and Lenaghan are cooking up some deal.'

Harold turned and looked back at the limousines. Aided by a street light, he could now make out two men wearing bowler hats leaning up against the middle car's exterior, surprised to see them in the freezing cold. Even more surprising was their overcoats were unbuttoned. Harold laughed. 'I don't know about you, Swifty, but if I was driving one of those cars I'd prefer to sit inside it rather than stand out in the cold with my coat undone.'

It was Swift's turn to laugh. 'They're not the drivers; they're the bodyguards. And their coats are unbuttoned because underneath they're carrying Thompson sub-machine guns.'

Harold knew of the weapons with their distinctively round magazines. He shook his head, bemused at his introduction to the London gangster underworld. Harold did not know at the time the two bodyguards were named Ignazio de Pascale and Lorenzo Martino. He was to kill them a mere eight days later. And in consequence, nine months on in November 1937, the Deputy Chief Justice of the Central Criminal Court of England and Wales, His Lordship Justice Samuel Prendergast, would sentence him to twenty-five years imprisonment with hard labour without eligibility for parole until he had served a total of eighteen years.

The orchestra played the final number of its set. Its members laid down their instruments and prepared to leave the stage. The dance floor had been full of high-spirited patrons, twisting and turning as they executed London's most daring dance steps. People were laughing excitedly as they made their way back to their tables. Harold stood back observing the throng. As he did, over the top of the crowd he saw Lenaghan and his male guest in what now appeared to be heated conversation. He watched Katrina, a strained look on her face, pick up the wine decanter and attempt to refill their guests' crystal glasses. The flat hand of the female hovering over her glass, all the while unsmiling and staring straight ahead, was an icy gesture of decline. And when Katrina refilled the man's glass he made no effort to acknowledge her, nor did he drink any of the beverage. Shortly after, the man threw down his table napkin; it was an act of angry finality. Almost immediately the man and the woman stood. Without a word to Lenaghan or Katrina they stalked from the club, their body language telling an unhappy story. Their hosts remained seated at the table looking bewildered. To Harold's eye, Lenaghan looked scared and Katrina upset.

A matter involving another reveller distracted Harold. By the time that was sorted Lenaghan and Katrina had both gone. Harold shrugged internally – whatever had gone on was none of his business. The orchestra returned and the night bubbled on.

The later it got, the more Harold had to do. Suddenly, he felt a tug at his sleeve. It was Lenaghan whose return to the floor Harold had not noticed. 'Where's Miller?' Lenaghan snarled. His eyes were red and his breath stank of cognac.

'Last I saw him was an hour ago, just before 1 am. He was over at the bar.'

'Go and find him. Tell him I want to see him immediately.' Harold hesitated. 'Now,' Lenaghan ordered.

'But what about all this?' Harold said, sweeping his arm in an arc to span the rowdy crowd.

'You can worry about the customers once you've found Miller.'

Harold headed to the club's entrance. Godwin was on door duty. *No point asking him*, Harold thought. He walked down to Miller's office, which was empty, before returning to the club floor, not to his own area *B* but to area *A*, currently patrolled by Swift. 'You seen Miller?' Harold asked of his colleague. 'Lenaghan wants to see him urgently.'

Swift was standing between two men who for some reason had taken a dislike to each other. Harold was amused by the spectacle. Here was Swift calmly conducting a conversation while his arms were extended so that a palm of each hand was firmly planted in the chests of the would-be protagonists, both of whom were railing volubly. 'He might be upstairs or in his office,' Swift said.

'Checked the office but he's not there. I'll try upstairs. Thanks.'

Harold made to leave. 'Harold,' Swift called after him, 'careful how you go.'

Harold smiled in the dark of the Riom barn, recalling how he bounded up the stairs of the club that night wondering what on earth Swift's warning was about. It soon became apparent.

Miller resided in a studio flat at the least preferred end of the upstairs corridor, owing to its proximity to a common toilet just down the corridor. Harold knocked on the door. No answer. *Should I or should I not try to open the door?* he thought. But not game to intrude into Miller's private residence, he rapped the door again, louder and longer. Still nothing. Then standing there in the early morning quiet, the noise of the club a dim hum below, he heard a sound. It came from behind him, from the storeroom down the corridor containing the club uniforms. Thinking he had misheard, perhaps subconsciously hoping, Harold ignored it. But then the sound of a female voice, husky as if with a head cold, reached his ears.

Harold later reflected it had been unwise of him to open the storeroom door. A sounder approach would have been to knock and wait until its occupants, whoever they were, came out. But whereas Harold was reluctant to intrude into Miller's private accommodation, the storeroom was common ground. Besides, he still had much to learn about the human condition.

On opening the door Harold was greeted by a sight he had never remotely contemplated. There were Miller and Katrina both as naked as the day they were born. Miller was supine on the floor, his feet pointing towards the door. Katrina was astride him, her back to the door. When she turned, her face was a combination of surprise and alarm. Her large breasts, appointed by erectly protruding nipples, continued to swing violently even after she stopped gyrating. Harold knew enough to realize he had interrupted the pair at a crucial stage of their encounter. He stood frozen with mortification, wishing Swift's warning had been more explicit.

'What the fuck?' Miller exploded, trying to sit up and look around Katrina to identify the intruder. Katrina quickly rolled off Miller and lay on her stomach in order to protect her modesty. Try as he might, Harold could not help looking at Miller's engorged and glistening member, fascinated as it shrivelled in an instant.

Miller bounced to his feet, a wild look in his eyes, his anger overcoming the vulnerability of his nakedness. Harold stepped back a pace; Miller's look told him he was about to have his neck broken. But then Miller's eyes widened and looked beyond him, out into the hallway. Harold turned to find Lenaghan, drunk and swaying, a pistol in his hand. 'That will be all, thank you, Harold,' Lenaghan said as if completing a piece of mundane business.

Harold returned to the floor. He was shaken by what he'd seen and wondered about the implications for him. Then the sound of a gunshot echoed through the club, followed by another. Patrons stopped and stared and a panic of sorts broke out as people began to race for the door. Godwin walked onto the floor only quickly to depart. Harold turned to see Swift in area *A* anxiously trying to discern the direction from where the shots had come. The club was rapidly emptying. Harold walked into the foyer and was nearly run down by a semi-clothed Miller, a suitcase under his arm from which items of clothing could be seen protruding. Miller charged out the door, his open coat flapping. Harold never saw him again.

Unsure what to do, Harold loitered in the foyer. Soon Godwin and Swift joined him. Harold would have liked to ask them what they thought was happening, but Godwin's hooded eyes discouraged this. Next, to Harold's amazement, a fully dressed and freshly made up Katrina walked down the stairs. She looked serenely beautiful and her eyes were clear. 'Mr Miller has resigned,' she told Harold, Godwin and Swift, 'with immediate effect. I'm to manage the club's closure tonight.' She looked at the grandfather clock in the corner of the foyer. 'It's 3:30 am,' she said. 'Please close up now and be here half an hour earlier on Monday so we can discuss revised security arrangements.' Katrina made no mention of Lenaghan or the pistol shots. Rather, she simply spun on raised heels and shimmied alluringly up the stairs.

Harold chuckled softly from within his straw cocoon in rural France, conscious of the *Maquis* warning to avoid making noise. But he couldn't help it. It was an involuntary reaction to the embarrassment he always felt when recalling his shocked naivety on learning there was more going on at The Sunset on Inverness than just the Katrina–Miller tryst.

The club's lock-up completed, Harold returned to his room. He was tired but couldn't sleep. Rising from his bed, he cautiously opened his bedroom door. Outside it was pitch-black and all seemed quiet. Taking up his club issue torch, Harold crept along the corridor and into the storeroom, gently closing the door behind him. The torch beam snaked around the room. Two fresh bullet holes were gouged in its back wall. *Shots to warn off Miller*, Harold thought. Suddenly, the telltale creak of floorboards under weight carried on the night air. Harold froze and turned off his torch.

After nearly twenty minutes he summoned the courage to cautiously open the storeroom door. The coast seemed clear and Harold decided it was safe to sneak back to his room. But just as he was about to set foot in the corridor, a shaft of light shot out from a doorway further down the hallway. It came from Swift's room. Harold stepped back into the storeroom, failing in his haste to close the door properly. The aperture was not large, less than an inch, but it was sufficient for Harold to see the hunched shape of Godwin pad ghostly by.

On Monday afternoon Harold, Godwin and Swift gathered in the foyer. No one spoke. In Godwin's company, Swift always directed a contemptuous stare at Harold whenever he was in the vicinity. In light of what he had seen from the storeroom in the early hours of Sunday, Harold now wondered about the extent of Godwin's hold over Swift.

From out of nowhere his thoughts turned to Robert, the lost son of Billy Fiddler from the Brixton Lodge, and his apparent sexual orientation. *But surely not?* Harold thought, denying for now the truth sitting in the pit of his stomach. Katrina's arrival interrupted his rumination. She waved the group into Lenaghan's office, who as ever was seated behind his large mahogany desk. As was his habit, Lenaghan indulged in little by way of formalities and made no reference to the Saturday night events beyond a casual mention of Miller's resignation. Harold shot a glance at Katrina, and she caught him, meeting his glimpse with a look of cool detachment.

'Now to the matter of Miller's replacement,' Lenaghan said after a time. 'I've decided to promote Bradshaw to chief of security.'

Harold could scarcely believe his ears. He'd given no consideration to any possibility other than Godwin taking on the role. Godwin was clearly likeminded. He stiffened in his chair. 'But Mr Lenaghan, that's not fair,' Godwin protested.

Here was Swift's cue. He jumped to his feet. 'I'll not work for anyone except Neville,' he declared, patently trying too hard.

Katrina watched on dispassionately. 'Why don't you two nancy boys just shut up,' she said, her taunt meaning to wound. 'Mr Lenaghan and I have made a decision. You can leave if you want, but I guarantee neither of you will get work in a club within fifty miles of London.'

Harold was aware of the *nancy boy* connotation. And that neither Godwin nor Swift objected told his heart what his head already knew. Even so, Swift's brief flinching glance at the floor shocked Harold. It spoke of unwilling participation in the relationship.

For his part, Lenaghan looked on in barely disguised admiration. All indications were he'd forgiven Katrina for her dalliance with Miller. Godwin restrained himself and forced a tepid smile to his lips. 'Of course, Mr Lenaghan,' he said. 'It's only that I like working here and I'm disappointed, that's all. I'm sure Francis feels the same way.'

'That's right. I was just disappointed too,' Swift said as prompted, putty in Godwin's hands and unable to muster anything original to say.

In the early evening, before the club opened, Harold moved into the studio flat formerly occupied by Miller. As instructed, he then returned alone to Lenaghan's office. 'You should know Katrina demanded I appoint you chief of security over Neville Godwin,' Lenaghan said. 'Frankly, I wanted Godwin but she was insistent.' Harold nodded, surprised Katrina should think so highly of him. 'Anyway,' Lenaghan continued, 'what's done is done. And now that you're in charge of security, I need to update you on a situation I have.'

Harold smiled inwardly. A *Dublin Zoo* as his father would have said.

'The Eyeties,' Lenaghan said simply, using a modestly uncomplimentary nickname for Italians. 'There's a new fella running the mafia over at Camden, a new *Don* as they say. He wants a slice of the club action in and around central London. He made an offer to buy this place. But it was well below the odds. The counter-offer I made was significantly higher, a bit inflated I do admit, hoping he'd fall somewhere between my price and his original offer. I invited him and his wife over last Saturday night so he could see The Sunset was a reputable establishment deserving of a decent price. But he was quite rude. Said the place was nothing more than a glorified music hall and if I had any sense I'd take his original offer while it was on the table. We argued and he stormed out, saying the original offer was now withdrawn. It's not the mafia way to walk away. For that reason, I want you as chief of security to start doing all front door duty, with immediate effect. That way you can keep your eye out and let me know if you see anything strange.'

Harold didn't ask about contacting the police. He suspected that, like him, Lenaghan would have good reasons to avoid the law. 'Who will monitor Godwin and Swift on the floor if I'm permanently stationed at the front?' he asked instead.

'Until we get a new person, I'll do that,' Lenaghan replied. This somehow aroused his ire, provoking a resort to cruder slang. 'It's more important you keep a lookout for any tricks those dago bastards might pull.'

'Okay, fine by me,' Harold said. He waited for Lenaghan to dismiss him.

But Lenaghan had more to say, choosing his words carefully. 'The argument upset Katrina.' Harold understood Lenaghan was referring to his disagreement with the mafia *Don*. 'She became distressed. I started drinking brandy after it and that cuckolding bastard Miller took advantage of her.' Lenaghan smiled wistfully. 'Still, that's life I suppose,' he said, seeming to indicate the topic was now closed. But then Lenaghan reconsidered. 'It's only ever happened this once ... you know, the storeroom ...,' he said, his voice trailing off.

Harold knew for sure Lenaghan's afterthought wasn't true. Swift had warned him in advance of what to expect going upstairs. Nonetheless, Lenaghan's lame attempt at obfuscation shocked Harold for the second time that day. What else was there hidden below The Sunset's surface he didn't know about?

Harold stood to leave.

'Before you go,' Lenaghan said, delving into his desk drawer and handing Harold a pistol and a box of ammunition. 'You might need these, for the Eyeties.'

The pistol was a Luger, not German-made but Swiss, a 6/29 semi-automatic handgun according to the ammunition box. Harold thought about asking Lenaghan where he got the weapon but reasoned he'd be told a load of poppycock if he bothered. He also considered telling Lenaghan he had never before held a gun let alone fired one. But Lenaghan beat him to the punch. 'That will be all,' he said, now finally dismissing Harold.

CHAPTER FIFTEEN

Secreted in the pitch-black barn in France, Harold recalled his surprise promotion to chief of security at The Sunset on Inverness and Neville Godwin's infuriated reaction to it. For a fleeting moment he wondered whether Godwin was still alive, given what later occurred between them. But Harold's contemplation did not reflect concern for Godwin's welfare; he didn't care one way or the other. The man was an abomination and Harold had no regrets about what he had done to him.

Harold had spent barely twenty pounds from the proceeds of the sale of the Scunthorpe cottage to Max Langdon before taking the job with The Sunset on Inverness. And by now he had recouped some of that amount in weekly savings. But having seen the effect of the Great Depression on his father not for a moment did he consider putting his money in a bank. Instead, Harold carried his current balance of 142 pounds on his person. The bank notes of the era were large and bulky and the club uniform trousers a slim fit. Whether he carried his billfold wallet in his back or side pocket, a lump bulged incongruously out of Harold's trousers. Sly Neville Godwin had noticed this. On recovering from the shock of being passed over for promotion, Godwin decided Harold's wad of cash should be the focus of his revenge.

After rising at noon each day, Harold routinely attended to his ablutions, initially in the common washroom he shared with Godwin and Swift and latterly in his flat's private bathing facility. While using the shared washroom, Godwin had observed how Harold always carried his sailor's duffle bag in which to store valuables. But now Harold had self-contained accommodation, Godwin calculated he might not be so careful.

Godwin had also gleaned from earlier conversations with Miller that in the depths of winter the flat's bathroom would fill with mist when the occupant drew a hot bath. As luck would have it, Godwin could see the unit's small bathroom window if he leant out of the window of his own room. Just after noon on the Wednesday of the week of Harold's promotion, not yet forty-eight hours since Lenaghan's announcement, Godwin opened his window and looked out. The third of February 1937 was freezing cold and Harold had opted for a hot bath. On seeing the clouded bathroom window, Godwin was galvanized; he hadn't planned to act this day but now seemed as good a time as any.

Kicking off his boots and in his stockinged feet, Godwin took the Bowie knife he kept under his mattress and peeked into the corridor. It was deserted although he could hear the house staff talking in the dining room. He needed to act quickly. A break and enter merchant from way back, it took Godwin less than ten seconds to silently spring open the door to Harold's rooms.

Stepping inside, he recalled from his one previously invited visit the flat consisted of three discrete areas: a combined sitting and dining space, with a laminated table abutting a wall featuring two cheap art works; to the left of the wall, set back from the sitting and dining area, was a sleeping cubicle; and to the wall's right a bathroom symmetrically balanced the sleeping area.

Looking around, Godwin could see the bathroom door was two-thirds open. Beyond the door in front of a green-tiled wall was a steel tub with Harold's raised knee visible above the water filling it. Godwin was driven by irrational hate and prepared to take risks. He crept through the living room to the sleeping area. On the single side table he saw a round-faced alarm clock with bells mounted on top, a torch and other items. He also saw the large, plump wallet containing Harold's money.

In an instant the money was out of the wallet and into Godwin's pocket. He was too anxious to leave to inspect the miscellany on the bedside table. Had he, he would have seen a 1915 silver Danish krone coin. And had Godwin opened the small cabinet at the foot of the bed he would have found a Luger 6/29 semi-automatic handgun and 100 rounds of ammunition.

Godwin tiptoed back to the unit's front door. Taking a deep breath he stepped into the corridor, locking the door behind him. The soft sound of the door latching sounded like a thunderbolt to the nervous Godwin. It wasn't of course but still loud enough to attract the attention of Francis Swift, who at that moment had walked out of the common toilet adjacent to Harold's studio flat.

Seeing Swift, Godwin froze. Swift turned expecting to see Harold only to find to his astonishment it was Godwin. The two stared at one another. Godwin recovered first. Holding the index finger of his left hand to his lips, he held the Bowie knife aloft in his right. The jerky throat-slashing gesture he made was no joke; this Swift knew for certain.

Harold was still naked when he noticed his money was missing. He did as might be expected, searching his bed and elsewhere in the flat. On finding nothing, he hurriedly dressed and rushed downstairs, not sure what he was hoping to find. Harold was conscious of running about wildly. 'It's a *Dublin Zoo*,' he told himself, trying to remain calm and think about who might have accessed his quarters while he was in the bath. Harold's thoughts turned to the house staff who cleaned the flat two times a week and had a door key. Racing back up the stairs to search for Katrina to follow-up on the possibility, he passed Godwin and Swift as they descended. Only when Harold reached the top did it register. In Godwin's company Swift always adopted a belligerent look whenever Harold was in proximity. But this time Swift's gaze was averted as if he were trying to avoid seeing Harold – even in his peripheral vision. Swift, Harold realized, had been fearful of making a facial expression that might implicate Godwin. Abandoning his search for Katrina, Harold instead drank a cup of tea in the dining room, thinking. He could feel the calm overtaking him; it was the same sensation he had experienced on entering the vagrants' camp in Scunthorpe prior to methodically carving up the Tattersall brothers.

Harold's main lead was Swift, whom he needed to get alone. But also he wanted others to know about the theft. He went first to Lenaghan. 'It's endemic in this business,' Lenaghan said unsympathetically. 'The trade attracts untrustworthy people.' Reluctantly, he agreed to advance Harold two pounds on his next week's salary. Katrina was more understanding when she reappeared after an evidently bountiful shopping expedition. She set off immediately to quiz the house staff, returning shortly after to report a nil return, which Harold knew she would.

Harold sat in his office. Suddenly, he was starving. Leaving the building he walked towards the Queensway in search of a meal. Turning into the thoroughfare he encountered Godwin and Swift heading back in the direction of the club. Harold did not know that a little over an hour earlier Godwin had off-loaded the stolen cash to a cut-out he trusted, principally because the cut-out feared him. 'Meeting in my office at 5:30 tonight,' Harold ordered abruptly, barely stopping to deliver his instruction.

Harold informed Godwin and Swift of the robbery at the scheduled 5:30 pm meeting, well aware they already knew about it. But it was the opening salvo in his plan to both recover his money and resolve the Godwin problem once and for all.

Godwin's sullen face gave nothing away when he denied any knowledge of the theft. Harold asked Swift for his thoughts, watching him closely. Swift was composed. The advance warning of the meeting had allowed him to prepare. He shook his head, lips pursed, steadfastly refusing to look at Godwin.

Harold addressed Godwin. 'I want you to do a stint on the front door tonight,' he said. 'For an hour starting at eight.'

Godwin was immediately suspicious. 'Why?'

'If you must know,' Harold replied with easily contrived heat, 'it's because I've something I must do for Mr Lenaghan.'

Godwin wasn't readily fazed, but Harold's anger did have an edge to it. 'All right,' he said, 'keep your shirt on.'

At twenty after eight Godwin arrived at the front door, late in open challenge to Harold's authority. But Harold let it go; he had bigger fish to fry.

Back on the club floor Harold looked around him. It was a Wednesday night and quiet. Lenaghan was nowhere to be seen. The nervous apprehension on Swift's face as Harold approached was telling. 'What happened to the money, Swifty?' Harold said gently once he'd sidled alongside.

'I told you I don't know anything about it.'

Harold placed a hand on Swift's shoulder. 'But you do, Francis, and we both know it. I also know you're a decent man who would never willingly go along with Godwin.'

'Godwin will kill me if I say anything,' Swift blurted, the steel in Harold's unblinking stare prompting his involuntary utterance.

'Look, Francis,' Harold replied, now appealing to Swift's common sense, 'this is your chance to be shot of Godwin. You can't live your life with him treating you like he owns you.'

Swift was petrified of Godwin. But he also recognized Harold's home truth. And above all, he wanted to do the right thing. Swift summoned his reserves of courage, speaking rapidly lest his nerve fail him before he could finish. 'Godwin broke into your flat when you were in the bath and stole your money,' he whispered. 'He told me he was going to off-load the cash and to wait for him in the Queensway. He came back after two hours but didn't say where he had been or who he gave the money to. I didn't ask. He got back just before we saw you this afternoon.'

Harold had now heard all he needed to hear. 'Thank you, Francis. You won't regret this. You have my solemn word.'

But Swift was not convinced. Beads of sweat had formed on his forehead. 'Without finding your stash on him or in his room, Harold, you have no evidence he took it.'

Harold winked at Swift. 'Lucky we're not in a court of law, isn't it?' He turned and walked away, reaching into his pocket as he did to touch his Danish krone coin.

On his return to the front door, Harold gave Godwin a hearty slap on the shoulder. 'Turns out Lenaghan wasn't ready for me, Neville,' his never before use of Godwin's Christian name sending Godwin's alarm sensors spinning.

As Godwin turned to leave, Harold slammed shut the club's front door. Godwin's sensors went into overdrive. The door closure signalled he and Harold were to settle their differences right now, this instant. Godwin came at Harold like the bull he was, head down and charging. But he forgot Harold was a southpaw. As such when Harold swayed to the right, as if giving himself room to throw a right-handed punch, Godwin committed to this trajectory and could not correct it when Harold coolly darted left. Harold's flashing left fist landed with brute force. Godwin went down like a sack of coal, his jaw now at right angles to the rest of his face. 'A word to the wise Nev, old son,' Harold whispered in the moaning man's ear, 'don't rush into fights with your head down. Now the name and address of the person to whom you gave the money, please.'

For all the pain of his broken jaw, Godwin made no answer. Harold rolled him roughly on his stomach and, taking Godwin's right arm, forced it up his back in the direction of his head. Godwin resisted and Harold pushed harder until Godwin's arm snapped, fracturing with a sound like splintering green timber. Godwin screamed. By now people had gathered, patrons and club staff alike. People were screaming along with Godwin. The noise was deafening. Lenaghan was halfway down the stairs, drawn by the hubbub, when Godwin lapsing in and out of consciousness and panting heavily said, barely audibly, 'Benny Shark. Solomon Gardens estate.'

Godwin had passed out when Harold took his left arm and also broke it. Onlookers were horrified at this last act of apparently gratuitous violence. Screams intensified and urgent entreaties to *Stop* rang out. But Harold had his reasons. He'd given Swift his word there would be no repercussions. Disabling Godwin for life, as he had the Tattersall brothers, delivered on that promise.

Lenaghan stood beside Harold, frantically flapping his arms against his sides. 'What the fuck are you doing?' he screeched.

'Godwin took my money, Mr Lenaghan,' Harold replied calmly.

With that, Harold walked away onto the club floor, passing Swift wide-eyed with fear. 'All that needs to be done, Francis, is done,' he said softly. 'You'll have a better life now.'

Had Harold stopped to survey the crowd gathered to watch his affray with Godwin, he would have seen Katrina looking on transfixed. He would have also noted her face was flushed and, with both hands behind her, she was sensuously rubbing her hips and buttocks.

The club was emptied out and closed. A rickety old ambulance carted Godwin off to nearby St Mary's public hospital. Lenaghan found Harold sitting at the bar drinking a glass of water. 'Well, a nice old pickle you've landed me in,' he said. Having seen Harold in full flight he was unwilling to say what he really thought. 'Between Miller and Godwin we're down two men and on top of that I've had to close the club for the night.'

Harold was matter-of-fact. 'I know a place over at Brixton where we can go tomorrow to recruit two new security staff. You'll be spoiled for choice, trust me.' Lenaghan grimaced but said nothing. 'And Wednesday nights are always quiet,' Harold continued. 'Business won't suffer too much for closing early tonight. In fact I suspect word about why we closed will spread like the plague, with a bit of spice added each time the story is retold. I'm betting The Sunset will be filled to the gunnels tomorrow night.'

Lenaghan considered this. He liked the idea of Harold assisting him recruit new security staff. Notwithstanding Harold's earlier antics, anyone he recommended for employment was sure to be a good choice. Lenaghan was also a man with a natural bent for public relations. He sensed Harold was probably right about the positive impact of the Godwin incident on business. Curious customers would come from near and far.

'Even so,' Lenaghan said, wanting to sound grudging, 'you've caused me a lot of headaches. Tomorrow we'll go to Brixton as you suggest. Provided we can find two new recruits you will ensure they're ready for immediate start, by Saturday night at the latest. Between organizing the new staff and managing the club with a skeleton security staff, you've got a busy couple of days in front of you.'

Harold nodded. 'One last thing, Mr Lenaghan, can you tell me the whereabouts of the Solomon Gardens estate? I need to make a visit there tonight.'

Harold fumbled around the Riom barn loft, unable to see in the dark, feeling for the water container they had left him. He gave another quiet laugh as he took a sip. But this time his chuckle was ironic and sour. It came from Harold's recollection that Solomon Gardens estate was a place he had come to know far too well. Located just north of Wormwood Scrubs, adjacent to the Scrubs Lane Bridge spanning the Great Western railway line, he could see it from his cell in the main prison, as if it were taunting him. He had given up looking at it for this reason. Although last year, after he'd been a *trustie* for about six months, before they removed him from prison to prepare him for the Marseille operation, Harold had gone there one day with a prison guard, a sort of outing they'd allowed him. It hadn't changed much.

Harold made his way as quickly as possible to White City underground, the station Lenaghan had told him was closest to Solomon Gardens estate. It took an age to find the place and was past midnight when he did. The complex had no functioning external lights. The light fittings on the few light poles Harold saw were all smashed. Harold could make out five blocks of flats, each of two levels, formed into an uneven rectangle.

Hemmed in by the buildings was a vacant square of land. Overgrown grass was visible in the moonlight, causing the square to resemble an unpaved quadrangle. It was difficult to tell exactly how many flats were occupied. Harold had intended to knock on doors and ask occupants if they knew where Benny Shark lived. This was proving to be easier said than done; each flat within each block was in total darkness, none apparently with electric light connected. And the mood of the common was also threatening. Harold told himself to be extra careful not to alarm any resident when trying to rouse them.

Harold's chosen approach was to concentrate on the centre block, starting with the ground floor flats and working up. Just as he was preparing to tap politely on the first door, he heard rowdy voices in the distance. Instincts of preservation told him to be cautious. He moved from the front of the building to its side and out of the moonlight. Dogs could be heard barking and Harold thought he heard a curse from within one of the flats. The rowdy voices were now louder. Soon the gang had reached the quadrangle. There were about a dozen young men, all seemingly as drunk as lords. Group members were jostling among themselves. Then one removed another's cap. There was little Harold could do when the man with the purloined hat ran in his direction, laughing loudly. Two others chased after him.

The three breakaways saw Harold at roughly the same time. They screamed like banshees, a wolf pack call causing the whole group to descend and encircle him. Harold stood with his back to the wall sizing up the snarling swarm. He scanned for the largest gang member and rushed at the selected target, punching him in the stomach and delivering a one-two combination to the head as the man doubled over. It was an effective strategy. The startled gang members were unable to stop Harold as he burst through their midst and sprinted into the night.

Not until he reached the relative safety of the White City tube station did Harold stop running. Lucky to have caught a late last train, he was relieved to be finally headed back towards Bayswater. Harold reflected as he went. Solomon Gardens, he decided, was not a place to go after dark. And on Thursday he was committed to going to Brixton with Lenaghan. Reluctantly, he accepted he would have to wait until Friday before he could return in the daylight hours. Harold was not to know an unanticipated development would prevent him from adhering to this timetable. But for now that was his plan. Harold's thoughts turned to his encounter with the estate gang and the pistol in his bedroom cupboard. It was then he decided he'd take the Luger 6/29 semi-automatic with him when he did return.

Harold and Lenaghan travelled to the Brixton hostel first thing on the morning of Thursday 4 February 1937; Lenaghan keen to get there before the residents dispersed for the day. Harold was weary. His little time in bed had been spent replaying the abortive attempt to recover his cash over and over in his mind.

The woman on duty was the same one Harold had met the night he arrived at the hostel. She remembered him and helpfully assisted to organize interviews. Lenaghan took care with his selections, endlessly quizzing Harold about why he preferred one candidate to another. By late afternoon, two men had been selected. Lenaghan told them to be at the club the next morning, Friday, to commence training. 'We'll need to get these fellows ready as soon as possible,' Lenaghan instructed the yawning Harold as they trained home. 'Make it your highest priority.'

Thursday night was just as Harold had predicted. A line of would-be patrons eagerly hoping for admission extended as far as the eye could see, while inside the club was packed. Lenaghan delighted in the upswing in business. He decided he could now levy an admission charge, a so-called cover charge, without deterring customers in any great numbers. The club's entire staffing complement was frantically busy. By 4 am Friday everyone was exhausted and happy to see the doors close.

Harold headed for bed as quickly as he could. The two new security staff were due to arrive at 10 am, in six hours' time, and he badly needed to get some sleep. Harold's plan was to ready the newcomers as soon as possible and then head to Solomon Gardens in the early afternoon while it was still light.

Lying on his straw bed in the loft outside Riom, hands behind his head, Harold became philosophical. He was thinking it was curious the way things turned out – how he had the 150 pounds Max Langdon had paid for the Scunthorpe cottage leading to the belting he subsequently gave Neville Godwin to thank for paving his way to Katrina's door. *Or more accurately hers to mine*, he thought.

Harold sat wearily at the dining table in his flat, unlacing his boots. Everything considered, it had been a demanding last couple of days. A light tap on the door caused him to look up. Still wearing one boot, he shuffled to it. It was Katrina. She pushed past him, quickly shutting the door behind her.

'Aren't you Frank's little pet, then?' she asked, smiling sweetly and standing close to Harold. He could feel her presence and smell her perfume. 'You made him a fortune tonight.'

Katrina's hands were now on Harold's biceps, kneading the muscles. 'Spose so,' he said for want of something better to say.

Katrina pushed her waist against his, then harder with circular movement. With that, Harold's fatigue vanished, as if by magic.

Katrina's voice was husky. 'I can't tell you what it did for me to see you thrash Godwin,' she whispered. 'Those legs and that arse of yours working overtime. Made me *sooo* randy. Why, I even let Frank mount me on Wednesday night.'

'What do you want?' Harold asked, conscious his voice was now also croaky and only too aware of his silly question.

Katrina's lips were on his. He didn't resist. Thoughts of Bessie in the hotel laundry in Scunthorpe had taken over. The couple staggered to his bed, ripping clothing from each other as they went. 'Mr Lenaghan?' Harold asked in one last futile attempt at prudence. But by now Katrina's mouth was at his loins.

Afterwards they lay in each other's arms, panting from exertion before falling asleep. Shortly after, Harold awoke with a start. His alarm clock told him it was 5:40 am. Harold gently woke Katrina. 'What are you going to tell Lenaghan?' he asked anxiously. 'Where are you going to say you've been?'

'Why, I'll tell him I was in here, with you,' Katrina muttered groggily, trying to turn on her side and continue sleeping.

'But what will he say about that? He tried to shoot Miller.'

Katrina was now wide awake. 'Miller hadn't just made him two thousand quid in a single night with the promise of more to come. There's only one thing Frank loves more than me and that's money.'

'Jesus,' Harold fretted, unconvinced by Katrina's explanation.

'You just keep the turnstiles ticking over, sweetheart, and everything will be fine,' Katrina said reassuringly. With that, she looked at Harold and smiled. 'Seeing that you've disturbed my beauty sleep ...' she said.

It was past 7 am before Katrina left Harold's quarters.

CHAPTER SIXTEEN

With yet another night of limited sleep and now beset by feelings of guilt, Harold was on edge as he descended the stairs for the 10 am arrival of the two new starters. He was grateful when both arrived on time. First item of business was a meeting with Lenaghan. Harold knocked tentatively on the office door.

'Come,' Lenaghan's voice boomed.

Harold ushered the recruits inside, announcing their arrival as he walked so as to obscure the awkwardness he felt. And when it became obvious Lenaghan was ignoring him, Harold grew even more uncomfortable. The meeting proceeded at a businesslike pace, with Lenaghan performing his usual intimidation routine for the benefit of the newcomers. Relieved when Lenaghan had finished, Harold took the new arrivals upstairs to the storeroom to select uniforms. He walked downstairs intending to wait in his office while they changed. To the nervous Harold's amazement Lenaghan was there.

'Got a minute?' Lenaghan asked.

Without waiting for Harold's answer, Lenaghan walked to the door and closed it. Harold winced. Was Lenaghan going to pull a gun on him? The two men stood facing one another. 'I knew for a long time of course that Miller was shagging Katrina,' Lenaghan said finally, a rueful look now on his face. 'But not until the meeting with the mafia fellow derailed did I do anything about it. I love her, you see, and didn't want to risk losing her.' Harold was struck by the change in Lenaghan, now seemingly vulnerable and without his usual bombast. 'Thought I might have had her to myself for a while after Miller sodded off,' Lenaghan continued, frowning. 'But now she informs me she's adopted you as her boy lover.' Harold said nothing. 'Be careful, Harold. She's a free spirit and will go wherever whim takes her. Don't fall in love. She'll break your heart if you do.'

Harold walked around his desk and sat down. Suddenly, his legs were as heavy as lead. 'I didn't intend for it to happen, Mr Lenaghan,' he said.

'Well, it did,' Lenaghan replied in a flash of sharpness. He quickly recovered himself. 'I had no idea what I was in for when I first met Katrina over a decade ago. I had just got a job as a junior manager at a club called The Rio near Piccadilly Circus owned by a Latin chap. She was a hostess there. The Latin, some sort of Lothario inevitably, was on with Katrina. But he was also work shy. He tried to pull an insurance scam by burning down the place but didn't fool anyone and got locked up for three years. Into Katrina's life stepped I. We went off to Birmingham, made a bit of money and two years ago returned here and bought this place. Miller wasn't Katrina's first indulgence and you won't be her last. The fact is, though, I can't contemplate living without her.'

Lenaghan pawed at the floor with his foot. 'So young Harold Bradshaw,' he said, looking up, 'although I can't stop Katrina from seeing you, not without the risk of her leaving me, I want you to know how painful and humiliating this is for me ... you and her. And in light of this, if you have any shred of decency the least you can do is to move heaven and earth to make this club a success. That's all I need to say. I don't propose to mention you and Katrina again.'

Frank Lenaghan was a cunning character whose loves really were money and Katrina in that order. He also knew Harold was the key to his club's financial success and, giddy with greed, had unburdened himself in order to make beneficial use of Katrina's seduction of his young employee. In that regard, Lenaghan had cannily identified Harold as a man with a wide streak of principle. That's why he had ignored Harold earlier, softening him up so as to prick his conscience. And Lenaghan's ploy proved to be spectacularly successful. For no sooner had he left than Harold was thinking, *Lenaghan's right. I do owe him over Katrina. From now on I'll make the club my priority. That'll mean getting these new starters sharp and ready today and looking for Benny Shark tomorrow.*

Friday night set a new record. Bolstered by Lenaghan's freshly instituted cover charge, revenue for this one night alone surpassed three-and-a-half-thousand pounds. Harold had teamed the recruits with Swift and left them to patrol the floor while he manned the front door. Harold didn't see Lenaghan until close to finishing time when he came downstairs to count the night's takings. Katrina had earlier flitted by. 'Why don't you give me the key to your flat?' she had suggested to Harold. 'That way I can be waiting in bed when you finish up later on.' Harold complied. And with that his perceived obligation to Lenaghan expanded like a gassed-up balloon.

Katrina was gone before Harold awoke around noon on Saturday. Clearing the air with Lenaghan had eased his mind and he slept soundly. But a sober mood quickly overtook him. He had to get to Solomon Gardens before it was dark and before this Benny Shark character frittered away his money. How Harold wished he had resolved the matter the previous Wednesday night after extracting the confession from Godwin. Events, however, had conspired against him. Thursday of course he was recruiting with Lenaghan at Brixton; and his plans for Friday had been stymied by his newfound devotion to Lenaghan, that stemming from his sampling of Katrina's carnal delights.

Harold headed for Solomon Gardens as quickly as he could that Saturday afternoon 6 February 1937. The Luger pistol issued him by Lenaghan was in one trouser pocket, its eight-shot magazine fully loaded; his Danish krone coin in the other. Even in daylight, the estate reeked of despair. Rubbish and old newspaper he hadn't seen last Wednesday night were strewn about. Harold saw a ragged woman nearby supervising a child kicking an equally dilapidated football. 'Looking for a fellow named Benny Shark,' Harold called out as he approached. The woman's dark hair suggested she was Irish. Harold never found out. Scooping up the child, she raced off without answering.

Looking around him, Harold saw a group of four sitting at the far end of the grassed square of land hemmed into a quadrangle by the estate's accommodation blocks. He set off in the group's direction, walking around the quadrangle's perimeter in preference to the unknowns of a direct path up its middle. As he neared, Harold could see the four were all boys, aged ten to twelve he estimated, Dickensian urchins all.

Suddenly, a voice close by and to his right boomed out, '*Eh*, what the fuck do you want?'

Harold turned and saw a large man with a protruding stomach standing on the threshold of one of the ground floor flats. He wore a dirty, blue roll neck sweater and his face was stubbled and unwashed. When he spoke, the man's mouth opened to reveal a set of ugly broken teeth.

'Looking for a Benny Shark,' Harold called back.

'What are you then, filth?'

'No,' Harold replied, deliberately laughing to emphasize the absurdity of the suggestion. 'I'm not a copper.'

The man was not prepared to share in the amusement. 'We don't like strangers wandering around here,' he said menacingly. 'So who are you? A private eye?'

Harold was also about to deny this suggestion when something told him that, although the man was an adult seemingly in his mid-thirties, he appeared to have a fascination with private detectives and their ilk. 'Didn't realize it was so obvious,' Harold replied.

The man was indeed a devotee of the *Dick Tracy* comic strip series, with a stunted mentality to match. And Harold's intuitive admission had now transformed him into one of the genre's gritty villains. 'I might be able to help if there's a drink in it for me,' the man said, seeking to extort payment by mimicking a line that recently had taken his fancy.

Harold had calculated during his earlier night visit that the complex hosted about 200 flats. In the daylight he could see most were vacant; the estate was like a ghost town. With so few residents he was sure the man would know everyone living there. Unfortunately for the man, Harold was also short of time and not a little annoyed he was being squeezed for money. After all, it was the theft of his cash that had brought him to Solomon Gardens in the first place. Harold strode to the man and pushed him hard in the chest, forcing him back against the building's fascia. In the one action he withdrew the Luger pistol from his pocket and forcefully inserted it into the uneven cavity that was the man's mouth. 'Benny Shark?' Harold hissed in his ear.

The man was shaking with fear, no longer in character. 'Benny's not here,' he mumbled, cheeks puffed and quivering as if trying to speak with a mouth full of pork pie. 'He got wind Wednesday night that someone was looking for him. It's you, ain't it?' the man asked, looking at Harold with wide, scared eyes. 'So he scarpered, that night. Don't ask me where.'

Harold was conscious of the group of boys nearby watching the confrontation. He was also conscious that his failure to complete the recovery task on Wednesday night stood to cost him his cash now that Benny Shark had disappeared. 'Where's Shark's flat?' Harold asked, determined at least to rummage through it and see what he could find. He withdrew the pistol from the man's mouth, allowing him to answer more easily.

'Second floor, over there,' the man replied, simultaneously gulping and pointing to an adjacent block. 'Number twenty-seven.'

Harold's hand snaked out and dragged the man forward by his hair, placing the barrel of the Luger pistol against his forehead. 'If you so much as hint to Benny Shark I've been here, I'll come back and kill you. Is that clear?' The threat was designed to ensure that if Shark returned unexpectedly in the next hour or so he wasn't alerted to Harold's presence in his flat, turning it over. For his part, the man's ready pledge to silence reflected a deep fear of being caught up in an all-too-real dispute between Benny Shark and the terrifying individual with the gun. He ran off the instant Harold released him, slamming the door of his flat behind him, his silence assured for a week.

With that, Harold turned to the watching boys shooing them away as if they were seagulls coveting his hot chips. Three of them retreated to a safe distance and stood watching as Harold stalked towards Benny Shark's flat. One, however, trailed behind. He was the oldest and the group's natural leader. Harold found the flat door closed but not locked. He stepped into a fetid hovel. A rat scurried from sight, followed by another, and toxic fumes stung Harold's eyes and itched his throat.

The sound of a young voice from behind him startled Harold. 'He's coming back tomorrow morning, you know.' It was the boy who had followed him.

'Who is?'

'Benny,' the boy said. 'For the fags.'

Harold looked at him questioningly.

'I was up late Wednesday night playing with my crystal set,' the boy said. 'I live over there.' He pointed directly across the quadrangle. 'Seen someone arrive and bang on Benny's door. Bang, bang, bang. Benny comes out and they run off together. In a great rush they were. But then the man who had knocked on the door started arguing with Benny. He was pointing to the flat, shouting something. I saw Benny stop running and come back and grab the other codger by his collar. I thought they were going to have a nice old punch on. Benny started shouting. He was like a foghorn; I could hear him real clear. "I told you, we have to go," he yelled. It was so funny the way he was rabbiting on. "We can't be carting six thousand fags around with us; they'll only slow us down. I'll come back on Sunday morning and get them, I promise. When things are quieter." '

Harold scanned the sparsely furnished room. His eyes settled on an off-white timber cupboard. Moving to it he found the closet was padlocked. 'Stand back,' Harold instructed the boy now standing by his side. With a powerful kick, the bottom of the door shattered as it gave way. Harold looked inside to find row after row of *Wild Woodbines* cigarettes all in their distinctively patterned ten-per-packet livery, 600 packets in all. Watched by the boy, Harold bundled most of the cigarettes into the empty Gladstone bag inside the cupboard. Those remaining, he stuffed in his trouser and jacket pockets. 'Don't tell anyone about this,' Harold instructed the boy. 'Not the other boys and certainly not your mother and father.'

'Got a Mum but ain't got no *Da*,' the boy said. 'Not one all the time, anyways.'

Harold suddenly warmed to the boy. In his own innocent way, he had just articulated his evidently hopeless lot in life. For a moment Harold thought of giving him a few packets of cigarettes to sell. But he soon realized this risked Benny Shark thinking the boy had taken the whole stash. Harold took a pound note from his pocket, half the salary advance given him by Lenaghan.

'What's your name?' he asked.

'They call me Slim,' the boy replied.

'Benny Shark and his friends will be wondering what's become of the cigarettes, Slim,' Harold warned. 'If I give you this quid, do I have your word you'll stay quiet about all this?'

The boy nodded. Harold was confident the lad was sufficiently street-smart to be trusted. 'Okay, off you go. And remember, not a word to anyone.'

Harold remained in Benny Shark's flat for an hour afterwards. For the boy's sake, he didn't want to be seen walking from the unit with him. And as well he now needed to plan for Sunday morning. Harold set about rearranging Shark's furniture.

Harold returned to the club as it was readying to open its doors. He quickly drew Swift aside and gave him the cigarettes. 'Sell these for me, Swifty, will you? We'll split the proceeds down the middle.' Harold was aware Swift had virtually no money. Katrina had told him. Godwin, she explained, not only used Swift as a sexual plaything but also took the majority of his earnings. 'Try that dodgy café on the Queensway,' Harold suggested. 'They sell fags and could be interested in a little hot property.'

Swift nodded his agreement. But he also looked enquiringly at Harold, asking why he would not be involved in the exercise. Harold saw this. 'I may have other matters to deal with next week,' he said, shrugging. Harold planned to deal with Benny Shark once and for all on Sunday morning. But if things went badly and somehow the police became involved, he would need to leave London in a rush. In which case, Swift was welcome to all the proceeds.

Patrons began to flood the club. They came in numbers never before seen. It was manic. New revenue and attendance records were set as the night wore on. Harold barely had a moment to spare. When he did get to have a hurried conversation with Katrina, he told her he would have to forego their liaison that night; a pressing task obliged him to leave as soon as the club closed on Sunday morning. She stared intently at Harold for a moment, assessing him. Then, understanding he was not lying, feigned her indifference and wandered off.

Within thirty minutes of the club closing Harold was headed for Solomon Gardens, having dallied long enough only to change into civilian clothes, load his Luger pistol and transfer his Danish krone, his good luck charm, to his new attire.

It was too early for trains, so Harold adopted the scout's pace approach to getting to the estate, alternately running and walking in short segments. It was dead quiet and the sun was not yet up when he crept into Benny Shark's flat. Harold took up position behind the broken down sofa he'd positioned so as to observe the flat's entrance through the observation hole poked in its fabric. It was over a two-hour wait. Just as Harold was beginning to wonder if Benny Shark might not return, he heard a noise outside. A man entered the flat, taking a furtive look up and down the estate as he closed the door. He was tall and lean and wore a brown jacket to protect against the cold.

Benny Shark held a key in his hand and moved directly in the direction of the cupboard. 'Fuck it, fuck it,' he uttered in a combination of dismay and alarm on seeing its smashed door. He ripped the flimsy timber apart with his hands as if vainly hoping to find the cigarettes elsewhere in the receptacle.

Harold understood Shark would go straight to the cigarettes. He left the sanctuary of his hidey-hole, crept along the pre-determined pathway and stood between Shark and the door. Shark turned standing bolt upright and tensing, first on sensing Harold's presence then on seeing him. 'The money Godwin gave you for safe keeping,' Harold demanded, 'give it to me.'

Shark's top lip curled in an angry sneer. A knife appeared in his hand. 'I'm gonna cut you, mate; I'm gonna cut you real bad.' He lunged at Harold teeth bared, weaving like the experienced street thug he was.

Harold was ready. He took the filthy blanket he had placed on top of a shelf the day before, casting it as if it were a fishing net. Shark raised an arm to deflect it. The distraction was fleeting but long enough. Picking up the wooden truncheon he had found in the flat and placed under the blanket, Harold brought it down on Shark's forearm. The cracking sound told them both the forearm had been fractured. Shark instinctively grabbed at the injury with the hand in which he held his knife. The surge of pain that swelled as the initial shock wore off caused him to bend forward.

Harold's next blow could have seriously hurt Shark, possibly killed him. But unlike Shark and Godwin before him, Harold's innate ability to remain calm while his every other sense was racing came to the fore. Much as with unruly patrons at the club, he regulated the force he applied so it was commensurate to the situation. First and foremost, he needed Shark conscious and able to tell him where the money was; and second, ever mindful of the Tattersall brothers in Scunthorpe, Harold wanted to avoid hurting Shark such that the law would get involved. Harold instead hit Shark a glancing blow on his good hand, causing him to drop the knife. Then he placed his leg behind the writhing man and pushed him hard, forcing Shark to the floor.

Harold stood with his boot on Shark's chest. 'The money?' he said softly, now holding Shark's knife.

'What money?'

Harold kicked at the fractured forearm, again and for a third time. Shark screamed on each occasion but otherwise remained resolute. Harold was puzzled; people like Benny Shark did not believe in honour among thieves. Suddenly, the reason for his stubbornness dawned. 'You're scared of Godwin, aren't you?' Harold said, realizing Shark was unaware of the extent of Godwin's injuries. 'Neville Godwin is now crippled,' Harold said. 'He will never again lift an arm above shoulder height.' Harold paused for emphasis. 'I made sure of that.' The momentary flicker in Shark's eyes told Harold Shark believed him. 'Yes, that's right,' Harold said. 'You don't need to put up with me prodding your broken arm because you're scared of Godwin. He's done with, finished for good.'

'King's Cross station,' Shark said, now anxious to cooperate. 'Locker key in my jacket.'

Harold stood back. 'Give it to me,' he commanded.

Using his good arm, Shark managed to sit semi-upright. From his jacket pocket he produced a small key.

Harold took it. Engraved on it were the words *London and North Eastern Railway*. 'Benny,' he said evenly, 'I'm prepared to believe you this once and let you go without hurting you further. I'll get rid of this, though,' Harold said, flourishing Shark's knife before opening the flat door and flinging the weapon far into the quadrangle. 'But there is one condition,' Harold said turning back to Shark, now pale and awkwardly reclined on his good arm. 'And that is you get as far away from London as your skinny legs will take you. You may not believe this, but I'm actually doing you a favour. Because it's not me you ought to be worried about; it's the people with who you did the cigarette job. You told your cronies about Godwin entrusting you with my money and it was one of them who warned you on Wednesday night about me beating up Godwin, wasn't it? But the person doing the warning also wanted you to take the *gaspers* with you. You, though, were too scared and wanted to get away as quickly as possible. Your compromise was to promise to come back today and pick up the fags. And now if you report the Woodbines have been stolen, they'll think you're lying. Even if they do believe you they'll blame you for their loss. Either way, they'll not be as generous as me. As sure as eggs are eggs, they'll break every bone in your body.'

Harold opened the locker at King's Cross railway station to find a small calico sack containing 142 pounds in paper notes. It was the exact amount Godwin had stolen from his flat. That not one penny was missing caused Harold to reflect on Godwin's hold over Shark as well as Swift, and likely many others. Godwin was a psychopath, a monster who would have continued to ruin people's lives unless someone stopped him. And Harold concluded, standing there in King's Cross station, fate had chosen him to be that someone.

For all that, Harold was pleased he had not resorted to firing his Luger pistol during his confrontation with Shark, with the attendant risk of attracting police attention. He now accepted it had been unnecessary to bring the gun with him – but that was with the benefit of hindsight. At the time he left for Solomon Gardens the possibility of Benny Shark carrying a gun could not have been ruled out.

At last Harold's eyes were starting to close. He had adjusted to the Riom barn's darkened confines and his retreat to earlier times had diverted his mind from the dangers he faced in France. And now two hours into his stay in the loft, Harold's pumping flow of adrenalin was slowing. A relaxed feeling comparable to that felt on recovering his money from Benny Shark began to take hold. Sleep came fitfully, nonetheless. Harold was acutely aware the Resistance people were upset over the administrative foul-up connected with his arrival, whatever it was. They were his lifeline; he had to be ready when they came back rather than risk further antagonizing them. Still the little over two hours' sleep Harold had proved invaluable. He was shaved, packed and ready to go as the sun started rising over the barn.

CHAPTER SEVENTEEN

Harold heard the man's footsteps and watched him approach through a gap in the barn's rough-hewn wooden doors. He wore a dark beret and proved to be a dour individual who said little before directing Harold to the van used the previous night. The tray floor section was lifted to reveal a void into which Harold, despite his bulk and suitcase, was told to squeeze. The man drove for about an hour, sometimes slowly, sometimes faster, indicating he was encountering other traffic. By the time he pulled up and released Harold from his uncomfortable confinement they were in suburban Riom, at the back of a stone house painted white. The man gestured for Harold to enter the house, and with no more drove off.

Once inside, Harold saw a French family eating breakfast at a small table – a man dressed in a dark three-piece suit, a woman and a girl of eight or nine. The man invited Harold to sit, offering him coffee and asking his wife and daughter if they would excuse them.

'I am Harold Lavigne,' Harold said once he and the man were alone. The other Resistance members knew Harold only as *Leon*.

'And I am Dr Claude Ravel,' the man said. 'For the purposes of this exercise, I am your second cousin on your late father's side. My wife's name is Sylvie and my daughter is Louane. Be sure to remember all our names. I am a banker here in Riom and you arrived yesterday by train from Paris where you reside. If questioned, I have been told to say you stayed with us overnight, for a social visit. Today you are proceeding to Lyon where you have a short business meeting before departing on the long trip southwest to Toulouse where you are to do a factory inspection. After that, I'm unsure of your movements.'

Harold, in fact, had two cover stories. One was for use while in Riom with the Resistance people, that which Claude Ravel had just enunciated. The other he was to use once on the train to Lyon and thereafter.

Ravel retrieved a small item from his waistcoat. 'This is a train ticket stub for travel from Paris to Riom. Keep it with the other tickets and receipts you'll collect as you go. We will leave in one hour.' Harold thanked Ravel who nodded curtly. 'From now on you are in the open,' he reminded Harold. 'Have your papers ready in case we encounter a road block.'

It was an odd time in France that morning of 5 September 1941 when Harold and Claude Ravel set out for the Riom city centre in Ravel's black Citroën coupe. Just sixteen months earlier the Germans had invaded the country. After a bloody month-long battle, the French had proposed an armistice and Hitler had agreed, not wanting to burden his forces with the day-to-day administration of all France. Under the terms of the truce, France was divided into two zones. The Germans controlled the northern half of the country, taking in Paris, and a strip of territory along its entire western seaboard guarding France's Atlantic coast. A pro-German regime located in the central French city of Vichy administered the southern zone, the so-called Free Zone, taking in cities such as Vichy, Riom, Lyon and Marseille. The Vichy regime was billed as the official government of all France and its overseas colonies. But in truth it was little more than a subset of the occupying German force.

Harold sat in the front passenger seat of Ravel's car. They travelled in silence. The large clock mounted on the watchtower above the entrance to the Riom Châtel–Guyon station showed twenty minutes after eight when the pair arrived. Ravel delayed only long enough to shake Harold's hand, as one might a distant relative. 'Good luck, my friend,' he said softly. '*Vive la France.*'

Harold purchased a second-class ticket to Lyon. As his instructors had coached him, he avoided any eye contact by focusing on an inanimate object in the near distance. In this way, they told him, he would not look furtive by walking with his head down. 'Also be sure to buy a newspaper,' they had added. 'It's something you can easily hide behind.'

The first test came when Harold walked to the platform to wait for his train. A Vichy policeman stood alongside the ticket collector at the platform entrance. 'Papers, please,' the policeman said. Harold produced his forged *Ausweis*, a German-issued pass permitting him to travel between the occupied and Vichy areas of France, steeling himself to remain calm despite the sweat rising in his armpits. The document declared him to be Harold Raymond Lavigne. 'A visitor from the occupied zone, I see,' the policeman said, eyeing Harold and evaluating him.

Harold laughed. 'A working visit, though. One's got to make a living somehow.'

The policeman did not return Harold's smile. 'Yet is that not a Marseille accent I hear?'

'You have a good ear,' Harold replied amiably, a chill tingling his spine at this first challenge to his identity. 'My mother was a *marseillaise*, and you never lose the language you learn as a child.' It was a line Harold had practised a thousand times.

The policeman appeared satisfied by the explanation. 'And how are things in Paris these days, dare I ask?' he said.

'Well, my office is in Chaillot just near the Arc and I live over the river in Nanterre. So, as you can imagine I spend half my life commuting. Unfortunately, the buses don't run as regularly as they once did.'

'Wouldn't know,' the policeman said dismissively. 'I've never been to Paris in my life.' With that, he turned his back on Harold to focus on other travellers.

Harold had been trained to avoid showing relief if and when his papers passed muster. With the trace of a smile still on his face he offered his ticket to the ticket collector. Once on the platform he took a seat and buried himself in his newspaper.

The train to Lyon was old and crowded. Passengers sat in groups of six, three abreast on hard wooden bench seats facing each other. There were no lights and the train's interior was dim and smelled musty. Most commuters settled down to try and sleep, to while away the two-and-a-half-hour trip in front of them. Harold did likewise, grateful to avoid the otherwise inevitable eye contact with those sitting opposite. But although weary, anxiety about what lay ahead denied him sleep. Instead, he settled for closing his eyes in order to rest them. 'Second class sleep is better than nothing,' his trainers had told him.

Encouraged by the relaxing effect he'd experienced in the barn outside Riom when thinking about the events preceding his insertion into France, Harold allowed his mind to drift back to the Sunday afternoon of 7 February 1937, after he had recovered his stolen money at King's Cross station. He recalled his benign intent that afternoon had been to return to The Sunset on Inverness, have a hot bath and eat dinner. But as he set out, Harold reflected, little did he know what lay ahead.

Little Italy in London's Camden borough, sometimes known as the Italian quarter, is a triangular district bordered by three main thoroughfares. On a laneway running through the heart of the area stood a four-storey, square warehouse of brown brick construction. The building's unprepossessing facade belied the fact that its top floor hosted a suite of modern offices. It was here that the mafia boss Don Carlo Castellaro attended to daily business. Don Carlo had been keeping a close eye on The Sunset on Inverness in the eight days since he and his wife had visited the club at the invitation of its owner, Frank Lenaghan.

The visit of course had not been a success. The club did have business potential, Don Carlo conceded to his trusted lieutenants the following Monday, and Lenaghan was right to argue it warranted a better price than he'd offered. But Lenaghan was a bumptious spiv in Don Carlo's estimation, prompting him to tell his senior operatives how he proposed to take the club for next to nothing. And now Don Carlo had been briefed that during the past week one of the club's security staff had savagely beaten a colleague in a dispute over money. He had also been informed that subsequently hordes of curious people had flocked to the club. He decided the upswing in The Sunset's popularity meant it was time to act, before it became too difficult to wrest the place from Lenaghan.

For this reason, Don Carlo ordered a raid on the club late on the afternoon of Sunday 7 February. The timing was chosen because The Sunset would be closed and by late afternoon on a wintry Sunday few people would be around. This limited the risk to members of the public when the Don's mafia gunmen raked the club with fire from their Thompson sub-machine guns. It also minimized the likelihood of witnesses needing to be paid off or otherwise dealt with.

The mafia raid was to involve two untraceable vehicles – a shooter's car and a trailing chase car. The shooter's car would carry three men, a driver and two gunmen, one gunman in the front passenger seat and the other in the back seat directly behind him. A lone driver would drive the chase car. The chase car with its three vacant seats was there to scoop up the occupants of the shooter's car in the event of a breakdown or other problem. The same applied in reverse so that, if necessary, there was a single vacant seat in the shooter's car for the driver of the chase vehicle. Don Carlo's central objective was to send Frank Lenaghan a message: get out while he could.

The *caporegime* entrusted with implementing the operation chose two senior crew members as his gunmen. Their names were Ignazio "Izzie" de Pascale and Lorenzo "Lorry" Martino, Don Carlo's bodyguards whom Harold had seen outside The Sunset eight days earlier and imminently was to kill. Izzie de Pascale had a younger brother called Giovanni, known as Johnny by those who liked him – which wasn't a legion of people. Johnny was just twenty-two. A vain, baby-faced and sulky manboy, he was the youngest and most spoilt of the seven siblings in the de Pascale family, of which Izzie at thirty-five was the eldest. Johnny idolized Izzie and yearned to emulate him. He was constantly badgering Izzie about involvement in mafia work. Judging that driving the chase car would be a relatively straightforward task, Izzie convinced the crew boss, the *caporegime*, to select Johnny for the job.

Dusk was approaching on Sunday 7 February when Harold arrived back in Bayswater from King's Cross railway station. His recovered money was snuggled in one front trouser pocket next to his Danish krone good luck charm, his loaded Luger pistol in the other. Harold had just turned into Inverness Terrace and was less than fifty yards from The Sunset when Izzie and Lorry seated in the slow-moving shooter's car passed him and seconds later opened fire on the club. Harold froze in disbelief. The sound of shattering glass and bullets ricocheting off bricks was deafening.

Johnny de Pascale up to now had been enjoying himself, singing lusty Italian love songs as he drove, chuffed finally to be a mafia soldier. The girls would be all over him once word got around. When the shooting started, however, Johnny now level with the walking Harold lost concentration. Not an experienced driver, his distraction caused him to confuse the accelerator for the brake, the effect of which was to mount his car on the footpath whereupon it crashed into a row of five steel garbage bins and stalled. The shooter's car, having completed its task, had accelerated up Inverness Terrace and was well past the club when its driver realized Johnny was not behind him. An animated discussion ensued, resulting in the shooter's car performing a U-turn.

By now Harold was at the door of Johnny's chase car. Johnny had not been hurt but was dazed and swearing fiercely in Italian. It took a moment to register, but when Harold heard him speak and observed his Mediterranean complexion, he grasped Johnny was Italian. Harold quickly summed up the situation, at least to the extent of realizing Johnny was a party to the attack on the club he'd just witnessed and that the perpetrators were the mafia of which Lenaghan had warned.

The returning shooter's car was about thirty yards away when Harold wrestled the protesting Johnny from the chase car. Harold felt violated. For all the faults of those who sailed in her, the club was his home. That apart, Harold was also insulted on Lenaghan's behalf, to whom he now owed an inflated sense of obligation and whom he felt he'd let down by allowing the club to be shot up. Johnny kicked Harold hard in the shins, causing Harold to fling the young man against the car with such force as to wind him. Harold knew the police would soon arrive. He planned to detain Johnny until then, prepared in the circumstances to risk questions about his own background.

The shooter's car had reached the struggling men. Its two passengers alighted, watched by Harold and Johnny who continued to struggle with their heads turned. One yelled, 'Johnny, Johnny.'

'Help me, Izzie, help me,' the thrashing Johnny screamed.

Harold's focus was now on the encircling men. The distinctively round magazines of their Thompson sub-machine guns seemed as large as flying saucers. Johnny was quick to take advantage of Harold's lapse. He bit Harold on the wrist, on the skin bared by Harold's coat riding up his arm. Harold took his injured hand off Johnny and wrung it in pain. His iron grip reduced to a single hand, Johnny managed to break free. He ran not to his brother but past him and like a rabbit disappearing down its burrow leapt head first into the back seat of the shooter's car.

Harold was all too aware that Johnny's escape was not the end of the matter. He vaulted across the bonnet of the stalled car just before a volley of sub-machine gun fire broke out. He looked around him. His options were restricted to moving left or right as the solid brick wall of the building behind him precluded backward movement.

Izzie and Lorry spoke rapidly in Italian and fanned out. Harold did not understand them. Had he, he would not have been surprised to learn the substance of their brief conversation was to the effect that Harold was a witness to the shooting who had to be killed.

Lorry moved to the left of the stalled car and Izzie to its right. The Italians were experienced gunmen, both with a healthy respect for weapons. Not realizing Harold was armed, they applied the safety catches to their weapons while taking up their positions. Their plan was to come at Harold from the left and the right, but not simultaneously because they knew that by firing at Harold at the same time they risked shooting each other. It was to be Lorry on Izzie's count of three who would jump forward first, intending to mow down Harold with a burst of fire. If Harold managed to elude Lorry, he would be blocked by the wall at his back and could only run to the right, where Izzie would be waiting to finish the job.

Lorry broke cover by springing out from around the back of the crashed car, levelling his now cocked sub-machine gun as he did. His eyes widened in mortification when he saw Harold, Luger pistol in hand, crouched and waiting for him. But Lorry's momentum prevented withdrawal. The recoil of the pistol jarred Harold's arm. When he looked, he saw Lorry spreadeagled on the footpath, his fallen sub-machine gun at his side. Harold stared at the body. The shot he had let loose was the first time he had fired the Luger, or any gun for that matter, and with his eyes shut as he pulled the trigger he hadn't seen his shot strike Lorry. For a moment Harold was unsure what had happened.

The sound of a pistol shot surprised Izzie. He had expected to hear the rattling of a Thompson sub-machine gun. Cautiously, he peered around the front of the car to see Harold pistol in hand staring at his fallen comrade. The click of the safety catch being released on Izzie's weapon alerted Harold who, with an agility known only to the young, flung himself flat on his stomach, wriggling under the car as he did so that his head faced its front where Izzie crouched. Izzie let go a burst of fire. The bullets spat at the pavement next to Harold, fragments of bitumen painfully pockmarking his face and ear. A game of cat and mouse ensued, with Harold under the car and Izzie now sitting on its bonnet, aiming to shoot Harold through the car's floor. In the eerie quiet that followed the distant sound of jangling bells and klaxon horns could be heard. It was the approaching police.

With that, the voice of a man speaking in Italian rang out, his tone one of extreme urgency. It was the driver of the shooter's car telling Izzie they had to go, and in the mafia operational hierarchy he had the last word on such matters.

CHAPTER EIGHTEEN

arold was jolted from his reverie by the jerk of the train as it slowed. He had been forewarned there would be a stop at Roanne about an hour from Riom and to expect a document check while the train was pulled into the station. Harold was pleased when two Vichy policemen appeared in his carriage and began politely asking travellers for their papers. 'If the Vichy police are accompanied by anyone in plainclothes,' the briefers had said, 'particularly persons wearing leather overcoats, then be on your guard. Because it'll be the Gestapo specifically looking for someone.' The instructors had been unable to offer Harold much in the way of concrete advice on what to do if he turned out to be the subject of a Gestapo search, beyond telling him to try and look confident at all times.

The document check went without a hitch. Shortly after, the train departed. As the knot in his stomach subsided, Harold's thoughts returned to his baptism of fire and what followed after he managed to kill Lorry Martino with his initial shot. That he had subsequently killed Izzie de Pascale, but only after first wounding him, Harold recalled, became a major point of contention at his trial – that and the illegal weapon he was carrying.

Don Carlo acted with alacrity in response to the botched raid on Frank Lenaghan's club. Favours were called in from politicians and policemen in the mafia pocket and bribes dispensed. The driver of the shooter's car and Johnny de Pascale were sent abroad. With the aid of compliant police, Don Carlo circulated a version of events whereby Izzie de Pascale and Lorry Martino were said to be freelancing, working in cahoots with Harold Bradshaw to shoot up The Sunset on Inverness because Bradshaw had developed a grudge against the club after a brawl there in the preceding days. Only one car was involved, and that vehicle had mounted the footpath on Inverness Terrace and crashed, probably as a result of the three men in it beginning to argue. The myth began to gain public acceptance, and soon it was the reality.

Harold's defence argued two vehicles had been involved. An Italian-speaking man drove the first car and the second, the crashed vehicle, was driven by a young Italian man called Johnny who had escaped in the first car. But the Crown had the wind of public outrage at its back, that skilfully confected by Don Carlo. It shrewdly avoided debate on whether other cars or persons were involved and instead pointed to Harold's admission he knew the police were close by and closing in. This gave the prosecutor leeway to argue Harold should have made more effort to avoid further shooting. Particularly pertinent was the fact that, on glimpsing Izzie de Pascale's boot from under the car, Harold had fired a round hitting Izzie's ankle. The Crown tactically conceded Harold could not have known Izzie's intention when he stepped onto the road surface. But equally, it contended, Harold should have waited to gauge the effect of Izzie's injury. Yet Harold had fired immediately Izzie fell to the road, three rounds in all, one fatally wounding the Italian.

In truth, Izzie was not a man given to leaving unfinished business, even when painfully wounded. As such the instant he hit the ground, he did level his weapon to fire a burst at the entrapped Harold. This exculpatory evidence, however, gained little traction. Rather, in seeking to depict Harold's action as an act of wilful killing and exploit the indignation dominating London's newspapers, the prosecution brought in an expert witness, a university professor whose specialty was the impact of wounds on biomechanics. The expert's evidence was to the effect that writhing in pain from an ankle wound, Izzie would have been unable to manoeuvre a notoriously cumbersome Thompson sub-machine gun so as to fire it. This was factual enough in essence but ignored the momentary period when Izzie was first wounded, that five-second window when his adrenalin was still pumping.

Harold had no hope. Humanly unable to ignore the prevailing public mood, the jury accepted the expert's evidence over his explanation. That's what sunk Harold. That and the fact he had wielded an unlicensed pistol, illegally imported into the UK as it turned out.

Indeed, that Harold should be walking the streets of London armed with an illegal weapon also significantly prejudiced the matter of his shooting of Lorry Martino. What should have been an open and shut case of self-defence became infected by the Crown's allegation of malice aforethought. A picture was painted of Harold as a societal threat, a man prepared to kill whenever and whomsoever he wished and who had equipped himself to do so. This swayed the jury. Harold's defence was rejected and a second murder conviction recorded.

The full stop to Harold's trial was a board of enquiry set up to investigate the incident, a political connivance designed to placate a shaken and angry citizenry. The firefight, the board concluded, was the result of a disagreement between small-time criminals, former allies who for reasons unclear had fallen out. No link to organized crime was uncovered. Certain findings were made concerning the illegal importation of weapons into the UK, with the Irish Republican Army conveniently branded as the main culprit in this regard.

The man next to Harold on the train to Lyon was sleeping, his head tilted towards Harold's right shoulder. But the train's wooden benches were uncomfortable forcing him periodically to adjust his posture. As the man shifted again, the wide brim felt hat resting on his knee fell at Harold's feet. He smiled apologetically at Harold as he bent to recover his headwear.

Harold looked at his travelling companion for the first time. About fifty and with a softness to him suggesting an office job but one, judging by his clothes, paying reasonably well. 'Not at all,' Harold said returning the smile.

'You're from Lyon?' the man asked, seeking conversation now he was awake.

Harold would have preferred the sanctuary of silence. He was grateful for the distraction provided by his reflection on past events and the comfort it brought. But he was also wary of being seen as standoffish. Who knew who this fellow might be or whom he might speak to? *A chance to test my new cover story now that I've left Riom,* Harold thought. 'I was born in Marseille but live in Paris these days,' he said. 'I'm a travelling salesman for *Maison de Vêtement*. Ever heard of it?'

'No,' the man replied. 'I've lived in Lyon all my life and can't say I have.'

'That'll be because MV sells haberdashery supplies to the wholesale market,' Harold said. 'We don't operate stores ourselves. I've only recently joined the firm and am undertaking a sales and familiarization visit to Lyon and then Marseille. I came from Paris to Riom yesterday and stayed overnight with a cousin in Riom.'

'My parents also live in Riom these days,' the man said with a maudlin air. 'They're quite old and I try to visit them once a month.' He brightened, seeking to change the subject. 'How is business these days?' he asked.

It was Harold's turn to act downcast. 'Slow,' he said with a Gallic shrug his mother would have been proud of. 'The war.' Having concluded the man was harmless, Harold embarked on a technical discussion about the difficulties in sourcing cotton and lace and decent machinists to work them. It was a device aimed at backing out of the conversation.

As hoped, the man's eyes started to glaze over. 'Well, good luck with it,' he said with a finality suggesting he too was intent on returning to solitude.

Harold was pleased. He could tell the man had unquestioningly accepted his cover story – *'Bore 'em to death,'* his instructors had told him – and with that the anxiety he might make a mistake receded. Harold recognized the nervousness; it was the exact same feeling he had experienced four years earlier when lying under the chase car on Inverness Terrace, when he heard the shooter's car depart and was waiting, willing for the gunfight to be over.

The police arrived just as Harold emerged from under the car and wearily placed the Luger pistol on its bonnet. Fearing more shooting, however, the officers took up defensive positions. By loudhailer they ordered Harold to raise his arms, walk to the middle of Inverness Terrace and lie face down. Only then did they close in, whereupon Harold was placed in handcuffs and transported to Bow Street police station. As the police car conveying him passed The Sunset on Inverness Harold could see no sign of life. He assumed those inside the club were still lying low and wondered if any of them had been harmed.

Long into the night two detectives interviewed Harold, older men who appeared to be senior officers. They probed Harold on his admission the Luger pistol was his. It made no sense to deny it; his fingerprints were all over it and residue from the gun could be found on his firing hand. Harold tried to explain the situation, how he had acted in self-defence. But his claim to have found the gun, offered in misplaced loyalty to Lenaghan, was a bad mistake. The fact that Harold had 142 pounds on him only compounded his problems. Unaware the police in Scunthorpe no longer had an interest in the assaults on the Tattersall brothers, Harold steadfastly avoided mentioning that the bulk of his money had come from the sale of his family's cottage. The obvious evasiveness raised police suspicions. That night, as a holding measure, he was charged with the possession of an unregistered firearm. By now a lawyer had been found for Harold, a volunteer retiree who was prepared to come into Bow Street on a Sunday night. He sought police bail for Harold. But the station sergeant was having none of that. Harold was remanded in custody, for now in the cells at Bow Street.

Early in the week that followed, Harold's volunteer lawyer told him he could face murder charges and likely the death penalty. He implored Harold to come clean on the gun and the cash. Harold was unwilling but the lawyer pressed him. Eventually, Harold admitted Lenaghan had given him the gun. And after two more days of stubborn reluctance to mention Scunthorpe, Harold finally opted for the perceived lesser of two evils and owned up to the source of his cash. He even named Max Langdon as the buyer of the cottage.

But by now it was too late. Don Carlo's disinformation campaign had taken root and the police big brass was demanding an early arrest. So compelled, the investigating detectives dismissed Harold's explanations as fabrications concocted in the days since his arrest. On Sunday 14 February 1937, a week after his arrest, the detectives finalized a brief of evidence and charged Harold with two counts of murder.

Harold was relocated to the remand section of Wormwood Scrubs prison the same night he was charged. After processing, a prison officer escorted him to the third landing, ushering him into a small, all-brick cell with a curved ceiling. The olive green paint on the cell walls was flaking in several spots, revealing roughly cemented brickwork beneath. The room smelled of dank, malodorous men and their tobacco.

Harold's train had now reached flat ground. Its steam engine hissed and puffed in seeming delight as it rollicked along towards Lyon. But Harold did not share in its elation. The loneliness of that moment, he reflected, when he had been placed in the stinking and decaying cell at Wormwood Scrubs, surpassed even the fleeting sense of abandonment he had felt at the barn near Riom when the Resistance people departed. And in the case of the prison experience, there was no salve to be found in memories of Katrina, principally because he was not alone. Three other men were inside, grainy figures illuminated by the dim light of a single bulb extending from the roof. 'This is Bradshaw,' the prison officer had said. 'He's innocent too, just like you lads.' He laughed, locking the cell door behind him as he went.

Two-tiered bunk beds stood on either side of the cell. Little more than an arm's length separated them. Beyond the beds a small, barred window – in daylight the cell's only source of natural light – was recessed to the depth of the cell's wall. To the front of the beds on one side was a night bucket and opposite it a small wall-mounted sink with a single rusty tap. Harold appraised his cellmates. On the lower berth of one two-tiered bunk was a young man barely old enough to be in an adult prison. He was pale-faced and terrified, looking only briefly at Harold before averting his gaze. A much older man sat on the top bunk. He nodded at Harold in cautious greeting. On the bottom of the other two-tiered bunk lay a thickset man in his thirties, a magazine resting cover up on his chest. The top bunk was strewn with what Harold correctly assumed were the man's possessions. He did not acknowledge Harold beyond staring coldly at him.

The woman sitting opposite Harold was returning to Lyon after a week at her sister's in Riom. Absorbed in her novel, she looked up to see a smile suddenly flicker across his face before it quickly faded. A sensitive soul, she wondered what he could be thinking about sitting there with arms folded across his chest and eyes closed. The woman would have been surprised to learn that, leaving behind thoughts of the despair which had gripped him when he was first placed in the cell at the Scrubs, Harold was reliving how on the very same night he had forged his prison *rep*.

Harold did not want trouble. In spite of everything, he still harboured a belief he would be exonerated on the grounds of self-defence. 'Looks like I'm up the top,' Harold said as inoffensively as he could to the coldly staring man on the bottom bunk. When the man made no answer, Harold tried again. 'Sorry, but I'm going to have to get you to move your things.'

'Fuck off,' the man snarled. He was vicious and intimidating. Harold could sense the boy and the older man on the other double bunk shrink in fear. He sighed inwardly, experiencing the sense of calm calculation that habitually overcame him ahead of physical conflict. As with Neville Godwin, Harold realized, the man was a problem needing to be dealt with, only in this instance the problem had to be dealt with right now.

Harold turned and took three short steps to the washbasin on which he placed the towel and soap he had been issued. Then in one unhurried stride, he moved to the night bucket and removed its lid as if planning to use it. It was a filthy contraption in need of a decent scrub. An inch or so of urine covered its bottom. Picking up the bucket, he darted to the man and tipped its contents over him. The startled man was infuriated, his face turning crimson with rage. Harold calmly picked him off with a powerful left fist as he sought to rise from his prone position. The man's cheekbone bulged in contusion as he sank to his knees on the cell's concrete floor. With that, Harold forcefully jammed the night bucket over his head, kicking him hard in the chest as he did.

'For tonight,' Harold said, leaning over the prostrate figure and removing the night bucket, the top of the man's nose and the area above his eyebrows bleeding lightly from their abrasions, 'I'm going to tie you to your bunk. And tomorrow you're going to arrange to have the screws shift you. Are we clear?'

'Yes,' the man said softly.

'Yes, what?' Harold demanded.

'Yes, sir,' the man said meekly, his demoralization now complete. Harold tied him, feet and hands, to the bottom bunk bed using his bed sheet. By the time it was lights out shortly after, Harold went to sleep confident he was safe from reprisal.

The older of Harold's cellmates was Freddie, a former bank clerk who had fallen afoul of fast women and slow horses. The younger man, Kenny, was a silly boy of sub-intelligence who liked to look in ladies' windows at night. When morning came Freddie and Kenny quickly spread the word, once Harold's bunkmate had paid half a pound of tobacco to a certain prison officer and been swapped with a doctor from Kensington who did abortions. The news spread like wildfire of how Harold at just twenty had done what many thought was impossible – belted up and humiliated the mad, bad standover man, Normie Norris.

In short order a reputation was born. Harold Bradshaw's calm flint-hardness became Wormwood Scrubs folklore among prisoners and prison officers alike. For long after the older lags regaled newcomers with stories of how Harold's *rep* was forged on his very first night at the Scrubs, while in the A-wing remand unit.

CHAPTER NINETEEN

The woman on the train to Lyon seated opposite Harold, the one who minutes earlier had glimpsed his face briefly light up, had returned to her book. Had she not done so, she would have seen a harsher emotion now in place. It was a grimace in the form of a hardening of his mouth. It was Harold recalling the end of Katrina.

In the week following his teardown of the hard man Normie Norris, and as the flurry of activity that had seen him end up in prison slowed, Harold began to feel slighted. True, he was pleased there had been no blowback from his confrontation with Norris. Indeed, the usually aloof prison guards, especially those who feared Norris, were now treating him with a modicum of respect as a result. Rather, Harold was growing irritated because he had heard nothing from Frank Lenaghan or anyone else at The Sunset on Inverness. For that reason, he was gratified when informed late in the week he had a visitor.

It was Francis Swift, his colleague from the club whom Harold had befriended and Neville Godwin had cruelly used, abused and stolen from. Nearly two weeks earlier, Harold had entrusted Swift to sell the cigarettes he had taken from Benny Shark's flat.

'It's been bedlam,' Swift said. 'Lenaghan was scared out of his wits. He and Katrina left the club the night it was shot up. He came back after a couple of days with an auctioneer who agreed to take the club's stocks of booze and cigarettes on consignment and even a few items of furniture as well. Lenaghan later returned with a real estate agent to put the property on the market. But between you and me, I hear the Camden mafia has put the frighteners on the real estate fellow and told him not to sell it to anyone bar a mafia front company. Lenaghan will be lucky if he gets one-twentieth of what it's worth.'

'And Katrina?' Harold asked shyly.

Swift smiled. 'I was shifting out of the club yesterday when she popped in to give me this.' Swift took a letter from his coat and gave it to Harold.

A prison officer approached from the rear of the visiting area, intending to confiscate the letter because it was forbidden for prisoners to receive mail in this way. But on seeing Harold was the recipient and thankful for his neutering of the dangerous Normie Norris, the officer nodded his assent and walked away. The note barely covered a third of a single page. *Darling Harold,* it read. *Frank and I have had to run away. I miss you and wish things could be different. But Frank will care for me in my old age and you and your thighs, my beautiful big boy, are just one of life's wonderful diversions. With much love K xxxx.*

'They're going back to Birmingham,' Swift said simply.

Harold stuffed the letter in his prison fatigues, feeling a powerful sense of loss wash over him. He knew Katrina was right to go with Lenaghan. Even so, the closing of this brief but unforgettable chapter in his life stung him. 'What did you do with the cigarettes, the Woodbines?' he asked Swift, trying to blot out painful memories of Katrina by changing the subject.

'Sold them to the dodgy café on the Queensway like you said,' Swift replied. 'Knockdown price of a shilling per packet. Thirty quid in all. I've kept half for myself.' Swift reached inside his trouser pocket and produced a handful of notes placing them on the table. 'Here's your share,' he said, pushing the fifteen pounds towards Harold.

Harold handed the notes back to Swift, knowing he had no job and would need all the proceeds. 'I don't want the cash, Swifty. I recovered what Godwin stole from me and provided you don't gamble there's precious little to spend it on in here.'

Swift stared at Harold for a time. 'Thank you, Harold,' he said eventually, taking back the money. 'I can go home to Dover now and start a new life.'

Swift stayed until the end of visiting hours, the two men occasionally sitting in comfortable silence. When it was time for Swift to go, they shook hands warmly. 'Thank you for everything, Harold,' Swift said, 'from the bottom of my heart.' His eyes brimmed with tears. This time they both knew he was referring to his liberation from Neville

Godwin's clutches. Swift turned and walked away, closing another chapter in Harold's life.

Harold's remaining time in the remand unit was relatively uneventful. Freddie, his older cellmate, went on to receive a three-year sentence following his conviction for embezzlement. He was moved to the main prison in May 1937. The doctor who did abortions and Freddie's replacement both managed to get bail shortly after. The prison guards, understanding Harold would cause trouble only if provoked, were happy to ensure his new cellmates were docile kinds unlikely to ruffle his feathers. Kenny, the retarded youth, was still on remand at the time of Harold's trial in November 1937.

Harold looked at his watch. All going well the train would dock at Lyon in thirty minutes. Most passengers were now awake and alert, looking forward to the end of their uncomfortable journey. Harold smiled politely at the man next to him and the woman opposite. They returned his acknowledgement. *The trip together,* Harold thought, *had created a bond; they were no longer strangers to each other.* Harold enjoyed the flush of comfort this gave him. It made him think of Archie.

Harold's reputation preceded him when, on sentencing, he was moved to the main prison. The fact he had been convicted of two murders, of mafia soldiers no less, enhanced his standing, at least in the eyes of the prison population.

Prisoners in the high security wing where Harold was transferred were accommodated two to a cell. The warders wisely followed the example of their remand unit colleagues and placed Harold in a cell with an amenable type. The man in question was a lifer by the name of Archie. He was fifty-two and rarely spoke. But he and Harold gelled well, respecting each other's privacy from the outset, and Harold appreciative of the fact that, virtually like no other prisoner, Archie did not smoke.

Even so, the Scrubs was no bed of roses. Violence and sexual assault were rife. And in the latter respect, Harold was of an age group favoured by rapist prisoners. Inevitably, his reputation notwithstanding, an attempted rape did occur in the shower block just before Christmas 1937. Harold received a nasty head laceration as a result. But he fared much better than his three assailants, all of whom endured lengthy stints in nearby Hammersmith hospital before emerging with permanently limiting injuries.

Harold was never harassed again in any substantial sense. Thereafter, other than messing with inmates, he kept largely to himself and out of trouble. Much that went on around him was unsavoury, cruel and heartless. But provided others left him alone, Harold did not interfere. The one exception to the rule came in April 1938 when a recently arrived young tough cornered Archie in the prison canteen and forced him to hand over the few pennies in his possession. That afternoon before lock-up,

Harold went to the perpetrator's cell, telling his cellmate to get lost and closing the cell door behind him. Prison officers were content to let matters take their course. Soon the money was recovered, with interest. The young hoodlum's ensuing transformation into a nervous and scared individual able only to eat soft food was a salutary reminder to all in the wing that Archie was not to be trifled with while Harold was around.

Harold's routine soon solidified into a way of life. Occasionally he read books, but with decreasing frequency. By the summer of 1938, not yet eighteen months since first being placed in the remand wing, Harold was spending long periods of time lying on his bunk. His cellmate, Archie, urged Harold to adopt a physical fitness regime as a defence against the torpor of prison life. 'You'll go stir crazy before you know it if you don't,' he warned.

Archie had lived for years on the fringes of the boxing world until murdering a rival in a contest of affections over a woman. He schooled Harold in exercises to be done in the confines of their cell after lock-up. Night after night, under Archie's watchful tutelage, Harold did five hundred push-ups, half as many sit-ups and a set of skipping exercises. The exercise was a godsend; it spared Harold the mental deterioration that so quickly and perniciously claimed the majority of other long-term prisoners.

Harold's train squeaked to a halt at Lyon–Perrache station. It was mid-morning on Friday 5 September 1941.

At the station exit Harold negotiated another checkpoint manned by a Vichy policeman. As with the check on the train, no words were spoken and the document inspection was perfunctory. Harold had been told to cross the Rhône River using nearby Pont Gallieni. From there he caught a number twenty-nine bus for five stops, recalling the directions he had recited over and over until they were chiselled into his memory. A short walk from the bus stop he found the hotel that was to be his resting place for the next two nights, just as his briefers had promised.

Harold's need to visit Lyon derived from an assessment made in London that, given the nature of his cover work, it would look odd and invite questions if he were to travel from the occupied zone yet go directly to Marseille and bypass Lyon, Vichy France's second-largest city behind Marseille. Moreover, it was judged of equal importance to create the impression that Harold was forging an orderly, unhurried pathway to Marseille from Paris. Hence the necessity for Harold's supposed overnight stay in Riom followed by his visit to Lyon before actually reaching Marseille.

To be sure, Harold's insertion at Riom and the unavoidable requirement for Resistance assistance, allied to the Lyon visit itself, did create some problems. But whatever the difficulties, Harold's stay in Lyon and the preceding arrangements were critically essential background, even for those involved in his insertion who were concentrated on secret alternative agendas.

The briefers preparing Harold had also drummed into him the importance of building work history while in Lyon, that which he could rely on when in Marseille. Immediately after checking into his hotel, therefore, Harold walked suitcase in hand to a nearby café. There he ordered lunch, asking the waitress if she could direct him to Rue Sala where Harold said with enough volume for others to hear, 'I have a business appointment.'

Harold was advised to take a taxi. This he did, lingering on the street to check his order book until the taxi disappeared. Harold spent the rest of Friday afternoon and all of Saturday identifying businesses suitable for his needs and writing up bogus orders. Several times he took taxis to various locations, keeping the payment receipts as evidence of an intention to seek later reimbursement. In this way any Vichy policeman, or even one of the numerous German soldiers prowling the streets, who bothered to perform a spot check would find in Harold's suitcase, in addition to his personal items and haberdashery samples, an order book reflecting commerce conducted with *bona fide* Lyon businesses and evidence of travel to call on these clients.

Of course there was never any expectation the order book ruse and receipts would withstand checks of greater depth. They were only ever designed to allay initial suspicions, those that if aroused would be sure to cause things rapidly to unravel.

Harold's time in Lyon concluded without incident. Several people in England were relieved when informed of this, none more so than those running secret alternative agendas.

As scheduled, Harold boarded a train for Marseille

mid-morning on Sunday 7 September 1941. Having passed unimpeded through several document checks in the last forty-eight-hours while diligently building cover, he was hopeful his travel south would go smoothly. Harold's train was not crowded and sported comfortable fabric seats. He settled back for the five-and-a-half-hour journey. Soon Harold began to mull things in his mind, trying to concentrate on his mission – why he was visiting Marseille and how to begin his task once there. But before long images of a naked Katrina intruded. Harold wrestled with them and their stirrings. His solution was to replay in his mind why he had been chosen for the Marseille job in the first place. Harold sat back, closed his eyes and literally thought of England.

Incarcerated behind Wormwood Scrubs' grim stone walls, Harold spent the remainder of 1938 conscientiously maintaining his training regimen as designed by Archie. Its physical and mental benefits contributed to his generally positive outlook, sullied occasionally by the thought he would be in prison until at least November 1955. Harold became an avid reader of newspapers, intrigued by Hitler's bellicose manoeuvres in Europe, those leading eventually to the onset of the European War in September 1939. Yet when the war did begin, Harold had no sense of being touched by its outbreak. It was an event occurring in the outside world, something as remote from him as if he were watching a film.

The war, however, did come closer to home in December 1939 when without explanation the Wormwood Scrubs remand wing was evacuated. In short order prisoners' cells were converted into offices and occupied by civilians. The prison grapevine soon identified the new arrivals as government intelligence officials. The interlopers were in fact members of the Radio Security Service, or RSS, a new War Office unit established to pinpoint radio transmissions by German spies within Britain. RSS personnel were placed at the Scrubs in what proved to be a mistaken belief the prison would afford protection from enemy bombing. For all that, the clearing of the remand wing did not overly affect Harold in the main prison. But the War Office's decision in February 1940 to commandeer all of Wormwood Scrubs did directly impact him, profoundly so in the long run, although initially only because it occasioned the transfer of most long-term inmates to rural facilities.

Wormwood Scrubs consisted mostly of poorly ventilated cells inadequately lit. Coincident with the prison's full civilian takeover a small team of prisoners was selected to stay behind to upgrade the facility to civil service standards and perform other tasks. Harold was among those chosen. He was young and strong, in no way obstreperous and still mentally agile. His one regret was being parted from Archie who had become something of a father figure to him. Archie himself hosed this down. 'This is an opportunity for something new and different,' he told Harold. 'You're not eligible for parole until 1955 and still have an awful lot of time to do. You'd be mad not to take it. Exercise might delay things, but without fresh stimulation sooner or later you'll end up just another senile old lag wasting his life.'

Another event late in 1938, one much less publicized than Hitler's inexorable march to war, was also destined to have profound significance for Harold. It concerned an industrial plant in the Norwegian city of Vemork. The plant had first opened in 1934. It produced heavy water, so known because of its excess of hydrogen relative to the chemical makeup of ordinary water. Although not radioactive in and of itself, heavy water was central to the then embryonic fields of nuclear medicine and nuclear energy. It was also an essential component in the production of atom bombs. By the end of 1938 the Vemork plant had reached peak operating capacity. It was now the only place in the world producing the commercial quantities of heavy water sufficient for the industrial-scale production of atomic weapons.

By the start of 1940 the Vemork plant had a heavy water inventory of nearly twelve tons. But Hitler was at the Norwegian door. French military intelligence knew an invasion was imminent. It went to some lengths to convince those in charge of the Vemork facility to resist German demands to sell their stock of heavy water and instead send it to France for safekeeping for the war's duration. Knowing it was only a matter of time before the Germans dispensed with the niceties of a business proposition and simply took the material, the Norwegians courageously agreed. The full heavy water inventory, sixty 200-litre barrels, was shipped to the Marie Curie Institute in Paris just ahead of the German invasion of Norway in April 1940.

But France was also vulnerable to invasion. And exactly a month after Norway fell, the Germans attacked. The French and their allies could not withstand the superior German forces, and soon capitulation was inevitable. Hurried arrangements were made to ship the heavy water to Britain, before France also fell under German control.

A man by the name of Henri Mittel was the load supervisor for the cartage contractor charged with removing the barrels of heavy water from storage in the Curie Institute and transporting them to Bordeaux. From there a British steamer would take the consignment to its new home in Falmouth, Cornwall. In the great scheme of things, Mittel was an unimportant figure with no formal authority. But his decision to syphon off twenty of the 200-litre barrels, four tons in all, and truck only the remaining forty barrels to Bordeaux was significant for Harold in a way that no one could ever have imagined.

Two powerful forces motivated Mittel – greed and fear. Although he didn't understand what heavy water was, he knew it was important. Mittel's primary aim was to sell the stolen portion of inventory, which he told workers to place on a separate lorry. But he also worried the Germans might decide to shoot those involved in denying them the stockpile and wanted some personal insurance against this. That is why on the first day of June 1940, the day the heavy water consignment was trucked to Bordeaux ahead of onwards shipping to Britain, Mittel set out for Marseille driving a lorry carrying the stolen twenty barrels. Why Marseille? Well, Mittel understood the city had not seen any fighting during the Great War. He mistakenly assumed the same would again apply. The second factor was Mittel had a cousin who ran a small farm at Allauch on Marseille's outskirts. The stolen heavy water, Mittel decided, could be stored discreetly at his cousin's farm, waiting to be called on as required.

In the prevailing state of affairs in France at the time – a mere two weeks later the Germans entered Paris – Mittel's theft went undetected in the chaos. True, the captain of the British ship that arrived in Bordeaux on 21 June 1940 to pick up the consignment was under the impression he was to receive sixty 200-litre barrels of heavy water. But those whom he questioned had been unable to explain the twenty-barrel discrepancy. The captain had no time to investigate further. Besides needing to load the heavy water, the ship was already carrying other valuables and a sizeable number of refugees. It was too dangerous to delay.

Immediately the forty barrels were on board, the ship sailed for Falmouth whereupon it disgorged the heavy water consignment. The arrival of a smaller number of barrels than expected prompted some head-scratching in the receiving laboratory, especially among the boffins who knew it took around four tons of heavy water to make an atomic bomb. Theoretically, they fretted, the missing material could result in Germany building such a weapon. But the import of nuclear fission was not well understood by the local political authority and, in the face of other pressing demands, the discrepancy was never investigated. Eventually, the Falmouth scientists came to accept there had been a miscommunication and the consignment had consisted of forty barrels all along. And like the British, the Germans, once in control of France, also came to assume the entire batch of heavy water had been transported to England.

The French–German armistice, which placed Marseille in the French Free Zone, was a factor very much in Henri Mittel's favour. The absence of an aggressive German policing presence in the city complemented the wider German belief there was no heavy water in France. In this comparatively benign environment, the generally less energetic Vichy police were unlikely ever to stumble across the twenty barrels hidden at his cousin's farm. Indeed, so apparently benign was the situation that a little over a year after spiriting the stolen material to Marseille, Mittel concluded the heavy water could be sold in the Vichy Zone without undue risk of alerting the Germans. And short of cash, that's what he decided to do.

For his part, Mittel's cousin on the farm at Allauch had been nervous from the outset about the possible ramifications of aiding and abetting his domineering relative. He was constantly badgering Mittel to remove the heavy water. As a matter of course, Mittel tended to ignore his cousin. But his relation's ongoing anxiety did remind him not to be cavalier, the seemingly amenable environment notwithstanding. This convinced Mittel he should not remove any drum from hiding for use as a sample to show potential buyers. The heavy water consignment had to remain in situ and be sold sight unseen in Marseille.

In early July 1941 Mittel took a week's leave from his Paris-based cartage job and made his way south to Marseille.

CHAPTER TWENTY

Harold's train initially made good speed across the lush farming flats south of Lyon en route to Marseille. After an hour, Harold became entranced by the scenery and was no longer thinking about his insertion into France. His contentedness grew when an attendant sold him a cup of ersatz coffee from a large urn. But as the train progressed the skies turned leaden and the countryside more mountainous. Under cloud cover and backed against the grey mountains the bucolic stone villages dominated by their high-spired churches looked less appealing. By the time Harold reached the city of Orange three hours south of Lyon his enchantment with the countryside was well in decline. A young but portly Vichy policeman conducted his document check while the train was in Orange station. As if to mark this return to reality, the man's bulk reminded Harold it was through another pudgy individual that the British had come to know of a possible stash of heavy water in Marseille.

France's physical division notwithstanding, countries such as Britain and the United States had initially recognized the Vichy regime as the legitimate government of all France. But Vichy–British diplomatic relations were soon severed when Britain sought to destroy French warships moored in Algeria at risk of German seizure. Despite this, British diplomats in adjoining Switzerland could still obtain transit permits from the Vichy Consulate in Geneva entitling them to pass through the Free Zone en route to London. The path taken was necessarily indirect. Diplomats usually travelled by road from Geneva to Marseille, via Evian on the Swiss–Vichy border, and thence by ship to Valencia in neutral Spain. From Valencia, they transferred to the British territory of Gibraltar, to the isthmus connecting the Rock to mainland Spain. From a newly built airfield there the RAF flew the diplomats to London. Diplomats commuting from London to Switzerland traced this route in reverse.

The Foreign Office courier was a *bona fide* British diplomat, albeit of low ranking. Based in London, the Vichy transit permit in his passport facilitated his monthly trips to and from the British Consulate in Geneva via the established routes. One weekday morning in early July 1941 the courier's diplomatic vehicle, driven by his security escort, arrived in Marseille from Geneva. It pulled into the Hôtel du Clou, a boutique establishment in the Marseille port district. The courier knew the hotel well, having used it frequently. He intended to take an early lunch before boarding the steamer that would take him and his clutch of sealed diplomatic bags to Valencia prior to wending his way back to London.

Henri Mittel was in Marseille at this time searching for a buyer for his stolen heavy water. A foreign government was his preference, the British particularly as Henri knew it was to Britain where the bulk of the heavy water consignment stored at the Curie Institute had been sent. Henri's cousin, anxious to be rid of the stolen material, was happy to assist. He knew a taxi driver, a Corsican who dabbled at the fringes of the law – mainly with relatives back home to smuggle Italian cigarettes into France. A meeting was set up. Henri needed to be more open than he preferred. But he did eventually glean from the Corsican that British diplomats often ate at the Hôtel du Clou when shuffling between London and Geneva. As such, Henri Mittel was lying in wait in the hotel foyer when the courier entered.

The exchange between the pair was brief. In truth, the courier was unnerved by the fleshy Frenchman with dark hair slicked over his balding pate and furtive, darting eyes. Mittel spoke in broken English. 'I have heavy water for sale. Twenty barrels, four tons altogether,' he spat out, staccato-like. His asking price was in English pounds, an even hundred of them – not as good as reichsmarks those days for transacting on the currency black market but better than worthless francs.

'Heavy what?' the courier asked politely, apprehensive about the approach and wanting to avoid a scene that conceivably could attract a Vichy policeman.

'Heavy water,' Henri replied.

The courier thought this to be a reference to alcohol. 'Don't touch the stuff, old chap,' he said pleasantly, terminating the conversation.

'It's stored here in Marseille, easy to ship,' Henri called to the courier's departing back in one last forlorn attempt to spark his interest.

And there it ended. Deflated, fat Henri Mittel shelved his sale plans and returned to Paris. He needed his job with the cartage firm and could not afford to spend more time in Marseille.

A Foreign Office security officer debriefed the courier once he was back in London. It was standard operational procedure. When the courier recounted his Marseille hotel encounter, his interlocutor exhibited no more than mild interest. 'Wine, was it?' he asked the courier.

'Think so,' the courier said. 'Some sort of high-powered hooch, heavy something or other.'

To his eternal credit, the Foreign Office debriefer sought specifics. And when the courier was able to recall the offer was for heavy water available in Marseille for immediate shipping, the debriefer, knowing the term, came alive. He pressed the courier for an accurate description of Henri Mittel and any other details he could remember. His final question was to ask the courier if he thought the offer was genuine, only to be met by indecisiveness.

'No fence-sitting, please,' the debriefer said. 'An opinion one way or the other.'

'At the end of the day,' the courier said after a time, 'I'd say not. Too shifty for my liking.'

That afternoon, the security officer wrote up the courier's report in a memorandum. The document circulated within the Foreign Office whereupon it was shared with various other government agencies.

Harold leant back against his headrest, happy the inspection of his papers at Orange had gone smoothly and pleased his train was again moving. Out of the blue he thought of Hugh Gregory. How nice it would be, he mused, if Hugh were travelling with him. But no matter. In the space of five short days he'd see Hugh in Marseille, albeit only briefly. So prompted, Harold's mind drifted back to when he and Hugh had first met.

By the time of Henri Mittel's abortive attempt to sell his heavy water consignment to the British courier in early July 1941, Harold had settled into his job with the Wormwood Scrubs maintenance detachment. In the absence of all bar twenty well behaved prisoners and their three prison officer supervisors, the Scrubs took on an atmosphere more resembling an office than a jail. Harold moved about, increasingly without supervision, frequently engaging in conversation with many of those now based at the prison.

One such person was a young army captain by the name of Hugh Gregory. At twenty-seven Hugh was three years Harold's senior. A tall, slim and good-looking man with sandy hair and hazel eyes, he was new to the army having been plucked six months earlier from the faculty of Modern History at Cambridge University, commissioned and then seconded to MI5, the UK domestic security agency. Over a period of two weeks in mid-July 1941, when Harold's work brought him into regular contact with Hugh, the pair began to chat. Their conversations were superficial at first but became more substantial as their familiarity grew. It was at this time that Harold, although still cautious about mentioning Scunthorpe, told Hugh how as a small child his mother, a *marseillaise*, had taught him the French language as spoken in the Marseille region.

Just days after Harold's disclosure, the Foreign Office memorandum recording Henri Mittel's approach to the British courier crossed Hugh Gregory's desk. His conversation with Harold was still fresh in his mind when on a hot afternoon on Monday 28 July 1941 Hugh attended a meeting in London's Baker Street, home to the secretive Special Operations Executive, the SOE, where the heavy water matter was on the agenda.

The SOE had been formed in July 1940 on the express orders of Prime Minister Churchill. Its job was to conduct guerrilla operations designed to sabotage and disrupt the German war effort, mostly in conjunction with Resistance elements in occupied countries. In the case of France, SOE operatives were inserted in various ways: by parachute; by road transits across the French–Spanish border; and occasionally by posing as diplomats.

The diplomatic insertion technique frequently led the SOE into conflict with the Foreign Office, particularly when Switzerland was involved. The Germans and the Vichy French were aware British agents posing as diplomats were entering France to connect with and organize the *Maquis* to strike against German installations in occupied France. Indeed, the conquering Germans were forever demanding that the Vichy authorities stamp out the practice. The Foreign Office worried the Swiss, themselves fearful of German invasion, could break off diplomatic relations with Britain as a result of SOE's activities. This would seriously damage Britain's standing with other neutral countries. Such relations were vital to the British war effort and the Foreign Office, charged with keeping the neutrals onside, was determined to do exactly that.

The meeting in the SOE's Baker Street office reached the heavy water agenda item. 'Absolutely out of the question,' the Foreign Office representative said, dismissing the SOE's opening gambit that an operative posing as a diplomat be infiltrated into Vichy France to investigate the apparent existence of a cache of heavy water. 'We all know what happened last February. I can tell you flatly the Swiss won't overlook a repeat instance; nor will Jerry. They'll be marching up the Quai du Mont-Blanc in the blink of an eye if we're not careful.'

The diplomat was referring to an ill-conceived SOE initiative reluctantly countenanced by the Foreign Office involving a female agent posing as a diplomat with a forged Swiss diplomatic visa in her passport. For one reason or another she panicked at the border crossing at Evian, was arrested by the Vichy police and handed to the Gestapo. The Foreign Office representative's reference to the prominent Geneva thoroughfare was a not-so-subtle reminder of the limits to German tolerance when it came to respecting Swiss neutrality.

For once the Foreign Office had an ally in the room in the form of the head of the War Office delegation. 'Harry makes a fair point, Nigel,' he intoned, vigorously stubbing out his cigarette as if to emphasize the point. 'And anyway, do you really want to send in someone whom you've trained up in all the *Boy's Own Annual* stuff on a reconnaissance mission that if the FO courier's to be believed might well turn out to be a wild goose chase?'

'Well, there is the small matter that the Huns could build an atom bomb if they lay their hands on four tons of heavy water,' the SOE colonel, Nigel, countered. 'We're working with the Norwegian Resistance to disable the plant at Vemork. But it's hard going. There's going to be a lot of time, money and lives expended before it's done, and it will be a bloody wasted effort if we blow up the fucking place ...,' he stopped suddenly to smile an apology at the young woman sitting behind the man heading the delegation from the prime minister's office, 'only for the Jerries to find they're already sitting on a stash of heavy water.'

'What about your chaps?' the man from the prime minister's office asked, addressing the UK overseas spy agency delegation, the contingent from MI6, the Secret Intelligence Service, the SIS.

By now the SIS delegation head had decided his people were not about to get involved in so uncertain a venture; there was too much to lose and quite likely nothing to be gained. 'I do agree,' he said, 'it is important to get to the bottom of this apparent offer to sell us heavy water. But for any of us to take on the task with so little to go on could be folly. At best we might find the heavy water is actually a batch of bath water some fat Frog hoaxer with slicked-over hair aims to flog to us; at worst we could be risking a valuable asset all for nothing.'

Finally, a man spoke, his voice carrying the slightest trace of a Scottish brogue. He wore the uniform of a major general and had been listening to the debate while puffing on a time-worn pipe with a curved stem. His name was Angus Carmoday and he headed a Top Secret special unit within the SOE. Just two weeks earlier, Prime Minister Churchill had personally handed him a *Close Hold, Top Secret* assignment. All others in the room were unknowing of the task, save for a Major Andrew Foulkes who sat directly behind Carmoday but against the wall, far from the table as if he found safety in his solitude.

'There are two simple truths pertaining, gentlemen,' Carmoday said, addressing the delegation leaders seated at the table, all men. 'The first is we can't ignore the possibility of a stockpile of heavy water in Vichy, apparently in Marseille. The second is that the uncertainty surrounding the offer to the FO courier by this French chap militates against inserting an asset in whom we've invested substantial resources.' He paused, lips pursed. 'I'm afraid we need to find an empty vessel capable of doing the job, and quickly.' An empty vessel was jargon for an expendable asset. 'After all, if there is heavy water around and the Germans uncover it, it could potentially win them the war.'

The general's call for urgent action surprised many around the table. There was an indisputably strong chance the sale offer was a hoax and Carmoday was renowned for not being easily panicked. But when Carmoday reiterated the need for urgent and immediate action, people were inclined to think he knew something they didn't. And indeed he did, although none of them could ever have guessed what it was. 'Any ideas?' Carmoday asked, opening up the issue for general discussion.

With that, Captain Hugh Gregory sitting behind the MI5 delegation leader cleared his throat.

Harold chuckled out loud before quickly gathering himself. A fellow passenger on his train to Marseille, a Frenchman of advanced years sitting opposite, had only minutes ago awoken from a nap and was now reading his newspaper. He glanced sharply at Harold, silently rebuking him for his noise. Harold smiled apologetically at the man. The cause of Harold's mirth was the recall of his original meeting with General Carmoday and Major Andrew Foulkes, strange cove him. But in his mind he had referred to Carmoday not by his real name. To this day, Harold knew of Carmoday only as Jones.

It was the early afternoon of Thursday 31 July 1941. 'You're wanted up at the governor's office,' said the prison maintenance gang member sent to summon Harold. Even though there was no longer a governor at Wormwood Scrubs, the warders and prisoners who remained behind still referred to it as such. 'A couple of important-looking geezers have arrived, apparently to see you,' he added, pulling a pretend scary face at Harold.

Harold shrugged. He had no idea who the visitors were. On reaching the office he was told to wait in an anteroom. After a short delay, the door opened and in stepped three men. The only one of the three Harold knew was Hugh Gregory.

'This is Mr Jones and Mr Brown,' Hugh said, keeping a straight face in an honourable attempt to disguise the fact that both names were fictitious. Jones, so-called, appeared to be in his mid-fifties. A big man dressed in Harris Tweed, he was actually Major General Angus Carmoday, the SOE officer on whom Churchill had recently foisted a *Close Hold, Top Secret* task. And in that regard the general was battling an inflexibly tight timeline.

Carmoday's companion, Brown, sported a blue double-breasted flannel suit. He was younger and taller than the general but just as thickset. 'Please be seated,' Carmoday instructed Harold, who had stood up in accordance with prison rules. Carmoday took a pair of horn-rimmed eyeglasses from the breast pocket of his suit and momentarily studied the file taken from his brief case. 'I understand you speak some French?' he asked, looking up at Harold.

Harold explained that he did and why, eyeing Hugh briefly.

'Would you be prepared to take a *wee* language test?' Carmoday asked in his soft Scottish timbre.

Harold nodded his assent, prompting Carmoday to look at the man calling himself Brown.

Brown was among the few others privy to the task Churchill had set General Carmoday. Yet he spoke convivially, as if embarking on a discussion about football. 'So, you're in here for killing two men with an illegally obtained Luger pistol?'

'Them or me,' Harold said simply. He had long given up trying to explain how he'd been forced to act in self-defence.

Brown nodded in apparent understanding. 'We also hear,' he said, again smiling amiably, 'that you're quite tasty?'

'Depends on the opposition,' Harold replied in modest appraisal of his physical prowess.

Brown found this amusing, laughing generously. 'Well, we might put you to the test shortly.'

'Got a brain left in your head?' Carmoday cut in, demanding and harsh, like the man without time to spare that he was. 'Our checks indicate you did well in school and could have gone to university but for the Depression. But you've been inside for over four years and doing porridge doesn't do much for the grey matter. Still think for yourself, can you, laddie?'

Carmoday's implicit reference to Scunthorpe made Harold wary. He still worried his assaults on the Tattersall brothers would one day return to lengthen his prison sentence. Eager to find safer ground, he voiced an opinion formed from his past reading of newspapers. 'I think in different circumstances Neville Chamberlain might have been a hero,' Harold said of the former British prime minister's infamously futile attempt to appease Hitler in September 1938.

Brown regarded Harold impassively – not so General Carmoday, or Jones as Harold knew him. 'We're here to offer you the chance to do a job for us,' he said, closing the file in front of him, evidently having detected in Harold's response signs of a still functioning mind. 'Do it to our satisfaction and we'll ensure you don't go back to prison.' Carmoday lit his pipe, drew smoke and lifted his head to exhale. 'But as a starting point we want to put you through your paces, some language and other tests, just to make sure you're our boy.'

Harold was relieved Jones had moved on from Scunthorpe. He was also greatly attracted to the offer that had now been tabled.

'It'll involve leaving home sweet home here in the Scrubs and coming down to Dorset,' Carmoday added. 'No prison staff will be involved; effectively, you'll be a free man. But don't get ideas of sneaking off or Brown here will break your neck. Up for it?'

Harold was about to give an emphatic *Yes*, but on glancing at Hugh Gregory he saw a set of troubled eyes in the instant before Hugh averted his gaze. 'Might need to sleep on it,' Harold replied cautiously, picking up on the cue but unsure what it meant.

An uneasy silence followed, broken by Brown. 'You may have heard that Archie whatsit, the lifer you were shacked up with in here, is doing well at a prison farm near York. But someone in the system wants to transfer him to Barlinnie in Glasgow and put him in with all the homo lifers. Blessed if I know why. Those lads are not fussy and have nothing to lose. They'll fuck his innards out in a week even though he's a wrinkly old scrubber.'

The raw coarseness of Brown's threat shocked Harold and rendered him momentarily speechless. He stared at Brown, while all the while Brown unblinkingly returned his gaze.

Brown spoke first, breaking the silence with unhurried menace. 'What I mean you ungrateful piece of shit is that unless you do what is required of you, we'll chuck your old mate in the sexual offenders' wing at Barlinnie, lock the door and forget about him. But your choice.'

Harold felt the calm descend on him, the signal he was poised to exert calibrated violence. His eyes fixed on Brown's Adam's apple knowing that should he unleash there would be little in the way of restraint in this instance. But he also knew that if he did Archie would be the one who suffered most. 'Right you are, then,' he replied instead.

'Excellent,' Carmoday said, as if there'd been no coercion. 'Go and pack, and try to get an early night. We'll be extracting you at zero six hundred hours tomorrow morning.'

CHAPTER TWENTY-ONE

Harold looked at his watch. He was well over four hours into the trip to Marseille and had just on an hour to go. He sat back and closed his eyes, only to be disturbed minutes later by the conductor passing through the carriage to announce that when the train stopped at Avignon all passengers were to remain on board. This could mean only one thing – another document inspection. Avignon was less than an hour from Marseille. Harold felt the tension mount in his shoulders, concerned that a check should be called so close to the train's final destination. And the more he thought about it, the more he worried.

On reaching Avignon two Vichy policemen entered Harold's carriage, but to Harold's relief without accompanying Gestapo. The policeman who examined Harold's papers was young and officious. It occurred to Harold that he and his colleague were part of the cadre of Vichy police who supported the Nazis. 'Where will you be staying in Marseille, Mr Lavigne?' the policeman asked when Harold volunteered his visit related to his job as a junior travelling salesman with a Paris-based company.

Harold offered the address of the Hotel Burgundy in Marseille's fifth arrondissement, where indeed he was to billet.

'Stayed there before?' the policeman asked. This simple question caused alarm bells to screech inside Harold's head. It had been asked in near flawless English.

Harold stared at the man, thinking of Hugh Gregory and how Hugh had drummed into him never to respond to spoken English. 'Condition your mind to ignore English,' he had said. 'Otherwise, the merest hint you understand it could trip you up.'

'*Excusez-moi?*' Harold replied, feigning a puzzled look.

The police officer turned and smiled smugly to his colleague across the aisle. It was a braggart's gesture, the sign of a man unsuited to authority. It then dawned on Harold that the two young officers were exercising their power for their own gratification. In order to flex their muscles, they had decided to detain the train at Avignon for an arbitrary document check.

The policeman handed Harold back his papers without another word. Harold nodded his thanks, fighting not to show emotion. As the train departed on the last leg of its journey to Marseille, he reflected on the stiff test the self-indulgent policeman had unwittingly set him. That he'd passed it with flying colours made Harold think of Athol House, grateful now for the rigour of his preparation. Only Harold didn't know the half of it – and never would.

Wormwood Scrubs was still in darkness when Harold was roused at 5 am on Friday 1 August 1941. Groggy with sleep, he had just enough time to wash and shave, eat quickly and collect his effects from the prison reception area. No question he was pleased to reclaim his money, all 142 pounds of it. But the thing most comforting for Harold was the recovery of the 1915 Danish krone coin, his good luck charm given to him by his father.

At 6 am sharp a black car driven by a uniformed soldier pulled up in front of the prison. Brown was in the front passenger seat. 'Ready?' he asked through the lowered window.

Harold nodded, his face stone hard.

Brown found Harold's lingering hostility amusing. He was a bachelor of forty-one who had been in the army since he was eighteen. He first tasted blood during the Malabar rebellion in India in 1921. Since then Brown had done a lot of dirty work for certain shadowy military units. The bad cop role suited his personality. He leant over to open the back door for Harold who climbed in, Brown thereafter ignoring him.

Two hours later, after passing through the south coast town of Weymouth, they arrived at a heavily guarded, austere brick building set in grounds. On production of Brown's pass, a military policeman granted the car entry beyond the high, barbed-wire-topped fence. 'Athol House,' Brown said abruptly as the driver pulled up. 'Secret SOE training facility.'

Colonel Frank Grimwade was the officer commanding at Athol House. He announced himself as such when he greeted Harold and ushered him and Brown into his office. Harold was surprised to see General Carmoday, whom he knew as Jones, already seated at a conference table. Harold, Grimwade and Brown joined him.

'Owing to the nature of our work,' Grimwade told Harold, 'we rely mostly on volunteers.' He pushed a piece of paper at Harold. 'As such, you are entitled not to sign this if you wish.'

'That's all been sorted, Frank,' Carmoday-cum-Jones cut in impatiently.

'Jolly good,' Grimwade said cheerily to Jones's barely disguised irritation, before turning to Harold, nodding at Brown on the way through. 'That being so, Major Foulkes can escort you to the orderly who will get you started.'

'I was actually *Brown* for the purposes of this exercise, sir,' the now revealed Foulkes said, shaking his head slightly, bemused that Grimwade should make so basic a gaffe.

An internal door in Grimwade's office opened after Harold and Foulkes departed. Captain Hugh Gregory stepped into the room, snapping his heels and saluting smartly. 'What do you think, Hugh?' Carmoday asked. 'Do you still think he's the one?'

'He's smart, resourceful and physically strong,' Hugh replied, purposely avoiding an assessment of Harold's chances of success. 'And has excellent language as best I can tell.'

General Carmoday looked at Grimwade and then at Hugh. 'I need to update you both on some recent issues we've had with the Resistance, specifically the networks in

Lyon and Marseille, Charlie and Oscar.' These were the SOE's operational networks in France, established to conduct hit-and-run guerrilla raids in the country's German-occupied zone. 'We're still in radio contact with both,' Carmoday continued, 'and certainly all their radio traffic looks in order. But only two nights ago we received an indication some Charlie network members might have been picked up. Where that leaves Oscar we're not entirely sure.'

Hugh nodded with serious calm, whereas Grimwade was less composed. 'Good God,' he cried. 'That's a rum show.' The differing reactions did not escape Carmoday.

'What does this mean for Harold's operation, sir?' Hugh asked Carmoday, knowing he'd been told about the Resistance only because the general had recently asked him to be Harold's sherpa, a mentor to guide him through his preparation.

Carmoday did not reply immediately. Instead, he loaded his pipe as if thinking about the question. 'With the doubts hanging over Charlie,' he said finally, 'and us still to gauge if there's been damage to Oscar, I'm reluctant to have Leon rely on Resistance assistance in either Lyon or Marseille. Other than arrival, therefore, his has to be a cold insertion.'

Hugh understood *Leon* was Harold's operational code name. He also knew a cold insertion was one where the operative was expected to fend for him-or herself. 'The news about Charlie and potentially Oscar is concerning, general,' Hugh said. 'But I have faith in Harold's ability to manage on his own in Lyon and Marseille provided we give him the necessary documentation and back story.'

'Yes, quite,' Carmoday replied. Another pause, this time one of the pregnant variety. 'But naturally we can't wait until Leon's back home to let us know if he's found any heavy water in Marseille and, if so, if he's managed to destroy it. Equally, in the absence of Oscar's assistance we don't want him lugging a radio transmitter about. We thought it best to put in someone like you to handle the reporting aspect. You'll know him better than most after working on his preparation and he'll have trust in you. We'd aim to insert you on expiry of his allotted search time in Marseille.'

'Sir, I need tell you I have only schoolboy French, nothing remotely like Harold's.'

Carmoday smiled briefly. 'We can get around that problem, Hugh, by inserting you under cover as a diplomatic courier heading up to Geneva.' Hugh's eyebrows rose. 'We think it would be relatively straightforward for Leon to come to the Hôtel du Clou,' Carmoday said, 'to meet you in the room where you'll be resting after your overnight boat trip from Valencia.' The Hôtel du Clou was the hotel in Marseille regularly used by Foreign Office diplomats, the one where in the foyer a little over three weeks earlier Henri Mittel had accosted the Foreign Office courier offering to sell his consignment of stolen heavy water.

'The meeting need only be for twenty minutes to half an hour,' Carmoday continued, 'until you've debriefed Leon. We'll give you a B2 to carry in your diplomatic consignment. You can send us a report from your room immediately afterwards and be on your way to Switzerland.

As soon as Leon is done with you he can go his own way and eventually back out via Spain as planned.' A B2 was a SOE-designed, long-range radio transceiver that fitted into a suitcase.

'General,' Hugh said, 'you do realize I don't have Morse?' This was a reference to Morse code, the means by which radio messages were transmitted.

'I do,' Carmoday confirmed. 'But there's nothing preventing you from learning the Morse for the letters *A*, *B* and *C*. They'll mean respectively: *found and destroyed*; *found and not destroyed*; or *not found*.' Carmoday smiled at Hugh. 'Keeping your reporting requirements simple enables us to get a readout on the state of play in good time.'

Hugh appreciated the need for reporting simplicity. But what if a report less cut and dried was required? Then a second thought overtook the first. 'But hasn't the Foreign Office vetoed SOE use of diplomatic cover involving Switzerland?'

'Those fairies,' Grimwade chimed in irreverently.

'What the FO doesn't know doesn't hurt it, Hugh,' Carmoday said wryly, ignoring Grimwade. 'One of our Bern people will come down to Marseille, on the QT so far as the FO is concerned, and meet you off the steamer in a car with Geneva consulate number plates. He'll take you to the Hôtel du Clou and drive you to a Geneva safe house after Harold's debrief. Next morning, he will return you to Marseille as if you're a regular courier.'

Hugh was unquestionably smart and of good British fibre; indeed, that's why Carmoday had personally selected him. But he was still burdened by notions of principle and fair play. That's why second thoughts had hounded him ever since putting forward Harold's name at the SOE meeting. At a minimum, Harold would have to enquire of Hôtel du Clou staff as to the name and whereabouts of the man said to have waylaid the Foreign Office courier, drawing him from the shadows. The risks entailed, Hugh came to believe, meant the job called for a fully informed volunteer. This accounted for Hugh's troubled eyes at Wormwood Scrubs when Carmoday made his unspecified job offer to Harold sugar-coated by the promise of prison release. And when Harold, on noting Hugh's doubts, had hesitated to accept the offer, Hugh felt in some way responsible for Foulkes's subsequent coercion of him; that's why he agreed to become Harold's sherpa. Now the thought of being in the field alongside Harold and sharing some of the risk was further balm to his guilty conscience. 'I'd be happy to be the communications cut-out, general,' he said.

Carmoday nodded. He knew character and had anticipated the response. 'We've scheduled Harold's departure for the night of 4 September, around five weeks from now. We'll parachute him into the Riom drop zone, have the Resistance do the pick up, hide him for the night and next day put him on the train to Lyon. Then he's on his own. We've given him the cover of a Paris-based travelling salesman because he must be able to move about Marseille if he's to search for the heavy water. But first, he'll spend two days in Lyon building essential background. Once in Marseille, he'll have four-and-a-half days, Monday to Friday lunchtime, to do the search before linking up with you.'

Hugh interrupted Carmoday before he could go on. 'Excuse me, general, but if Harold will have no Resistance assistance after insertion, where will he stay in Lyon and Marseille?'

Carmoday was impressed by Hugh's attention to detail. Many others would simply have assumed arrangements had been made. The general was now beginning to wish he could avoid using him. But it was too late to find someone else with the same spread of personal qualities. 'Good question, Hugh,' Carmoday said, careful to remain even. 'Just between us, one of our people from Switzerland recently had reason to make a short trip to Paris. While there, he rang hotels in Lyon and Marseille to make bookings posing as someone from Harold's Paris office. We have a friendly in the *Banque des pays du Nord* in Paris whom we use infrequently. The source arranged a credit with counterpart banks in Lyon and Marseille. The hotels will debit these once Harold's in the house. Handy, because the source gets a telex when that occurs and has a way of letting us know, thereby confirming Harold's arrival in each city. Bit hush some of this, you'll appreciate.'

And indeed, General Carmoday was not keen to elaborate. His tale of an SOE officer visiting Paris and making Harold's accommodation arrangements was true. But his suggestion this was incidental to other secret work was not. Carmoday's invention was in fact designed to obscure the critical importance he attached to Hugh's reporting task, to it being an integral element of the *Close Hold, Top Secret* task the general had before him. Now Carmoday was relying on Hugh's self-discipline to forestall further questions, one of the many attributes that had prompted the general to select Hugh in the first place, for the *real* role he was to play.

While Carmoday stoked his pipe, Hugh considered the general's explanation of how an SOE officer while in Paris on other business had also been tasked to make Harold's bookings. But Carmoday spoke again before he could fully digest it. 'You should plan on disembarking in Marseille on the morning of Friday 12 September,' Carmoday said. 'The meeting with Harold will be that afternoon at the Hôtel du Clou. After debriefing him you'll send us the report, reseal the radio in the diplomatic bag and set out on the drive to Geneva.'

Hugh nodded in understanding, but by now something was niggling at him. He looked at Carmoday seeking a hint as to what it might be, only to see an inscrutable face. Finally, Hugh realized it was Harold's accommodation arrangements that were unsettling him. Conjecture abounded as to whether a consignment of heavy water actually existed. This was precisely why Harold, a so-called *expendable*, had been press-ganged into conducting the heavy water search. Yet the general said an SOE officer on unrelated secret duty in Paris had made telephone calls into the Vichy Zone, assuredly German-monitored, and activated a rarely used banking source. This type of asset mobilization, Hugh realized, was incompatible with an empty vessel operation involving an expendable like Harold. But for now Hugh kept his counsel. He was dismissed pending further instructions. In the interim he was to see the orderly about a training course on radio transmitter operation. This direction served only to revive Hugh's earlier concern – the perceived inadequacy of his *A*, *B* or *C* reporting orders.

Grimwade spoke first when he and Carmoday were alone, nodding at the door through which Hugh had departed. 'I like Hugh. I think he'll do the courier impersonation perfectly well.'

Carmoday didn't answer. Instead he said, 'Let's go outside, Frank. There's something important we need to discuss.'

The two walked out to the building's grounds, where they selected a bench in a remote corner near the boundary fence. Carmoday's face was set hard. 'I was soft-pedalling in there a few minutes ago, I'm afraid. It's actually been confirmed that the Charlie network in Lyon has been betrayed. It seems a task force of Gestapo and hard line Vichy police raided the safe house a week ago; got the radio, two local commanders and found the weapons store. It's clear the Germans know the radio security practice and are now playing the network back against us.'

Grimwade's eyes had widened in alarm. 'Can I ask how you know this, general?'

The question pleased Carmoday; it was the opening he needed. 'It's a long story, Frank, but for a time we've had a watcher in place in Lyon. He's not a network member but an American asset, one they run from their embassy in Vichy. Every now and again, if we're especially nice to them, the Americans will sound out the source for us. The agent is a Vichy policeman based at police headquarters.

He has family in Guadeloupe, the French territory in the Caribbean, and provides the Americans with information in return for payments to his relatives back home.'

'Are you sure the source's information is reliable?'

'As much as we can be. After not hearing from Charlie for a couple of days, we had the Americans send someone across to consult the source on our behalf. One of their diplomats got there a few days after the raid on the safe house, before the Germans had extracted the messaging trap from the network radio operator and started re-transmitting. When the Yank caught up with his source, he was told about the raid. The source said someone in the Resistance had given up Charlie, but who exactly and from which network he didn't know. We received the American's report last night.'

'Jesus,' Grimwade uttered, rocking back and forth as if in pain.

Carmoday nodded wearily. 'The Minister of War was personally on the blower at five this morning, on the orders of the prime minister. He demanded an immediate resolution of the problem, namely the unearthing of the traitor and an assessment of the Resistance networks. "No higher priority; whatever it takes," were his exact words.'

'Heavens to Betsy, general,' Grimwade exclaimed. 'Where do we start?'

'The problem's much of our own making, Frank. The network structure currently in place, while no doubt efficient, doesn't properly compartmentalize Charlie in Lyon and Oscar in Marseille from each other or from the logistics network.'

Grimwade understood the logistics network was the Foxtrot network centred on Riom. Foxtrot was responsible for the reception of personnel, weapons and explosives air-dropped into Vichy France and their safe transport to the operational networks in Lyon and Marseille, Charlie and Oscar. It was the network slated to assist Harold when he parachuted into France.

'The structure's main strength, its cohesion,' Carmoday continued, 'has proven to be its greatest weakness, the result of us being slow to grasp the extraordinarily lax security practice of some in the Resistance. Those in Foxtrot have come to know the identities of many in Oscar and Charlie. As such, it's impossible to say if Charlie was given up by one of its own or whether it was someone in Foxtrot, or whether it was someone from Oscar in Marseille who learned of the Charlie safe house through a Foxtrot member with loose lips.'

'But general,' Grimwade said, a puzzled look on his face, 'didn't you earlier imply to Hugh Gregory and me there were no concerns over Foxtrot by saying there were only doubts hanging over Charlie and perhaps Oscar? I mean you told Hugh we're using Foxtrot for Harold's reception, didn't you?'

'If Hugh was to get into a fever over Harold's arrival,' Carmoday said bluntly, 'he and Harold would soon be chin-wagging and we'd end up with neither of them inserted. But the truth is there are doubts hanging over all three networks, Foxtrot, Charlie and Oscar alike.'

Grimwade was baffled as to why the general so badly wanted Hugh to do the reporting, to the extent of misrepresenting Foxtrot's situation and possibly placing Harold at risk. But Carmoday's hard voice warned against further questions. 'What news of Golf?' Grimwade asked instead. The Golf network was located at Luchon in the foothills of the Pyrenees Mountains, on the border between southern France and Spain. It had been set up to manage the border, to oversee the infiltration and exfiltration of SOE agents over the Pyrenees to and from neutral Spain.

'I'm confident Golf is intact,' Carmoday replied. 'It's a standalone network that has no contact with the three other units.' *It had better be,* he thought. *Foulkes will be passing through there shortly.* Major Andrew Foulkes was the man introduced to Harold as Brown, the SOE assassin whose real name Grimwade had inadvertently revealed that morning.

'So how do we proceed from here?' Grimwade asked.

'We have to assess the health of Foxtrot and Oscar, Frank,' Carmoday said. 'Only if they're clear will we know the traitor's in Charlie. The question of poor security practice, especially idle chatter, will have to be addressed. But it is quite distinct from the infinitely more serious problem of network collaborators. Our first priority must be to test Foxtrot and Oscar for traitors. And to do that we'll need to offer up some bait.'

'What did you have in mind?' Grimwade asked.

'Leon,' Carmoday said simply.

Grimwade still hadn't quite caught on. 'Leon what?'

Carmoday hid his exasperation. 'The Germans will know we might have cottoned on to Charlie's compromise. They won't have their informant break cover for nothing.

We have to offer something worthwhile to make them act once Harold's given up.'

Grimwade stared blankly at Carmoday. 'Who's giving up Harold?'

'We are, Frank, you and me. Sorting out the Resistance networks now trumps the heavy water matter. And to be candid, if we didn't have the Resistance problem I wouldn't be putting in anyone to follow up on the heavy water without more to go on. But we do have this Resistance issue and the starting point is to test Foxtrot. Harold's insertion via Foxtrot is the means we're going to use. That's why it's essential not to raise Hugh and Harold's concerns over Foxtrot. Be clear on that.'

Grimwade was, although still uncertain about exactly where Hugh fitted in.

'Two days before Harold leaves,' Carmoday said, 'you'll send a message to Foxtrot advising he will be parachuted into the Riom drop zone on 4 September and instructing it to secrete Leon for the night and next morning put him on the train to Lyon. You'll also prescribe the main elements of background cover we want: overnight stay with a distant relative; short meeting in Lyon the next day followed by travel to Toulouse; and the relative having no knowledge of subsequent movements.

'But when we do task Foxtrot,' Carmoday continued, trying not to lose Grimwade, 'we'll emphasize Harold *must* be on the train to Lyon early the next day. We'll spell out that his transit in Lyon is not to Toulouse as per his cover but to another destination, without specifying where or how. We'll also explain Harold's real transit involves someone very important and a tight one-hour transit window. If the informant's in Foxtrot, the Germans will know of Leon in advance and his supposedly vital transit in Lyon. They'll want to know whom he's meeting, where he's going, and so on. There'll be conspicuous police and Gestapo activity in Lyon as they gear up to surveil him off the train.'

Carmoday watched Grimwade, waiting for him to point out the deliberate planning flaw. 'Except if we're sending the message on 2 September,' Grimwade said eventually, speaking slowly as he thought it through, 'someone in Foxtrot could inadvertently spill the beans on Harold's insertion to a traitor in either Oscar or Charlie before he arrives on 4 September.'

Carmoday was relieved. He was beginning to wonder if Grimwade would ever spot the error. 'That's a good point, Frank,' he said with a pretence of vigour. 'An excellent point in fact. Let's rethink this. Harold's in on the night of 4 September, right?' Grimwade agreed. 'If your initial message to Foxtrot on 2 September indicates he's going in on *11 September*, saying we want him on the train the next day will indicate travel to Lyon on 12 September. Whether they find out from a traitor or because of idle chatter, that's what the Germans will be planning for.'

Carmoday could sense Grimwade's energy rise. He fed it as he went. 'But when Foxtrot comes up for its radio schedule at 9 pm Riom time on 4 September,' Carmoday said, 'three hours before Harold is due to jump, we'll send a correction advising the error's just been detected and Leon in fact will be there tonight, 4

September. Apologies for getting his week of departure wrong, etcetera. Foxtrot won't be happy but three hours is still long enough for its people to get out there, do the pick up, hide him for the night and, on 5 September, put him on the train to Lyon. In that case, Foxtrot's compromise will be evident from the frantic activity in Lyon shortly after the correction is sent on 4 September, as the Gestapo brings forward its operation to surveil him off the train. What do you think?'

'By George, I think you're right,' Grimwade said excitedly. 'The three-hour notice of Harold's actual arrival gives the Foxtrot people no time to informally transact with Oscar and Charlie. But any traitor in Foxtrot will have an established channel to a Gestapo controller. If there's a rapid build-up of Gestapo and Vichy police activity in Lyon immediately after we advise Harold's amended arrival time, the traitor has to be in Foxtrot.'

Thus was born the administrative error, Harold's mistaken drop date and the last minute correction to it, which so annoyed the Foxtrot Resistance who received him when he did parachute into the Riom reception zone late on 4 September 1941. 'It's messy, Frank,' Carmoday said. 'But we must have the heavy water search cover. Good work spotting the earlier planning error; it's thanks to you we've found a solution.' With that, as Carmoday intended, Frank Grimwade now owned the error.

Carmoday briefly allowed Grimwade time to bask in his success. 'And shortly after Harold goes in,' he said on resuming, 'we'll have the Americans sound out their Lyon police source. If the source reports an activity spike after

9 pm on 4 September when we advise the arrival error it will confirm a Foxtrot traitor.'

Grimwade nodded sagely. *He's well on board now,* Carmoday thought, judging it was time to warn Grimwade about the thing he feared most but could not avoid because of Harold's critically essential background needs. 'But remember,' Carmoday warned, 'Foxtrot must believe Leon made a short transit of Lyon on 5 September to parts unknown. Even if Foxtrot has no traitor, we simply can't rule out network gossip after Harold's arrival.'

'Yes, yes, I see your point,' Grimwade said with matching seriousness, and Carmoday sincerely hoped he did.

Inadequate separation between Foxtrot and the networks Charlie in Lyon and Oscar in Marseille was indeed responsible for the Charlie network's compromise. But General Carmoday did not tell Grimwade that he already knew a traitor in Oscar, aided by a Foxtrot operative's injudiciousness, had betrayed Charlie. Nor did Carmoday disclose it was this liking of some in Foxtrot for indiscreet chatter that obliged him to mount the network integrity test, specifically the American sound out of their Lyon police source, even though Foxtrot was unsullied by a traitor.

And least of all did Carmoday explain how his charade linked to Prime Minister Churchill's *Close Hold, Top Secret* operation, of which Grimwade was necessarily unaware. The tie-up stemmed from the fact that Carmoday and Major Andrew Foulkes judged Harold as most vulnerable to Foxtrot's bad security habits during his first three days in France. That was why the network was to be told Leon would come and go from Lyon on 5 September in the space of an hour to an unknown destination: to make Foxtrot's people unsure of Harold's whereabouts, in which case a German search for Harold arising from idle chatter would reflect Foxtrot's uncertainty by focusing further afield than Lyon.

Even so, Carmoday and Foulkes accepted that were Harold exposed during his first seventy-two hours Churchill's operation would have to be aborted. They based this on the belief that if alerted in the first three days, the Germans would have ample time to locate Harold, regardless of where they searched, such that he would be detained before the early hours of 12 September when, known only to Carmoday and Foulkes, Churchill's secret task was to trigger. Should the Foxtrot integrity test reveal chatter in the key first seventy-two hours, therefore, Harold was to be deemed as lost and with that the one-shot window for Churchill's operation would close.

But Carmoday and Foulkes had also calculated that, by three days on from Harold's arrival, Foxtrot would be distracted by other tasks, diverting its attention from Harold and substantially reducing the likelihood of network chatter about him. This, they assessed, would elevate Harold's survival prospects to a fifty-fifty proposition. And at fifty-fifty, Carmoday and Foulkes agreed, to bet on Harold reaching Marseille and getting through to the 12 September trigger point was a risk worth taking.

CHAPTER TWENTY-TWO

Harold's beating heart had slowed in the hour since the scare of the document check at Avignon. But now with the train about to reach Marseille, he was conscious his apprehension had revived. 'Just put one foot in front of the other when you get there,' Hugh had counselled. 'Don't think too far ahead.' The train ground to a halt in a cloud of hissing steam. Harold grimaced slightly while retrieving his suitcase from the luggage rack. Affecting a leisurely manner, he stood politely aside to allow other passengers to bustle off the train ahead of him.

Stepping onto the platform around 4:30 pm on Sunday 7 September 1941, Harold willed himself to be alert. A bored policeman briefly examined his papers at the station exit and waved him through, whereupon Harold followed his briefers' instructions and reached the Marseille fifth arrondissement. There he soon located the Hotel Burgundy. It was a small hotel that had once known grandeur. But now it was tired and neglected, as if the owners had decided it should blend in with the area's spread of industrial development. Harold could not have known that at that very instant an American diplomat from the US Embassy in Vichy had also reached his hotel – in Lyon.

The American diplomat checked into Lyon's upmarket Champvert Hotel. Three hours later he sat at the hotel bar nursing a glass of Pernot wine. A man passing behind lightly brushed his back. The diplomat finished his drink and walked casually outside, as if to take the evening air. After strolling two blocks he paused to take in the scene, looking with relaxed interest in one direction then another. With that, he proceeded to the next corner and turned right where, with a glance over his shoulder, he darted into an unlit alley midway up the street. The pathway extended for a city block, linking two of Lyon's major thoroughfares and giving daytime access to workers servicing the office buildings and hotels backing onto it. Walking swiftly now, almost running, the diplomat continued up the service lane until he could see a main artery up ahead. Calming himself, he slowed to a creep looking for the open doorway. He had used it before but now the laneway was pitch-black. On locating the entrance, he stepped inside into an even darker area that he knew from past experience was a stairwell.

The man who had brushed by him in the hotel bar spoke first. 'Yes?' he said in an abrupt whisper, speaking with the lightest of creole lilts. 'Why another meeting so soon after the last?' The questioner was an off-duty Vichy policeman stationed at Lyon police headquarters. He was originally from Guadeloupe as General Carmoday had earlier told Frank Grimwade. It was through code words in telephone calls from relatives that the Americans arranged unscheduled meetings with him.

'Friends of ours are wondering if suddenly on the night of 4 September, from about 9 pm onwards, Gestapo or Vichy units started gearing up to surveil someone due off the train from Riom mid-morning 5 September?' the diplomat said softly.

'No. The station's been dead quiet for a week.'

'What about in the three days since 4 September? Any hint of an urgent search for a man believed to have been briefly in Lyon on 5 September but whose whereabouts are now unclear?'

'None. And trust me, I would know about things like that.' The policeman worked in the police communications centre and was privy to all bulletins and other alerts.

'Are you one hundred per cent sure?' the diplomat asked.

'*Certainement.*'

'Okay. Thanks. See you in a month as per the normal schedule, unless advised differently.'

The diplomat stepped into the alley and walked to the nearest thoroughfare. Back in his hotel room, he placed a call to his embassy in Vichy, knowing it would be monitored.

'Duty officer,' a voice said when the connection finally materialized.

'Hi Kevin,' the American diplomat said. 'It's Bill Preston. I'm over in Lyon for meetings with the mayor and others tomorrow. Have the ballgame scores come in yet? My brother in Chicago was going to last night's Cubs' game. He's a diehard fan.'

Kevin laughed. 'He'll be happy. Cubs eleven to two in the ninth over the Cardinals.'

Kevin now cabled Washington to say *nil return*. The diplomat's reference to the Chicago Cubs meant no traitor and to his brother meant no chatter. Had he enquired of the New York Yankees or mentioned his father, Kevin would have sent a longer despatch marked *Most Urgent*.

The American *nil return* reached Angus Carmoday at midnight London time Sunday 7 September 1941. The general was waiting, knowing no traitor lurked within Foxtrot but dreading news of network chatter. Carmoday picked up the telephone. 'Foxtrot's clear,' he said cryptically to Frank Grimwade, awoken in his Athol House flat. 'And no chatter since arrival,' he added, pretending an aside to mask his huge relief. The general was now willing to take his chances on Harold's luck holding for a tad over four more days, until early 12 September when Churchill's *Close Hold, Top Secret* operation would trigger. 'The next step is to test Oscar,' Carmoday told Grimwade. 'Trickier. See you at oh six hundred. Have a pot of tea ready.' Over five weeks had elapsed since Carmoday had sold Grimwade the Foxtrot network integrity test pretext. He was well prepared.

Carmoday and Grimwade did indeed share a cup of tea on the morning of Monday 8 September before walking into the Athol House grounds and taking up the same bench they had occupied when discussing Harold's role in testing the Foxtrot network. Carmoday got straight to the point. 'We can expect the banking source's confirmation of Harold's arrival in Marseille in the next couple of days,' he said. 'As such, we should plan to initiate the Oscar integrity test at the 5 pm radio schedule this coming Thursday, 11 September.' Had Carmoday been more open, he would have told Grimwade the trigger for Churchill's *Close Hold, Top Secret* operation was about to be primed.

'At the 11 September radio schedule,' Carmoday told Grimwade, 'you will send Oscar a message advising Harold Lavigne is in Marseille on an unspecified mission and task Oscar to take him from the Hotel Burgundy to the network's radio on the morning of Friday 12 September to send a report to London. Harold being unaware of this 11 September message is the key. If there is an Oscar traitor, the Gestapo will be alerted to him by the early evening of 11 September. It would give the game away were Harold not seen to be acting consistent with his cover.'

By now Grimwade had visibly blanched. 'Never lose perspective, Frank,' Carmoday said on seeing the bleak reaction. 'Harold's an expendable. He's the price we have to be prepared to pay if there's a traitor to be uncovered.'

'Yes, I know,' Grimwade said dejectedly. 'It's just such a pity.'

Grimwade's obvious misgivings worried Carmoday. Worse was to come. *Best to spit it out,* the general thought, *and see how he reacts*. 'But even if there is a traitor in Oscar,' Carmoday continued, gently now, massaging Grimwade, 'the Gestapo won't act immediately unless they're convinced it's worth their while. After all, nabbing Harold straight away will reveal the Oscar network is betrayed.'

'Fine,' Grimwade said, ponderously wondering how Carmoday planned to compel the Germans to show their hand should Oscar be compromised and, now he had thought about it, confused by the need for Oscar to assist Harold make a report. Hadn't the general arranged weeks ago for Hugh Gregory to debrief Harold in Marseille and radio a report independent of the Resistance? 'So, how do you plan to get the Germans to react and where does Hugh Gregory fit into all this?' Grimwade asked apprehensively.

Carmoday took an extra deep breath. Here was the really messy part. 'Before closing down the 11 September radio schedule you will QTA the instruction to Oscar to take Harold to the network's radio.' QTA was one of a family of three-letter codes commonly used by Morse code operators. It meant: *cancel the preceding message*.

'Then,' Carmoday continued, 'you'll send a replacement message advising Oscar an SOE officer, work name of Graham Grantham, will arrive in Marseille on the morning of Friday 12 September under cover as a diplomatic courier. Grantham is Hugh of course. We'll tell Oscar Grantham will debrief Harold at the Hôtel du Clou that afternoon and instruct it to send a Morse operator to Grantham's room at 2:30 pm to transmit his report on the B2 radio set he'll carry in his diplomatic luggage.'

Grimwade's eyes widened in horrified amazement. Carmoday nodded in confirmation. 'If the traitor is in Oscar, our intention to send in Hugh specifically for the reporting purpose will convince the Germans Harold's insertion is important enough for them to act. We'll ensure Foxtrot has no contact with Oscar for twenty-four hours after you send the 11 September message, thereby isolating Oscar from the other networks. If the Germans react to the news of Hugh's insertion we can be confident there's a traitor in Oscar.'

'But ... but,' Grimwade warbled, 'Gregory's one of us, not an expendable. The Germans won't settle just for Harold. If Oscar's compromised, they'll wait until Hugh's arrived and also nab him.'

'Yes, sadly that's true,' Carmoday said with grim simplicity.

Grimwade fell silent. For weeks he had wondered about Hugh's actual role, only now to find Carmoday planned to treat him as an expendable. 'I don't know if in good faith I can do this, general,' Grimwade said finally. 'And anyway,' he asked, suddenly suspicious, 'why did you have me initiate the messages to Foxtrot and why am I to send this second lot to Oscar? Why can't they be sent from Baker Street HQ, for example?'

Carmoday sighed. It would have been so simple to tell Grimwade he had been chosen for his incompetence. Harold's mistaken drop date sent to Foxtrot and the late-notice correction to it were pure Frank Grimwade. So too was the 11 September tranche of messages to be sent to Oscar in Marseille. Grimwade's cancellation of his initial message and his replacement second missive were sure to convey, as Carmoday intended, the first communication had been sent in error.

Carmoday's logic was simple. SOE's work involved people of many nationalities. Already one Nazi spy, a Pole working in the Baker Street central registry, had been detected and quietly removed. Carmoday knew for sure there would be others. But any enemy agent buried in SOE's ranks who sighted the Foxtrot and Oscar messages would also note Frank Grimwade was recorded as the originator. Unaware Carmoday had carefully crafted the despatches expressly to highlight Grimwade's distinctive hallmarks, and knowing that Grimwade administered the Athol House training facility, with a little luck any sleeper would assume the messages were a training drill.

And even should a Nazi spy uncover that Grimwade's messages were operational, either to locate a consignment of heavy water or flush out a Resistance traitor, Carmoday reasoned that was where it would end. In SOE circles, Grimwade was a renowned plodder. His involvement was Angus Carmoday's rolled gold insurance. If somehow a hint of Prime Minister Churchill's momentous *Close Hold, Top Secret* operation emerged, no informer, however imaginative, would suspect messages sent by Frank Grimwade of association with it.

'I need a stout fellow like you, Frank,' Carmoday said, aiming to flatter Grimwade. 'Someone I can trust to get the job done with no fuss. We need to sort out this traitor business asap.'

Grimwade had made it to colonel in the army catering corps. And his appointment to administer Athol House was one of those bureaucratic accidents that occasionally occur in large organizations. To be fair, he had made a reasonable fist of things. It was just that the man had no feel for operational work, not a jot. Carmoday watched Grimwade grapple with his dilemma, thinking he could hardly entrust the colonel with the sort of task Major Andrew Foulkes was to undertake forty-eight hours after Hugh Gregory's arrival in Marseille. The general was a hard man with a low threshold of tolerance for fools. Praise from him was rare and valued. Carmoday was banking on Frank Grimwade being powerless to resist his blandishments.

Carmoday's was an astute assessment. 'You've a safe pair of hands in me, general,' Grimwade said after a time, once he could no longer deny Carmoday's kudos, beaming now.

'Good chap,' Carmoday said, forcing a warm smile to his lips. 'I have to return to London urgently. But I'll be back soon with the Oscar messages for you to send on 11 September.'

General Carmoday did return to London as he said he would, but not to SOE's Baker Street headquarters. Rather, he had his driver drop him at Battersea Park train station. The general watched the car drive off, waiting until it was completely out of sight before taking the short walk to Boating Lake in nearby Battersea Park. Selina was waiting. She was a tallish woman of about forty who had aged well. Her hair was dark as were her eyes, and she had lost none of her continental dress sense in the two years she'd been resident in Britain. Selina smiled at Carmoday as he approached. 'Angus, my darling,' she said in accented English, 'you do look so tired. Are those awful Germans keeping you up at night?' She extended a hand, the back of which Carmoday dutifully kissed.

'Are you ready?' Carmoday asked. The couple sat next to a quaint, apex-roofed boathouse. 'You'd better be. I expect to have confirmation Leon's in Marseille by Wednesday at the latest. You should plan on going in Thursday morning.'

'I believe so,' Selina replied. 'I've settled on how best to get your Leon from his grubby little Hotel Burgundy back to the apartment in Rue Fauchier, taking into account it will be the middle of the night during curfew.'

The Hotel Burgundy, of course, was the establishment in Marseille's fifth arrondissement where Harold was now ensconced under his travelling salesman cover. And the Rue Fauchier apartment was home to a Corsican woman known to Carmoday who had fought for the Republicans alongside Selina and her husband during the Spanish civil war. The Corsican woman was also someone whom Selina's husband had bedded frequently. Selina had come within a whisker of shooting her on discovering her husband's infidelity. But deciding it took two to tango, she relented. Ironically, the two women thereafter became close friends. In mid-August, Carmoday had sent Selina to Marseille to renew acquaintances with her Corsican friend, and do other things, crossing into France from

Spain and back again within the space of seventy-two hours.

Carmoday also knew from first-hand experience he could rely on Selina. 'All that matters,' he said, 'is keeping Leon from the clutches of the Germans from the early hours of Friday 12 September, when you extract him from his hotel, until noon on Sunday 14 September, about sixty hours in all. I hardly need tell you that when Leon doesn't show at the Hôtel du Clou for the 12 September meeting the Gestapo will go into overdrive looking for him. Every informant in Vichy France will be mobilized. And also be aware that from the early evening of 11 September, the Gestapo and Vichy police will be watching the Hotel Burgundy.'

Selina smiled flirtatiously at Carmoday. 'Trust me when I say I can still get into any man's room I choose, day or night. All I need is a name and a room number and I'm as good as in there.' She sniggered at this teasing, knowing that Carmoday found her attractive while also knowing he would never make a pass at her. Such a dedicated professional, *mon dieu.*

Carmoday refused to rise to the bait. 'His work name is Harold Lavigne,' he said straight-faced. 'But we won't know his room number. You'll need to ascertain it in advance of the extraction, taking care not to alert those watching the hotel.'

Selina was momentarily serious. 'I can handle that. Once I have him out and back to the apartment I will set the chalk mark on the *Parc Longchamp* tram stop. But to do that your Mr Lavigne must follow my instructions unquestioningly when I use the code. There'll be no time for arguments.'

'Understood,' Carmoday said. 'We'll impress on him that you're acting with my express authority and he's not to quibble. We'll ram this down his throat just before he leaves.'

'And what of the code, Angus?'

'*Dublin Zoo*,' the general said simply.

'A strange choice,' Selina mused.

'Long story,' Carmoday replied. 'But it's to do with his father.'

Carmoday first met Selina in Spain in 1938 when she and her husband, both French communists from Marseille, were fighting Franco's Nationalists. Carmoday was in charge of military intelligence at the British Embassy in Madrid at the time. Selina became his source once a Nationalist victory was inevitable, passing information on Republican strategy knowing the British were in bed with Franco and wanting to end the pointless suffering. Selina's husband never made it; shot dead in March 1939 just days before the war's formal end as he and Selina, and innumerable Republican others, fled into France. Marseille was a dangerous place for Republican informers in those days, even uncovered ones, and Carmoday arranged to have Selina whisked to England. She had arrived barely two years ago, just as Hitler was about to invade Poland and trigger World War II.

After that Carmoday lost contact with her. But on SOE's formation, he tracked her down to a pub in Marble Arch where she worked as a barmaid by day, returning at night to a bedsit in St John's Wood. There was apparently a man in her life at this stage but Carmoday never met him. And by the time he started using Selina as a talent spotter among the French left bank community in London, the consort appeared to have disappeared. Carmoday soon realized Selina had lost none of her wiles or her beauty. That's why he operationalized her. She had now made the recent sortie into France, to make contact with the Corsican woman in the Rue Fauchier apartment, as well as other preparations. The venture was not a major task in the great scheme of things but dangerous enough to convince Carmoday Selina still had her iron nerve and velvet-gloved ruthlessness.

Carmoday and Selina sat in silence, reflectively watching the pedal boats in the distance. 'Are you going to tell me why it's so important to keep Leon out of German hands for a couple of days, Angus?' Selina asked after a time, smiling coquettishly.

'You know the rules, Selina,' Carmoday said firmly.

And in any event, Carmoday wasn't about to tell Selina that the head of the Irish Army intelligence directorate, Tommy Noonan, had secretly contacted him seven weeks ago, in July. In an out-of-the-way Dublin pub, Noonan had confided how a high-ranking Gestapo officer, aiming to convince Ireland to abandon its neutrality, had recently bragged to him of British feebleness. In the process, the German had let slip that a month earlier, in June, the Gestapo had recruited an informant from the senior ranks of the SOE's Oscar network in Marseille and how, on overhearing incautious remarks by a visitor from the Foxtrot network, the traitor had learned the location of the Charlie safe house in Lyon. 'No name mentioned,' was Noonan's terse reply to Carmoday's expected question, before hastening out the pub's back door lest the two were seen in private conversation.

Nor was Carmoday likely to open up on the secret plan subsequently approved by Prime Minister Churchill designed to take advantage of the traitor. It involved inserting Major Andrew Foulkes into France on Saturday 13 September via the Spanish–French border crossing at Luchon. Once over, handpicked operatives from the Golf network would transport Foulkes to Marseille. By late Saturday night Foulkes would be installed on the top floor of a three-storey building adjacent to Marignane airport. It was from Marignane mid-morning Sunday 14 September that Field Marshal Philippe Pétain, head of the Vichy Government, was to board a plane taking him on a tour of France's North African colonies.

Foulkes's task was to assassinate Pétain, using the high-powered rifle equipped with telescopic gunsight the Golf people would provide. Pétain was a French icon, an acclaimed Great War hero. Since becoming the internationally recognized prime minister of collaborationist France, he had adroitly used his status to portray himself as the champion of all French people, metropolitan and colonial alike. But Pétain's death would create a leadership vacuum, which Churchill intended Charles de Gaulle, leader of the anti-Nazi Free French Forces, to fill with messages of liberation and nationalism broadcast into France on *Radio Londres* from his exile in London. And although de Gaulle's rhetoric would appear to target divided continental France, Churchill's secret imperative was France's North African colonies. Only Churchill, Carmoday, Foulkes and four others – all trusted Churchill advisers – knew of the plan. Churchill believed that unless the pro-Vichy colonies of Algeria, Morocco and Tunisia fell in behind de Gaulle, the Allies would never drive Rommel's Afrika Korps from North Africa, with catastrophic implications for Britain's essential Middle East oil supplies.

Harold Bradshaw's role in all this? Well, the Germans appreciated that Pétain brought considerable personal influence to bear in keeping France's North African colonies loyal to the pro-German Vichy regime. In deference to his importance, the garrison of German troops in Marseille was normally deployed around the Marignane perimeter any time Pétain flew out of the airport. In truth, this was mainly pandering to Pétain's vanity. But the Germans were nothing if not thorough; it was common knowledge they always searched the surrounding buildings, particularly those with line of sight vision to the airfield's parking area. This included the three-storey building where by Saturday night 13 September Major Foulkes would be in position, waiting to shoot Pétain on Sunday morning as he walked across the tarmac to his departing aircraft.

But when Harold, having disappeared from his hotel in the small hours of Friday 12 September, failed to attend the meeting that afternoon with Hugh Gregory at the Hôtel du Clou the Germans would react. Hugh would be taken into custody. And when poor Hugh specially chosen for his stoicism, courage and patriotism preferred to die rather than give up his perceived reason for Harold's insertion, namely to search for a batch of heavy water, the Gestapo would be convinced it absolutely had to know the reason for Harold's presence in Marseille.

A massive manhunt would ensue whereby ritualistic priorities would quickly give way to those of the real variety. The German garrison and most of Marseille's more reliable Vichy police would be deployed to hunt for the missing Harold. Provided Selina could ensure Harold remained at large until Sunday at noon, supervision of Pétain's departure would be left to Vichy police not engaged in the search, officers far less diligent than the fastidious Germans. In that case, there would be no in-depth security measures masquerading as pomp and ceremony.

CHAPTER TWENTY-THREE

In the early evening of Sunday 7 September, sixteen hours before Carmoday's meeting with Selina in Battersea Park, Harold checked into the Hotel Burgundy in Marseille, recalling as he did the clerical sergeant at Athol House issuing his forged *Ausweis* in the name of Harold Raymond Lavigne – the German-issued pass permitting Harold's travel between France's occupied and Vichy zones. 'Best to keep your real given names, sir,' the sergeant had said. 'That way if someone asks you to state your full name, you'll respond instinctively giving you a split second to prepare to trot out your adopted surname.'

Harold lay on his bed, resting before dinner. But after an hour alone in his hotel room his mind began to wander. The voice of doubt became louder, unchecked by outside influences. Harold thought of Athol House and Hugh's obvious if unexpressed concern over his lack of direction on the so-called policy aspects of the heavy water search. It was then Harold decided to defer his search for a day and spend Monday building cover just as he had in Lyon.

It was security to which he could cling when he tackled his assignment, more work history he could fall back on.

Harold sailed through his preliminary testing at Athol House, graded *exceptional* in both language aptitude and physical condition. With that, his training proper commenced. Hugh Gregory was seldom far from his side, regularly accompanying Harold on the Whitley bomber flights to Scotland where in the dead of night Harold parachuted into the frigid night air. The mock interrogations that followed came unannounced, often in the early hours as an exhausted Harold sought to sleep. Afterwards, Hugh would offer advice: how Harold needed to be more natural when explaining his job as a junior travelling salesman for *Maison de Vêtement*, his Paris-based employer; things like the company's address and the name of its managing director needed to roll smoothly off his tongue; ditto for where he lived in Paris. 'Name a prominent landmark close to the apartment,' Hugh said. 'Tell them in an instant the floor you're on and have a resigned smile ready to go when admitting the apartment has no telephone connected.'

The friendship between Hugh and Harold quickly grew; soon Hugh had adopted the elder brother mantle. In late August Harold was informed that, owing to issues with the Resistance network, he would be reporting to Hugh at the Hôtel du Clou in Marseille on the afternoon of Friday 12 September 1941, eight days after parachuting into France.

Yet like any big brother worried about a younger sibling, Hugh could not ignore the gnawing feeling all was not right with the operation. First there had been his inadequate *A, B* or *C* reporting instruction. Then there had been General Carmoday's explanation of how an SOE agent in Paris on unrelated business had taken risks and used vital assets to make Harold's hotel bookings in Lyon and Marseille, even though Harold was an expendable in whom such resources were not usually invested.

The uncertainty bothering Hugh prompted him at dinner that same late August night to quiz Harold on his instructions for conducting the heavy water search. 'Tell me exactly, Harold,' Hugh said, 'what directions have you been given?'

Harold shrugged. 'The briefers have emphasized the first step in the search is to identify the man who made the sale offer to the Foreign Office courier. The starting point is the Hôtel du Clou, using the courier's description of him. The hotel is a small boutique outfit. The concierge stationed in the foyer is the hotel staff member most likely to have witnessed the exchange. But I'm only to make enquiries during business hours, consistent with my cover work. I'm also to finish my investigations by noon on Friday 12 September, which makes sense now I know I'm reporting to you at the Hôtel du Clou at 2:30 pm.'

'Yes, that's all good advice. But what if you do locate this fellow who apparently made the sell offer? I mean, are you to reason with him, threaten him or promise him money? This obviously is not a question for the briefers. It's what I'd call a policy aspect requiring a decision from on high.'

When Harold admitted he had been given no particular guidance, Hugh's puzzlement deepened. 'Okay,' Hugh said, leaving aside that conundrum for now, 'what are you supposed to do if you find the heavy water?'

'They had an expert in to show me photographs of heavy water containers. I'm to count the number of barrels, note any markings and then puncture the barrels and tip out the water.'

'And when are you supposed to do this? The briefers have said you're to search for the seller only during business hours. But what if you have no option but to destroy the heavy water at night, after curfew? This is another policy aspect you need to be clear on. Have you had any word on this from senior people?'

Harold shrugged again. 'Not really,' he said. 'All I've been told *ad nauseam* by the briefers is that to be on the streets of Marseille after night curfew without a sound reason will guarantee arrest with inevitable consequences to follow.'

Hugh understood Harold's prison background had conditioned him not to question authority figures like Carmoday and Grimwade. Even so, Hugh was perplexed. Carmoday in particular was usually assiduous when it came to dotting the Is and crossing the Ts. But Hugh was not about to disparage his superiors, no matter how steeply his worry was mounting. He changed the subject, trying to push the troubling thoughts from his mind. Hugh's brow, however, remained furrowed and this did not go unnoticed by Harold.

On 2 September 1941, two days before Harold's departure, Hugh was summoned to provide General Carmoday with a final update on Harold's progress. 'For someone five months short of his twenty-fifth birthday,' Hugh said, 'his ability to assimilate all that has been thrown at him has been quite remarkable.'

Carmoday showed no emotion although he was torn; short of a miracle, he'd soon be sending both Harold and Hugh to their deaths. 'That's good, Hugh,' he said levelly. 'He seems well prepared. How are your own preparations coming along?'

Hugh smiled. He was pleased, grateful even, to be linking up with Harold in Marseille. 'I'm about as ready as I will ever be, sir,' he said. Even so, Hugh was determined to raise his concerns with Carmoday, starting with the policy aspect questions. 'Permission to speak frankly, general,' he said.

'Go on,' Carmoday replied, reaching for the security shield of his pipe.

'Sir,' Hugh said, 'I've become worried by Harold's lack of instruction on how to deal with the seller of the heavy water, should he unearth him, and what to do if destroying the cache means skulking around after dark. He's been repeatedly warned how dangerous it is to be out at night in Marseille after curfew without a watertight explanation for it. I do think he needs clear direction on these aspects, policy questions on which the briefers can't help him.'

Carmoday grimaced. 'I think you underestimate Harold, Hugh.' And even though Carmoday spoke calmly, his preceding frown told Hugh the general thought he had better things to do with his time than answer such questions. 'Others have spoken to Harold and he understands he's got to use his initiative,' Carmoday said. 'No one can write a script for him. In the event the seller won't be cajoled one way or another, Harold may have to force him to cooperate. Harold's skilled enough to do that and moreover has the gift not to lose his nelly and apply more force than necessary. And if destroying the stuff requires after-dark work, he knows we expect him to find a way. Never forget Harold's a unique blend of power, restraint and intelligence.'

Hugh observed Carmoday closely as he answered, and despite the general's measured explanation his continued fiddling with his pipe did nothing to allay Hugh's concerns. But Hugh was too respectful of Carmoday to press him. *Best to leave sleeping dogs lie*, he thought. Clearly, though, something was going on about which Carmoday had decided neither he nor Harold had a need to know. This same *something going on*, Hugh concluded, was also surely responsible for the asset mobilization associated with Harold's accommodation in Lyon and Marseille and the oddly limiting reporting task he'd been handed.

But for all that, Hugh's *something going on* conclusion did convince him he and Harold were involved in a game of higher stakes than previously thought. It was in this moment that he decided to take his own precautions. He would include in the diplomatic consignment he carried to Marseille his army-issued side arm. 'Sorry, sir,' Hugh said, pretending embarrassment. 'I wasn't aware Harold had been briefed on these issues. He didn't mention it to me. No doubt he was practising good security.'

In fact, General Carmoday had earlier ordered Colonel Frank Grimwade to brief Harold in terms identical to those Carmoday had just summarized for Hugh. And heavily pre-occupied, Carmoday had been obliged to accept Grimwade's assurance he understood that briefing Harold was vital to maintaining the heavy water search cover.

Grimwade of course did not know the plan to root out the Resistance traitor under cover of Harold's supposed heavy water search was itself a feint for Churchill's *Close Hold, Top Secret* plan to assassinate Field Marshal Pétain. But he was also flushed with pride that the general should enlist him in what he believed to be the real secret operation – the effect of which was to dangerously inflate his self-confidence. As ever with Frank Grimwade and operational matters, the unilateral decision he made was a poor one. In the days since speaking to Carmoday, Grimwade decided not to brief Harold on how to deal with the heavy water seller and complications in destroying the material. His rationale was that because Harold's insertion was bait to uncover a Resistance traitor and not to search for heavy water, the briefing was redundant and could be foregone.

Meanwhile in Marseille, too long cooped up alone in his hotel room, Harold was now riven with doubt. He shelved plans to eat dinner and instead, as they had taught him, sought to break out of his downward spiral with a hot bath.

Harold felt the steaming water's soothing effect. Soon he was reflecting on how the time since his removal from Wormwood Scrubs had passed in a blur. It had been a joy to be away from the prison – the relative freedom, better food and the many new and varied tasks, all of which he had tackled with boyish enthusiasm.

The reminiscence gave Harold cause to compare his resort to a hot bath with his ability at Athol House to contain his anxiety. Being away from Wormwood Scrubs, he concluded, had reawakened him to life, to an outside world of endless possibilities. This had bred in him a fierce determination to avoid returning to prison that was sufficient to overcome discouraging thoughts about what lay ahead. Harold shrugged causing bath water to lap onto the floor. *It was natural to be nervous,* he told himself, *now he was on the ground in Marseille and cheek by jowl with the abounding risks.*

Harold began to slumber. And when he did the aching desire he could not be rid of resurrected. After all, he was twenty-four and in peak condition. The physical training at Athol House each morning before breakfast was vastly more demanding than the push-ups, sit-ups and skipping Harold had done in prison while his cellmate Archie dutifully kept count. Visions of Katrina from The Sunset on Inverness rushed to him. It was one thing to quell the sensation while half scared to death in a barn outside Riom or when travelling on trains, but quite another to confront it in the privacy of a hot bath in his hotel room.

Earlier, on 3 September twenty-four hours ahead of his departure, Harold was taken to a room to be joined shortly after by the man he still knew as Jones – General Carmoday. To Harold's surprise, Major Andrew Foulkes entered the room behind Carmoday, making no effort to acknowledge Harold. Foulkes sat not at the table with Carmoday and Harold but in the background. Harold had not seen him since the morning when they drove down to Dorset from Wormwood Scrubs. As usual, Foulkes was frosty and remote.

'From all reports, you're ready to go,' Carmoday said immediately he sat down.

'Yes, sir,' Harold replied. He was now more soldier than prisoner, even if the institutional language was the same.

Carmoday refilled his pipe before speaking. 'Harold,' he said in a fatherly tone Harold had not heard before, 'there's one other matter I wanted to discuss, just between us, and Andrew here,' he said, directing his thumb over his shoulder at Major Foulkes. 'No one else need know about it, not even Hugh. Understood?'

'Yes, sir,' Harold said, wondering what secret Jones and Foulkes should want to keep from others involved in the operation, Hugh especially.

Carmoday motioned to Foulkes, who spoke from the back of the room. 'Before visiting you in the Scrubs a while back,' Foulkes began, 'General Jones and I went to Scunthorpe to check out your background. We visited a fellow called Trimble, the butcher who was your employer. He was in the hospital, cancer I'm afraid. I suspect he's in a better place by now.'

Harold was not surprised by Foulkes's revelation he and Jones had visited Scunthorpe. Carmoday, as Jones, had said as much at Wormwood Scrubs when first interviewing him. But the mention of Mr Trimble did cause Harold's eyes slightly to widen.

Foulkes saw this and smiled. 'Trimble refused to implicate you, if that's what you're worried about. But his evasiveness did suggest there might be something to the snippet we picked up in earlier conversation with the wife of the landlord of the Lion and Castle pub – Bessie someone – that you extracted a pound of flesh, shall we say, from the ruffians believed to have killed your mother.'

Harold flinched as if he'd been hit. He had always feared the assaults on the Tattersall brothers would rebound on him. And Foulkes's mention of his mother's murder had also swathed him in bitter memories. Suddenly, the fact that his parents lay in humble graves in Scunthorpe disturbed Harold. He resolved to rectify this, whether that was in the few hours remaining before he left or after he was returned to prison.

Carmoday broke in on seeing Harold react, playing his accustomed good cop to Foulkes's bad. 'I can assure you, Harold,' he said, 'we have no interest in chasing down rumours about your dim, dark, distant past.'

'But?' Harold asked, looking directly at Carmoday.

'But nothing,' Carmoday replied, leaving Harold hanging.

So why tell me you know about the Tattersalls? Harold thought.

Had he bothered, Carmoday would have explained that Foulkes's veiled reference to the Tattersalls targeted Harold's transparent resolve not to be returned to prison and reminded him of his – Carmoday's – leverage in this regard. Carmoday would have also explained the theatrics were necessary to ensure Harold adhered religiously to the instruction he was about to deliver. Here was Carmoday fulfilling his undertaking to his secret agent Selina that, unthinkingly and unquestioningly, Harold would obey her orders when she extracted him from the Hotel Burgundy in the early hours of Friday 12 September. For as Carmoday knew better than any other, Harold's extraction was the lynchpin on which hinged the *Close Hold, Top Secret* operation to assassinate Field Marshal Pétain.

'Andrew,' Carmoday said instead, 'only raised Scunthorpe because this Trimble chap told us you were fond of using the term *Dublin Zoo* to describe a tricky situation. He said the habit had been passed down to you by your father.' This time Harold smiled at the recollection. 'As such,' Carmoday continued, 'I've decided *Dublin Zoo* should be the failsafe code to be used by a certain asset who will be in Marseille when you are there.'

Carmoday paused, wrestling with the thought that once cut adrift by Selina Harold had virtually no hope of eluding the Germans. Drawing on his Scottish doughtiness, the general pulled clear of his funk. 'All going well, you won't need any help,' he said. 'That is, once you've made your report to Hugh on 12 September you should proceed to the Spanish border at Luchon and cross over as soon as feasible. In the interim, if you do need some help, and our operative can provide it, that person will use the *Dublin Zoo* code when approaching you. You should faithfully follow the instruction of anyone using the *Dublin Zoo* identifier because the asset will be acting with my express authority. I want to be very clear on this point. If someone utters the words *Dublin Zoo*, you are to follow their instructions to the letter, immediately and without question or exception.'

Monday 8 September 1941 dawned bright and sunny in Marseille. Thanks to his hot bath, Harold had slept well and, on waking, enjoyed a hearty breakfast of cold cuts, fresh bread rolls and coffee. He was looking forward to being out of his hotel room and away from its depressing confines. Harold knew the Vichy authorities would conduct document checks at various locations around the city. But his forged papers had survived numerous inspections and he had trust in them. So long as he kept to building cover only a stroke of bad luck could undo him.

True to form, Monday passed without incident. Harold moved unimpeded around Marseille and comfortably negotiated the three document checks he experienced. He continued working at his cover during the morning of Tuesday 9 September. Around noon he made his way to the port district. It was conspicuously distant from Marseille's commercial hub, but after all the purpose of being in the city was to visit the Hôtel du

Clou. At the briefers' insistence, Harold had repeatedly practised claims to being lost in case of challenge. The hotel was as the Athol House people had described. Seated in the foyer of the small establishment, Harold noted no doorman, only a concierge's desk in one corner and an intermittently staffed reception counter in another.

After thirty minutes, Harold approached the concierge. 'Good afternoon,' he said, 'I'm waiting for a colleague, Monsieur Huppert. We were to have lunch in the restaurant. My name is Harold Lavigne. Has a message been left for me by chance?'

The concierge looked beneath his desk. 'I'm sorry, but no.'

'He's about my height, 180 centimetres,' Harold said, using the Foreign Office courier's description of Henri Mittel. 'And about ninety kilos, I'm afraid,' Harold added, sniggering, hoping to build rapport with the concierge. 'A little plump, you see.'

But unbeknown to Harold, the concierge's wife was also a little plump and he was sensitive about it. He resented that this fit young man should make fun of someone just because they carried a few extra kilos. Unsmiling, he shook his head.

'No?' Harold said, pressing the concierge. 'He's a balding chap who tries to cover his patch by slicking down his hair, which is quite dark.' The concierge didn't answer. 'I think the last time we ate here was about two months ago, in July,' Harold continued. 'Unfortunately, my friend Huppert ran into an old business rival; they had words here in this very foyer.'

By now the concierge had decided he didn't appreciate Harold's persistence. And in truth, Harold had been slow to heed the messages conveyed by his body language. 'I've said I can't help you,' the concierge answered, this time with unmistakable iciness. With that, Harold backed off and walked from the hotel. Once outside he began to shake, realizing he had overplayed his hand and the danger in this.

Harold started back towards central Marseille. Two blocks into his journey, he came across the Marseille Cathedral. Harold could scarcely believe his eyes as he recalled his mother's reminiscences about its distinctive architecture, all those years ago when he was a toddler in Scunthorpe. The building was as grand and ornate as she had described. And coming across it also told Harold he was in the area of the city where his mother had grown up. But with worries now swelling over his ham-fisted approach to the concierge, Harold was anxious to be on his way and lingered only briefly.

As he walked, Harold began to hear his mother's voice in his head, loud and lifelike. The distress he always felt when thinking of her sad and unfulfilled life began to consume him. How glad he was that before he left for France he had given Hugh the 142 pounds he had with him when arrested back in early 1937. Hugh was to organize the relocation of his parents' remains from their current graves to a joint burial plot in the Scunthorpe Great War servicemen's cemetery and the erection of a large marble headstone: *Loving Mother and Father of Harold* it would read.

Thinking of his mother's truncated life reminded Harold of the existential implications for him in his bungled exchange with the Hôtel du Clou concierge. He tried to console himself with the thought that the exercise had made clear the concierge either hadn't seen or couldn't or wouldn't remember the incident with the Foreign Office courier. Harold mulled over his options. He supposed the next step was to talk to other hotel staff, taxi drivers, deliverymen and the like.

But now with his anxiety still mounting over the concierge incident, Harold's confidence was deserting him. The prospect of loitering in doorways trying to speak to strangers suddenly scared him. It was this mindset that prompted Harold to abandon the heavy water search for the time being. He would fall back on the security of building cover until he could seek Hugh's advice and reassurance when they met in three days' time. Armed with Hugh's wise guidance, Harold theorized, he would then recommence the search. Jones, Foulkes and Co. in London might not approve of his unilateral decision to delay his exit from France. But provided he completed the task satisfactorily, Harold was sure they would not grizzle too much.

Wednesday 10 September. Harold rose early as his cover required, his mood buoyed. He had temporarily abandoned the risky heavy water search and the checks on the preceding days had reaffirmed his trust in his papers and cover story. Clearing his head, however, had also created space in his mind for other thoughts, not least of which was the brief time spent the day before in the area of Marseille where his mother had grown up. He began to think he could risk another visit to the port area, to find his mother's family home, the address of which he knew by heart, relying on his cover story of being lost if necessary. By mid-afternoon the idea emerged that he actually owed it to his mother to do so. The repeated warnings given him by Hugh and others, to avoid being needlessly off track from the path where his cover work would take him, fought with the temptation swirling inside Harold's head. And for now prudence won out.

Harold dreamt that night of visiting his mother's childhood home. Throughout the morning of 11 September he continued to resist the growing enticement. Over lunch, Harold wrote up more bogus orders in his order book. To add more, he rationalized, would be overkill. It was of course the first sign that Harold was about to succumb.

Before long Harold was in the back lanes of the Marseille port district. And when shortly after he located his mother's family home, years of pent-up emotion spilled over. Harold, it transpired, had inherited from his parents a predisposition to mental aberration, and now the thought of his mother weaning him in this very dwelling enlivened it for the first time. The mother-child bond formed in infancy, usually dormant in adults, stirred within him. Soon the sensation transformed into a powerful sense his mother was by his side, overwhelming Harold psychologically. He had not forgotten the risks of being in Marseille. But another compartment of his mind had opened within which he believed he was in the company of his mother.

Over the next two hours, the mission and his mother vied for Harold's attention, each obtaining roughly equal shares. But by the time Harold, fortunate to have escaped detection while wandering randomly, arrived back at the Hotel Burgundy just on six in the evening of Thursday 11 September 1941 the mother area of his brain was in the ascendancy. With that, complacency set in, reflected in Harold's excited conversation with the hotel manager in which he told of earlier visiting his mother's childhood home. Harold planned to have an early night followed by a day of exploring Marseille, his illusory mother in tow.

An hour before Harold returned to his hotel on the night of 11 September, Colonel Frank Grimwade radioed the Oscar network in Marseille advising an SOE agent by the name of Harold Lavigne was staying at the Hotel Burgundy. Oscar was to contact Lavigne next morning, Friday 12 September, and take him to the network's radio to file a report to London. Grimwade then cancelled this message with the QTA code and, in its stead, sent another indicating an SOE agent, Graham Grantham – the work name given Hugh – would arrive in Marseille mid-morning 12 September per the SS Santa Maria out of Valencia. Grantham would be posing as a British Foreign Office courier and was to debrief the agent Harold Lavigne at the Hôtel du Clou that day. The Resistance was now to send a Morse operator to Grantham's hotel room at 2:30 pm – first floor, room eight – to transmit his report on the radio set contained in his diplomatic baggage.

Of course when Grimwade sent these messages General Carmoday already knew, courtesy of his counterpart in the neutral Irish Republic service, that a traitor had infiltrated Oscar. Not so Colonel Grimwade who believed the communications were designed to ascertain if in fact Oscar was compromised at all.

CHAPTER TWENTY-FOUR

Two pivotal events straddling Frank Grimwade's cancelled and change-of-plan messages to the Oscar network took place in Marseille on Thursday 11 September 1941. Although seemingly distinct, the two were closely interrelated. The first involved the late-morning arrival at an apartment in Rue Fauchier of a woman calling herself Mona Barbier. She was in fact General Carmoday's agent Selina, the Frenchwoman he had rescued from Marseille in 1939 at the end of the Spanish civil war. Mona, so-called, was fresh off the train from Luchon having crossed into France from Spain early that morning with papers indicating she was a schoolteacher returning from an education conference in Madrid. She came to the apartment posing as an old school friend of the occupant, the Corsican woman who had been Selina's *confrère* in Spain.

The second matter concerned an early evening meeting between a Gestapo Standartenführer and a native of Marseille, a man age forty-eight, who was third in command of the Oscar network. He had access to all network communications. He was also the Oscar traitor. The man had been spying for the Germans for the past three months because of a long-standing hatred of the British owing to a family matter dating back many years, but commencing his treachery only once convinced Germany would win the war.

The traitor gave his Nazi controller the details of the two messages received from Frank Grimwade barely an hour ago. As an Oscar network strategist, he was closely involved in planning Resistance operations even if he left their actual conduct to the younger *Maquis*. 'I have already selected the Morse operator to attend the Hôtel du Clou tomorrow afternoon,' he said, 'for this 2:30 meeting between the agents Grantham and Lavigne.'

'Fine, let that proceed,' the German replied. 'In the interim, I'll organize surveillance of this Lavigne character and see what it produces. When this second British agent arrives, we'll pick up both at the Hôtel du Clou tomorrow afternoon. If we don't know beforehand, we'll find out then why they're in Marseille.'

'And your plans for the Morse operator?'

The Standartenführer shrugged. 'Probably best that he dies trying to escape.'

The traitor smiled. 'I agree. I've actually chosen a young woman. But no matter.'

Harold was still in his room around half past six on the night of 11 September when two Gestapo officers arrived at the hotel demanding to see the hotel lodger register. They declined to answer the manager's query about the reason for their visit. 'Routine inspection,' they said when the manager knew quite well it wasn't. After noting Harold's room number, the Gestapo pair returned to a Renault sedan parked fifty metres down the street, climbing into its back seat. A Vichy police officer in plain clothes was seated behind the car's steering wheel. The vehicle was in fact an unmarked surveillance car belonging to the Marseille gendarmerie. A brief conversation ensued after which the Vichy policeman, an inspector, alighted from the car and walked to a non-descript man in non-descript clothes who waited unobtrusively in a doorway on the other side of the road.

'Room 206, second floor,' the inspector said to the non-descript man. 'Go and see if he's in.'

Harold was in his underwear cleaning his suit, tidying up before going out to eat, when he heard the tap on his door. He quickly wrapped a towel around himself. The enquiry should have been a warning but it went undetected owing to Harold's distracted state of mind. 'No, no, this is not Mr Braudel's room ... Not at all, don't think anything of it ... *Au revoir.*'

'Young man, mid-twenties, about 180 centimetres but solid, eighty-five, ninety kilos,' the non-descript man reported from the Renault's front passenger seat. 'Dark complexion, black hair quite short and black eyes. A business suit on the bed, black or possibly dark blue. I glimpsed a brown suitcase. Can't say if there was other luggage.'

'We'll wait,' the Gestapo officer in charge said. He was the same Standartenführer who thirty minutes earlier had met with the Oscar traitor. He took a packet of cigarettes from his pocket, offering one to his colleague while ignoring the Frenchmen sitting in the car's front seats. The Germans smoked in silence. 'Your people had better be ready if he leaves,' the Standartenführer said to the Vichy inspector after a time, his voice laced with menace.

'There are three of them in position across from the hotel,' the inspector replied politely, 'and one in the foyer.' He inclined his head towards the non-descript man next to him. 'Maurice has given them the description. And a little later we'll station someone on the second floor close to his room.' The inspector disliked the Gestapo, particularly when they took control of investigations and treated the Vichy police as their personal workforce. But this Standartenführer fellow was a pig and a dangerous pig at that. There was nothing to gain and a lot to lose in upsetting him.

Twenty minutes later, a torch flashed from up ahead. 'Target's on the move,' the inspector said, flashing the Renault's headlights in acknowledgement. 'Our people are about to follow.'

'Right,' the Standartenführer said. 'Let's go. You two,' he said, addressing the Frenchmen as the four men hurried up the street, 'stay at the front of the hotel and find a way to delay him if we're not finished when he returns.'

The Gestapo officers surveyed Harold's room. There was little of interest other than the brown suitcase. 'Looks like he's a salesman from Paris, judging by this sales book and the orders from businesses here and in Lyon,' the Standartenführer said.

'Do you think there's any chance we've got the wrong person?' his junior colleague asked.

'Doubt it,' the Standartenführer answered. 'But we don't have time to check out these orders. We'll wait for tomorrow's meeting at the Hôtel du Clou. Until then we'll keep a close eye on this Lavigne and see what that reveals.'

The Gestapo had long departed Harold's room when he returned from eating. They had taken care to leave the room as they found it. And in any event, lulled into a false sense of security by his current illusion of being in Marseille with his mother, Harold had taken no precautions. But not so the hotel manager who, on tiptoe, had followed the Gestapo pair to the second floor to learn that the subject of their interest was the guest in room 206, the gregarious young man with whom he had spoken at length earlier in the evening, Harold Lavigne.

The hotel manager was still on duty an hour later, working the reception desk until his night clerk arrived at 8 pm. He emerged from the reception office when General Carmoday's agent Selina rang the front counter bell at twenty minutes before eight. She had chosen this time because the demands on the reception desk would be few, leaving the person staffing the desk free to be moulded to her needs.

Selina had two plans, although she much favoured the first over the second. Both took into account General Carmoday's warning the hotel would be under Gestapo and Vichy police surveillance; this forewarning vouched for by the swarthy man seated in the hotel lobby closely watching Selina. The manager greeted Selina warmly, evidently smitten by her allure. Noting this, Selina put her preferred option into effect. 'I'm looking for Mr Claude Douin, a hotel guest,' she said. 'I have a message for him.' The manager confirmed a reservation for Mr Douin but indicated he had not yet checked in. Selina fluttered her eyes. 'It's possible his train is delayed,' she said as if mildly distressed. Selina had made the booking when in Marseille in mid-August renewing acquaintances with her Corsican friend. 'Perhaps you could ensure he receives my message? Until what time will you be here tonight?'

The beguiled manager smiled at Selina. 'I finish at eight, leaving me just enough time to get home before curfew. But my night clerk could deliver a message,' he said. 'I am the hotel manager, you see,' he added, hoping his importance would impress Selina. The boast pleased her more than the man could ever have imagined, but not in the way he intended.

'Why, thank you, that is very kind of you,' Selina replied with a comely smile. She handed the manager an envelope containing a note telling the non-existent Douin to be at a non-existent business address by 9 am the next day.

On leaving the hotel Selina walked to a nearby bus shelter she had identified back in August. It was far enough away from the hotel to avoid the gaze of any policemen but still close enough to see its entrance in the distance, and the regular comings and goings of people at the shelter meant her lingering there would not be too obvious. Equally, though, Selina knew that like the manager she needed to be off the street by 9 pm when curfew started. She was relieved, therefore, when shortly after 8 pm she saw him leave the hotel. Had he not appeared before she had to leave, Selina would have been obliged to implement her second plan. The manager walked on the opposite side of the street but fortunately in her direction. When he reached the spot where Selina was now waiting, his eyes widened first in pleasant surprise and then in instinctive caution.

'You again, madam, can I be of further assistance?'

'There is a young man called Harold Lavigne staying at your hotel,' Selina said gravely. 'He has taken liberties with me and now, I find, with another woman. Yours is a small hotel and I anticipate you will know his room number, information I am prepared to pay for if necessary. He will not be expecting to see me and I want to confront him while he is off-guard.'

The manager now was deeply concerned. Selina's approach coming on top of the Gestapo interest in Harold Lavigne was too great to be a coincidence. Lavigne, the manager decided, was trouble. The more the manager thought about it, the more he worried the Gestapo might think he was implicated in Harold's activities. Then he recoiled. Was this a Gestapo test to see if he could be trusted to keep quiet about its visit to the hotel?

Selina saw the manager's reaction. 'I can see you're worried about the police monitoring the hotel,' she said, abandoning her cheated lover persona. 'That is why, besides giving me Lavigne's room number, I also want you to unlock the padlock on the grille blocking access to the hotel basement from the canal. As the manager, I'm sure you have access to the key.'

Selina's reference to the canal was to the *Canal de Marseille*. It was an ancient complex of aqueducts and tunnels bringing water to Marseille from the Durance River to the north. A network of tunnels 160 kilometres in length snaked beneath the city. In many places, the tunnels could be accessed from private property, including the apartment block on Rue Fauchier, home to Selina's Corsican friend. As a younger woman, a girl really, Selina had explored the tunnel network with her doctor boyfriend-cum-husband. She was a refugee from a well-to-do banking family and he a committed socialist; hence her drift into communism and eventual involvement in the Spanish civil war. Selina had reconnoitred the canal when in Marseille in mid-August and found a padlocked grille blocking ingress to the hotel. Herein was the reason for preferring her first plan to the second. Unlike the second option, the first did not involve the cumbersome and telltale use of bolt cutters on a hardened steel padlock should no one be able or willing to open it.

Selina's awareness of the *Canal de Marseille* and the way she spoke made the manager think she was Resistance. The world weighed more heavily on his shoulders. 'Why do you want me to unlock the grille?' he asked apprehensively.

'I need to remove Lavigne from the hotel tonight and propose to use the lazy Susan to move between the basement and his floor, thereby bypassing the policeman stationed in the foyer.' The lazy Susan was a small service elevator in which food and laundry was shuffled between floors, a dumbwaiter as the Americans cared to call it. Selina had inspected it during a quick dash downstairs via the hotel foyer later on the same August day she had scouted the canal entrance.

The thought of Harold leaving the Hotel Burgundy was music to the manager's ears, enough to overcome his trepidation. 'Yes, I do have the key to the canal grille,' he said. 'And risky as it is, I'm prepared to take the chance and go back to the hotel now and open it. Lavigne is in room 206 on the second floor.' The manager paused. 'The elevator is at the end of the corridor furthest from his room. But be aware another policeman is now stationed on the floor close to Lavigne's room. I'll leave it to you how to get around that.'

Selina retreated to the bus shelter and watched the manager walk back to the hotel. Gathering himself and affecting confidence, he puffed out his chest as he entered, laughing as he did. 'I'm back, Pierre,' he said to the night clerk, loud enough for the Vichy policeman in the foyer to hear. 'I've left the damn key to my apartment in my office.' With that, the manager walked quickly to his office located down the corridor from the reception office behind the front counter. Opening a key safe, he took a large key from its hook and crept downstairs to the basement, carrying a torch. Nervously fumbling, he opened the padlock and scurried back up the stairs, returning the key to its hook and closing the key safe.

Straightening his jacket and brushing back his hair, the manager returned to the front counter. 'Couldn't remember where I'd put it for a moment,' he told the night clerk, again loud enough for the benefit of the Vichy policeman. 'But here it is,' he said, holding aloft the house key he'd had on him all the time. 'Must run,' the manager said. 'I'm getting late for curfew.' As he emerged from the hotel, the manager squeezed his nose with his left hand, signalling to Selina the steel grille was now open. Selina boarded the next bus to arrive and made her way back to the Rue Fauchier apartment.

At midnight on Thursday 11 September, Selina left the apartment. She wore dark trousers and a dark sweater and sported rubber-soled shoes that made no sound. On entering the canal tunnel underneath the apartment block, she took a moment to get her bearings. Then aided by the torch she carried she walked for ninety minutes, intermittently scaling piles of rubble as she went. Periodically, she emerged from the tunnel for a few seconds at a time to check her navigation. Finally, Selina reached the stretch of canal running underneath the street siting the Hotel Burgundy. Counting off the number of buildings she had memorized when exploring the canal in mid-August, she came upon the hotel entrance. Selina was gratified when the steel grille opened, albeit grudgingly.

Stepping into the void of the hotel basement Selina stood stock still in the pitch-dark listening for signs of activity. When satisfied there were none she flashed her torch briefly before moving to the lazy Susan. It was call button operated. On arrival, items were placed in the elevator's carry space of around three-and-a-half-feet square. The desired floor was selected by an external button, which once pressed automatically closed the elevator's doors sending it on its way. Selina climbed into the carry space and from a crouched position reached out at full stretch to press the second-floor button.

The sound of the arriving lazy Susan woke the Vichy policeman on the second floor. He had been slumbering in a soft chair. It took him a moment to locate the service elevator at the far end of the corridor. When he did its dimpled steel doors were closed. Pressing the call button to open it, he peered inside. Nothing. That was the last thing he remembered until regaining consciousness three hours later. The flashlight Selina expertly wielded caught him flush on the temple, recalling as she struck the man her mentor in Spain once telling her it wasn't how hard you hit them but where.

Placing the torch in her trouser pocket, Selina withdrew the set of lock picks she carried. In under a minute, she was standing inside Harold's darkened room.

Harold was sound asleep worn out by the vast distance he had walked the previous day. At first he thought he was dreaming when the gloved hand pressed against his mouth, causing him to struggle for breath. '*Dublin Zoo,*' came a voice in his waking ear.

'Wh ... aat?' he mumbled through the glove.

'*Dublin Zoo,*' the voice repeated, now distinctively female.

Harold blinked in the dark, trying to rid his eyes of sleep.

'*Dublin Zoo,*' Selina said for a third time. 'Get dressed. We've got to go. Now.'

'Who are you?' Harold whispered, pulling on his trousers and fumbling for his shoes. General Carmoday's implied threat to return him to prison had imprinted on Harold's brain that he should unhesitatingly obey anyone using the *Dublin Zoo* code.

'Explanations can wait,' Selina answered. 'Quickly, we have to leave. Leave everything; none of it is any use to you now.'

Harold had fully dressed. Reflexively checking his papers were inside his coat jacket, and not yet realizing they were now useless, he followed Selina from his room. The prostrate man by the lazy Susan reinforced Selina's authority. 'Climb in,' she ordered. 'The lift will stop at the basement. I'll follow.' Harold did as instructed, fitting into the tiny space only with difficulty.

Standing in the dark of the basement waiting for Selina Harold patted his coat pockets. Then with greater urgency he slapped at his other clothing. The Danish krone coin, his good luck charm, Harold realized, was still on the bedside table in his room.

'Someone has betrayed you to the Germans,' Selina whispered, closing the grille and snapping shut the padlock in order to leave no trace of hotel staff involvement in Harold's extraction. 'Follow me. We need to move quickly.'

With her flashlight blinking on and off, the result of damage caused to it when she struck the Vichy policeman, Selina led Harold through the maze of tunnels. Nearly two hours later they reached the Rue Fauchier apartment.

Selina ushered Harold into a bedroom. 'Wait here and be quiet,' she whispered. 'I'll be back shortly.' Selina returned to the tunnel, to a spur separate from the pathway she and Harold had negotiated. From underneath the *Parc Longchamp* tram station Selina emerged, quickly and stealthily, to draw a chalk cross on the station shelter, announcing Harold's successful extraction to the initiated.

It was 4:30 am on Friday 12 September 1941 and Churchill's *Close Hold, Top Secret* operation had just been triggered.

CHAPTER TWENTY-FIVE

Six hours before Harold and Selina began making their way along the *Canal de Marseille*, Captain Hugh Gregory had boarded the SS Santa Maria in Valencia for the fifteen-hour overnight trip to Marseille. He carried with him four canvas diplomatic bags, all with compressed lead seals, the largest containing a B2 radio transceiver in a made for purpose suitcase. And taped to the back of the suitcase, in a leather pouch, were Hugh's six-shot service revolver and a supply of ammunition. Under the diplomatic rules pertaining, neither the Spanish nor the Vichy authorities were permitted to inspect the consignment.

It was close to dawn when Selina returned to the waiting Harold in the unlit bedroom of the Rue Fauchier apartment. A curtain tethered at either end of the room provided separation, as if in poor imitation of a hospital ward. Selina whispered to Harold he should sleep, hushing his barrage of questions and explaining only that a Resistance traitor in the Oscar network had informed the Germans about him. This made sense to Harold as he knew that Hugh's insertion had been arranged because of Resistance concerns. He lapsed into an uneasy slumber as did Selina on the other side of the screen, both too wound up to sleep soundly.

Selina's Corsican friend had reluctantly agreed to allow Harold to remain in the apartment until noon on Sunday 14 September. 'But not a second more,' she had said, fearful a collaborating neighbour would detect Harold's unexplained presence and inform the authorities. The Corsican woman worked as a cleaner Monday to Friday and had left for the day when Harold and Selina roused from their slumber. 'My name is Mona,' Selina said, practising good security. 'You can wash and shave in here.' Selina pointed to her side of the curtain, to a sink and shaving material once belonging to the Corsican's boyfriend before his eviction a year ago. 'You must stay in the bedroom and not come out under any circumstances,' Selina ordered. 'I'll bring you food. The Germans will be searching for you. After a day or so, they'll assume you've escaped Marseille and be looking elsewhere. I have fresh papers for you. By Sunday afternoon it should be safe to head to Luchon and cross into Spain.'

Harold's new papers did indeed give him another identity. But Selina and General Carmoday both knew his description would be widely circulated and that Harold would not last long once he left the apartment. Recognizing this, Selina's insistence he stay isolated in the bedroom was aimed at preventing Harold, who had no idea where he was, from ever leading the Gestapo back to the Rue Fauchier hideout.

'What about my task?' Harold asked, not sure what Selina, as Mona, knew or didn't know.

'Consider it aborted,' she said.

Harold was momentarily panicked. What would Hugh think when he didn't arrive for today's 2:30 pm meeting? Then he calmed. Hugh could not be betrayed, Harold believed, because the Oscar network was unaware of him. Logically, Hugh would continue on to Switzerland once it was obvious he, Harold, would not be attending the Hôtel du Clou.

As to who made the first move was never clear. For her part, Selina's feelings had stirred when she observed Harold shaving and noted his passing resemblance to her late husband. In Harold's case, it was over breakfast. *An attractive older woman so like Katrina from The Sunset on Inverness*, he had thought. And when Selina confided her real name, the intimacy of the gesture caused the aching desire Harold could never conquer to begin to throb. Then there was the closeness of their confinement and the fact they were both tired, a little scared and in need of human warmth. A look here, a look there; a glance held slightly longer than necessary; a brush of hands and a smile. Both resisted responsibly, but there was no denying the edginess of the sexual tension. Did Selina place herself in Harold's arms? Hard to say. But when Harold leant forward to kiss her, there was no pull back. Selina, as with Katrina, was a liberated woman who took her pleasure where she found it. It was just after 11 am on Friday 12 September 1941 when first physical contact was made. A mere ten kilometres away, Captain Hugh Gregory was disembarking at the port of Marseille.

Two plainclothes Gestapo watched Hugh from a distance. They were assistants to the same Standartenführer who had monitored Harold at the Hotel Burgundy. Hugh loaded his diplomatic consignment into a vehicle bearing British Consulate, Geneva licence tags. The driver was as Carmoday had said an SOE officer from Bern. He had met Hugh alongside and would convey him to the Hôtel du Clou.

'He's arrived at the hotel,' the Gestapo pair reported back to the Standartenführer. 'The driver is in the room with the diplomatic consignment while the agent is taking lunch.'

'Let him enjoy it,' the Standartenführer said. 'It will be his last decent meal.'

Since being told in the early hours of the morning that Harold had eluded the Vichy police at the Hotel Burgundy, the Standartenführer had dispensed with the French incompetents. He now relied on a platoon of eighteen crack German troops, as well as his two colleagues who had observed Hugh on arrival and trailed him to the Hôtel du Clou.

At a restaurant in Madrid, Major Andrew Foulkes was also dining. Earlier, in a short conversation with a certain Spanish gentleman, the man told of a telephone call that morning from a Marseille-based colleague, a Spanish journalist, and how in code the journalist had reported a chalk mark on the *Parc Longchamp* tram station. Now that Churchill's *Close Hold, Top Secret* operation was a confirmed *Go,* Foulkes opted for a hearty lunch. He had just ordered the lemon sole and a glass of dry Fino sherry.

Hugh returned to his room at around 1 pm so that, consistent with the diplomatic courier cover, his driver might also eat lunch. Hugh quickly broke open the seal on the diplomatic bag containing the radio suitcase and sat the transceiver on a small table, festooning its single wire antenna around the room, over the cheap art works adorning the walls. That done, he removed his Smith and Wesson service pistol and its ammunition from the pouch taped to the back of the suitcase and placed them in his suit jacket pockets. Lastly, he took out the sealing tool and lead seals also secreted in the bag, those with which Hugh would reseal the radio in the diplomatic consignment once Harold had been debriefed and the *A, B* or *C* reporting message sent. The tool and broken seals would later be secreted in the supposed consulate vehicle, which in that guise was also subject to diplomatic immunity. Hugh was tense, but not overly so. He had mastered the requisite

Morse code and once Harold arrived for his interview, the driver would stand guard outside the door.

At 2:30 pm sharp, a light tap was heard. Hugh dismissed as nerves the warning flashing to his brain that Harold would give the door a more masculine rap. He opened it, a smile on his face to greet Harold, only for his jaw to drop. A young woman, thirty at most, stood before him. 'I am here to send the message,' she whispered in accented English.

Hugh took the woman's arm, dragging her inside the room and shutting the door. 'Something's not right,' he said, turning to the driver a puzzled look on his face. But for Hugh the puzzlement quickly turned to the ugly realization he had been right all along. The operation was not only flawed but also, somehow, relatedly compromised. His first thought was of Harold.

By now Hugh's driver had withdrawn his own weapon. Holding the gun behind his back, he opened the door and peered cautiously into the corridor. 'Can't see anything,' he said, looking back at Hugh.

Hugh's pistol was also in his hand. The terrified woman explained she was *Maquis*, a Morse operator sent to the room on the SOE's instruction. Hugh knew for certain this was no cockup, but as to the whys and wherefores of it he had no idea.

'What do we do?' the driver asked, the squeak in his voice betraying his anxiety.

'We wait,' Hugh said, his ability to think under pressure contrasting with the driver's rising panic. 'We'll give Leon until three sharp. Then we go. In the interim,' he said, 'we should plan an escape route out of here. But first, let me do this.'

The driver looked on as Hugh took a piece of paper from the hotel stationary and scrawled on it before slipping the note under the hotel room door. Had the driver seen it, he would have read two words: *Dublin Zoo*. It was Hugh's desperate attempt to warn Harold.

Harold had been sleeping in Selina's arms. He jolted awake and looked at his watch. It was ten after three in the afternoon. Harold was instantly riddled with guilt. He had abandoned Hugh at the Hôtel du Clou while here he was indulging in an assignation. At the very least, he should have arranged for a message to be passed to Hugh to alleviate the angst he would surely still be experiencing even though now, presumably, on his way to Switzerland.

Selina was still sleeping. Harold walked into the apartment's sitting room overlooking Rue Fauchier. He pulled back the curtain in time to see an open troop transport full of German soldiers drive by led by a command vehicle. The German patrol could mean anything Harold tried to tell himself. But he knew with startling certainty what it meant. The Germans had uncovered the plan for Hugh to transmit a message from the hotel. They were now on high alert and combing the city, no doubt looking for him. But what of Hugh? Harold wanted to believe he was safely en route to Switzerland.

But the grimmer likelihood that Hugh had been captured was too stark to ignore.

Harold shook Selina awake. In crisp sentences, he told her about the planned rendezvous with Hugh. 'The Germans are out on the streets. They know the plan. I have to find out what has happened to Hugh.' Selina knew from Carmoday that the scheduled meeting at the Hôtel du Clou was never meant to take place. But until Harold spoke, revealing his deep agitation, she had no idea just how close he and Hugh had become.

Shortly before 3 pm, while Harold and Selina were still sleeping, the Standartenführer had reached the same conclusion as Hugh Gregory and his driver in room eight on the first floor of the Hôtel du Clou: the missing Harold was a no show. 'Go and get them,' the Standartenführer told the platoon commander. Four men were to enter Hugh's room through the front door, backed by another six in the corridor. The commander stationed his remaining eight squad members outside, beneath room eight's window, waiting for abseilers using knotted sheets.

The German troops saw Hugh's *Dublin Zoo* warning to Harold on the piece of paper under the door. But they didn't understand it and it delayed them only briefly. The door crashed open with a screech of splintering timber. A German soldier charged into Hugh's room, three others close behind. On seeing the pistol in the hand of Hugh's driver, the front German killed him with a burst from his sub-machine gun. Hugh downed the soldier with a shot catching him in the throat, causing the following Germans to scramble out of the room.

With that, and at Hugh's urging, the Morse operator clambered onto the ledge outside the window. But as she tried to scurry along it as per Hugh's hastily devised escape route to a point above the *porte-cochere* – the decorative canvas shelter overarching the hotel entrance which was to break her fall when she leapt clear of the hotel – she slipped and fell to the ground. The eight German soldiers below rushed to her lifeless body. As they did two men emerged from a small van nearby and began firing into the group. They were the operator's escort, Resistance the Oscar traitor had been obliged to send to watch her back. And from a distance, they could not know the woman was already dead. Hugh took this in from his precarious crouched position on the outside window ledge. In the chaos below no one was paying him attention.

The German soldiers inside the hotel had regrouped. Taking up a room clearance formation, they re-entered Hugh's room. Glancing back through the window, Hugh saw them and fired three rapid shots into the room before flattening himself against the wall. A cry of pain was followed by withering fire shattering the window's glass and timber frame. Hugh moved crab-like along the ledge but as he did a volley of shots from a German soldier leaning out the window of his room caught him in the right thigh. Hugh kicked open the window of the room adjoining his. Bleeding profusely, he fell inside. The room was vacant. Ripping a pillowcase in half, he wrapped it around his injured thigh. Hugh considered his options. The hotel corridor would be full of German soldiers. Outside, where the gunfight raged, was his only hope.

Fuelled by survival instincts, Hugh scrambled through the window and literally skipped along the window ledge until he was above the *porte-cochere*, whereupon he tumbled into the cacophony. The Standartenführer's two Gestapo assistants saw him reach the ground and ran towards him. Hugh shot them both, their death cries only adding to the confusion. Then he went, limping, towards the nearby port, the pain intensifying all the while and knowing he was leaving a trail of blood. Hugh's quest for freedom took him not to the ship berthing area from whence he had come but towards a series of warehouses. He could not have known it, but Hugh was hobbling towards the port area where in April 1916 Harold's father Albert had first courted Rita, Harold's mother.

The Germans had lost four of their number to the Resistance attack. It had taken some time to neutralize the threat. But Hugh's blood trail told them he was headed for the port. The Standartenführer was beside himself with rage at Hugh's escape and the fact that Hugh had killed a further two soldiers along with his two assistants. He ordered the Vichy police to provide reinforcements.

Without help, Hugh would have soon been discovered. But a nervous Frenchman saved him, a stevedore working at one of the warehouses who hated the Germans enough to take the risk. The first thing the stevedore did was to lay Hugh on the floor of a warehouse and slit open his trouser leg. Then using a low-pressure hose he washed the wound. The bullets, two of them, had passed through the fleshy part of Hugh's leg. The gash was gaping, ugly and had torn muscle, causing massive bleeding. But the bone was intact. The man retied the pillowcase Hugh had used at the hotel until it was a tourniquet staunching the flow of blood, and secured it in place over the top of Hugh's flapping trouser leg. Now leaving no trail of blood, he helped the barely mobile Hugh into an adjacent warehouse. There he unscrewed a floor plate and motioned to Hugh to climb into a cavity barely fifty centimetres in height, little more than a foot-and-a-half. '*Bonne chance, mon ami*,' he said before racing off. Minutes later, Hugh could hear the sound of German voices as the search for him began.

Harold became insistent that efforts be made to determine Hugh's fate. Only too aware of the danger in this, Selina knew she should deflect the demand even if it meant formal recourse to the authority invested in her by General Carmoday. But she could not. Selina had first met her husband when he was around Harold's age. Most of all she remembered the excitement and danger they shared, and the passionate sex it spawned. 'Wait for tonight,' she heard herself tell Harold. 'I will speak to my Corsican friend.'

The Corsican woman was mortified. 'No, no, absolutely not,' she said. 'I'm not getting involved in your business.'

Selina reminded the Corsican of Spain, of sparing her life after her affair with Selina's husband was revealed. 'I've never once asked you for anything in return,' Selina said. 'Now all I want is some assistance in gathering information.'

Debate raged, until eventually the Corsican wilted.

Around the time the Corsican left the apartment early on the morning of Saturday 13 September to visit her brother, Major Andrew Foulkes crossed into France from Spain. He proceeded to a bar in Luchon whereupon the nervous owner quickly ushered him into a back room.

The Corsican woman returned at noon. Her brother was making enquiries. He would call by the apartment in a few hours to report his findings. The Corsican's brother was a taxi driver by day and smuggler and thief by night. Like most of his compatriots, he was a soldier of fortune, not much interested in the politics of war and rather more focused on the activities of the Corsican mafia in Marseille. The Corsican network prospered largely because of its hard-edged ruthlessness, but also because it was an efficient intelligence machine; not much of what went on in Marseille escaped its attention.

In the late afternoon, the Corsican's brother and one other man arrived at the apartment. They sat with Harold, Selina and the Corsican woman in the apartment's sitting room.

'There was a gunfight yesterday afternoon at the Hôtel du Clou,' the brother said, 'involving the Gestapo, Resistance and a British diplomatic courier just arrived from Spain. Several German soldiers, some Resistance and the courier's driver were killed. Word has it the courier was wounded but escaped to the dock area. So far as I know, he hasn't been found although there's a whisper about the French police have him. But that would mean defying the Gestapo, which is unlikely. Either way, he's dead or as good as dead. The Germans spent last night arresting *Maquis*. They tell me the whole Marseille network has been rounded up.'

'Hugh,' Harold gasped hoarsely, head bowed, shaking and now accepting that Hugh was dead. 'What a *Dublin Zoo*,' he whispered fighting back tears, his anguish sufficiently raw to stir sympathy even in the two usually immovable Corsican males.

'One further thing, though, which might be of interest,' the Corsican brother added, his uncharacteristic empathy provoking an attempt at consolation. 'Early this morning the Germans apparently took one of the Resistance, a man, to a safe house in Bon-Secours.' Harold looked up, surprised. 'Yes,' the brother said noting Harold's interest spark. 'It's entirely possible that person is a German informant. For the sake of appearances, they had to arrest him last night with all the others. But the prison's a lice-infested rat hole so they've quietly taken him to a place in the suburbs where he'll be more comfortable.' The brother then proceeded with a convoluted explanation that Selina seemed to understand as to the safe house's location.

Silence ensued as Harold digested the information. Anger rose in him quickly followed by the onset of the calm he always felt before going into battle. He might never know the full story, he reasoned, but it was now clear the same Resistance traitor who had informed on him had also betrayed Hugh. Lost in thought, Harold was slow to realize the second Corsican, the brother's hitherto silent companion, was speaking to him.

'So, you're English?' the second Corsican asked.

'Yes,' Harold replied. Hugh's fate had numbed him; there was no longer any point in trying to pretend he was French.

The second Corsican was in fact the taxi driver whom Henri Mittel had consulted the preceding July after arriving in Marseille to search for a buyer for his stolen heavy water consignment. 'A fellow I know has a farm at Allauch, about twenty kilometres from here on the city's outskirts,' the second Corsican continued. 'He introduced me to his cousin, a man called Mittel. This Mittel came from Paris looking to sell the British something he'd thieved, something he has stored at the Allauch farm. I regularly drop fares at the Hôtel du Clou and told Mittel how British diplomats often stage through the hotel when coming and going to Geneva. But I understand when Mittel approached a British diplomatic courier he got the brush-off. Curious then, isn't it, that yesterday's shoot-out at the Hôtel du Clou also involved a British courier? I'm betting the two matters are connected.'

Harold was momentarily astonished despite the pall of despair gripping him. 'You mean you know where the heavy water is?'

'If you're talking about whatever Mittel has stolen, then yes.' Harold's blank stare prompted the man to offer more. 'The farm's located at the far eastern end of Boulevard Gueidon,' he said. 'You can't miss it.'

Harold knew of Boulevard Gueidon, having in recent days trudged up and down the portion of it hosting several of Marseille's fashion houses. But in truth, he was only mildly interested that the thoroughfare extended to the Allauch farm; his curiosity about the heavy water and where it was hidden had waned in virtually the same moment it had flowered. Right now, Harold's thoughts were dominated by the loss of Hugh.

Harold turned his gaze to the Corsican woman's brother, the hard look in his eyes betraying his intention. Harold had decided that just as the Tattersalls had paid for the death of his mother and his father's related suicide, the Resistance traitor was now going to pay for Hugh's death.

I want two things,' Harold said. 'A gun and for you to take me to this safe house in Bon-Secours as soon as it is dark.'

The brother laughed. 'A gun, fine. But if you think I'm going to drop you at the front door of the Bon-Secours safe house you are mistaken. The place will be alive with Germans.'

'Okay,' Harold said. 'Drop me close by and point me in the right direction.'

'I would go no closer than five kilometres to the house and from that distance you'd be lost in a matter of minutes,' the brother scoffed.

'I'll come with you, Harold. I know exactly where the place is.' It was Selina. The voice inside her head was screaming, demanding she tell Harold it was madness to seek revenge against the Resistance traitor, that the odds were insurmountable and the only possible outcome was his death. But the words refused to issue. And with that, Selina yielded. She would do as Harold wished and at the cost of the task Carmoday had set her, just as she had forsaken her comfortable middle-class life and gone to Spain for her husband. The liberated, emotionally contained Selina had fallen in love.

By now Harold was exhausted by his grief and the significance of Selina's offer of assistance. Too tired to generate vigour, he shook his head gently. 'It's too dangerous for you, Selina,' Harold said softly, pleading with her.

But Selina was not listening. 'Two guns and a sharp knife, please,' she said to the Corsican woman's taxi driver brother. 'You can drop us five kilometres from the safe house just before the 9 pm curfew.'

And that was that. The Corsican men left and Harold returned to the bedroom. From there he heard the Corsican woman speaking. 'When you two leave tonight, Selina,' she said, 'please don't come back.'

Selina's softly spoken agreement reached Harold's ears. The thought that within three hours they would leave the sanctuary of the apartment, never to return, caused Harold to pat his trouser pocket. He was instinctively feeling for the Danish krone coin given to him by his father.

But in the instant he reached for his good luck charm, Harold felt only a sense of nakedness, briefly as if it were a gust of wind. And accompanying the sensation, a pang of intense foreboding wafted across him. Harold had experienced the feeling only once before. It was little more than a day ago when he had stood in the dark of the Hotel Burgundy basement waiting for Selina, when he realized that in the rush to escape his hotel room he'd left his talisman on the bedside table.

CHAPTER TWENTY-SIX

Harold and Selina crept through the dark. It was just after 10 pm on Saturday 13 September 1941. They were in a quiet residential area and it was curfew; no one else was around. The safe house was a single-level villa at the top end of a narrow, steeply inclining road. Tightly shut metal doors embedded in a gothic portico topped by a stone pediment offered room enough for a small motor vehicle to enter. At the back, the dwelling's high concrete wall abutted a flatter laneway. Tall, rectangular, wooden doors provided access, with the wall tapering sharply from its high point above the doors to a height of about six feet. Luxuriant foliage further protected the front and rear boundaries. The towering concrete walls on either side of the villa, separating it from its neighbouring buildings, were both secured by three strands of barbed wire running their entire length. It was from the back laneway, at the end of the fence furthest from the doors, that Harold silently hoisted himself up to peer inside, one foot in Selina's interlinked hands.

'Sentry at the back gate facing the villa, another outside the villa's back door facing the gate,' Harold reported once dismounted. 'The guard detachment's transport vehicle is parked inside at the front and there's a military motorbike and sidecar inside the back gate.'

'Bound to be a sentry on the front porch,' Selina said, 'and Germans in the front rooms as well.'

Harold's heave of breath in the dark reflected the difficulty facing them. 'Too much light and activity at the front,' he said. 'And the sides are too high. The back's quieter and not as brightly lit. We've got to get in there, somehow. The positioning of the sentries, though, means they've got the back area covered.'

The sound of tearing material startled Harold. It was Selina ripping at the blouse she wore, so that the full swell of her breasts was in view. She handed Harold her pistol but carefully placed the dagger knife she carried down the back of her skirt. 'Hit me,' she whispered to Harold. 'Short and hard, make my nose bleed.' Harold hesitated, unsure what to do. 'Do it, quickly,' Selina urged.

Harold cupped a hand gently behind her head. The smack of fist on flesh and bone was muted by Harold's shirtsleeve over his knuckles. Selina buckled slightly. He held her in his arms, deep affection coursing through him. 'Give me a minute,' she whispered. Soon she recovered enough to wipe some of the blood smearing her face onto her blouse.

Selina rapped on the large wooden doors. 'Help, help,' she cried, low and plaintively, enough for the sentry inside the gate to hear.

The wooden doors opened an inch. 'My husband has beat me because he has discovered I have a German boyfriend,' she whispered in German. 'I live over there and saw you people arrive this morning. Please protect me.' No one did a damsel in distress quite like Selina.

The German sentry stared at Selina, her heaving breasts visible in the weak light. 'Karl,' he called to his colleague at the villa's back door, softly so no one inside the house would hear. 'I'm letting this lady in. She has a problem and needs the protection of the Reich.' He sniggered at his perceived cleverness. 'And she likes Germans,' he added suggestively.

The sentry from the villa's back door, Karl, approached. He too eyed Selina now resting up against the first sentry. A little older than the back gate sentry, he exercised natural authority. He nodded his approval for his younger colleague's plan. 'Take her in there,' he whispered, pointing in the direction of an open doorway off to the side that had once been staff quarters.

The Germans laid Selina on the floor, forcing up her skirt until her panties were visible. The older sentry grasped Selina's breast under her brassiere. She smiled up at him and touched his erect penis over the top of his trousers. 'Me first,' he said urgently to the younger man. 'Keep a watch for the others. We don't want any interruptions.'

The younger man stood with his back to Karl and Selina, peering around the doorway. The older man removed his boots, hopping from one foot to the other, never taking his eyes off Selina. He had one leg out of his trousers and one leg in them and was powerless to react when Selina suddenly sprang to her feet, lunged forward and cut his carotid artery. A grunt followed by the sound of him dropping dead alerted the younger man who turned in time for Selina's dagger to strike him under the rib cage. She buried it all the way to the hilt. He too was dead before he hit the ground. Selina moved to the large wooden gate and opened it. 'Coming?' she whispered into the dark where Harold was waiting.

Harold and Selina tiptoed to the villa's back door, each now holding a sentry's rifle. Sounds of male voices speaking German drifted towards them. Both knew that once inside there was no further need for stealth. The back door creaked slightly as they slipped into a semi-darkened passageway. Harold held up the little finger on his right hand, then his ring finger and finally his middle digit. With that, they stormed into a sitting room where five Germans sat playing cards. Harold killed three and Selina two. Throwing down his rifle, Harold withdrew his pistol from his belt and shot the spellbound German sentry on the veranda, frozen still as he stared through the window.

'The bedrooms, quick,' Harold ordered. There were, in fact, three bedrooms. Harold burst into one. The first thing he saw was the jacket of an officer's field grey uniform hung from a hook in the wall, on top of which a peaked cap was also suspended. To Harold's right, a man lay on the bed in trousers and a singlet, now in the throes of waking from sleep. Harold quickly summed up he was the German officer in charge of the detachment who had been allocated his own room. As the officer scrambled for his side arm, Harold calmly cut him down.

Selina was not so lucky. Three soldiers occupied the bedroom she entered. She killed one but then her rifle jammed. A second German shot her in the stomach as she sought to take her pistol from her clothing. Harold heard the kerfuffle and knew Selina was in trouble. He raced to the bedroom where from the doorway he shot dead the German standing over Selina. In the mayhem, Harold failed to notice that the third German had crawled under a bed where he was hiding fearfully.

Taking Selina in his arms, Harold carried her to the sitting room and laid her gently on the floor. She was groaning and blood was flooding out of her. Harold may have had an ability to maintain calm during physical combat, but he was an altogether different proposition when trying to tend to Selina's wounds. Panicked, he looked about wildly for something to stem the flow of bleeding. All Harold could think of was the German officer's uniform jacket. He raced back into the officer's room and grabbed the jacket before returning to Selina and kneeling by her side. Only then did he realize that in his haste he had also brought the German officer's peaked cap with him. Throwing it aside, Harold tried to press the jacket against Selina's stomach. But its mass made it difficult to compress, plus something bulky in the jacket's side pocket was further impeding him. Harold realized it was a set of keys. In frustration, he also cast the jacket aside. A cotton tablecloth on a small table caught his eye.

He removed it with a violent tug, sending glasses and ashtrays smashing to the floor.

As Harold applied this more accommodating poultice a bell began to ring, loudly and irritatingly. The Resistance traitor in the third bedroom, aided by the delay while Harold tended to Selina, had cautiously crept from his bed where he had been cringing in fear to activate the panic button in his room. It rang an alarm bell not only at the house but also alerted Gestapo headquarters in central Marseille to a problem at the safe house.

Harold found the bell on the front porch where literally he shot it, sparks and flame preceding its silence. In the quiet, the sound of running footsteps on marbled floor reached his ears. He darted back inside as the back door slammed, catching the fleeing man as he opened the tall, wooden back gates. Harold dragged him into the house, to the sitting room where Selina lay. Only once in the light did Harold look at the man. To his breathtaking bewilderment, Harold found himself staring at the frightened face, eyes downcast, of someone the spitting image of him, older to be sure, but near identical all the same.

The man was too scared to look at Harold. 'Don't kill me, please don't kill me,' he pleaded, speaking to the floor. 'I only spied for the Germans because they made me, threatened me.'

The man's admission he was the Resistance traitor almost prompted Harold to shoot him on the spot. But equally, Harold was befuddled by the man's uncanny similarity to him. 'What's your name?' Harold asked hoarsely, needing to satisfy his rocketing curiosity.

'Axel,' the man said in an obvious attempt to hide his identity.

Harold shook him so hard his head oscillated raggedly.

'Axel Tzanetis,' the man panted begrudgingly.

Harold stared at him in disbelief. 'Did you have a sister?' he asked, his mouth dry, already knowing the answer.

For the first time Axel studied Harold. 'You're Rita's son,' he said, his incredulity briefly defeating his fear. 'The bastard son.'

The two men stared at one another, each unsure what to say. At their feet Selina stirred, coughing frothy blood as she tried to speak. Harold pushed Axel into a chair. 'Stay there,' he ordered forcefully before kneeling at Selina's side.

'You have to go, Harold,' Selina rasped. 'The Germans will be here shortly. Give me a machine pistol and some stick grenades. I'll hold them up as long as I can.'

Tears coursed down Harold's face. 'No, no. I have to take you with me.'

Selina's smile was at once sad and beautiful. 'I've seen enough dying people to know when it's my turn.' She stared at Harold's distraught face. 'It's a *Dublin Zoo*,' she gasped, her weak laugh bringing up more blood. Harold shook his head, too distressed to think. 'I'm so glad I helped you, Harold,' Selina said. 'But I can't be moved; we both know that.'

'I'll carry you.'

Another gentle laugh further caused frothy blood to seep from Selina's mouth. 'You'll do no such thing.' She struggled to speak. 'Kiss me, Harold, and then go, please.'

Harold hesitated, torn between Selina's pleading and not wanting to leave her side. She placed a hand on his shoulder and pushed gently. 'Go now, please. While you can.'

Harold stood wearily and rummaged through the uniforms of the dead soldiers. 'Here's a Mauser machine pistol, a dozen clips of ammunition and six stick grenades,' he said, gulping hard. 'I'll leave them next to you.'

Brushing Selina's hair Harold kissed her tenderly on the forehead, his tears mingling with the blood on her face. The bubbling emotion, contained until now, rose in his throat and choked him. 'Goodbye, Selina,' was all he could say.

'Goodbye, Harold,' Selina mouthed with silent affection, now unable to speak.

In the second bedroom, the German soldier hidden under the bed heard and understood Harold and Selina's tortured farewell. And like them both, he also heard the distant sirens.

His face strained with torment, Harold turned to the terrified Axel cowering in his chair. 'Who belongs to the motorcycle and sidecar in the backyard?'

'The officer in charge of the detachment rides it,' Axel whispered in a quavering voice.

Harold turned and picked up the discarded officer's jacket and peaked cap, extracting the set of keys from the jacket as he did. 'Can you drive the motorcycle?' he asked Axel.

'No,' Axel responded, but too quickly.

Harold rounded on Axel, forcing him to stand and twisting his arm up his back. Had Axel been less scared, he might well have continued to plead incompetence. But he feared one more misstep could be his last. 'Stop,' he yelled in pain. 'Yes, yes, I can drive it.'

Harold released him. 'Put on that uniform jacket,' he said, pointing to an item of clothing hanging over the back of a chair, 'and the *stahlhelm*.' Harold was referring to a coal scuttle-shaped steel helmet on the chair, of the type that was standard issue to German soldiers.

Harold allowed himself one last glance at Selina as he and Axel left. It was as if she were in a laboured sleep. He knew she would die soon and this propelled him. In the backyard, Harold gave Axel the keys to the motorcycle. Both were wearing German military jackets, Harold the officer's peaked cap and Axel the steel helmet. 'Let's go,' Harold said, pointing to the open wooden gates. 'We're going on a night ride to Allauch. We have some heavy water to dispose of.'

Why Harold chose this course of action was later the subject of much discussion by a board of inquiry. The testimony of the Corsican woman, Selina's friend who was interviewed a year after the war ended, made clear Harold knew the whereabouts of the farm belonging to

Henri Mittel's cousin where the heavy water was secreted. The woman specifically told of the Corsican taxi driver, her brother's colleague, giving Harold precise directions in the hours before the romantically entwined Harold and Selina left for the Bon-Secours safe house.

Some board members wondered, in light of this testimony, if Harold had envisaged a future life with Selina and wanted to destroy the heavy water to safeguard against a return to jail; after all, he had substantially departed from his search orders. But when the German soldier who had survived the carnage at Bon-Secours was unearthed, the man who had hidden under the safe house bed, the question was emphatically answered in the negative. He told of Harold and Selina's tearful parting and how on leaving Harold had placed weapons by her side. Harold, it was agreed, knew Selina was past the point of no return. So why then did he not kill Axel Tzanetis and try to make good his escape?

The wise heads finally decided the answer lay in complex human psychology. Two important considerations arose. One was that when Harold located his mother's family home in the Marseille port district she was re-born in his imagination, and soon his figment of her was alongside him, relishing being back in the city of her birth after years of loneliness and isolation. Harold had said as much in his garrulous conversation with the Hotel Burgundy manager – another witness interviewed after the war – on the night of Thursday 11 September 1941, on his return to the hotel after exploring the port area. From this the psychiatrists assisting the inquiry extrapolated that Selina's whisking Harold from the hotel and what followed had temporarily suppressed but not eradicated the illusion his mother was by his side. And when confronted by Axel, the illusion reasserted itself. In consequence, the psychiatrists concluded, there existed in Harold's mind the very real consideration, however fanciful, that killing his mother's eldest brother would destroy her immensely deserved moment of enjoyment.

The second factor was Hugh, the big brother Harold had never had. At the time that Harold made his decision in the Bon-Secours safe house to take Axel to the heavy water, he believed Hugh had perished shortly after arriving in Marseille. In this, the extent of Harold's upset was reflected in the Corsican woman's recall of his distraught use of the *Dublin Zoo* expression when told by her brother that, effectively, Hugh was dead. The conclusion to be reached, the experts decided, was with Selina dying Harold had calculated the best he could salvage from the situation was to destroy the heavy water. Only then would Hugh, who had come to Marseille to play a part in the heavy water operation, have not died in vain.

The powerful BMW motorcycle raced through the streets of Bon-Secours onto Boulevard Gueidon before heading for Allauch, twenty kilometres away. Axel drove and Harold sat in the sidecar, his pistol pointed at Axel's side. It was curfew to be sure. But the Maltese cross on the motorcycle's sidecar and the silhouetted images of Harold the German officer and Axel as his other ranks driver facilitated their unimpeded passage, initially at least. From behind them, Harold heard explosions coming from the safe house until finally there was silence. He would never know that Selina got four of them before the grenade she was trying to throw slipped from her grasp and fell out of reach, the ensuing explosion killing her.

But Selina did buy Harold time enough to get away. Even so, the speeding motorcycle soon raised the suspicion of a Vichy police patrol, which reported its sighting. At the Gestapo's behest, the patrol was instructed to tail its riders. 'Heading east towards Allauch on Boulevard Gueidon,' was the patrol's next radioed report.

It was well after 11 pm on Saturday 13 September and the farmhouse was in darkness when Harold and Axel arrived. A man timidly poked his head out of his front door when Harold pounded on it. His apprehension deepened when he observed the intensity in Harold's eyes. 'The heavy water, where is it?' Harold demanded urgently.

This was the moment Henri Mittel's cousin had always dreaded. He cursed that Henri should be safe and snug in his bed in Paris while he was confronted by an agitated young man holding a pistol to the back of a clearly unwilling companion. The extraordinarily close resemblance of the younger gunman to his reluctant accomplice only added to an already surreal situation. But the cousin soon let it go; he had a higher order imperative. 'It's in the shed at the back,' he said, recognizing this was his chance once and for all to be rid of the barrels and the burden they were. 'I'll get a lamp and take you there.'

And there they were, all twenty barrels. Harold remembered their markings from his Athol House briefings. 'Get me something to cut them open,' he commanded. The cousin produced an axe from inside the shed. 'Have you got tin snips?' Harold asked.

'Yes, but not here.'

'Get them.'

The cousin didn't need a second bidding. He ran like a scolded cat into the house where he locked the door and barricaded it with his sofa. On the still night air, he heard sirens in the distance and knew this could mean only one thing – Germans.

Axel sneered at Harold. 'He won't be back, you know.'

Harold was unconcerned. His attention was on the approaching Germans, guided unbeknown to him by the Vichy police patrol that had followed him and Axel to the farm and parked a short distance up the road. Harold handed Axel the axe. 'Smash a hole in each barrel,' he ordered. 'I'll empty them.'

Axel swung at the first barrel, puncturing its top. He turned to a second barrel while Harold emptied the contents of the first. But as Axel bashed at the second container, the axe handle sheared off at the point where it was inserted into the metal axe head. Harold rushed to retrieve the axe head, his pistol now in his trouser belt pressing against the small of his back. As he leant over to pick it up, Axel brought the axe handle down on Harold's head, wielding it like a baseball bat. The force of the blow drove Harold to his knees. Warm, sticky blood began to cascade down the back of his neck.

Axel deftly plucked the pistol from the kneeling Harold's belt. 'So, dear nephew, the tables are now turned,' he said gloatingly. 'There's a detachment of German soldiers about to arrive and won't I be popular? I'm not completely sure why these barrels are so important but my German friends are bound to be extra pleased with me for finding them, and you. Ideally, they'd like you alive but the fact I'm your uncle makes for complications. Wonderful soldiers the Germans, but suspicious people all the same. I'd prefer just to claim a freakish but meaningless resemblance with you, the dead English spy, and leave it at that.'

'Why have you sided with the Germans, Axel?' Harold asked. He surprised himself with the question before recognizing that now he was certain to die, he needed to know the truth.

'You, in a word,' Axel replied. 'My sister was defiled by your father, an ugly, little, limping Englishman, and you are the product of that illicit union. Ever since the day Rita introduced your father to our family I have hated the British. That's why I joined the Resistance and worked so hard to win their confidence, waiting until I was certain the Germans would win the war and I could betray the British in payback for your father's filthy pawing of my sister.'

Harold was still kneeling, his hands clasped at the back of his head. He stared at Axel knowing that to beg for mercy would give Axel too much pleasure. 'Get on with it, then,' he said deadpan, willing his nerve to hold.

Axel raised the pistol. Harold continued to bead him with defiant eyes. '*Dublin Zoo*,' he said out loud as Axel's finger tightened on the trigger, as if summarizing his life.

The sound of the shot ringing out was loud enough to reach the police car parked further up the road. 'Someone's shooting,' they radioed in.

The back of Axel's head exploded like a watermelon hit with a sledgehammer. Staring at Axel, awaiting his own denouement, Harold at first wondered if Axel's toppling forward was the result of a heart attack. Then he saw the gaping hole in the back of his head. And with Axel's death, the compartment in Harold's brain creating the illusion of being in Marseille with his mother closed as if it had never been opened, snapping him back to the sober reality that Rita was dead and had been since 1936.

Now truly awake to his situation, Harold looked searchingly into the dark trying to comprehend how it was that someone had just shot Axel. After some seconds he could make out a figure still in the firing pose, arms outstretched and both hands gripping the butt of a pistol, with one forefinger on the weapon's depressed trigger. The figure moved forward, into the light, limping severely. It was Hugh Gregory.

CHAPTER TWENTY-SEVEN

The German search for Hugh was thorough at first. They followed his blood trail from the Hôtel du Clou to the port area, ransacking from top to bottom those warehouses in which traces of blood could be found. But after a time, still unable to find Hugh, the searchers panicked a little, worried he might have again escaped their clutches and fearful of the Standartenführer's wrath in the event. 'He'll head for the berthing area,' one soldier declared. 'That's his only means of escape, to stow away on a departing ship.' Within the increasingly anxious German search party, the speculation soon took root.

To be sure, the Germans did search the warehouse where Hugh lay hidden in the floor cavity, trying to quiet his breathing and ignore the pain of his wounded leg. Indeed, on two separate occasions German soldiers had stood on the section of floor directly above him. But the absence of any blood indicating Hugh had been inside the warehouse and the Germans' growing desire to move to the port berthing area meant the search was distracted and haphazard. And aware that Vichy police were about to arrive at the warehouses, the Germans soon departed, eager to begin searching ships moored at the port.

The Vichy police contingent arriving at the port area that late afternoon of Friday 12 September was led by the same police inspector who had sat with the Standartenführer in the unmarked Renault the night before, when surveillance was first placed on Harold at the Hotel Burgundy. As a result of Harold vanishing from the hotel at a time when Vichy police under the inspector's command had been entrusted with his monitoring, the Standartenführer was contemptuous of the French officer. 'Glad you could make it,' he said sarcastically, looking at his watch.

The inspector was tired and frustrated. He'd been woken at 3 am with the news that one of his officers at the Hotel Burgundy had been knocked out and the British agent Harold Lavigne was missing. And now the heavy-handed Germans had provoked a gunfight here in the heart of the Marseille port district and were demanding the Vichy police drop everything and clean up the mess. This was sovereign France – not a German colony. The Standartenführer's rebuke was just one thing too much, enough to cause the inspector's usual reserve to desert him. 'You arrogant bastard,' he seethed. 'Why don't you just fuck off back to Berlin and your beer halls and delusional rallies?'

The Standartenführer could scarcely believe his ears. No Frenchman had ever dared to insult him. 'You pathetic *hosenscheisser*,' the Standartenführer spat. 'Don't you speak to me like that. Get your people searching right now before I have you shot for insubordination, here on the spot.' With that, the Standartenführer stormed off.

The inspector watched him go. He knew enough German to know the Standartenführer had used a derogatory expression to denigrate him as a coward. And the inspector also knew the risks associated with losing his temper with a senior Gestapo officer. But the Rubicon had been crossed. He would never again kowtow to the Germans, preferring to die instead.

Still stewing over his confrontation with the Standartenführer, the inspector began to deploy his patrol. By now Hugh was close to death. He had suffered severe blood loss and his blood pressure was dangerously low. If he didn't eat soon, he would die. The inspector divided his twenty men into four sub-units of five, allocating each an area of the warehouse precinct. One sub-unit had a sniffer dog. In short order, a Vichy policeman ran to the inspector. 'The dog's found someone under the floor in the third warehouse along,' he reported breathlessly.

Hugh blinked when the torchlight was shone in his face. The game was up; he was powerless to resist as the police dragged him from his hidey-hole. 'Have any of you told any of the others?' the inspector asked the sub-unit members gathered around Hugh. All five shook their heads.

'Good,' the inspector said. 'Let's keep it that way.' The officers nodded in unison. 'Put the floor plate back in place,' the inspector ordered. 'We'll take him away with a minimum of fuss. We are French police working in a French jurisdiction. It is our job to arrest and interrogate suspects, not the Gestapo's.'

The five policemen looked at one another. A chord had been struck. One began softly to sing *La Marseillaise* and the others joined in. Bewildered and sick, Hugh hung limply in the arms of two officers waiting for the finish of the national anthem's impromptu rendition. When it did, the sergeant in charge of the sub-unit walked inconspicuously from the warehouse to a police vehicle parked in front of the Hôtel du Clou. In the now fading early evening light, he brought it to the warehouse. Hugh was bundled into the back seat and laid down flat. The car drove off with the inspector seated in the front passenger seat.

Hugh was placed in a cell in an out-of-the-way police station in the Marseille suburb of La Viste. A doctor was called, whereupon he connected Hugh to glucose and saline drips and tended his wound with a sulfate antibiotic dressing. Hugh was left to rest for the night.

In the late afternoon the next day, Saturday 13 September, the doctor returned to the La Viste police station. Around the same time, Harold and Selina were in discussion with the Corsican taxi drivers in the Rue Fauchier apartment; and Major Andrew Foulkes was en route to Marseille from the border city of Luchon.

'I see you've managed to keep down some food,' the doctor said in English, indicating he knew Hugh's nationality. 'That's a good sign.'

Hugh was wan and tired but still managed a smile. 'Where am I doctor?'

The doctor made no response. He was fearful of the German reaction should they discover he had treated the Englishman and was still unnerved that the Corsican taxi driver who drove him to the station just before curfew on the night of Friday 12 September had pointedly mentioned the Hôtel du Clou shooting.

'You will likely make a full recovery if you have a few weeks of bed rest. But if you don't rest, the bleeding will start again, infection will set in and because you're already weakened, you'll almost certainly die.' The doctor smiled professionally. 'Good luck,' he said, signalling he wouldn't be coming back.

Hugh spent the evening alone in the cell, except for a brief moment when the officer in charge of the station brought him a meal. The officer was an old friend of the inspector's and had agreed as a favour to hold Hugh over the weekend for questioning. But the inspector's friend had made his agreement conditional on Hugh being handed over to the Germans first thing Monday morning. Withholding the prisoner any longer than that, he told the inspector, risked serious repercussions.

This arrangement in place, the junior gendarme manning the desk was surprised when the inspector walked into the La Viste police station late on the night of Saturday 13 September. The young police officer was even more surprised when the inspector informed him he would be taking Hugh into his personal custody. The junior tried to protest the irregularity but the inspector sternly pulled rank. Hugh limped handcuffed from his cell and was placed in the back of the inspector's car. The inspector drove off only to stop a short time later. Un-cuffing Hugh, he told him to sit in the front seat.

At this precise time late on the night of 13 September, Major Andrew Foulkes lay on the top floor of a three-storey building overlooking Marseille's Marignane airfield. He had been in place for an hour now and, using a light tower as his reference, had already calibrated the gunsight on the high-powered weapon at his side. Satisfied all was in readiness, Foulkes rummaged in his shirt pocket and withdrew a small vial containing several white pills, swallowing two.

'Your compatriot, Harold, is causing a certain amount of mayhem at the moment,' the inspector said in English as he drove, answering Hugh's puzzled look. 'In consequence, it is no longer fair to my colleagues for you to stay at the station.' He smiled grimly. 'After I drop you off, I'll go to my friend the La Viste station commander. We will erase any trace of you ever being at the station. Those who know of your presence there will keep their mouths shut on fear of being shot by the Germans.'

'Drop me where?' Hugh asked.

The inspector turned up the volume of the police radio in his car. The airwaves were fairly buzzing. 'I'm hearing that

Harold has not only shot up a Gestapo safe house but has also kidnapped a Gestapo agent, commandeered a motorcycle and gone to a farmhouse at Allauch. Here,' he said, handing Hugh a map with a large red cross marked on it. 'Why he has done any of this, I really don't know.' The inspector took a deep breath. 'I'll take you to the back of the property. That way you can manage the short walk to the farmhouse. You can join your countryman and take your chances with the German contingent soon to address the problem that is *bon Ar ... old*.'

Hugh looked at the inspector and shook his head. 'You know as well as me I'm in no condition to fight Germans. I'd be lucky if I could walk a hundred yards without needing a blood transfusion.' Hugh stared at the inspector who remained expressionless, looking straight ahead. 'You'll need to drop me somewhere else.'

'That's impossible, I'm afraid,' the inspector said flatly, before turning to look at Hugh. 'Provided the Germans neutralize you and Harold, they'll observe political niceties and not enter into further correspondence with the Vichy police about you two. But if one or both of you got away, well that's a different story.'

'So why take me to the farmhouse if you need me eliminated? Why not just give me to the Gestapo?'

A Gallic shrug answered the questions. 'Yesterday I made a stand against the German in charge of the search for you and later ordered you be taken into our custody without his knowledge or approval. My men respected me for this. Even if I wanted to, I'm in no position to hand you to the Germans on a plate. It's a question of personal and national integrity.'

'But Harold and I don't have a hope in hell, especially as I'm ill,' Hugh protested. 'You've already told me a contingent of German troops is on its way to the farmhouse.'

The inspector gave another shrug. 'In the glove compartment,' he said, 'is your service pistol and some rounds of ammunition. We found them under the floor at the warehouse. Take them with you. They might help.'

Hugh sat in silence as the inspector drove on. He was desperately unwell. But equally the thought of being reunited with Harold was drawing him like a moth to a flame, forestalling further argument. Hugh gave his own shrug. He would take his chances alongside Harold at the farmhouse.

A police roadblock loomed up ahead. The inspector parked the car and spoke to the officer in charge, who seemed to be offering directions. A short time later the inspector pulled up in a rural laneway running between two fields. He motioned for Hugh to get out of the car. 'There's a gate over there,' he said pointing through the gloom. 'Go through it and keep walking straight. Once you're over the rise, you'll be able to make out the farmhouse about half a kilometre away.' By now both Hugh and the inspector could hear sirens on the night air. The inspector had to go. 'I won't wish you good luck,' he said to Hugh. 'But I will say I'm sorry it's turned out this way.' Then he was gone.

Hugh walked as quickly as his leg would allow him, stopping occasionally to gather his strength. Even so, the movement over uneven ground soon had him breathless and feeling nauseous. His body tingled and a fever-like sweat soaked his shirt and stung his eyes. As Hugh breasted the rise, he could hear the sound of male voices speaking French, angry and strained. The voices appeared to be coming from an area in front of the farmhouse. Suddenly, a shaft of light could be seen coming from an outbuilding of some description about a hundred yards away. Hugh was conscious he was now wobbling, as if drunk. He stopped for a moment to steady himself and wiped his brow. Then, after withdrawing his service pistol from his belt, he crept forward.

In the moonlight, Hugh could see the building was a small tin shed with a crooked lean. The light source, which he correctly surmised was a lamp, was placed to the right-hand side of the shed as Hugh viewed it, meaning the left side approach was in complete darkness. Hugh crept to the shed's darkened side. He heard a man's harsh voice. On cautiously peering around the shed, Hugh saw Harold kneeling, his hands clasped behind his head and the back of a man in the process of raising a pistol to fire it. Several olive-green barrels could be seen. In that instant, Hugh knew Harold had found the heavy water but for reasons unclear was about to be shot as a result. Taking a deep breath to steady his woozy head, Hugh stepped clear of the shed, his service pistol raised. He killed Axel Tzanetis just one millisecond before Axel would have executed Harold.

'Hugh,' Harold exclaimed, when the limping figure emerging from the gloom could be made out. 'How ... what?' Hugh was too exhausted to answer. Instead, he plodded forward and fell into Harold's arms.

The two embraced with deep brotherly masculinity. As they did high-powered lights sprang to life in the near distance.

'Germans,' Harold said to Hugh's knowing face.

'Harold,' Hugh said urgently, 'we're in one of your *Dublin Zoos*, I'm afraid. Our options are to surrender or fight.' He looked at Harold with frank honesty. 'Either way, we're done for.'

Harold nodded grimly. 'Yes, we are,' he said. 'I lost my Danish krone yesterday, my good luck charm, and ever since have been feeling as if my father is no longer looking over me.' Resigned amusement overtook Harold and he smiled broadly. 'From then on I suspected things might end badly.'

They both roared with laughter, brothers-in-arms now at terms with their destiny.

'Let's at least destroy the heavy water,' Hugh suggested as if proposing a boyish prank.

'Let's indeed,' Harold said.

'Hugh,' Harold called as they began to remove the remaining barrels from the shed. 'Did you arrange for a new joint grave and a nice big headstone for my parents as we discussed?'

Hugh laughed, weak and labouring for breath from his exertion. 'I did. But you actually owe me a few quid; it cost 150 pounds, eight more than you gave me.'

Harold laughed back. The fact that he and Hugh were together in a fight to the death had swelled him with unaccountable happiness, and the knowledge his parents were now appropriately resting only added to his contentment. And when from out of nowhere Harold recalled his mother's avowed belief in the afterlife, his sense of joy became irrational exhilaration, spurred by the sudden conviction he would soon see his parents and be reunited with Selina.

Hugh and Harold re-loaded their pistols and began firing shots into the nineteen barrels that along with the emptied container they had assembled in a semi-circle in front of the shed at their backs. Soon all the barrels were punctured, on their sides and leaking their contents.

The sound of shooting caused the Germans to delay momentarily. But when the white phosphorus flares lit up Harold and Hugh's position as if in broad daylight, the soldiers became more aggressive. Fanning out across the paddock they advanced towards the shed unleashing crushing small arms fire as they came. The flimsy fort Harold and Hugh had built shredded, and with that any remaining heavy water in the twenty barrels dribbled out.

Hugh died first, a blaze of fire ripping at his head and torso, flinging him backwards. Harold followed fifteen seconds later, standing at full height protectively astride his fallen comrade firing blindly in the direction of the illuminating arc lights.

It had just turned midnight on Saturday 13 September 1941.

The announcer on Radio-Paris, the French national radio service, cleared his throat. It was 6 am on Sunday 14 September and he was about to read the first news bulletin of the day. 'And finally,' he said, concluding the bulletin, 'the Prime Minister, Field Marshal Pétain, has cancelled plans to visit French territories in North Africa owing to a severe head cold. The visit will be rescheduled at a later date. Now to the weather ...'

And Major Foulkes? Never heard of again. In 1955 a team of hikers discovered human remains on a remote walking path in the Pyrenees Mountains, three kilometres from Spain on the French side of the border. Only bones remained, indicating the body had been there for some time. No documentation could be found. Toxicology tests showed high residual levels of methamphetamine in the bones, revealing the deceased had regularly ingested chemicals capable of causing prolonged waking, abnormal energy levels and feelings of invincibility. Taken for any duration, the chemicals were known to severely damage the heart, lungs and other vital organs.

In January 1946 the SOE was absorbed into the Secret Intelligence Service. General Carmoday retired at this time and returned to Scotland, living in isolation and dying with his secrets in 1980 at the grand age of ninety. But he had one reprise, an appearance before an inquiry into the ultimately frustrated Pétain assassination attempt, the operation ordered by Churchill without war ministry approval of which Attlee Labour had learned on taking government after the war.

It was this board of inquiry that interviewed the Corsican woman who owned the Rue Fauchier apartment in Marseille, the former German soldier who had survived Harold and Selina's attack on the safe house at Bon-Seccours, and the manager of the Hotel Burgundy in Marseille who had assisted Selina in Harold's covert extraction from the hotel. Among others, Frank Grimwade, formerly officer commanding at Athol House, the SOE secret training establishment in Dorset, also appeared. Grimwade was to die of heart disease at age fifty-eight, five years to the day after the inquiry first convened in June 1946.

Prime Minister Attlee established the inquiry once it became clear that Pétain, imprisoned for life on the *Île d'Yeu* for his wartime collaboration, would die there. With some, most notably President Truman of the United States, claiming Pétain's cooperation with the Germans had saved France from total destruction, Attlee wanted clean British hands.

The inquiry focused on whether British interests of the day warranted Pétain's assassination, taking into account the operation came at the cost of four British agents, with a fifth agent missing and also believed killed. This grouping consisting of course of Harold, Hugh, Hugh's SOE driver, Selina, and the then missing Major Andrew Foulkes. Owing to its sensitivity, the panel sat *in camera* under the chairmanship of none other than the current Lord Chief Justice of England and Wales, Sir Samuel Prendergast KGMG CB KC OBE.

The board's findings were politic and cleverly balanced the operation's various pros and cons. On one hand, the report noted that, indirectly, the mission did result in the destruction of a cache of heavy water the Germans might otherwise have used to produce an atomic weapon and the elimination of a Resistance traitor. On the other, any outright criticism of the operation, of which there was some, especially in light of Rommel's subsequent defeat in North Africa, was softened by the concession its planners lacked the benefit of hindsight. Sir Samuel's final report was handed down on 14 March 1947.

That same night at dinner in their Kensington home, after their adult children had left the table, Sir Samuel told his wife Lady Millicent he had been dealing with a matter touching on the death of Albert and Rita Bradshaw's son, Harold. As with Harold's parents, Sir Samuel confided discreetly, his death was also the result of sadly tragic circumstances. 'It was a disaster in every respect,' Sir Samuel said. 'A *Dublin Zoo*.'